Helvétius, William Hooper, John Adams

A Treatise on Man

his intellectual faculties and his education - Vol. 1

Helvétius, William Hooper, John Adams

A Treatise on Man
his intellectual faculties and his education - Vol. 1

ISBN/EAN: 9783337381578

Printed in Europe, USA, Canada, Australia, Japan

Cover: Foto ©Andreas Hilbeck / pixelio.de

More available books at **www.hansebooks.com**

A

TREATISE

O N

M A N,

H I S

INTELLECTUAL FACULTIES

A N D   H I S

E D U C A T I O N.

A Pofthumous Work of

M.   H E L V E T I U S.

Honteux de m'ignorer,
Dans mon être, dans moi, je cherche à pénétrer.
VOLTAIRE, Difc. VI. de la Nat. de l'Homme.

Tranflated from the FRENCH, with additional Notes,

By   W.   H O O P E R,   M. D.

V O L.   I.

L O N D O N,
Printed for B. LAW, AVE-MARIA-LANE; and
G. ROBINSON, PATER-NOSTER-ROW.
MCCLXXVII.

PREFACE.

MY inducement to engage in the following work, was merely the love of mankind and of truth; from a perfuafion, that to become virtuous and happy, we wanted only to know ourfelves, and entertain juft ideas of morals.

My defign can hardly be miftaken. Had I publifhed this book in my life-time, I fhould, in all probability, have expofed myfelf to perfecution, without the profpect of any perfonal advantage.

That I have continued to maintain the fame fentiments which I advanced in my Treatife on the Underftanding, is the confequence of their appearing to me the only rational principles on the fubject, and of their

Vol. I.　　　A　　　　being

being generally adopted, fince that time, by men of the greateſt learning and abilities.

Thoſe principles are farther extended, and more accurately examined, in the preſent work than in the former; my reflection having ſuggeſted a number of new ideas, while I was employed in the compoſition. Such thoughts as are leſs intimately connected with the ſubject, are thrown into notes, at the end of each ſection; thoſe only being retained in the text, which were of an explanatory nature, or ſerved to remove objections, which could not be directly anſwered, without greatly encreaſing the limits, and retarding the progreſs of the work.

The ſecond is the moſt encumbered with notes, becauſe the principles it contains being chiefly controvertible, required the ſupport of a greater accumulation of proof.

It is not improper on this occaſion to obſerve, that there are ſeveral reaſons which may render a work contemptible in the opinion of the public; ſuch as, that the author has not taken ſufficient pains to merit approbation;

bation; that he is defective in abilities, or
chargeable with difingenuity. I can fafely
affirm, that I have nothing with which to
reproach myfelf on the latter of thofe heads.
It is only in prohibited publications that truth
is now to be found; for in others, falfehood
is difcernible. The greater number of authors is in their writings, what men of the
world are in their converfation: folicitous
only to pleafe, they are wholly indifferent,
provided they attain their purpofe, whether
it be by means of falfity or truth.

A writer who is defirous of the favour of
the great, and the tranfitory applaufe of the
prefent hour, muft adopt implicitly the current principles of the time, without ever at-
tempting to examine or queftion their authority; and from this fource arifes the want
of originality, fo general among literary
productions. Books of intrinfic merit, and
which difcover real genius, are the phæno-
mena but of very few periods in the fpace
of many ages; and their appearance, like
that of the fun in the foreft, ferves only to
render the intervening darknefs more con-
fpicuous. They conftitute an epoch in the

hiftory

hiftory of the human underftanding, and it is from the principles they contain, that future improvements in fcience derive their origin.

It would ill become me to fay any thing in praife of this work; I fhall, therefore, only obferve, in refpect to its principles, that I have advanced no fentiment which was not fuggefted by my own reflection, nor affirmed any propofition which I do not believe to be true.

In expofing fome prejudices, I may be thought, perhaps, to have conducted myfelf with too little referve. I have treated them with the fame ingenuous freedom, which a young man is apt to ufe towards an old woman, whom he is under no inducement either to flatter or depreciate. Through the whole inquiry, truth has been my principal object; and this confideration, it is to be hoped, will ftamp fome value on the work. A fincere love of truth is the difpofition moft favourable for difcovering her.

I have all along endeavoured to exprefs my ideas with perfp'cuity; nor ever facrificed any

fen-ſentiment to popular prepoſſeſſion. If, there-fore, the book be void of merit, it ought to be imputed to the fault of my judgment, and not to a depravity of heart. It is few, I believe, that can with juſtice ſay ſo much in their own favour.

To ſome readers this work will appear to be written with great boldneſs. There are periods in every country when the word *prudent* bears the ſame ſignification with *vile*; and when thoſe productions only are eſteem-ed for their ſentiments, which are written in a ſtyle of ſervility.

It was once my intention to have publiſhed this book under a fictitious name, as the only means of reconciling with my own ſafety the deſire I entertained of rendering ſervice to my country. But, during the time I have been employed in the work, a change has happened in the circumſtances and government of my fellow-citizens. The diſorder, which I hoped in ſome meaſure to remedy, is become incurable : the proſpect of public utility is vaniſhed, and I defer the publication of the work, till its author be no more.

A 3   My

My country has at length submitted to the yoke of despotism. She will never again produce any writer of extraordinary eminence. It is the characteristic of despotic power to extinguish both genius and virtue.

The people of this country will never more signalize themselves under the appellation of French : the nation is now so much debased as to become the contempt of Europe. No fortunate crisis can henceforth ever restore her liberty. She will die of the consumption. Conquest alone can afford a remedy proportioned to the virulence of her disease ; and the efficacy even of this, it is chance and circumstances which must determine.

In all nations there are certain periods when the citizens, undetermined what measures they ought to take, and remaining in a state of suspense between a good and bad government, are extremely desirous of instruction, and disposed to receive it. At such a time, if a work of great merit makes its appearance, the happiest effects may be produced : but the moment once past, the people, insensible to glory, are, by the form of

their

their government, irrefiftibly inclined towards ignorance and bafenefs. Their minds are then like parched earth : the water of truth may rain upon them, but without producing fertility. Such is the ftate of France.

Henceforth, among the French, the eftimation of learning will daily decline, with its utility ; as it can only ferve to fhew in a ftronger light the mifery of defpotifm, without fupplying the means of evading it.

Happinefs, like the fciences, is faid to advance progreffively over the world. Its courfe is now directed towards the North. There great princes cherifh the feeds of genius, and genius is ever accompanied with a high degree of public felicity.

Nothing can be more oppofite than the ftate of the fouth and north parts of Europe at prefent to each other. Clouds of thicker darknefs are perpetually overfpreading the South, produced by the mifts of fuperftition and of Afiatic defpotifm. The horizon of the North becomes every day more bright and effulgent. A Catharine II. and a Frederick,

A 4   render

render themfelves dear to humanity. Convinced in their own minds of the value of
truth, they encourage the cultivation of it
in others, and afford their patronage to every
effort by which it may be farther invefti-
gated.   It is to fuch fovereigns that I dedicate
this work : it is by the aufpicious influence
of thofe that the world can be enlightened.

The former brightnefs of the South becomes
more dim, while the dawn of the North fhines
forth with increafing radiance.   It is the
North that now emits the rays which penetrate even to Auftria.   Every thing there
haftens towards an extraordinary change.
The affiduous application beftowed by the
emperor on alleviating the weight of the impofts, and improving the difcipline of his
army, fhews plainly that he entertains a defire of becoming the darling of his fubjeĉts ;
that he wifhes to render them happy at home,
and refpeĉtable to foreign nations.   The
efteem for the king of Pruffia, profeffed from
his earlieft years, afforded a prefage of his
future virtues !   Efteem always indicates a
fimilarity of difpofition to the objeĉt of it.

C O N-

C O N T E N T S.

V O L U M E I.

CONTENTS.

Chap.

CONTENTS.

CONTENTS.

That

CONTENTS.

Chap.

CONTENTS.

Chap.

CONTENTS.

CONTENTS.

That

CONTENTS.

CONTENTS.

SECTION IV.

Men commonly well organifed, are all fufceptible of the fame degree of paffion: the inequality of their capacities is always the effect of the difference of fituation in which chance has placed them.

CONTENTS.

Chap.

CONTENTS.

it

CONTENTS.

lore

CONTENTS.

CONTENTS.

VOLUME II.

SECTION V.

OF the errors and contradictions of thofe, whofe principles differing from mine; refer the unequal degrees of underftandings to the unequal degrees of perfection in the organs of the fenfes,

None having wrote better on this fubject than M. Rouffeau ; I take him for an example of what I advance.

It refults from his contradictions, that juftice and virtue are acquifitions.

That his humanity is always the confequence either of fear, or of his education.

Chap.

CONTENTS.

CONTENTS.

SECTION VI.

Chap.

CONTENTS.

Chap.

CONTENTS:

CONTENTS,

CONTENTS.

CONTENTS.

That

CONTENTS.

That

CONTENTS.

CONTENTS.

CONTENTS.

SECTION IX.

Of the poffibility of laying down a good
plan of legiflation. Of the obftacles
ignorance oppofes to its publication.
Of the ridicule it throws on every new
idea; and every profound ftudy of morality and politics. Of the inconftancy
it fuppofes in the human mind; an inconftancy incompatible with the duration
of good laws. Of the imaginary danger
to which (if we believe ignorance) the
publication of a new idea, and efpecially

CONTENTS.

CONTENTS.

CONTENTS.

CONTENTS.

CONTENTS.

Chap.

CONTENTS.

O N

ON

M A N;

H I S

INTELLECTUAL FACULTIES

A N D

HIS EDUDATION.

C H A P. I.

Of the different points of view from which we may consider man: of the influence of education.

THE science of man, taken in its utmoft extent, is immenfe; the ftudy of it is long and painful. Man is a model expofed to the view of different artifts; every one furveys it from fome point of view, no one from every point.

The painter and the mufician confider man; but merely with regard to the effect that colours and founds have on his eyes and his ears.

Corneille, Racine, and Voltaire have ftudied him, but only in relation to the impreffions that are excited in him by actions of greatness, tenderness, pity, rage, &c.

Moliere and Fontaine have confidered mankind from other points of view.

In the ftudy that the philofopher makes of men, his object is their happinefs. This happinefs is dependent on the laws under which they live, and the inftructions they receive.

The perfection of thefe laws and inftructions fuppofes a preliminary knowledge of the human heart and mind, with their various operations; in a word, of the obftacles to the progrefs of the fciences of morality, politics, and education.

Without this knowledge, what means are there to render men better and happier? The philofopher fhould, therefore, remount to the fimple and productive principle of their intellectual faculties and their paffions, the only principle that can inform him of the degree of perfection to which laws and inftructions can carry them, and fhew him what is the power of education over them.

I regard the underftanding, the virtue, and genius of man, as the product of inftruction. This idea prefented in the Treatife of L'Efprit appears to me invariably true; but perhaps it is not fufficiently proved. It is granted me, that education has more influence over the genius and character of men, and of nations, than was imagined; and this is all that has been granted me.

The

The examination of this opinion will make the firſt part of this work. To educate mankind, furniſh their minds, and render them happy, we muſt know of what inſtructions and what happineſs they are ſuſceptible.

Previous to the entering on this inquiry, I ſhall ſay a few words.

   1. On the importance of this queſtion.

   2. On falſe ſcience, to which is alſo given the name of education.

   3. On the dryneſs of the ſubject, and the difficulty of treating it.

C H A P. II.

Of the importance of this queſtion.

IF it be true that the talents and the virtues of a people determine their power and their happineſs, no queſtion can be more important than this, to wit,

If in each individual his talents and his virtues be the effect of his organiſation, or of the education he receives.

I am of the latter opinion, and propoſe to prove here what perhaps is only advanced in the treatiſe of L'Eſprit. If I can demonſtrate that man is, in fact, nothing more than the product of his education, I ſhall doubtleſs reveal an important truth to mankind. They will learn, that they have in their own hands the inftrument of their greatnefs and their felicity, and that to be happy and powerful nothing more is requifite than to perfect the fcience of education.

But by what means fhall we difcover whither man be in fact the produce of his education ? By a thorough difcuffion of the queftion.   If this exa-mination fhould not give the folution, we ought ftill make it ; for it will be ufeful, as it will com-pel us to the ftudy of ourfelves.

Mankind are, but too often, unknown to him that governs them ; yet to guide the motions of the human puppet, it is neceffary to know the wires by which he is moved.   Without this know-ledge, what wonder is it that his motions are frequently fo contrary to thofe the legiflature requires.

If fome errors fhould creep into a work that treats on man, it will ftill be a valuable work.

What a mafs of light does the knowledge of mankind throw upon the feveral parts of govern-ment.   The ability of the groom confifts in know-ing all that is to be done to the animal he is to manage ; and the ability of a minifter, in knowing all that is to be done in the management of the people he is to govern.

The fcience of man makes a part of the fcience of government. (1) The minifter fhould connect it with that of public affairs. (2) It is then that he will eftablifh juft laws.

Let

Let philofophers therefore penetrate continually more and more into the abyfs of the human
heart, let them there fearch out all the principles
of his actions, and let the minifter, profiting by
their difcoveries, make of them, according to
time, place, and circumftances, a happy application.

If the knowledge of mankind be regarded as
abfolutely neceffary to the legiflature, nothing can
be more important than the examination of a
problem which implies that knowledge.

If they who are perfonally indifferent to this
queftion, fhall judge of it only as relative to public intereft, they will perceive that of all the obftacles to the perfection of education, the greateft
is to regard our talents and virtues as the effect of
organifation. No opinion is more favourable to
the idlenefs and negligence of inftructors. If organifation make us almoft entirely what we are,
why do we reproach the mafter with the ignorance and ftupidity of his pupils? Why, he will
fay, do you impute to education the faults of nature? What anfwer will you make him? When
you admit a principle, how can you deny its immediate confequence?

On the contrary, if we prove that talents and
virtues are acquifitions, we fhall roufe the induftry of the mafter, and prevent his negligence;
we fhall render him more affiduous in ftifling

the

the vices, and cultivating the virtues of his
pupils.

The genius moſt ardēnt in carrying the
inſtruments of education to perfection, will perceive perhaps in an infinity of thoſe minute
articles, now regarded as inſignificant, the hidden
feeds of our vices, our virtues, our talents, and
imbecilities ; and who can ſay to what point genius may then carry its diſcoveries ? (3) Of this
we are certain, that we are as yet ignorant of
the true principles of education, and that it is at
the preſent day reduced almoſt entirely to certain falſe ſciences, to which even ignorance is
preferable.

C H. A P.   III.

Of falſe ſcience, or acquired ignorance.

MAN is born ignorant ; he is not born a ſot;
and it is not even without labour that he
is made one. To be ſuch, and to be able to extinguiſh in himſelf his natural lights, art and method muſt be uſed ; inſtruction muſt heap on him
error upon error ; he muſt have multiplied his
prejudices by a multitude of lectures.

If ſottiſm be the common condition of mankind
among the poliſhed nations, it is the effect of a contagious

gious inftruction; it is becaufe they are educated by men of falfe fcience, and read fottifh books; for it is with books as with men, there is good and bad company. The good book is almoft every where prohibited (4) Senfe and fpirit urge its publication; bigotry forbids, for bigotry would command the world; fhe is, therefore, interefted in the propagation of folly. Her aim is to blind mankind, and bewilder them in a labyrinth of of falfe fcience. It is not enough that men be ignorant; ignorance is the middle point between true and falfe learning. The ignorant man is as much above the falfely learned, as he is below him of real fcience. The defire of fuperftition is to render man ftupid; her fear is that he become enlightened. Now to whom will fhe commit the care of making him a brute? To the fcholaftics, for of all the fons of Adam they are the moft ftupid and conceited (5). "The mere " fchool divine, according to Rabelais, holds the " fame rank among men as that animal does " among beafts, who neither labours like the ox, " nor bears a burden like the mule, nor barks at " the thief like a dog, but like the ape, foils " all, breaks all, bites the paffenger, and is " noxious to every one."

The fcholaftic is powerful in words, and weak in argument, therefore, what fort of men does he form? Such as are learnedly abfurd and ftupidly proud (6). With regard to ftupidity, I

have

have already faid it is of two forts, one natural, the other acquired; the one the effect of ignorance, the other of inftruction. Now of thefe two forts of ignorance or ftupidity, which is the moft incurable? The latter. The man who knows nothing may learn; it is only requifite to excite in him the defire of knowledge. But he who is falfely learned, and has by degrees loft his reafon when he thought to improve it, has purchafed his ftupidity at too dear a rate ever to renounce it *. His mind overloaded with the weight of a learned ignorance, can never mount up to the truth; it has loft the fpring that fhould raife it up. The knowledge he muft acquire is connected with that he muft forget. To place a certain number of truths in his memory, it is frequently neceffary to difplace the fame number of errors. Now this difplacement requires time, and if be at laft effected, the man is formed too late.

We are aftonifhed at the age the Greeks and Romans acquired maturity. What various talents did they difplay in their adolefcence? At twenty, Alexander, already a man of letters and a great general, undertook the conqueft of the Eaft. At the fame age Scipio and Hannibal formed the greateft projects, and executed the

---

* A young painter having drawn a picture in the bad manner of his mafter, fhewed it to Raphael, and afked what he thought of it? I think, fays Raphael, if you knew nothing, you would foon know fomething.

moft

moft difficult enterprifes. Before the age of maturity Pompey, the conqueror of Europe, Afia,
and Africa, had filled the earth with his glory.
Now how did thefe Greeks and Romans become
at once men of letters, orators, generals, and minifters of ftate ? How did they qualify themfelves for all forts of employments in their republics, exercife them, and even frequently abdi-
cate them, at an age when no one in our days is
capable of affuming them ? Were the men of antiquity different from the moderns ? Was their
organifation more perfect ? No doubtlefs. For
in the fciences, and the arts of navigation, phyfics, mechanics, the mathematics, &c. we know
that the moderns excel the ancients.

The fuperiority the latter have for fo long
a time preferved in morality, politics, and legiflation, is therefore to be regarded as the effect of
their education. The inftruction of youth was
not then confided to fcholaftics, but philofophers.
The object of thefe philofophers was to form
heroes and great politicians. The glory of the
pupil was reflected on the mafter ; that was his
reward.

The object of an inftructor is no longer the
fame. What intereft has he in exalting the mind
and foul of his pupil ? None. What is his aim ? To
weaken their natural abilities, to make them fuperftitious ; to disjoint, if I may be allowed the
expreffion, the wings of their genius ; to ftifle in
their

their minds all true fcience, and in their hearts every patriotic virtue (7).

The golden ages of thefe fchool divines were the ages of ignorance, whofe darknefs, before Luther and Calvin, covered the earth. Then, fays an Englifh philofopher, fuperftition reigned over all nations, " Men were changed, like Nabuchadnez-
" zer, into brutes, and being like mules, bridled
" faddled, and loaded with heavy burdens, they
" groaned under the weight of fuperftition ; but
" at laft fome of thefe mules began to kick, and
" throw off at once their loads and their riders."

No reformation can be hoped in the plan of inftructions fo long as it is confided to the fcholaf-tics.   Under fuch tutors the fcience taught will never be any thing more than the fcience of errors ; and the ancients will preferve that fuperiority over the moderns in morality, politics, and legif-lation, which they owe not to the fuperiority of their organifation, but, as I have already faid, to that of their inftruction.

I have now fhewn the futility of falfe learning, and have evinced the importance of this work. It remains to fpeak of the drynefs of the fubject.

CHAP.

CHAP. IV.

Of the dryness of the subject, and the difficulty of treating it.

THE examination of the question I have proposed requires a refined and deep discussion. Every discussion of this sort is tiresome. That a man who is a real friend to humanity, and already habituated to the fatigue of attention, should read this book without disgust, I should not be surprised, and his approbation would doubtless content me, if from the beginning, to render this work useful, I had not proposed to make it entertaining. Now what flowers can be thrown on a question so serious and important. I. would instruct the man of common capacity, and in almost every nation men of this sort are incapable of attention: from hence proceeds disgust; and it is in France especially that this sort of men are the most common.

I past ten years at Paris; the spirit of bigotry and fanaticism reigned then not there. If I may believe the public report, it is now the spirit of the times. With regard to people of fashion, they are more and more indifferent to works of reflection. Nothing affects them but a ridiculous description (8), which satisfies their malignity without disturbing their indolence. I renounce, therefore,

the

the hope of pleafing them. Whatever pains I might take, I fhould never diffufe fufficient entertainment over a fubject fo dry and ferious.

I have obferved, however, that if we judge of the French nation by their works, either the people are lefs light and frivolous (9) than they are thought to be, or the fpirit of the men of letters is very different from that of the nation. The ideas of the latter appear to me grand and elevated ; let them, therefore, write on, and reft affured, notwithftanding national partialities, that they will every where find juft judges of their merit. I have only one thing to advife them, and that is, fometimes to dare to defpife the opinion of a fingle nation, and to remember, that a mind truly great will attach itfelf to fuch fubjects only as are interefting to the whole race of mankind.

This of which I here treat is of that nature. I fhall only repeat the principles in the treatife of L'Efprit, to examine them more thoroughly, to prefent them in a new point of view, and to draw new confequences from them,

In geometry every problem not fully refolved, may become the object of a new demonftration. It is the fame in morality and politics.

Let no one therefore decline the examination of a queftion fo important, and whofe folution moreover requires the expofition of truths hitherto but little known.

Is

Is the difference in the minds of men the effect of their different organisations or education? That is the object of my inquiry.

SECTION I.

The education neceffarily different in different men, is perhaps the caufe of that inequality in underftandings hitherto attributed to the unequal perfection of their organs.

CHAP. I.

No two perfons receive the fame education.

I Still learn; my inftruction is not yet finifhed: When will it be? When I fhall be no longer fenfible; at my death. The courfe of my life is properly nothing more than a long courfe of education.

What is neceffary that two individuals fhould receive precifely the fame education? That they fhould be in precifely the fame pofitions and the fame circumftances. Now fuch an hypothefis is impoffible : it is therefore evident, that no two perfons can receive the fame inftructions.

But why put off the term of our education to the utmoft period of life? Why not confine it to the time exprefsly fet apart for inftruction, that is, to the period of infancy and adolefcence?

I am

I am content to confine it to that period ; and
I will prove in like manner, that it is impoffible
for two men to acquire precifely the fame ideas.

C H A P. II.

Of the moment at which education begins.

IT is at the very inftant a child receives motion and life that it receives its firft inftruction : it is fometimes even in the womb where it
is conceived, that it learns to diftinguifh between
ficknefs and health. The mother however delivered, the child ftruggles and cries ; hunger gripes
it, it feels a want, and that want opens its lips,
makes it fieze, and greedily fuck the nourifhing
breaft. When fome months have paffed, its fight
is diftinct, its organs are fortified, it becomes by
degrees fufceptible of all impreffions ; then the
fenfes of feeing, hearing, tafting, touching, fmelling, in a word, all the inlets to the mind are
fet open ; then all the objects of nature rufh
thither in crowds, and engrave an infinity of ideas
in the memory *. In thefe firft moments what
can be true inftructors of infancy ? The divers
fenfations it feels : thefe are fo many inftructions
it receives.

* See Mr. Buffon's eloquent and admirable difcourfes
on man.

If

If two children have the fame preceptor, if they are taught to diftinguifh their letters, to read and repeat their catechifm, &c. they are fuppofed to receive the fame education. The philofopher judges otherwife : according to him, the true preceptors of a child are the objects that furround him; thefe are the inftructors to whom he owes almoft all his ideas.

C H A P. III.

Of the inftructors of childhood.

A Short hiftory of the infancy of man will bring us acquainted with them. He no fooner fees the light than a thoufand founds ftrike his ears ; he hears nothing but a confufed noife ; a thoufand bodies offer themfelves to his fight, but prefent nothing but objects imperfectly defined. It is by infenfible degrees the infant learns to hear and fee, to perceive and rectify the errors of one fenfe by another *.

Being conftantly ftruck by the fame fenfations in the prefence of the fame objects, he thereby

---

* The fenfes never deceive us ; objects conftantly make the impreffions on us they ought to make. If a fquare tower appears round at a certain diftance, it is becaufe at that diftance the rays reflected from the tower ought to be confounded, and make it appear as it does; it is becaufe there are certain cafes in which the real forms of bodies cannot be afcertained without the united teftimony of feveral fenfes.

acquires

acquires a more complete remembrance of them, in proportion as the fame action of the objects are repeated on him; and this action of them we fhould regard as the moft confiderable part of his education.

The child in the mean time grows; he walks and walks alone; numberlefs falls then teach him to preferve the equilibrium of his body, and to ftand firm on his legs; the more painful the falls, the more inftructive they prove, and the more adroit, attentive, and cautious he walks.

The child grows ftrong; he runs, he is already able to leap the little canals that traverfe and water the garden. It is then that by repeated trials and falls he learns to proportion his leaps to the width of the canals.

He fees a ftone fall into the water and fink to the bottom, while a piece of wood floats on the furface : by this inftance he acquires the firft idea of gravity.

If he take the ftone and the wood out of the water, and by chance they both fall on his feet, the unequal degree of pain occafioned by their fall, engraves more ftrongly on his memory the idea of their unequal weight and hardnefs.

If he chance to throw the fame ftone againft one of the flower-pots placed on the border of a canal, he will then learn that fome bodies are broke by a blow that others refift.

There

There is therefore no man of difcernment who muft not fee in all objects, fo many tutors charged with the education of our infancy *.

But are not thefe inftructors the fame for all? No. The chance is not precifely the fame for any two perfons; but fuppofe it were, and that two children owed their dexterity in walking, running, and leaping to their falls; I fay, that as it is impoffible they fhould both have precifely the fame number of falls, and equally painful, chance cannot furnifh them both with the fame inftructions.

Place two children on a plain, in a wood, a theatre, an affembly, or a fhop. They will not, by their mere natural pofition, be ftruck precifely in the fame manner, nor confequently affected with the fame fenfations. What different fubjects moreover are by daily occurrences inceffantly offered to the view of thefe two children.

Two brothers travel with their parents, and to arrive at their native place they muft traverfe long chains of mountains. The eldeft follows his father by the fhort and rugged road. What

---

* If I have here defcribed the feveral ftates of infancy in a curfory manner, it is becaufe I am fearful of tiring the reader. What imports him to know the time the child is in paffing through the feveral periods? It is fufficient that they are paffed through. It is by no means neceffary that my narration fhould be as long as the infancy of man.

does he fee? Nature in all the forms of horror; mountains of ice that hide their heads among the clouds, maffy rocks that hang over the traveller's head, fathomlefs caverns, and ridges of arid hills, from whence torrents precipitate with a tremenduous roar. The younger follows his mother through the moft frequented roads, where nature appears in all her pleafing forms. What objects does he behold? Every where hills planted with vines and fruitful trees, and vallies where the wandering ftreams divide the meadows, peopled by the brouzing herds.

Thefe two brothers have, in the fame journey, feen very different profpects, and received very different impreffions. Now a thoufand incidents of the fame nature may produce the fame effects. Our life is nothing more, fo to fay, than a long chain of fimilar incidents; let men not ever flatter themfelves, therefore, with being able to give two children precifely the fame education.

What influence moreover may a difference in inftruction, occafioned by a trifling difference in furrounding objects, have on the mind? Who does not know that a fmall number of diffimilar ideas, combined with thofe two men already have in common, can produce a total difference in their manner of feeing and judging?

Suppofing, however, that chance fhould conftantly offer the fame objects to two perfons, does it prefent them when their minds are precifely in the

the fame fituation, and when confequently thofe objects will make the fame impreffions on them ?

C H A P.   IV.

Of the different impreffions objects make on us.

THAT different objects produce different fenfations is felf-evident. Experience, moreover, teaches us that the fame objects excite in us different impreffions, according to the moment at which they prefent themfelves; and it is, perhaps, to thefe different impreffions, that we are principally to attribute the diverfity and great inequality that is to be found in men educated in the fame country, in the fame habits and manners, and who have moreover the fame objects before their eyes.

There are in the mind certain moments of perfect repofe, when its furface is not agitated by the leaft breath of paffion. The objects that then prefent themfelves fometimes engage our whole attention; we examine more at leifure their different appearances, and the impreffions they make on our memory are much more complete and durable.

Occurrences of this fort are very common, efpecially in early youth. A child commits a fault, and for punifhment is fhut up by himfelf

in a chamber.   What does he do? He fees in
the window fome pots with flowers, he plucks
fome of them, he confiders their colours, and remarks their fhades; his idle fituation feems to
give an additional difcernment to his fight.   It is
then with the child as with the blind; if the latter have commonly the fenfes of hearing and feeling more keen than other men, it is becaufe he
is not like them difturbed by the action of the
light upon his eyes, becaufe he is the more attentive, and more concentered within himfelf; and,
laftly, to fupply the fenfe he wants, he is, as M.
Diderot remarks, more interefted to improve thofe
fenfes that remain.

The impreffions that objects make on us depend principally on the moment at which thofe
objects ftrike us.   In the example juft mentioned,
it is the attention that the child is, fo to fay,
forced to give to the only objects that are expofed
to his fight, which makes him difcover in the colours and form of the flowers, thofe nice differences that a diftracted view, or a fuperficial glance
would not have permitted him to obferve.   It is
thus that a punifhment, or fome fimilar incident,
frequently determines the tafte of a young man,
and makes him a painter of flowers; by firft giving him fome knowledge of their beauty, and
then a love for thofe pictures that reprefent them.
Now to how many like incidents is the education of youth liable? and how can we imagine
them

them to be the fame in any two indviduals?
How many other caufes, moreover, prevent two
children, whether at home or at college, from
receiving the fame education ?

C H A P. V.

Of a collegiate education.

CHILDREN that have been brought up in
the fame college, are fuppofed to have
received the fame education. But at what age
do they enter the college? At feven or eight
years. Now at that age they have already charged
their memories with ideas, which being partly owing
to chance, and partly acquired in the parental
abode, arife from the ftate, the character, the
fortune, and wealth of their parents. Can we
then be furprifed that children entering a college with ideas frequently fo different, fhould difcover more or lefs ardour for ftudy, more or lefs
tafte for certain branches of fcience; and that the
ideas they have already acquired being united
with thofe they receive in common in the fchools,
fhould produce in them a confiderable alteration ?
From ideas thus altered, and combining again
among themfelves, muft frequently arife unexpected productions. From hence that inequality

C 3   in

in minds, and that diverfity of taftes obferved in the pupils of the fame college *.

Is it the fame of domeftic education ?

C H A P.   VI.

Of domeftic education.

THIS fort of education is doubtlefs more uniform ; it is more the fame. Two children are brought up under their parents, have the fame preceptor, nearly the fame objects before their eyes ; and read the fame books. The inequality of age is the only difference that appears to have any influence on their inftruction ; would you rendered that ineffectual ? Suppofe then thefe two brothers to be twins ? But have they had the fame nurfe ? What does that fignify ? It fignifies a great deal. How can we doubt the influence of the difpofition of the nurfe on the child ? At leaft they made no doubt of it in Greece, as is evident by the confequence in which the Lacedæmonian nurfes were held.

---

* I have elfewhere obferved, that it is to chance, that is to fay, to what is not taught by a mafter, we owe the greateft part of our inftruction. He whofe knowledge fhould be confined to the truths he learns from his governor, or his tutor, and to the facts contained in the fmall number of books that are read in the claffes, would doubtlefs be the moft ignorant child in the world.

In

In fact, fays Plutarch, if the Spartan does not cry even at the breaft ; if he be infenfible to fear, and already patient under fufferings, he owes it to his nurfe. In France, where I live, as in Greece, the choice of a nurfe therefore cannot be matter of indifference.

But fuppofe the fame nurfe to have fuckled thefe twins, and to have brought them up with the fame care. Is it to be imagined, when returned to their parents, the father and mother will have precifely the fame degree of affection for thefe two children ? and that the preference imperceptibly given to one of the two, will have no influence on his education ?

Suppofe, moreover, that the father and mother fhould regard them equally, will it be the fame with the domeftics ? Will not the tutor have a favourite ? and will the fondnefs that he fhews for one of the two children be long unnoticed by the other ? The different paffions, or patience of the mafter, and the foftnefs or feverity of his lectures, will they have no effect on the children ? In the laft place, will thefe two twins enjoy the fame ftate of health ?

In the career of the arts and the fciences, fuppofe them both to fet off with an equal pace, if the firft be ftopped by fome diforder, and fuffer the other to advance too far before him, his ftudies will become difguftful to him. If a child

lofe

lofe the hope of pre-eminence, if he be obliged
in a certain fenfe, to acknowledge a number of
fuperiors, he becomes thereby incapable of a vigorous application: even the fear of punifhment
is then ineffectual. This fear caufes a child to
contract a habit of attention, makes him learn to
read, and perform all that he is enjoined; but it
will not infpire him with that ardour for ftudy
which is the only pledge of great acquirements. It
is emulation that produces genius, and a defire of
becoming illuftrious that creates talents. It is
from the moment when the love of glory fires the
breaft, and takes poffeffion of the man, that we
are to date the progrefs of his intellectual faculties.
I have always thought that the fcience of education is, perhaps, nothing more than a knowledge
of the means of exciting emulation, which may
be lighted up or extinguifhed by a fingle word. A
commendation beftowed on the care with which
a child examines an object, and the exact defcription he gives of it, has fometimes been fufficient to excite in him that fort of attention to
which he has afterwards owed the fuperiority of
his underftanding. A collegiate, or domeftic
education is therefore never the fame for any two
individuals.

From the education of childhood we will
proceed to that of youth. Let not this examen
be regarded as fuperfluous. This fecond education is the moft important: mankind have then
other

other inftructors, with whom it is proper to be acquainted.

It is in youth, moreover, that our taftes and our talents are formed. This fecond education, the leaft uniform, and the moft abandoned to chance, is, at the fame time, the moft proper to confirm the truth of my opinion.

C H A P. VII.

Of the education of youth.

IT is at leaving the college and entering the world that the education of youth begins. It is lefs uniform than that of childhood, but more dependent on chance, and doubtlefs more important. The youth is then attacked by a greater number of fenfations : all that furrounds him ftrikes him, and ftrikes him forcibly.

It is at the age when certain paffions fpring up, that all the objects of nature agitate and impel him the moft ftrongly. It is then that he receives the moft efficacious inftruction ; it is then that his taftes and his character are determined ; and, laftly, that being more free, and more himfelf, the paffions excited in his heart determine his habits, and frequently all the future conduct of his life.

In children the difference of underftanding and character is not always very obvious. En-

gaged

gaged in the fame fort of ftudies, fubject to the fame difcipline, and moreover without paffions, their exterior is fufficiently fimilar.

The feed, that by fpringing up, fhall one day make fo much difference in their taftes, is either not yet formed, or at leaft is yet imperceptible. I compare two children to two men fitting on a bank, but with their backs to each other. If they rife up and walk in the direction they fat, they will infenfibly become further diftant, and foon lofe fight of each other, unlefs by again changing their direction, fome accident make them again approach.

The refemblance of children in fchools or colleges is the effect of conftraint. When they leave the college the conftraint ceafes. Then begins, as I have already faid, the fecond education of man; an education the more directed by chance, as youth on entering the world find themfelves in the midft of a greater number of objects. Now the more the furrounding objects are multiplied and diverfified, the lefs can the father or the mafter depend on the refult of their impreffion, and the lefs part the one and the other have in the education of a young man.

The new and principal inftructors of youth are the form of government under which they live, and the manners that form of government gives to a nation.

Mafters

Masters and pupils are all subject to these inſtitutors; these are the principal, but, however, not the only inſtructors of youth ; among these I also reckon the rank a young man holds in the world, his wealth or indigence, the societies with which he is connected *; and, laſtly, his friends, his books, and his miſtreſſes. Now it is on chance that depend his opulence, or poverty, and the choice of his ſociety (10), his friends, his books, and his miſtreſſes. It is on chance, therefore, that depends the choice of the principal part of his inſtructors. It is chance, moreover, that places him in this or that poſition, excites, extinguiſhes or modifies his taſtes and paſſions; and that has, conſequently, the greateſt part in forming his character. The character of a man is the immediate effect of his paſſions, and his paſſions are often the immediate effects of his ſituations.

The moſt ſtriking characters are ſometimes the produce of an infinity of little accidents. It is from an infinity of threads of hemp that the largeſt cables are formed (11). There is no change that chance cannot produce in the character of a man. But why do theſe changes almoſt always

---

* Does a man ſearch for the company of the learned ? Does he live habitually with thoſe of ſuperior abilities ? He becomes enlightened. It is to a deſire I always had to converſe with ſuch men, ſaid to me one day a celebrated author, that I owe my feeble talents.

operate

operate in a manner unperceived by himself? Because to perceive them, he must have a most severe and penetrating eye on himself. Now pleasure, idleness, ambition, poverty, &c. equally divert him from this observation. Every thing turns him away from himself. A man has, moreover, so much respect for himself, so much veneration for his own conduct, as being the consequence of such sagacious and profound reflection, that he can rarely permit himself to examine it : pride forbids, and pride is readily obeyed.

Chance has, therefore, a necessary and considerable influence on our education. The events of life are frequently the produce of the most trifling incidents. I know this assertion disgusts our vanity, which constantly assigns great causes to effects that appear to it of great consequence. To destroy the illusions of pride, I shall prove, by the aid of facts, that it is to the most trifling incidents the most illustrious citizens have sometimes owed their talents. From whence I conclude, that chance acts in a like manner on all mankind, and if its effects on ordinary minds are less remarked, it is merely because minds of this sort are themselves less remarkable.

CHAP.

C H A P. VIII.

Of the chances to which we often owe illustrious characters.

FOR my first example, I shall cite M. Vaucanson : his pious mother had a spiritual director, who lived in a cell, to which the hall where the clock was placed served as an antichamber. The mother paid frequent visits to this director. Her son waited for her in the antichamber : there alone, and having nothing to do, he wept with weariness, while his mother wept with repentance. However, as we commonly weep and weary ourselves as little as possible, and as in a state of vacation there are no sensations indifferent, young Vaucanson was soon struck with the uniform motion of the pendulum, and desirous of discovering its cause. His curiosity was roused ; he approached the clock case, and saw, through the crevices, the wheels that turn each other ; discovered a part of the mechanism, and guessed at the rest. He projected a similar machine, which he executed in wood with a knife, and at last was able to make a clock more or less perfect. Encouraged by this first success his taste for mechanics was determined. His talents displayed themselves, and the same genius that enabled

him

him to make a clock in wood, fhowed him the poffibility of forming a fluting automaton.

A chance of the fame fort allumined the genius
of Milton. Cromwell died, his fon fucceeded
him, and was driven out of England. Milton par-
ticipated his ill-fortune ; he loft the place of fecre-
tary to the protector, was imprifoned, releafed,
and driven into exile. At laft he returned, retired
to the country, and there, in the leifure of retreat
and difgrace, he executed the poem which he had
projected in his youth, and which has placed him
in the rank of the greateft of men.

If Shakefpeare had been, like his father, always
a dealer in wool ; if his imprudence had not obliged him to quit his commerce, and his country ;
if he had not affociated with libertines, and ftole
deer from the park of a nobleman ; had not been
purfued for the theft, and obliged to take refuge
in London ; engage in a company of actors ; and,
at laft, difgufted with being an indifferent per-
former (12), he had not turned author ; the prudent Shakefpeare had never been the celebrated
Shakefpeare ; and whatever ability he might have
acquired in the trade of wool, his name would
never have reflected a luftre on England.

It was a chance nearly fimilar that determined
the tafte of Moliere for the ftage. His grandfather loved the theatre, and frequently carried
him thither. The young man lived in diffipation ;

the

the father obferving it, afked in anger, if his fon
was to be made an actor.   Would to God, replied the grandfather, he was as good an actor
as Montrofe.   Thofe words ftruck young Moliere; he took a difguft to his trade, and France
owes its greateft comic writer to that accidental
reply.   Moliere, a fkilful tapeftry-maker, had
never elfe been cited among the great men of his
nation.

Corneille loved; he made verfes for his miftrefs, became a poet, compofed Melite (13),
then Cinna, Rodogune, &c. is the honour of
his country, and an object of emulation for pofterity.   The difcrete Corneille had remained a
lawyer, and compofed briefs that would have
been forgotten with the caufes he defended.
Thus it is, that the devotion of a mother, the
death of Cromwell, deer-ftealing, the exclama-
tion of an old man, and the beauty of a woman,
have given five illuftrious characters to Europe *.

I fhould never have done if I would enume-
rate all the writers celebrated for their talents,
and who owed thofe talents to fimilar incidents †.   Many philofophers adopt my opinion

---

* It will doubtlefs be faid, that fimilar incidents would
not produce fimilar effects but on men organifed in a
certain manner; I fhall anfwer this objection in the next
fection.

† *It will not be improper, however, to add here one more instance; Newton, in his younger days, was a student at Cam-
bridge,*

on this particular. M. Bonnet * compares with
me, genius to a lens, that burns in one point
only. Genius, according to us, is but the produce of a ftrong and concentered attention to any
art or fcience; but from whence does this attention proceed? From a lively tafte we feel
for that art or fcience. Now this tafte is not the
mere gift of nature †. Is a man born without
ideas? He is born alfo without taftes. We may,
therefore regard them as acquifitions arifing from the
fituations in which we are placed ‡. Genius then,
is the remote produce of incidents or chances
nearly fimilar to thofe I have cited (14).

M. Rouffeau is not of this opinion: he is, however, himfelf an inftance of the power of chance.

_bridge, but during the time of the plague retired into the country:
As he was reading under an apple-tree, one of the fruit fell and
ftruck him a fmart blow on the head. When he obferved the
fmallnefs of the apple he was furprifed at the force of the ftroke.
This led him to confider the accelerating motion of falling bodies;
from whence he deduced the principles of gravity, and laid the
foundation of that philofophy which will reflect honour on the
Englifh nation, when, perhaps, the names of Creffy, Agincourt,
and Blenheim will be utterly forgotten._

* See his Analytical Effay on the Faculties of the Mind.

† If children have feldom the tafte we would give them,
it is the fault of their inftructors, and not that of their organifation.

‡ The only difpofition to fcience a man has at his birth,
is the faculty of comparing and combining. In fact, all the
operations of his mind are neceffarily reduced to the obferving of the relations objects have to him, and among themfelves. In the next fection I fhall examine what this faculty
is in man.

On

On entering the world fortune placed him in the train of an ambaſſador. A bickering with that miniſter made him quit the political career (15), and follow that of the arts and ſciences. His choice lay between eloquence and muſic; equally adapted to ſucceed in both thoſe arts, his taſte remained for ſome time undetermined; a particular ſeries of circumſtances made him at laſt prefer eloquence; a ſeries of another kind would have made him a muſician. Who knows if the favours of a fair chantreſs would not have produced that effect (16). No one at leaſt can affirm, that love could not have made an Orpheus of the French Plato. But what particular incident made M. Rouſſeau enter the career of eloquence? I do not know: that is his ſecret; all that I can ſay is, that in this purſuit his firſt ſucceſs was ſufficient to determine his choice.

The academy of Dijon propoſed a prize for eloquence. It was a whimſical ſubject * ; the queſtion was, *Whether the ſciences be more hurtful than uſeful to ſociety?* The only ſtriking manner of treating this queſtion was to take part againſt the ſciences. M. Rouſſeau was ſenſible of this ; and made on this ſubject an eloquent diſcourſe, that deſerved and obtained great en-

---

* He that propoſed this prize probably thought, that the only way to become equally eſtimable with any other, was to prove, that any other is as ignorant as himſelf.

comiums *.   This fuccefs made the remarkable
period of his life.   From hence arofe his glory, his
misfortunes, and his paradoxes.

Charmed with the beauty of his own difcourfe,
the maxims of the orator (17) foon became thofe
of the philofopher; and from that moment, devoted to the love of paradoxes, nothing was difficult
to him.   Was it neceffary to maintain, in order
to defend his opinion, that the man abfolutely
brutal, without art, without induftry, and inferior to every known favage, is notwithftanding
more virtuous and happy than the polifhed citizen
of London or Amfterdam ? he was ready to maintain it.

The dupe of his own eloquence, and content with the title of an orator, he renounced
that of a philofopher, and his errors became the
confequence of his firft fuccefs.   The leaft caufes
have often produced the greateft effects.   Chag-
rined at laft by contradictions, or perhaps too

* *A man who is mafter of a fine ftyle, and is well verfed in
fophiftry, will always fhine by taking the paradoxical fide of a
queftion. He that fhould attempt to prove that we fee the light
of the fun at mid-day, how juftly foever his arguments were ranged and how beautiful foever his language, would have but few
readers. Whereas, he that fhould affert we fee the fun's light at
midnight, and fupport his affertion in a pleafing language, by
fomething like argument, would have many admirers. For the
human mind, though not convinced, is always pleafed to find the
appearance of argument where it has no right to expect any argument at all.*

fond

fond of fingularity, M. Rouffeau quitted Paris and
his friends: he retired to Montmorenci (18). He
there compofed and publifhed his Emelius ; and
was purfued by envy, ignorance, and hypocrify.
Efteemed by all Europe for his eloquence, he
was perfecuted in France. They applied to him
this paffage, *cruciatur ubi eft, laudatur ubi non
eft* *. Obliged at laft to retire to Swifferland,
and continually more irritated againft perfecution,
he there wrote his famous letter addreffed to the
archbifhop of Paris. Thus it is that all the ideas
of a man, all his glory, and all his misfortunes, are
frequently formed into a feries by the invifible
power of a firft event. M. Rouffeau, therefore,
as well as an infinity of illuftrious men, may be
confidered as one of the chefs d'œuvres of
chance.

Let me not be reproached with having ftopped
to confider the caufes to which great men have fo
frequently owed their talents ; my fubject obliged
me to it. I fhall not grow tedious by details. I
know that the public is fond of great talents, and
that the trifling caufes by which they are produced appears of little confequence. I fee with pleafure a river roll its waves majeftically through the
plain, but it is with labour my imagination mounts
to its fource, to fee it affemble the volume of

---

* This fentence is applicable to almoft every philofopher
whofe writings have obtained the public efteem.

waters

waters neceffary to its courfe. Objects prefent
themfelves to us in maffes; it is with wearinefs
we attend to their decompofition. I cannot perfuade myfelf without difficulty, that the comet
which traverfes with fuch rapidity our mundane
fyftem, and menaces its ruin, is nothing more
than a certain compofition of invifible atoms.

In morals, as in phyfics, we are ftruck by the
great alone : we conftantly affign great caufes to
great effects; we would make the figns in the
zodiac anounce the fall or revolution of empires.
Yet how many crufades have been undertaken or
fufpended ; how many revolutions accomplifhed
or prevented ; how many wars kindled or extinguifhed, by the intrigues of a prieft, a woman,
or a minifter. It is for want of fecret anecdotes,
that we do not every where find the glove of the
duchefs of Marlborough *.

Let what I here fay of empires be applied to
individuals : it will appear in like manner,, that
their exaltation or difgrace, their happinefs or
mifery, are the produce of a certain feries of circumftances, of an infinity of chances unforefeen,
and is apparently infignificant. I compare the

* The phyficians fay, that a great acrimony in the femi-
nal matter was the caufe of the violent paffion of Henry VIII.
for women. It is therefore to this acrimony England owes
the deftruction of popery. Hiftory would perhaps degrade
its dignity, if it were always to fearch out in this manner
the fecret caufes of great events : but it would be far more
inftructive.

little

little incidents that produce the great events of our lives, to the hairy fibres of a root that infinuate infenfibly into the clefts of a rock, and there increafe that it may one day fpring up.

Chance *, therefore has, and always will, have a part in our education, and efpecially in that of men of genius; therefore, would you increafe their number in a nation, obferve the means that are ufed by chance to infpire mankind with a defire of becoming illuftrious. This obfervation made, place them exprefsly and frequently in the fame pofitions that chance places them but feldom: this is the only way to make them numerous.

The moral education of mankind is now almoft entirely abandoned to chance. To render it perfect, the plan muft be directed by public utility, and founded on fimple and invariable principles; this is the only method to diminifh the influence it receives from chance, and to obviate the contradictions that are found, and muft necefarily be found, among all the various precepts of modern education.

---

* I muft inform the reader, that by the word Chance, I mean the unknown concatenation of caufes proper to produce fuch or fuch an effect, and that I never ufe the word in any other fenfe.

CHAP.

CHAP. IX.

Of the principal caufes of the contradictions in the precepts of education.

IN Europe, and efpecially in the catholic countries, if all the precepts of education are contradictory, it is becaufe public inftruction is there confided to two powers, whofe interefts are oppofite, and whofe precepts therefore muft be different and contradictory:

The one is the fpiritual power,

The other is the temporal power.

The ftrength and grandeur of the latter depends on the ftrength and grandeur of the empire it commands. The real ftrength of a prince con- fifts in the ftrength of the nation; when that ceafes to be refpected, the prince ceafes to be powerful. He defires, and ought to defire, that his fubjects be brave, induftrious, learned, and virtuous. Is it the fame with the fpiritual power? No; its intereft is not the fame. The power of the prieft depends on the fuperftition and ftupid credulity of the people. It is of little fignifi- cance to him that they be learned; the lefs they know the more docile they will be to his dictates. The intereft of the fpiritual power is not connect- ed with that of a nation, but with that of a fect.

Two

Two nations are at war; what is it to the pope which is the master and which the slave, if the conqueror and conquered are both to be subject to him? If the French sink under the power of the Portuguese; if the house of Braganza mounts the throne of the Bourbons, the pope sees nothing in it but an increase of his authority. What does the sacerdotal power require of a nation? A blind submission, a credulity without bounds, a puerile and contagious fear. Whether the nation renders itself renowned for its talents and patriotic virtues, is what the clergy concern themselves little about. Great talents and great virtues are almost unknown in Spain, Portugal, and in all parts where the spiritual power is most formidable.

Ambition, it is true, is common to both powers, but the means by which it is gratified are very different. To raise itself to the highest point of grandeur, the one must exalt the passions of men, and the other debase them.

If it be to a love of the public good, to justice, to riches, and glory, that the temporal power owes its warriors, its magistrates, its merchants, and men of letters; if it be by the commerce of its towns, the valour of its troops, the equity of its senate, and the genius of its literati, that the prince renders his nation respectable among others, the strong passions directed to the general good then serve as the basis of his grandeur.

The

The ecclefiaftic corps, on the contrary, found their grandeur on the deftruction of thofe very paffions. The prieft is ambitious, but ambition is odious to him in the laity; it thwarts his defigns. The project of the prieft is to extinguifh every defire in man, to make him difguft his wealth and power, and by that difguft to appropriate both of them to himfelf (19). Of this we are certain, that the fyftem of religion has been conftantly directed by this plan.

At the time that chriftianity was eftablifhed, what did they preach? *The community of property.* Who offered himfelf as the depofitary of the goods that were to be in common? The prieft. Who violated the depofit, and made himfelf the proprietor? The prieft. When the rumour of the end of the world was fpread abroad, by whom was it authenticated? The prieft. The report was favourable to his defigns, he hoped, that ftruck with a panic, mankind would be anxious about one matter only (a matter in reality of importance) that of their falvation. Life, they faid, is but a paffage: heaven is our inheritance; why then fhould we give ourfelves up to earthly pleafures? If difcourfes of this kind did not entirely detach the laity from earthly enjoyments, it at leaft weaned them from the love of their relations, of glory, of the public good, and of their country. Heroes then became rare; and fovereigns, ftruck with the hope of mighty poffeffions in Heaven, confented

confented fometimes to commit to a prieft a part of their terreftial authority. The prieft feized it, and to preferve it depreciated true glory and true virtue. It was no longer permitted to honour fuch characters as Minos, Lycurgus, Codrus, Ariftides, Timoleon ; in a word, the defenders and benefactors of their country. Other models were propofed, 'other names, were infcribed in the calendar ; and inftead of the ancient heroes, were feen the names of St. Anthony, St. Crif-pin, St. Claire, St. Fiacre, St. Francis (20); in fhort, the names of all thofe folitary wretches, who, dangerous to fociety by the example of their ftupid religion, retired to cloifters and deferts, there to vegetate and end their ufelefs days.

By fuch models the priefts hoped to accuftom mankind to regard this life as a fhort journey. They then hoped that being without defires for terreftrial goods, and without friendfhip for thofe they fhould meet on their journey, they would become equally indifferent to their own happi-nefs and that of their pofterity. In fact, if life be nothing more than a baiting-place, why fhould we be fo interefted in the affairs that con-cern it ? A traveller does not repair the walls of an inn where he is to pafs one night only.

To fecure their grandeur, and fatisfy their ambition, the fpiritual and temporal powers muft, therefore, in every country, employ very

different

different means. Charged in common with the inſtruction of the public, they muſt engrave on the hearts and minds of men precepts that are contradictory, and relative to the intereſt that one has in kindling, and the other in extinguiſhing the paſſions *.

That theſe two powers, however, equally preach probity, I allow. But they do not attach the ſame meaning to the word; and modern Rome, under the government of the pope, has not certainly the ſame idea of virtue that the ancient Romans had under the conſulate of the elder Brutus. The aurora of reaſon begins to appear; men now know that the ſame words do not every where convey the ſame ideas. What therefore is now required of an author? That he annex clear ideas to the terms he uſes. The reign of the dark ſcholaſtics may diſappear; the theologians will not perhaps always impoſe on the people and governments. Of this we may reſt aſſured, that they will not at leaſt preſerve their power by the means they have acquired it. Circumſtances have changed with the times: the neceſſity of the paſſions is now confeſſed; it is found, that by their preſervation, that of empires is ſecured. Paſſions are, in effect, ſtrong deſires,

* To attempt to deſtroy the paſſions of men, is to attempt to deſtroy their action. Does the theologian rail at the paſſions? he is the pendulum that mocks its ſpring, and the effect that miſtakes its cauſe.

and

and thefe defires may be either conformable or contrary to the public welfare. If avarice and intolerance be hurtful and criminal paffions, it is not fo with the defire to render ourfelves illuftrious by talents and patriotic virtues (21). By annihilating the defires, you annihilate the mind ; every man without paffions has within him no principle of action, nor motive to act.

You are, O catholic clergy! rich and powerful upon the earth, but your power may be deftroyed with that of the nations you command. By degrading them ftill more, they may be conquered by others, and will ceafe to be under your fubjection. Even your own intereft requires that men fhould continue to be excited by paffions and wants ; to ftifle them in man you muft change his nature.

O venerable theologians! O brutes! O my brethren! abandon the ridiculous project: ftudy the human heart, examine the fprings by which it is moved, and if you have not yet any clear idea of morality and politics (22), forbear to teach them. Pride has led you too long aftray : remember the ingenious fable of the birth of Momus. The moment he faw the day, fays a great poet, the infant god filled Olympus with his cries ; the celeftial court was ftuned : to quiet him, each one gave the child a play-thing. Jupiter, who had juft then created man, gave him to Momus, and ever fince man has been the

puppet

puppet of folly.   Now among the puppets of this
fort, the moft rueful, proud, and ridiculous, is a
doctor of divinity (23).   O theological puppet !
do not perfift in deftroying the paffions, they are
the vital principles of a ftate (24).   Employ
yourfelf in promoting the general good ; endeavour to trace out a plan of inftruction, whofe clear
and fimple principles fhall all center in the happinefs of the public.

How far diftant are we from fuch a plan of
inftruction ? Parents and mafters, with little harmony among themfelves, are equally ignorant of
what children ought to be taught.   Their ideas
of education are yet all confufed, and from
thence arifes that glaring contradiction in all their
precepts.

C H A P.   X.

*Examples of contradictory ideas or precepts inculcat-
ed in early youth.*

IF, in order to fhow more fenfibly the
contradiction in all the precepts of our education, I am obliged to defcend to a more
familiar ftyle, the fubject will plead my excufe.
It is in the religious feminaries deftined for the
inftruction of young ladies, that thefe contradictions are moft glaring.   Suppofe therefore I

enter

enter a convent : it is eight in the morning, the hour of conference ; there is held a difcourfe on modefty ; the fuperior of the convent proves, that a boarder fhould never look at a man. The clock ftrikes nine ; the dancing-mafter is in the parlour. Mind your fteps, he fays to his fcholar, hold up your head, and always look at your partner. Now which of thefe is fhe to believe? the dancing-mafter or the miftrefs of the con- vent ? The fcholar does not know; and there- fore acquires neither the grace the firft would give her, nor the referve that is preached to her by the other. Now from whence do thefe con- tradictions arife, but from the contradictory de- fires of the parents, who would have their daugh- ter at once agreeable and referved, join the pru- dery of the cloifter to the graces of the theatre ? That is, they would conciliate irreconcilables *.

The Turkifh education is, perhaps, the only one that is confentaneous with what is required of women in their own country (25).

The principles of education will be variable and indeterminate fo long as they do not regard one certain point. What point is that? The greateft public utility ; that is, the greateft plea-

---

* A girl is required to be fincere and ingenuous. A hufband is provided for her; fhe does not like him ; fhe declares it free- ly : it is taken amifs. The parents, therefore, would have her true or falfe, according as it is their intereft that fhe fhould be the one or the other.

fure,

fure, and the greateft happinefs, of the largeft number of citizens.

Do parents lofe this point of view ? They wander here and there in the paths of inftruction. Fafhion is their only guide. They know that to make their daughter a mufician they muft pay a mafter of mufic, but they do not know that to give her juft ideas of virtue they muft in like manner pay a mafter of morality.

When a mother undertakes the education of her daughter, fhe tells her in the morning, while putting on the rouge, that beauty is nothing ; that virtue and talents are all *.   At that moment company enters to the mother's toilet ; every one praifes the young lady's beauty, but not once a twelvemonth a word is faid about her talents and virtue †. The only recompence moreover that is promifed to her application and her virtue, is the ornaments of drefs, and yet they would have the young girl be indifferent to her beauty. . Into what confufion muft her ideas be thrown by fuch conduct !

---

* Do they perfuade a girl that without talents fhe will never get a hufband ? to-morrow fhe hears that the moft ftupid of her companions has made an excellent match, becaufe fhe had a large fortune, and that without a fortune no one can be married.

† If they commonly praife nothing but beauty in a daughter, it is becaufe beauty is really the moft interefting and defireable quality in her we vifit, and to whom we are neither hufband nor friend ; and with women the men are always on a vifit.

The

The education of a youth is not more confentaneous: the firft duty prefcribed him is the obfervance of the laws; the fecond, their violation, when he is offended; in cafe of an infult, he is to fight, under pain of being difhonoured. Do they prove to him, that it is by fervices rendered his country, he will obtain the confideration of this world, and the felicity of the next; what models do they propofe for his imitation? A monk, a fanatical and flothful dervife, whofe intoleration has filled empires with trouble and defolation.

A father recommends to his fon fidelity to his promife. A theologian then comes and tells the young man, that we are not bound to keep our promife to the enemies of God; for which reafon Lewis XIV. revoked the edict of Nantz given by his anceftors; that the pope has decided this queftion, by declaring every treaty made between catholic princes and heretics to be void, and by giving the former the power of violating thofe treaties whenever they have fufficient ftrength.

A preacher proves in the pulpit, that the God of the Chriftians is the God of truth; that it is by their hatred to falfehood his worfhippers are known (26). He defcends from the pulpit, and then owns, that it is quite prudent to obferve a refervation (27); that he himfelf in praifing the truth, takes great care how he fpeaks it (28). In fact, the man who fhould write the true hiftory

of

of his times, in a catholic country, would fet all
thefe worfhippers of the God of truth againft him
(29). In fuch a country, a man to guard himfelf
from perfecution, muft either be dumb, a fool, or
a liar.

Suppofe a preceptor, by force of application,
fhould infpire his pupil with candour and humanity ; his fpiritual director enters, and tells
him that we may pardon mankind their vices,
but not their errors ; that in the latter cafe indulgence is a crime, and that every one who does
not think as he does fhould be burned.

Such is the ignorance and contradiction of a
theologian, that he declaims againft the paffions
at the very moment he would excite emulation in
his pupil. He then forgets that emulation is a
paffion, and a very ftrong paffion too, if we judge
by its effects.

In every part of education, therefore, there is
contradiction. What is the caufe ? An ignorance of
the true principles of this fcience ; they have nothing
but confufed ideas about it. Mankind fhould be
elucidated ; the prieft oppofes it. Does the truth
dawn a moment upon them ? Its rays are abforb-
ed in the darknefs of fcholaftics. Error and crime
both fearch for obfcurity, the one in words (30),
the other in the night. Let not however all the
contradictions of our education be charged to
theology ; there are fome alfo that arife from the
vices of government. How will you perfuade a
                                              youth

youth to be faithful to fociety, and to keep the fecret of another, when even in England, the government, under a moft frivolous pretext, opens the letters of private perfons and betrays the public confidence? How can you flatter yourfelf with an expectation of infpiring him with a horror for fpies and informers, when he fees them honoured, rewarded, and penfioned.

When a young man comes from the college, and mixes with the world, he is expected to render himfelf agreeable, and conftantly preferve his chaftity. At the period that the paffion of love is moft fenfibly felt, muft a young man be indifferent to women, and live in the midft of them without defire * ? Can parental ftupidity imagine that when government builds a theatre for operas, and cuftom fets it open to young men, that, fond of their virginity, they will always behold with an eye of indifference, a fpectacle in which the endearments, the tranfports, and magical power of love, are painted in the moft brilliant

---

* If they would really damp the defires of love in a young man, what fhould they do? Inftitute violent exercifes, and infpire youth with a tafte for them. Exercife is in this cafe the moft efficacious lecture. The more we perfpire, the more of the animal fpirits we exhauft, the lefs vigour remains for love. The coldnefs and indifference of the favages of Canada, proceeds from the fatigue and inanition produced by their long and wearifome huntings.

colours, and enter their minds by all the organs of the fenfes †.

I fhould never have done if I would make a catalogue of all the contradictions in the European education, and efpecially in that of the Papifts.   In the thick fog of errors, how fhall we difcover the path of virtue? The Catholic, therefore, frequently wanders from it.   So that without fixed principles in this matter, it is to his fituation, to books, to friends, and to the miftreffes that chance has given him, that he owes his virtues or vices.   But is there any method of rendering the education of men more independent of chance ? and if there be, how is it to be attained ?

Teach nothing but the truth.   Error is continually at contradiction with itfelf : the truth never.

Do not abandon the education of the people to two powers, who having two oppofite interefts, conftantly teach two contradictory moralities (31).

By what fatality, it will be faid, have almoft all nations confided to the priefthood the moral

---

† Let it not be imagined, from what is here faid, that I am for deftroying the opera, or the drama. I only mean to condemn the cc-tradiction in our cuftoms and precepts. I am neither an enemy to the theatre, nor in this matter of the opinion of M. Rouffeau. The theatres are inconteffibly pleafing.   Now there is no pleafure that in the hands of a wife government may not, by being made the recompence of virtue, become its productive principle.

instruction

inftruction of their youth! What is the moral
of Papifts? A medly of fuperftitions. However there is nothing the facerdotal power cannot
execute by the aid of fuperftition. For by that
it robs the magiftrates of their authority, and
kings of their legitimate power : it is by that it
fubdues the people, and acquires a power over
them which is frequently fuperior to the laws;
and finally, by that it corrupts the very principles
of morality. What remedy is there for this evil ?
There is but one. This fcience muft be entirely
refounded. A new fpirit muft prefide over the
formation of its new principles, and every part
of it muft be directed to the public welfare.

It is time that under the title of the holy minifters
of morality, the magiftrates fhould found it on principles that are fimple, clear, and conformable to
the general profperity, and of which all the inhabitants may form ideas equally juft and precife.
But will the fimplicity and uniformity of thefe
principles agree with the different paffions of
men ?

Their defires may be different, but their manner of regarding objects is effentially the fame.
They fee well and do bad. Every one being born
with a juft difcernment difcovers the truth,
when it is prefented to him in a clear light.
With regard to youth, they have more avidity for
it, as they are lefs accuftomed to break it, and
have lefs intereft to fee objects different from what

E 2   they

they really are. The minds of young people cannot be drawn from the truth without force. To produce this effect, all the patience and all the art of modern education are required; and even then they see by fits the light of natural reafon, and the falfity of thofe opinions with which their memories are charged. Why then do they not efface thofe, and fubftitute in their place new ideas? Such a change of ideas requires time and pains, and is too difficult a tafk for the greateft part of mankind, who frequently defcend to the grave before they have acquired clear and precife ideas of virtue.

When will they have juft ideas? When the religious fyftem fhall coincide with the national profperity: when religions, the habitual inftruments of facerdotal ambition, fhall become the felicity of the public. Is it poffible to conceive of fuch a religion? The examination of this queftion deferves the attention of the fagacious part of mankind. I fhall therefore, en paffant, take a view of the falfe religions.

CHAP. XI.

Of falfe religions.

"EVERY religion, fays Hobbes, founded on "the fear of an invifible power, is a tale, that, "avowed by a nation, bears the name of religion,
"and

" and difavowed by the fame nation, bears the name " of fuperftition." The nine incarnations of Wift-nou are religion in the Indies, and tales at Nuremberg.

I fhall not make ufe of the authority of this definition to deny the truth of religion. If I believe my nurfe and my tutor, every other religion is falfe, mine alone is the true *. But is it acknowledged for fuch by the univerfe? No: the earth ftill groans with the multitude of temples confecrated to error. There is no one that is not the religion of fome country.

The hiftories of Numa, Zoroafter, Mahomet, and fo many other founders of modern worfhip, teach us that all religions may be confidered as political inftitutions, which have a great influence on the happinefs of nations. I therefore fuppofe, as the human mind ftill produces, from time to time, new religions, that it is a matter of importance, in order to render them the leaft detrimental poffible, to point out the plan that fhould be followed in their formation.

All religions are falfe, except the Chriftian: but I do not confound that with papifm.

---

* Perhaps this affertion will appear abfurd. This abfurdity, however, is common to all men. The ridicule in me, as in them, is the effect of pride. If each one thinks his religion the beft, it is becaufe each one fays to himfelf: *They who do not think as I do, are wrong.* I therefore exprefs myfelf in the fame manner as others.

CHAP.

C H A P.   XII.

Popery is of human inſtitution.

PAPISM in the eyes of a man of ſenſe is
nothing more than mere idolatry (32).   The
Roman church without doubt regarded it as no
other than a human inſtitution, when, it made of
that religion a ſcandalous uſe, an inſtrument of
its avarice and ambition, that ſerved to promote
the criminal projects of the popes, and legitimate
their avidity and pride.   But theſe imputations,
ſay the papiſts, are calumnies.

To prove them to be true, I aſk if it be probable that the heads of the monaſtic orders regarded their religion as divine, when to enrich
themſelves and their convents, they forbade the
monks to inter any one in holy ground who died
without making them a bequeſt? If they were
themſelves the dupes of a doctrine publicly pro-
feſſed, when they made themſelves proprietors (33)
of goods, that in quality of ſtewards for the poor,
they ought to have divided among them?   If
the popes thought they really practiſed juſtice and
humility, when they declared themſelves the diftributors of the kingdoms of America, over which
they had no ſort of right?   When by a line of
demarkation, they divided that part of the world
(34) between the Spaniards and Portugeſe? Laſtly, when they pretended to reign over princes,
direct

direct them in temporal matters, and be the arbitrary difpofers of their crowns? O papifts!
examine what has been the conduct of your church
in all ages. Has it fought to entertain a Roman
garrifon in every kingdom, and to attach a great
number of men to its intereft? (it is the practice
of every ambitious fect.) It has inftituted a great
number of religious orders; erected and peopled
a great number of monafteries; and laftly has
had the artifice to quarter this ecclefiaftical militia
in the countries where it was eftablifhed.

The fame motive that made it defire the
multiplication of the fecular clergy, has multiplied the facraments: and the people, in order
to receive them, were obliged to augment the
number of their priefts. They foon equalled that
of the grafs-hoppers of Egypt. Like them they
devoured the harvefts; thefe priefts, fecular and
regular, being maintained at the expence of the
catholic nations. To bind thefe priefts more
clofely to its intereft, and to enjoy their affection without a rival, the church obliged them to
live a life of celibacy, without wives and without children; but otherwife in a ftate of eafe and
luxury, that made their condition continually
more pleafing to them. This was not all; the
Roman church, ftill farther to increafe its riches
and power, endeavoured, in the name of
St. Peter, or fome other, to raife contributions
in every kingdom. By this method it in effect

E 4 opened

opened a bank between earth and heaven, and under the name of indulgences, received ready money for bills drawn on heaven and payable to order.

Now, as we have feen in every age the facerdotal power facrifice virtue to the luft of wealth and power : when we read the hiftory of the popes, and fee their policy, their ambition, their manners, in a word their whole conduct, and find it fo different from that prefcribed by the Gofpel, how can we imagine that the chiefs of this religion have had any other defign than to get poffeffion of all the power and wealth of the earth (35) ?

After examining the manners and conduct of the monks, the clergy, and pontifs, a proteftant may, I think, fhow, for the juftification of his belief, and the advantage of nations, that papifm was never any thing more than a human inftitution. But why have religions been hitherto merely local ? Is it not poffible to conceive of one that may become univerfal ?

C H A P. XIII.

Of an univerfal religion.

AN univerfal religion cannot be founded but on principles that are eternal and invariable, that are drawn from the nature of men and

things,

things, and that, like the propofitions of geometry, are capable of the moft rigorous demonftration. Are there 'fuch principles, and can
they be equally adapted to all nations ? Yes,
doubtlefs : or if they vary, it will be only in fome
of their applications to thofe different countries
where chance has placed the different nations.

But among the principles or laws proper for
all focieties, which is the firft and moft facred ?
That which fecures to every one his property,
his life, and his liberty.

When a man is an uncertain proprietor of his
land he will not till his field, he will not cultivate his orchard : the nation foon becomes ravaged and defolated by famine. Is a man the uncertain proprietor of his life and liberty ? He that
is in continual fear, is without fpirit and without
induftry : folely concerned for his perfonal prefervation, and wrapt up in himfelf, he does not regard
what paffes without him : he does not ftudy the
fcience of man, nor remark his defires and his
paffions. It is, however, from this preliminary
knowledge that the laws moft conformable to the
public profperity are to be deduced.

By what fatality have laws fo neceffary to fociety, remained unknown, even to the prefent
day ? Why has not heaven hitherto revealed
them ? Heaven, I anfwer, requires that man
by his reafon fhould co-operate to his own happinefs, and that of the numerous focieties of the
earth

earth (36); and that the mafter-piece of an excellent legiflation fhould be, like that of other
fciences, the product of genius and experience.

God has faid to man, I have created thee, I
have given thee fenfations, memory, and confequently reafon. It is my will that thy reafon,
fharpened at firft by want, and afterward enlightened by experience, fhall provide thee fuften-
ance, teach thee to cultivate the land, to improve the inftruments of labour, of agriculture,
in a word, of all the fciences of the firft neceffity. It is alfo my will, that by cultivating this
fame reafon, thou mayft come to a knowledge of
my moral will, that is, of thy duties toward fociety, of the means of maintaining order, and
laftly of the knowledge of the beft legiflation
poffible.

This is the only natural religion to which I
would have mankind elevate their minds, that
only which can become univerfal, that which is
alone worthy of God, which is marked with his
feal, and that of the truth. All others muft
bear the impreffion of man, of fraud and falfehood *. The will of God, juft and good, is
that the children of the earth fhould be happy,

---

* *This is evidently to be underftood of mere natural religion,
and has nothing to do with that which is revealed ; for the queftion here is not, whether the revealed religion be true or falfe ;
but how a natural religion, that would be univerfally ufeful,
might be eftablifhed.*

and enjoy every pleafure compatible with the public welfare.

Such is the true worfhip, that which philofophy
fhould reveal to the world. No other faints would
belong to fuch a religion than the benefactors to
humanity ; fuch as Lycurgus, Solon, Sydney,
the inventors of fome ufeful art, fome pleafure
that is new, but conformable to the general intereft : none would be rejected as reprobate, but
the enemies to fociety, and the gloomy adverfa-
ries to the pleafures.

Will the priefts * one day become the apoftles
of fuch a religion ? Their intereft forbids. The
clouds that hover over the principles of morality
and legiflation (which effentially are the fame fcience) have been brought thither by their policy.
It is on the ruins of the greateft part of religions
that found morality muft be founded. Would to
God that the priefts, fufceptible of a noble ambition, had fearched in the conftituent principles
of man, the invariable laws by which nature and
heaven directs that the happinefs of focieties be
eftablifhed ! Would to God that the religious
fyftem may become the palladium of public felicity ! It is to the priefts that thefe cares fhould be
confided. They would then enjoy a grandeur
and glory founded on public acknowledgement.
They might then fay to themfelves each day of

* The author means the Roman priefts, to whom it is plain
he every where refers.

their

their lives, it is by us that mankind are happy. Such a grandeur, such a lasting happiness appeared to them mean and despicable. You might, O ministers of the altar! become the idols of intelligent and virtuous men! you have chose rather to command over bigots and slaves; you have rendered yourselves odious to good citizens, by becoming the plague of nations, the instruments of their unhappiness, and the destroyers of true morality.

Morality founded on true principles is the only true natural religion. However, if there should be men whose insatiate credulity (37) cannot be satisfied without a mysterous religion; let the friends of the marvellous search out among the religions of that sort, one whose establishment will be least detrimental to society.

C H A P. XIV.

Of the conditions, without which a religion is destructive to national felicity.

AN intollerant religion, and one whose worship requires a great expence, is undoubtedly a prejudicial religion. Its intollerance must, in process of time depopulate the nation, and the sumptuous worship exhaust its wealth (38). There are Roman Catholic countries where they reckon near fifteen thousand convents, twelve thousand

thoufand priories, fifteen thoufand chapels, thir-
teen hundred abbeys, ninety thoufand priefts employed in ferving forty-five thoufand parifhes,
and befide all thefe an infinity of abbés, teachers
of feminarifts, and ecclefiaftics of every kind. The
total number amounting to at leaft three hundred
thoufand men, whofe charge * would maintain a

* In every country where they count 300,000 monks, curates,
priefts, canons, bifhops, &c. they muft coft the ftate, in lodg-
ing, cloathing, feeding, &c. one with another, half a crown
per day. Now, to fupport this, what prodigious fums muft
the priefthood raife on the nation, in rents, tenths, penfions,
impofts for maffes, reparations of churches and chapels, paro-
chial and conventual treafuries, feats in churches, offerings,
marriages, baptifms, burials, charities, difpenfations, mif-
fions, &c.

The tenths alone that the clergy draw from the cultivated
lands of a country, are nearly equal to what is received by all
its proprietors. In France the arpent * of cultivated land, let
at five fhillings and fix pence, or fix fhillings, yields about
twenty or twenty-two minots of corn of three bufhels each.
The prieft for his tenth takes two; the price of thefe two minots, or fix bufhels, may be, one year with another, eight or nine
fhillings. The prieft moreover takes as much ftraw as may
amount to five fhillings; befides his tenth of oats and their ftraw
amounting to twenty pence or two fhillings: total fifteen fhillings that the prieft takes in the three years for the fame land,
that yields the proprietor in the fame time fixteen or eighteen
fhillings, out of which he is to pay the tenth, fupport his farm,
make good the deficiencies of unlet land, and lofs by far-
mers, &c.

From this calculation it is eafy to judge of the immenfe riches
of the clergy; fuppofe we reduce the number to 200,000 ?
Their maintenance will then amount to 25,000 pounds fterling per day, and confequently to nine millions one hundred
and twenty-five thoufand pounds per annum. Now what a fleet

* The arpent contains one hundred perches fquare, of eighteen feet each.

formidable

formidable army and marine.   A religion thus expensive to a state (39) cannot long be the religion of an enlightened and well governed nation (40). The people that submit to it will labour only to maintain the ease and luxury of the priesthood; each of its inhabitants will be nothing more than a slave to the sacerdotal power.

and army might be maintained with this sum ?   A wise government, therefore, cannot be desirous of supporting a religion that is so expensive and burdensome to the subject. In Austria, Spain, and Bavaria, and perhaps even in France, the priests, (deduction being made for interest paid to annuitants) are richer than the sovereigns.

What remedy is there for this abuse ?   There is but one; and that is to diminish the number of the priests. But there are religions (and the Roman Catholic is of this sort) whose worship requires a great number. In this case the worship should be changed, or at least the number of the sacraments diminished. The fewer priests there are, the fewer funds will be necessary for their maintenance. But these funds are sacred. Why ? Is it because they are in part usurped from the poor ? The clergy are only the depositaries. Therefore no taxes should be levied on these funds, but such as are absolutely necessary for government. I would observe further, that the temporal power being expressly appointed to watch over the temporal happiness of the people, it has a right to the administration of such legacies as are left to the poor, and to reassume all the funds of which the monks have defrauded them. But what use shall be made of them ? Apply them to the actual support of the wretched; either by charities or diminution of taxes, or by the purchase of small possessions, which distributed among those whom poverty has deprived of their property, will, by making them proprietors, render them citizens.

These long notes will not perhaps, afford much entertainment to an Englishman. They should however afford him a sensible pleasure, when he reflects how much happier the inhabitants of this country now are, than their ancestors were a very few centuries past.

A religion

A religion, to be good, therefore, fhould be tolerant and little expenfive (41). Its clergy fhould have no authority over the people. A dread of the prieft debafes the mind and the foul: makes the one brutifh and the other flavifh. Muft the minifters of the altar be always armed with the fword? Can the barbarities committed by their intollerance ever be forgotten? The earth is yet drenched with the blood it has fpilt! Civil tollerance alone is not fufficient to fecure the peace of nations: the ecclefiaftic muft concur in the fame intention. Every dogma is a feed of difcord and injuftice that is fown among men. Which is the truly tolerant religion? That which like the pagan has no dogma, or which may be reduced, like that of the philofophers, to a found and elevated morality; which will, doubtlefs be one day the religion of the univerfe.

It is requifite, moreover, that a religion be gentle and humane:

That its ceremonies contain nothing gloomy or fevere:

That it conftantly prefent fpectacles that are pompous, and feftivals that are pleafing (42):

That its worfhip excite the paffions, but fuch paffions only as tend to the public utility; the religion that ftifles them produces Talapoins, Bonzes, and Bramins; but never heroes, illuftrious men, and noble citizens.

The

The religion that is joyful, fuppofes a noble
confidence in the goodnefs of the Supreme Being.
Why would you have him refemble an Eaftern tyrant? Why make him punifh flight faults with
eternal torment? Why thus put the name of the
Divinity at the bottom of the portrait of the devil?
Why opprefs the foul with a load of fear, break its
fprings, and of a worfhipper of Jefus, make a vile,
pufillanimous flave? It is the malignant who paint
a malignant God. What is their devotion? A
veil for their crimes.

A religion departs from its political purpofe,
when the man who is juft, humane toward his
brethren, and diftinguifhed for his talents and his
virtues, is not affured of the favour of heaven:
when a momentary defire, a burft of paffion, or
the omiffion of a mafs, can deprive him of it for
ever.

Let not the rewards of heaven be made the
price of trifling religious operations, which convey
a diminutive idea of the Eternal, and a falfe conception of virtue; its rewards fhould never
be affigned to fafting, hair-cloth, a blind fubmiffion, and felf-caftigation.

The man who places thefe operations among
the virtues, might as well place thofe of leaping,
dancing, and tumbling on the rope. What is it
to the public whether a young fellow flog himfelf or make a perilous leap?

As

As they formerly deified the fever, why not deify the public good? Why has not this divinity his worſhip, his temple, and his prieſts; (43) and laſtly, why make a virtue of ſelf-denial? Humanity is in man the only virtue truly ſublime: it is the principal, and perhaps the only one with which religions ought to inſpire mankind, as it includes almoſt all others.

Let humility be held in veneration by a convent: it favours the meanneſs and idleneſs of a monaſtic life (44). But ought this humility to be the virtue of a people? No: A noble pride has ever been that of a renowned nation. It was the ſpirit of contempt, with which the Greeks and Romans regarded the ſlaviſh nations; it was a juſt and lofty opinion of their own courage and force, that concurring with their laws, enabled them to ſubdue the univerſe*. Pride, it will be ſaid, attaches a man to the earth: ſo much the better; pride is therefore uſeful. Let religion, far from

---

* *That the Romans owed much of their exaltation to this ſpirit is very certain, but it is not ſo certain that they made a right uſe of it, or at leaſt did not carry it to an exceſs; for as Lord Bolingbroke obſerves, in his Letters on the Study of Hiſtory, when ſpeaking of the Roman nation, during the career of their conqueſts. They had not then learned the leſſon of moderation;* " *An inſatiable thirſt of* " *military fame, an unconfined ambition of extending their empire,* " *an extravagant confidence in their own knowledge and force, an* " *inſolent contempt of their enemies, and an impetuous, overbearing* " *ſpirit, with which they purſued all their enterprizes, compoſed at* " *that time the diſtinguiſhing character of a Roman; and their* " *ſages had not then learned, that virtues in exceſs degenerate into* " *vices.*"

oppofing, encreafe in man an attachment to things terreftial ; let every citizen be employed in promoting the profperity, the glory and power of his country ; and let religion be the panegyrift of every action that promotes the welfare of the majority, fanctify all ufeful eftablifhments, and never deftroy them. May the intereft of the fpiritual and temporal powers be for ever one and the fame ; may thefe two powers be reunited, as at Rome, in the hands of the magiftrates (45) : may the voice of heaven be henceforth that of the public good : and may the oracles of God confirm every law that is advantageous to the people!

C H A P.   XV.

Among the falfe religions which have been leaft detrimental to the happinefs of fociety?

THE firft I fhall mention is that of the Pagans : but at the time of its inftitution, this pretended religion was nothing more than the allegorical fyftem of nature. Saturn was Time, Ceres, Matter ; and Jupiter, the generating Spirit (46). All the fables of mythology were mere emblems of certain principles of nature. When we confider it as a religious fyftem, was it fo abfurd to adore, under various names, the different attribues of the Divinity * ?

---

* We are aftonifhed at the abfurdity of the Pagan religion : pofterity will one day be far more aftonifhed at the religion of the Papifts.

In the temples of Minerva, of Venus, Mars, Apollo, and of Fortune, whom did they adore? Jupiter, by turns confidered as wife, beautiful, powerful, enlightning and fertilifing the univerfe. Is it more rational to erect, under the names of St. Euftache, St. Martin, or St. Roch, temples to the Supreme Being? But the Pagans kneeled before ftatues of wood or ftone. The Catholics do the fame; and if we may judge by exterior appearances, they frequently exprefs more veneration for their faints than for the Eternal.

I am willing to allow moreover that the Pagan religion was the moft abfurd. It is wrong for a religion to be abfurd: its abfurdity may have mifchievous confequences. This fault however is not of the firft magnitude; and if its principles be not entirely oppofite to the public good, if its maxims may be made agreeable to the laws, and the general utility, it is even the leaft detrimental of all others. Such was the Pagan religion. It never oppofed the projects of a patriotic legiflature. It was without dogmas, and confequently humane and tolerant. There could be no difpute, no war among its fectators that the flighteft attention of the magiftrates would not prevent. Its worfhip moreover did not require a great number of priefts, and therefore was not neceffarily a charge to the ftate:

Their Lares or domeftic gods, fufficed for the daily worfhip of individuals. Some temples erect-

ed

ed in large cities, fome colleges of priefts, fome
pompous feftivals, were fufficient for their rational
devotion.   Thefe feftivals, in the vacation from
rural labours, gave the inhabitants an opportunity
to vifit the cities, and became thereby a feafon of
pleafure.   Though thefe feafts were magnificent,
they were rare, and confequently but little expenfive.   The Pagan religion had not therefore
any of the inconveniencies of Papifm.

This religion of the fenfes was befide the moft pro-
'per for mankind, the beft adapted to produce thofe
ftrong impreffions that it is neceffary for the legiflature fometimes to excite in the people. The imagination being thereby continually kept in action,
nature was held in entire fubjection to the empire
of Poefy, which enlivened and invigorated every
part of the univerfe.   The fummits of the mountains, the wide extended plains, the impenetrable
forefts, the fources of the rivers, and the depths
of the feas, were peopled by the Oreades, the
Fauns, the Napes, the Hamadryades, the Tritons,
and Nereides.   The gods and goddeffes lived in
fociety with mortals, took a part in their feafts,
their wars, and their amours; Neptune fupped
with the king of Ethiopia.   The Nymphs and
the Heroes fat down among the Gods.   Latona
had her altars.   The deified Hercules efpoufed
Hebe.   Thefe celebrated heroes inhabited the
fields and the groves of Elyfium. Thefe fields,
fince adorned by the fiery imagination of the prophet,

phet, who tranfported thither the Houres, were the abode of various and illuftrious men of every fort. It was there that Achilles, Patroclus, Ajax, Agamemnon, and all thofe heroes that fought under the walls of Troy, were ftill employed in military exercifes; it was there that Pindar and Homer ftill celebrated the Olympic games, and the exploits of the Greeks.

The fort of exercife and fong that had been the occupation of the heroes and poets on the earth, in a word, all the taftes they had contracted, accompanied them in the infernal regions. Their death was not properly any other than a prolongation of their life.

According to this religion, what muft have been the moft earneft defire, the moft cogent intereft of the Pagans? That of ferving their country by their talents, their courage, their integrity, their generofity, by all their virtues. It became a matter of importance to render themfelves dear to thofe with whom they were to continue their exiftence after death. Far from extinguifhing that enthufiafm a wife legiflation infpires for virtue and talents, it was by this religion more ftrongly excited. The ancient legiflators convinced of the utility of the paffions, had no defire to ftifle them. What fort of men would you look for among a people without defires? Merchants, captains, foldiers, men of letters, able minifters? No: none but monks.

A people

A people without induftry, courage, riches, and fcience, are born the flaves of any neighbour that has boldnefs enough to put on their fetters. Men muft have paffions, and the Pagan religion did not extinguifh in them the facred and animating fire. Perhaps the Scandinavian, a little different from the Greek and Roman, led mankind to virtue by a more efficacious method. Reputation was the god of this people. It was the only divinity from whom the inhabitants expected their reward. Every one afpired to be the child of Reputation. Every one honoured the bards, as the diftributors of glory, and the priefts of the temple of renown *. The filence of the bards was dreadful to warriors, and even to princes. Contempt was the lot of every one that was not the child of Reputation. Flattery was then unknown to the poets. The fevere and incorruptible inhabitants of a free country, they had not then debafed themfelves by fervile eulogies. No one among them even dared to celebrate a name that the public efteem had not already confecrated. To obtain this efteem, a man muft have rendered fome fervice to his country. The religious and powerful defire of an immortal fame, therefore, excited men to render them-

---

* The advantage of this religion over fome others is ineftimable; as it rewards thofe talents and actions only that are ufeful to our country; and the heaven of other religions, is the reward of fafting, folitude, maceration, and other ftupid virtues that are ufelefs to fociety.

felves

felves illuftrious by their talents, and their virtues. What advantage muft not fuch a religion, that was at the fame time more pure than the Pagan, procure to a nation!

But is a religion of this fort to be eftablifhed in a fociety already formed? The attachment of a people to the prevaling worfhip is well known, and their horror againft a new religion. What method can be taken to change the received opinions?

The method is perhaps more facile than may be imagined. If in a nation reafon be tolerated, it will fubftitute the religion of Renown in preference to all others. But if it fhould fubftitute mere Deifm, what advantage will it not have given to humanity *! But will the worfhip, rendered to the Divinity, remain a long time pure? The people are groveling; fuperftition is their religion. The temples elevated at firft to the Eternal, will foon be confecrated to his feveral perfections; ignorance will make of them as many gods. Be it fo: and fo far let the magiftrate permit them to go: but arrived there, let the fame magiftrate, attentive to direct the progrefs of ignorance, and more efpecially of fuperftition, keep it always in view; let him obferve what form it affumes, and oppofe the eftablifhment of

---

* *That is, how much better is it that men fhould be mere Deifts than Papifts: not know Chriftianity, than make it fubfervient to wicked and contemptible purpofes.*

F 4   every

every dogma, every principle inconfiftent with found morality, that is to fay, with the public utility.

Every man is jealous of his fame. If the magiftrate, as at Rome, unites in his perfon the double office of fenator and minifter of the altar (47); the prieft in him fhould be conftantly fubordinate to the fenator, and religion conftantly fubordinate to the public happinefs.

The abbé of St. Peter has faid, the prieft cannot be really ufeful but in quality of an officer of morality. Now, who can better fill that noble function than the magiftrate? Who better than he can fhow the motives of general intereft, on which are founded particular laws, and the indiffolubility of the bond that unites the happinefs of individuals with that of the public.

What influence would not a moral inftruction, given by a fenate, have on the minds of the people? With what refpect would not the latter receive the decifions of the former? It is from the legiflative body only that we can expect a beneficent religion, one moreover that is tolerant and not expenfive, and that offers no ideas of the Divinity but what are grand and folemn : that excites the foul to a love of talents and virtue ; and laftly, that has not, like the legiflature, any other object than that of the felicity of the people. Let fagacious magiftrates be clothed with temporal and fpiritual power, and all contradiction between religions

and

and patriotic precepts will difappear : all the people will adopt the fame principles of morality,
and will form the fame idea of a fcience in which
it is fo important for all of them to be equally inftructed.

Perhaps many ages will pafs by before the
alterations that are requifite for human happinefs can be made in the falfe religions.   What
has happened to the prefent hour ?   That men
have nothing but confufed ideas of morality :
ideas that they owe to their different fituations,
and to chance, which never gives to two men
precifely the fame feries of circumftances, nor
ever permits them to receive the fame inftructions, and acquire the fame ideas.   From whence I
conclude, that the inequality actually perceived
in the underftandings of different men, cannot
be confidered as a proof of their unequal aptitude
to acquire it.

NOTES.

N O T E S.

1. (page 4.) THE science of man is the science of philosophers; to whom the politicians think
themselves, in this respect, far superior. They in fact know
more of the cabals of a cabinet, and in consequence conceive
the highest opinion of their own abilities. If they are curious
to know their merit, let them write on man, and publish
their thoughts : the esteem they will be held in by the public
will teach them what esteem they ought to have for themselves.

2. (ibid.) The minister knows the detail of affairs better
than the philosopher. His informations of this sort are more
extensive : but the latter has more leisure to study the heart of
man, and knows it better than the minister. They are both,
by their different species of study, destined to elucidate each
other. The minister who would promote the public good,
should be the friend and protector of letters. Before it was
forbid at Paris to print any thing but Catechisms and Alma-
nacs, it was to the numerous pamphlets of intelligent men,
that France, they say, owed the advantage of exporting corn,
which was demonstrated by men of science. The minister,
who was then at the head of the finances availed himself of
their informations.

3. (p. 6.) To whatever degree of perfection education may
be carried, let it not be imagined however that all who are
able to receive it may be made men of genius. By the aid of
instruction an emulation may be excited among the people, they
may be habituated to attention, have their hearts opened to
humanity, and their minds to truth; in a word, all the people
may be made, if not men of genius, at least men of understanding and sensibility. But, as I shall prove in the course
of this work, this is all the improved science of education can
perform, and it is enough. A nation composed in general of
such sort of men would be, without dispute, the first in the universe.

4. (p. 7.) At Vienna, Paris, Lisbon, and in all the catholic countries, they permit the sale of operas, dramas, ro-
mances, and even some good books of geometry and medicine.

cine, but of every other fort, the work of fuperior merit, and
that is regarded as fuch by the reft of Europe, is prohibited.
Such are thofe of Voltaire, Marmontel, Rouffeau, Montefquieu,
&c. In France, the approbation of the cenfor, is for an author
almoft always a certificate of his ftupidity. It announces a
book without enemies, which at firft will be received with approbation, becaufe no one troubles himfelf about it, becaufe
it does not excite envy, nor wound any one's pride; and contains nothing but what all the world knows. The general
eulogy of the moment of publication, almoft always excludes
that of futurity.

5. (p. 7.) The fcholaftic, fays the Englifh proverb, is a
mere afs, that having neither the meeknefs of a Chriftian, nor
the reafon of a philofopher, nor the affability of a courtier, is
nothing more than an object of ridicule.

6. (ibid.) What is the fcience of fcholaftics? it is to abufe
words, and render their fignification uncertain. It was by the
virtue of certain barbarous terms that the magicians formerly
deftroyed enchanted caftles, or at leaft their appearance. The
fcholaftics, heirs of the power of the ancient magicians, have,
by virtue of certain unintelligible words, in like manner given
the appearance of a fcience to the moft abfurd reveries. If
there be a way to deftroy their enchantments, it muft be by
obliging them to give a precife definition of the terms they
ufe. Were they forced to annex clear ideas to their terms,
the magic of their fcience would vanifh. We fhould, therefore, miftruft every work where frequent ufe is made of the language of the fchools; that in common ufe is almoft always
fufficient for thofe that have clear ideas. He that would inftruct, and not deceive mankind, fhould fpeak their language.

7. (p. 10.) There are but few countries where the fciences
of morality and politics are ftudied. Young people are feldom
permitted to exercife their minds on fubjects of this fort. The
priefts are unwilling they fhould contract a habit of reafoning.
The word rational is now fynonimous with incredulous. The
clergy probably fufpect that the arguments for faith, like the
little wings of Mercury, are too weak to fupport it. To be a
philofopher, fays Malbranche, we muft fee clearly; and to be
faithful, we muft believe blindly. Malbranche did not perceive that he made a fool of his firm believer. In fact, where-
in does a fottifh credulity confift? in believing without fufficient evidence. They will tell me here of the faith of Charbonnier.

bonnier. He was in a particular situation. He talked with
God, who gave him an inward light. Every man except this
Charbonnier, who boasts of a blind faith, and a belief on *hear-*
/ay, is therefore a man puffed up with infatuation.

8. (p. 11.) Let us sometimes amuse ourselves with the paintings of ridicule. There is nothing better. Every excellent
piece of this fort supposes a large share of discernment in him
that drew it. What does society owe him ? a tribute of gratitude and applause proportionate to the evils his ridicule has
banished, by exposing this or that defect. A nation that
should regard this matter as important, would be itself ridiculous. " Of what consequence is it, says an English author,
" that a certain citizen is singular in his humour : that a petit
" maitre is curious in his dress, or a coquet affected in her
" behaviour ? she may white-wash, paint, and patch her face,
" and lie with her gallant, without affecting my property :
" the incessant flutter of a fan does not injure my constitution "
A nation too much busied with the coquetry of a woman, or
the fatuity of a petit maitre, is evidently a frivolous nation.

9. (p. 12.) All nations have reproached the French with their
frivolity. " If the French, said Mr. Saville formerly, are fri-
" volous, the Spaniards grave and superstitious, the English
" serious and profound ; these properties are the effects of their
" forms of government. It is at Paris that the man curious
" in trinkets and dress ought to fix his abode : it is at Madrid
" and Lisbon they ought to reside who love to give themselves
" discipline, and see their brethren burnt alive ; and lastly it is
" at London they should live, who would think, exert that facul-
" ty which principally distinguishes the man from the brute. Ac-
" cording to this author, there are but three subjects worthy of
" consideration : nature, religion, and government. Now, as the
" French, says he, dare not think on these subjects, their books,
" insipid to men, can afford entertainment only to women. Li-
" berty alone enobles the spirit of a nation, and the spirit of a
" nation that of its writers. The minds of the French are with-
" out energy. The only estimable author among them that I
" have a regard for is Montaigne. Few of his fellow-subjects are
" worthy to admire him : to feel him we must think, and to think
" we must be free*."

10. (p. 27.)

* *A great part of that universal respect which is paid to the writ-*
ings of Montaigne arises, I imagine, from his unparalleled frankness.
It is

10. (p.27.) The jesuits afford a striking example of the power of education. If their order has produced few men of genius in the arts or sciences; if they have had no Newton in physics, no Racine in Tragedy, no Huygens in astronomy, or Pot in chymistry; no Bacon, Locke, Voltaire, Fontaine, &c. it is not that the religious of this order never find among their scholars those who discover the greatest genius. The Jesuits moreover, from the tranquility of their colleges, have not their studies molested by any avocations, and their manner of living is the most favorable to the acquisition of talents. Why then have they given so few illustrious men to Europe? It is because surrounded by fanatics and bigots, a Jesuit dare not think but after his superiors: it is, moreover, because forced to apply themselves for years together to the study of the casuists and theology, that study, so repugnant to sound reason, destroys its efficacy on them. How can they preserve on the benches a just judgment! the habit of sophistry must corrupt it.

11. (ibid.) If all the Savoyards have in a manner the same character, it is because chance has placed them in situations nearly similar, and that they almost all receive nearly the same education. Why are they all travellers? because there is no living without money, and they have none at home. Why are they laborious? because they are without assistance, and without protection in the countries were they transplant themselves; and bread is not to be had without labour. Why are they faithful and diligent? because to be employed in preference to the natives, they must surpass them in diligence and fidelity. Why, in the last place, are they all economists? because having, like other men, an attachment to their native country, they go out beggars to return rich, and live on what they have accumulated. Suppose, therefore, we had the greatest desire to inspire a young man with the virtues of a Savoyard, what is to be done? place him in a similar situation; and let a part of his education be confided to misfortune and indigence. Want and poverty are the only instructors whose lessons are always heard, and whose

We see his inmost thoughts; and there is in the human mind such a strong relish for the truth, when it does not oppose our interest, that wherever we are sure we see it, we are sure to be pleased. Montaigne wrote whatever he thought; most authors write whatever they think will please their readers.

counsels

counfels are always efficacious.   But if the national manners
will not permit him to receive fuch an education, what other
muft be fubftituted for it ? I do not know: no other can be fo
certain.   We fhould not be furprifed, therefore, if he do not
acquire any of the virtues we defire him to have. Who can wonder at the want of fuccefs in an education that is infufficient.

12. (p.30.) Shakefpeare never played but one part well, which
was the ghoft in Hamlet.

13. (p. 31.) See the extract in the Dictionary of Moreri, and
the extract from the Republic of Letters: Jan. 1685, " It was to
" a lady to whom was given at Rouen the name of Melita, that
" France owes the great Corneille."   It is in like manner to
love that England owes the celebrated Hogarth.

14. (p. 32.) The greater part of men of genius would have it
believed that their early youth announced what they fhould one
day be : this is their foible.   Would they pretend to be of a
fuperior race to the reft of mankind ? be it fo.   Let us not
difpute this point with their vanity : we fhall affront them;
but let us not believe it on their mere affertion ; we fhould deceive ourfelves.   Nothing is more elufory and uncertain than
thefe firft prognoftics. Newton and Fontenelle were but indifferent fcholars.   The claffes are filled with clever children,
the world with foolifh men.

15. (p.33.) The life or death, the favour or difgrace of a pa-
tron, frequently determine our future ftate and profeffion. How
many men of genius do we owe to accidents of this fort.
Falfehood, meannefs and frivolity reign in a court ? do men
live there without regard for truth, humanity, and pofterity ?
Who can doubt but difgrace or oppreffion may be fometimes
falutary to a courtier; he may recollect in exile what man owes
to himfelf ; and freed from the diffipations of a court, a habit
of ftudy and meditation may chance to produce in him the development of the moft exalted talents. *(See on this head Ld. Bolingbroke's Reflections on Exile.)*

16. (ibid.) M. Rouffeau is not infenfible; his very railing
againft women is a proof of it. Every one of them may apply to
him this verfe.

" Tout jufqu'à tes mepris, m'a prouve ton amour."
   All, even thy difdain, declares thy love.

*It is proper to add here, that M. Rouffeau has fince made the great-
eft atonement a man can make for railing at women ; that of marrying.*

17. (p. 34.) M. Rouffeau in his works has always appeared to
me lefs folicitous to inftruct than feduce his readers. Every where
                                                          the

the orator, and seldom the reasoner, he forgets that though it is sometimes permitted to make use of eloquence in philosophic discussions, it is only when the importance of an opinion already received is to be strongly imprest on the mind. Was it necessary, for example, to rouse the Athenians from their stupor, and arm them against Philip? It was then incumbent on Demosthenes to exert all the powers of his eloquence: but when a new opinion is to be examined, reason alone should be employed: he that is then eloquent is wrong. Does the English house of commons always pay a due attention to the different use that should be made of eloquence, and the spirit of discussion?

18. (p. 35.) M. Rousseau became acquainted at Montmorency with Marshal Luxembourg; that nobleman had an affection for him, and honoured his talents, protected him, and by that protection acquired the right of acknowledgment from all men of letters. Let not learned men blush to extol the truly great, why should they refuse praise were it is deserved? if the people have need of instruction, the literati have need of protectors. The friendship of Marshal Luxembourg could not, it is true, protect M. Rousseau from persecution. Perhaps the influence of that nobleman was not sufficiently strong; or perhaps the protector of the good and great is not so powerful as the hypocrisy of the bad. It may be added to the eulogy of M. Luxembourg, that he never lavished his favours on those insects of literature who reflect disgrace on their protector.

" If great men chuse indifferently, says Lord Shaftesbury,
" any subject for their bounty, and are pleased to confer their
" favour on some one pretender to art, or promiscuously to such
" of the tribe of writers, whose chief ability has lain in making
" their court well, and obtaining to be introduced to their ac-
" quaintance This they think sufficient to instal them patrons
" of wit, and masters of the literate order. But this method
" will, of any other the least serve their interest or design. The
" ill placing of rewards is a double injury to merit; and in
" every cause or interest, passes for worse than mere indiffe-
" rence or neutrality. There can be no excuse for making an
" ill choice. Merit in every kind is easily discovered when
" sought. The public itself fails not to give sufficient indica-
" tions, and points out those geniusses which want only coun-
" tenance and encouragement to become considerable. An
" ingenious man never starves unknown; and great men must
" wink hard, or it would be impossible for them to miss such
" advan-

" advantageous opportunities, of fhewing their generofity, and
" acquiring the univerfal efteem, acknowledgments, and good
" wifhes of the ingenious and learned part of mankind."
" Advice to an Author, Sect. I. p. 229.

19. (p. 40) More than half a million fterling feized in Spain on
two procurators of the jefuits at Paraguai, fhows that in preaching a contempt for riches, the jefuits have not been the dupes
of their own fermons.

20. (p. 41.) Of all legends the moft ridiculous are thofe the
monks write of the founders of their orders. They fay, for example,
" That at the fight of a fawn purfued by the wolves, St. Omer
" commanded them to ftop, and they immediately obeyed."

" That St. Florent having no fhepherd, ordered a bear he
" met by the way to feed his fheep, and the bear led them to
" the pafture every day.

" That St. Francis greeted the birds, talked to them, and
" commanded them to hear the word of God, and the birds
" hearing the difcourfe of St. Francis, were exceedingly
" glad, ftretching out their necks, and opening their beaks.

" That the fame St. Francis paffed eight days with a grafs-
" hopper; fung a whole day together with a nightingale;
" cured a mad wolf, and faid to him, Brother wolf, you ought
" to promife me that you will not hereafter be fo ravenous as
" you have been; which the wolf promifed by bowing his head;
"St. Francis then faid to him, Give me your pledge, and at the
" fame time held out his hand to receive it, and the wolf gent-
" ly lifting up his right paw, put it on the hand of the faint."
They write alfo that many other faints took delight in talking with brutes.

21. (p. 43.) They certainly do not attach a clear idea to the word
paffions, when they regard them as detrimental. This is a mere
difpute about words. The theologians themfelves have never
faid that the lively paffion of the love of God is a crime. They
have not condemned Decius for vowing himfelf in the field of
battle to the infernal gods. They have never reproached
Pelopidas with that animated love of his country which armed
him againft the tyrants, and engaged him in a moft perilous enterprize. Our defires are our motives, and it is the force of
our defires which determines that of our virtues and vices. A
man without defire, and without want, is without invention
and without reafon. No motive can engage him to combine
or compare his ideas with each other. The more a man ap-
proaches

proaches that ftate of apathy, the more ftupid he becomes. If the fovereigns of the Eaft are in general fo ignorant, it is becaufe difcernment is the child of defire and want. Now the Sultans feel neither the one nor the other. There is no pleafure which a fimple act of their will does not procure: invention therefore is almoft always ufelefs. The only inftance in which it becomes neceffary, is, when defirous of the title of a conqueror, they would ravifh the fcepter from fome neighbouring potentate. In every other circumftance to require fagacity in a defpotic prince, is to require an effect without a caufe. To reckon in an arbitary government on the capacity of a monarch born to the throne, is abfurd. So that without the chance of a very extraordinary education, there are few fovereigns at once abfolute and intelligent. Therefore hiftory commonly, in the number of great monarchs, reckons only fuch as Henry IV. Frederic, Catherine II. &c. and thofe among the princes, whofe education has been fevere, and who have had a fortune to make, and a thoufand obftacles to furmount.

22. (p. 43.) A bigot may excel in geometry, and a certain fort of painting; but when we confider the prefent contradiction between the intereft of the public, and the intereft of the prieft, a man cannot, without inconfiftency, be at once religious and a ftatefman, a faint and a good citizen, that is to fay, an honeft man. This is a truth that will be demonftrated in the courfe of this work.

23. (p. 44.) It was formerly the petit maitre who knew all things without learning any thing; now it is the theologian. Afk him about the nature of animals: they are, he will fay, mere machines. But by what argument does he fupport this affertion? has he, in quality either of fportfman or philofopher, ftudied the conftitution and manners of animals? No. He has brought up neither dog nor cat, not fo much as a fparrow: but he is a doctor, and, from the moment he took his degree, he has thought himfelf, like the emperor of China, obliged by the etiquet of his rank, to anfwer to all that is afked him; *I knew it.* The ftoical fage was fuppofed to be verfed in all arts and fciences; he was the univerfal fcholar. The theologian is the fame; he is poet, mathematician, philofopher, watchmaker, &c. That he may have all thefe talents I agree: but not to read his verfes, and buy his watches. Will he permit me to give him a word of advice: it is, before he talks of animals, to confult the works of M. Buffon, and three or four

letters in the Journal Etranger, by an accurate obferver and a good writer: and that he forbear to attack my fentiments on this point. I have given, they fay, a mind and reafon to brutes. That is a favour I did the doctors. What was your acknowledgment, O ungrateful mortals!

24. (p. 44.) The property of defpotic government is to weaken the movements of the paffions in man. A confumption is therefore the mortal malady of thefe empires and governments, and the people fubject to them have not, in general, either the confidence or courage of republicans. Even the latter have not excited our admiration, but in thofe critical moments when their paffions were in the higheft effervefcence. In what times did the Hollanders and the Swifs perform actions more than human? When animated by the two violent paffions of vengeance, and a hatred of tyrants. Paffions are neceffary to a people: this is a truth of which every body is now convinced, except the Guardian of the Capuchins.

25. (p. 45.) The Turk fuppofes woman to be formed for the pleafure of man, and created to irritate his defires. Such, he fays, is the evident defign of nature. Therefore that in Turkey that they fhould permit art to add to the beauty of their women, that they fhould even enjoin them to improve the methods of pleafing, is quite natural. What abufe can be made of beauty that is confined in a feraglio? Suppofe, if you pleafe, a country were the women are in common. In fuch a country, the more methods they fhould invent to feduce, the more they would multiply the pleafures of man. Whatever degree of perfection of this kind they might attain, we may be fure that their coquetry would have nothing contrary to the public good. All that could be then required of them, would be that they fhould preferve fo much veneration for their beauty and their favours, as to beftow them only on men diftinguifhed by their genius, their courage, or their probity. By this method their favours would become an encouragement to talents and virtue. But in Turkey if the women may, without inconvenience, inftruct themfelves in all the arts of delight, is it the fame in fuch a country as Europe? Where they are not fhut up, nor common? where, as in France, every houfe is open; is it to be imagined, that by the women's multiplying the arts to pleafe, they would much augment the happinefs of their hufbands? I doubt it: and till fome reformation is made in the laws of matrimony, what art might add

to

to the natural beauties of the fex, would perhaps be inconfiftent with the ufe that the European laws permit them to make
of it.

26. (p. 47.) There are men who pretend to veracity, by
virtue of their calumnies; whereas nothing is more oppofite to
truth than flander: the one, always indulgent, is infpired by
humanity; the other, always fevere, is the daughter of pride, of
hatred, malevolence, and envy. The tone and gefture of de-
traction always difcover its parent.

27. (ibid.) If we cannot without a crime, conceal the truth
from the people and the fovereign; what man has ever been
without reproach in this refpect.

28. (ibid.) If on reading the ecclefiaftic hiftory, a young
Italian, fhocked at the follies and villanies of the popes, fhould
doubt of their infallability. What an impious doubt! his preceptor would exclaim. But, replies the pupil, I fpeak what I
think; and have you not always forbad me to lie? Yes, in ordinary cafes; but in favour of the cnurch falfehood is a duty.
And what intereft have you in the pope? A very great one,
replies the preceptor. If the pope's infallibility be acknowledged, no one can refift his will. The people muft obey him implicitly. Now what confideration does not this refpect for the
pope refleft on all the ecclefiaftic body, and confequently
on me?

29. (p.48.) Whoever in writing hiftory alters the facts, is a
bad citizen. He deceives the public, and deprives it of the
ineftimable advantage it might receive from that biftory. But
in what nation can we find a juft hiftorian, and a real adorer of
the God of truth? is it France, in Portugal, or Spain? No: it
is only in a free and reformed country.

30. (ibid.) Why are the theological difputes about grace in-
terminable? Becaufe, luckily for the difputants, neither one
fide nor the other have any clear ideas of what they talk
about. Do they prefent fuch as are more clear in their defini-
tions of the Divinity? Cardinal Perron, after having in a fet
difcourfe proved the exiftence of a God, to Henry III. faid to
him, If your majefty pleafe, I will now prove his non-exiftence
juft as clearly.

*There is fcarce any propofition that may not be proved either
true or falfe, in words; but this fort of proof is very different from
hat which enforces conviction on the mind. All the arguments
the meft fubtle wit can imagine, will never convince a thinking*

man, that there is not one eternal, infinite, omnipotent, creating Power; though they may so confound his ideas that he may not be able to untangle the sophistry.

Quibbles of this kind, especially when applied to subjects of importance, are a scandalous abuse of the rational faculty, and discover an insolent contempt of the party to whom they are offered.

31. (p. 50.) Why do the most part of sensible people regard all religions as incompatible with sound morality? Because the priests of every religion set themselves up as the only judges of the goodness or badness of human actions; it is because they would have the decisions of theology regarded as the real code of morality. Now the priest is a man, and in that quality judges in conformity to his interest; and his interest is almost always opposite that of the public; therefore the greatest part of his judgments are unjust. Such, however, is the power of the priest over the minds of the people, that they have frequently more veneration for the sophistries of the school, than for the sound maxims of morality. What clear ideas can the people form about them. The decisions of the church, as variable as its interests, involve them continually in confusion, obscurity, and contradiction. What does the church substitute for the true principles of justice? Ridiculous ceremonies and observances. So that Machiavel in his Discourses on Livy, attributes the excessive iniquity of the Italians to the falsity and contradictions in the moral precepts of the Catholic religion.

32. (p. 54.) Man, says Fontenelle, has made God after his own image, and could not make him otherwise. The monks in like manner have fashioned the celestial court after those of oriental monarchs: the prince is there invisible to the greatest part of his subjects, and accessible only to his courtiers. The complaints of the people do not reach him but through the ears of his favourites. The monks have, in like manner, environed the throne of the Monarch of the universe, by those they call saints, and would not have the celestial favours obtained but by the intercession of these saints. But what must be done to render them propitious? The priests assembled for this purpose decide, that the images of the saints in wood, sculptured or unsculptured, should be placed in the churches, and that the people should kneel before them, as before the Almighty; that the exterior signs of adoration should be the

same

fame for the Eternal and for his favourites; in fhort, that honoured by the Chriftians, as the Penates and the Fetiches by the Pagans, and Savages, St. Nicholas in Ruffia, for example, and St. Janvier at Naples, fhould be treated with greater refpect than God himfelf. It is on thefe facts that are founded the accufations brought againft the Greek and Latin churches. It is to the laft efpecially, that we owe the re-eftablifhment of Fetechifm. Thus France has a national Fetiche in St. Dennis, and a Fetiche of its capital in St. Genevieve; and there is no community, nor even inhabitant, that has not his particular Fetiche under the name of Peter. Claud, Martin, &c.

33. (p. 54.) There are no frauds, falfehoods, tricks, betraying of confidence, in fhort, no methods more bafe and villainous than thofe the priefts have employed to encreafe their wealth. The Capitularies collected by Baluze, vol. ii. inform us by what means the clergy of France formerly acquired their tenth, "They produced a letter, which they faid came down "from heaven, and was wrote by Jefus Chrift; in which our "Saviour threatened the Pagans, the Sorcerers, and thofe who "did not pay the tenth, to blaft their fields with fterility, "and to fend flying ferpents into their houfes, to devour the "breafts of their women." This firft letter not fucceeding, the priefts had recourfe to the devil. They produced him (fee the fame Capitularies, vol. i.) in an affembly of the nation, and the devil becoming at once apoftle and miffionary, and zealoufly concerned for the welfare of France, endeavoured to recall them to their duty by falutary caftigations. "Open your "eyes at laft, faid the clergy, the devil himfelf was the author "of the laft famine; it was he that devoured the corn in the "ear: dread his fury. He has declared, in the midft of the "fields, with dreadful howlings, that he will inflict the moft "cruel punifhment on thofe hardened Chriftians who refufe "the tenth." So many impoftors on the part of the clergy prove that, in the time of Charlemagne, none but the pious fouls paid the tenth. If the clergy were fuppofed to have had a right to levy it, they would not have had recourfe to God and the devil. This fact makes me recollect another of the fame fort: it is a fermon of a vicar on the fame fubject. "O, my dear parifhioners, he faid, do not follow the example "of the wretched Cain, but much rather that of the good Abel. "Cain would never pay the tenth, nor go to mafs. Abel, on

"the

" the contrary, always paid it with the faireſt and beſt, and
" never once miſſed a maſs." Grotius, on the ſubjeƈt of tenths
and donations, ſays, " that the ſcruple of Tiberius in accept-
" ing ſuch gifts, ſhould make the monks aſhamed of their
" rapacity."

34. (p. 54.) The popes by their ridiculous pretenſions on
America, have given the example of iniquity, and authoriſed
all the aƈts of injuſtice the Chriſtians have therè exerciſed.

When there was one day, an examination in the houſe
of Commons, whether a diſtriƈt ſituate on the confines of Canada, belonged to France, one of the members got up and ſaid,
" This queſtion, gentleman, is the more delicate, as the French,
" as well as we, are fully perſuaded that the land in queſtion
" does not belong to the natives of the country."

35. (p. 56.) After theſe faƈts, though the papiſts may ſtill
boaſt of the great perfeƈtion to which their religion carries the
morals of mankind, they will make no proſelytes.   To ſhow
the pretenſions of the papiſts, let them be aſked what is the objeƈt of the ſcience of morality ? It will appear that it cannot
be any thing elſe than the *public good*; for if we require virtues
in individuals, it is becauſe the virtues of the members make
the felicity of the whole body.   Now it is evident that the
only method to render the people at once learned, virtuous, and
happy, is to ſecure the property of individuals by ſound laws,
to excite their induſtry, to permit them to think and communicate their thoughts. But is the papiſtical religion the moſt favourable to ſuch laws ? are the inhabitants of Italy and Portugal
more ſecure in their lives and properties than thoſe of England?
Do they enjoy a greater a greater liberty of thought? Are their
governments founded on better principles of morality, and are
they leſs ſevere, and conſequently more reſpeƈtable ? Does not
experience prove on the contrary, that the Lutherans and Cal-
viniſts in Germany are better governed and more happy than
the Catholics ; and that the proteſtant Cantons of Switzerland
are more rich and powerful than thoſe of the papiſts.   The reformed religion therefore tends more direƈtly to the happineſs of
the public, than the Catholic ; and is more favourable to the
objeƈt of morality.   It therefore inſpires better morals, and
ſuch as have no other tendency than to promote the felicity of
the people.

36. (p. 58.)

36. (p. 58.) There are great, and there are small societies. The laws of the latter are simple, because their interests are clear. They are conformable to the interest of the majority, because they are made by the consent of all; they are, lastly, very exactly observed, because the happiness of each individual is connected with their observance. It is good sense that dictates the laws of small societies; it is genius that plans those of large communities.

But what can determine men to form such large communities? Chance; an ignorance of the inconveniences attending such societies, a desire to conquer, a fear of being subdued, &c.

37. (p. 60.) Shaftesbury in his Treatise on Enthusiasm, mentions a bishop, who not finding, in the Catholic catechism, enough to satiate his enormous credulity, was forced to have recourse to the tales of the fairies.

38. (ibid.) It is with popery as with despotism, they each of them devour the country were they are established. The most certain method of debilitating the power of England or Holland, would be to establish there the Catholic religion.

39. (p. 62.) If our religion, say the papists, be very expensive, it is because its instructions are greatly multiplied. Be it so: but what is the produce of these instructions? Are mankind the better for them? No. What is to be done to make them so? Divide the tenths of each parish among those who cultivate their lands best, and perform the most virtuous actions. This division of the tenths will produce more labourers, and more honest men, than all the preachments of the curates.

40 (ibid.) The History of Ireland informs us, vol. i. p. 303. that it was, at a distant period, constantly exposed to the voracity of a most numerous clergy. The poets, the priests of the country, enjoyed all the advantages, immunities, and privileges of Catholic priests; and like them, were maintained at the public expence. These poets in consequence, multiplied to such a degree, that Hugh, then king of Ireland, found it necessary to discharge his subjects from such a heavy burden. That prince loved his people, and was a man of courage; he determined, therefore, to annihilate the priests, or at least greatly diminish their number, and succeeded in the enterprize.

In Pensylvania there is no religion established by government: each one adopts that he likes best. The priest is no

charge

charge to the state. The individuals provide them as they find it convenient, and tax themselves accordingly. The priest is there, like the merchant, maintained at the expence of the consumer? He who has no priest, and consumes no part of the commodity he deals in, pays not part of his expence. Pensylvania, therefore, is a model from which it would be proper to copy.

41. (p. 65.) Numa himself instituted but four. vestals, and a very small number of priests.

42. (ibid.) There is the same difference between paganism and popery, said an Englishman, as between Albani and Calot: the name of the former makes me recollect a pleasing picture of the birth of Venus; that of the other, a grotesque painting of the temptation of St. Anthony.

43. (p. 65.) Under the reign of Numa, the Romans consecrated a temple to Fidelity; the dedication of this temple kept them for some time faithful to their treaties.

44. (ibid.) Whoever affects such great humility, and accustoms himself early to regard life as a pilgrimage, will never be he any thing better than a monk, nor ever promote the happiness of the human race.

45. (p. 66.) The reunion of the spiritual and temporal powers in the hands of the same arbitrary sovereign may be dangerous, it will be said; I believe it. Every arbitrary prince, in general, solely solicitous to gratify his caprice, is but little concerned for the felicity of his subjects. He will frequently make use of the spiritual power to legitimate his pleasures and his cruelties: but it will not be the same if this power be confided to the body of magistrates.

46. (ibid.) Why was Jupiter supposed to be the last of the children of Saturn? because order and generation, the successors of chaos and sterility, were, according to the Pagan philosophers, the last product of time. Why was Jupiter, in quality of generator, called the god of the air? because, said the philosophers, vegetables, fossils, minerals, animals, in a word all that exists, transpire, exhale, corrupt, and fill the air with volatile principles. These principles being heated and put in action by the solar fire, the air must then produce a new generation by the salts and spirits received from the putrefaction. The air, therefore, the only principle of generation and corruption, appeared to them as an immense ocean agitated by nu-

merous

merous different principles. It is in the air, according to them, the feeds of all beings float, which conftantly ready to re-produce, wait for that purpofe the moment when chance fhall difpofe them in a convenient matrix. The atmofphere appeared to them, to ufe the expreffion, always alive; being charged with an acid to corrupt, and with feeds to engender. It was the vaft recipient of all the principles of animation. The Titans and Janus, according to the ancients, were in like manner the emblem of chaos. Venus or love, that of attraction, the productive principle of order and harmony in the univerfe.

47. (p. 72.) The reunion of the temporal and fpiritual powers in the fame hands, is indifpenfable. Nothing is done againft the facerdotal body by merely making it more humble. Who does not entirely annihilate it fufpends, and not deftroys its influence. A body is immortal; a favourable circumftance, fuch as the confidence of a prince, or a revolution in the ftate, is fufficient to reftore its primitive power. It will then revive with a vigour the more redoutable, as by being inftructed in the caufes of its abafement, it will be more attentive to overthrow them. The ecclefiaftical body in England is at prefent without power, but it is not annihilated. Who then can affirm, faid a certain nobleman, that it will not one day reaffume its original ferocity, and again caufe as much blood to fiow as it did formerly *. One of the greateft fervices that could be rendered to France, would be to employ a part of the extravagant revenues of the clergy to the liquidation of the national debt. What could the clergy object, if careful of their welfare, they were to preferve their benefices during life, and if after that they were to be alienated? Where would be the evil of bringing fo large a quantity of riches again into the circulation.

* Our author will be excufed this wild fuppofition, as being a foreigner, and not fufficiently acquainted with our excellent conftitution. Such an alteration in the power of the clergy, would totally deftroy that equilibrium in which the effence of our liberty confifts.

SEC-

S E C T I O N   II.

All men, commonly well organifed, have an
equal aptitude to underftanding.

C H A P.   I.

As all our ideas proceed from the fenfes ; the under-
ftanding has been confequently regarded as the ef-
fect of more or lefs fenfibility in the organifation.

WHEN we learn from Locke, that it is to
the organs of the fenfes we owe our ideas,
and confequently our underftanding; and when
we remark the difference in the organs and in the
underftandings of different men, we may conclude,
in general, that the inequality of their underftand-
ftandings is the effect of the unequal fenfibility of
their organs.   An opinion fo probable, and fo
analogous to facts * muft be the more generally
adopted, as it favours human indolence, and prevents the pain of a fruitlefs fearch.

* It is by the aid of analogies that we fometimes make the
greateft difcoveries: but in what cafes fhould we be content with
a proof by analogy ? When it is impoffible to procure any other.
This fort of proof is frequently fallacious.   Have we conftantly feen animals generate by the coupling of the males with
the females ? We conclude from thence, that it is the only method by which animals can propagate.   To undeceive ourfelves,
we fhould with the moft accurate and fcrupulous attention
enclofe

If contrary experiments, however, prove that the fuperiority of underftanding is not in proportion to the greater and lefs perfection of the fenfes, we muft fearch for the explication of this phenomenon in fome other caufe.

Two opinions concerning this fubject divide the learned of the prefent age. The one fay, *The underftanding is the effect of a certain fort of interior temperament and organifation.* But no one has, by a feries of obfervations, yet determined the fort of organs, temperament, or nourifhment that produces the underftanding*. This affer-

---

enclofe a vine-fretter in a phial†: we fhould divide the polypus, and prove by reiterated experiments, that there is another method by which animals can regenerate.

* Some phyfiologifts, and among them M. Laufel de Magny, have faid, that the ftrongeft and moft courageous temperaments were the moft acute. Yet no one has ever mentioned Racine, Boileau, Pafchal, Hobbes, Toland, Fontenelle, &c. as ftrong and courageous men. Others pretend that the bilious and fanguine are at once the moft ingenious, and leaft capable of a conftant attention. But can we fay, at the fame time, incapable of attention, and endowed with great talents? can it be imagined, that without application, Locke and Newton had ever made their fublime difcoveries?

Some again have remarked, that the cogitative and ingenious are ordinarily melancholic: but have not perceived that they took in them the effect for the caufe, that the ingenious is not

† *Our author is certainly right in directing thefe obfervations to be made with the moft fcrupulous attention; and after all perhaps they will be far from conclufive. Who can fay that the femen of the infect here mentioned cannot pervade glafs, when we know that body is permeable by other fubftances, fuch as the magnetic and electric effluvia, as well as light.*

tion being vague and deftitute of proof, is then reduced to this, *The underftanding is the effect of an unknown caufe, or occult quality, to which is given the name of temperament cr organifation.*

Quintilian, Locke, and I, fay:

The inequality in minds or underftandings, is the effect of a known caufe, and this caufe is the difference of education.

To prove the firft of thefe opinions, we muft fhow, by repeated experiments, that the fuperiority of the underftanding does really belong to fuch a fort of organ or temperament: Now thefe proofs are yet to be made. From whence it follows, that if from the principles I lay down, the caufe of the inequality in minds or underftandings can be clearly deduced, we ought to give the preference to the latter opinion

Now when a known caufe can explain a fact, why fhould we have recourfe to one that is unknown, to an occult quality, whofe exiftence, always uncertain, explains nothing that we cannot explain without it?

fo, becaufe he is melancholic, but melancholic becaufe the habit of meditation made him fo.

In the laft place, many have made the underftanding depend on the fenfibility of the nerves: but women have very lively fenfations. The fenfibility of their nerves fhould therefore give them a great fuperiority over men. Are their underftandings really fuperior? No. Befide, what clear idea can we form after all, of the greater or lefs fenfibility of the nerves?

To

To prove *that all men equally well organifed, have an equal difpofition for underftanding** ; we muft remount to the principle by which it is produced : what is it ?

* Mr. Locke was doubtlefs partly convinced of this truth, when he faid, fpeaking of the unequal capacity of under-ftandings, he thought he faw lefs difference between them, than is commonly imagined. " I think, fays he, in the fecond page " of his Education, we may affert, that in a hundred men, there " are not more than ninety, who are what they are, good or bad, " ufeful or pernicious to fociety, but from the inftruction they " have received. It is on education that depends the great " difference obfervable among them. The leaft and moft im-" perceptible impreffions received in our infancy, have confe-" quences very important, and of a long duration. It is with " thefe firft impreffion, as with a river, whofe water we can " eafily turn, by different canals, in quite oppofite courfes, fo " that from the infenfible direction the ftream receives at its " fource, it takes different directions, and at laft arrives at " places far diftant from each other: and with the fame " facility, I think, we may turn the minds of children to what " direction we pleafe." In this paffage Locke does not indeed exprefly affirm, that all men equally well organifed, have equal aptitude to mental capacity : but he here fays, what he had been, as it were, a witnefs of, and what daily experience had taught him. This philofopher had not reduced all the faculties of the mind to the capacity of fenfation, which is the only principle than can refolve this queftion.

Quintilian, who had been for fo long a time charged with the inftruction of youth, had ftill more practical knowledge than Locke, and is more bold in his affertions. He fays, Inft. Orat. lib. i. " It is an error to think that there are few men born " with the faculty of difcerning the ideas offered them, and " that the greateft part lofe their time and pains in endea-" vouring to conquer the innate idlenefs of their minds. The " greateft number, on the contrary, appear equally well orga-" nifed,

All the senfations of man are material. Perhaps I have not fufficiently explained this truth
in my treatife on the Mind. What then fhould I
here propofe ? To demonftrate rigoroufly, what,
perhaps, I have there only afferted, and prove that
all the operations of the mind are reducible to
fenfation. It is this principle, that can alone explain to us how we owe our ideas to our fenfes ;
and at the fame time that it is not, however, as is
proved by experience, to the extreme perfection
of thofe fenfes, that we owe the greater or lefs extent of our underftanding.

If this principle will reconcile two facts, in appearance fo contradictory, I fhall conclude, that
the fuperiority of the underftanding is not the
produce of temperament, nor of the greater or lefs
perfection of the fenfes, nor of an occult quality,
but that of the well known caufe, education, and

" nifed to think and retain with promptitude and facility. It is
" a talent as natural to man, as flying is to birds, running to
" horfes, and ferocity to favage beafts. The life of the foul is
" in its activity and induftry, from whence it has received the
" attribute of a celeftial origin. Minds that are ftupid and
" incapable of fcience, are in the order of nature to be regard-
" ed as monfters and other extraordinary phenomena : minds
" of this fort are rare. From whence I conclude, that there are
" great recourfes to be found in children, which are fuffered to
" vanifh with their years. It is evident therefore that it is
" not of nature, but of our negligence we ought to complain."
The opinions of Quintilian and Locke, both founded on experience, and the proofs I have urged to demonftrate this
truth, ought, I think, to fufpend on this fubject the too precipitate judgment of the reader.

in

in short, that inftead of vague affertions fo frequently repeated, we may fubftitute very determinate ideas.

Previous to the particular examen of this queftion, I think, in order to make it more clear, and
to avoid all conteft with the theologians, I fhould
firft diftinguifh between the mind, and what they
call the foul.

C H A P.   II.

Of the difference between the mind and the foul.

THERE are no two words perfectly fynonimous.   This truth being unknown to
fome, and forgot by others, has caufed the words
Mind and Soul to be frequently confounded.
But what is the difference between them ? and
what is the foul ? Are we to regard it, after the
ancients, and the firft fathers of the church, as a
matter extremely refined, and as the electric fire
by which we are animated ? Were I here to re-
count all the opinions of different nations, and
different fects of philofophers, concerning it, they
would altogether form nothing but vague, obfcure, and trifling ideas. The only people'that
expreffed themfelves with fublimity on this fubject, were the Parfis.*   When they pronounced a

* A people of Cambya, in the empire of the Mogul.

funeral

funeral oration over the tomb of some great man, they cried " O earth! O, common mother of human " beings, take back what to thee appertains of the " body of this hero : let the aqueous particles that " flowed in his veins exhale into the air, and fall- " ing in rain on the mountains, replenish the " streams, fertillise the plains, and roll back to " the abyss of the ocean from whence they pro- " ceeded! Let the fire concentered in this body " rejoin the heavenly orb, the source of light and " heat! Let the air confined in his members, " burst its prison, and be disperfed by the winds " in the mundane space! And lastly thou, O " breath of life, if perchance thou art of a nature " separate from all others, return the unknown " being that produced thee! or, if thou art " only a mixture of material elements, mayest " thou, after being disperfed in the universe, " again affemble thy scattered particles, to form " another citizen as virtuous as this hath been!"

Such were the noble images, and sublime ex- preffions employed by the enthusiasm of the Par- fis, to express the ideas they had of the soul. Philosophy, less bold in its conjectures, dares not describe its nature, and resolve the question. Phi- losophy cannot advance without the staff of ex- perience : it does indeed advance but constantly from observation to observation, *and where obser-* *vation is wanting it stops.* All that philosophy knows,

knows is, that man feels, that he has within him a principle of life, and that without the wings of theology, he cannot mount to the knowledge of this principle.

Whatever depends on obſervation appertains to metaphyſical philoſophy ; all beyond belongs to theology * or ſcholaſtic metaphyſics.

* Some have doubted whether the ſcience of God, or theology, be in faɛt a ſcience. All ſcience, they ſay, ſuppoſes a ſeries of obſervations. Now what obſervations can be made on a Being that is inviſible and incomprehenſible ? Theology is therefore no ſcience. In faɛt, what do we underſtand by the word God ? The unknown cauſe of order and motion. Now, what can we ſay of an unknown cauſe ? If we attach other ideas to the word God, we ſhall fall, as Mr. Robinet has ſhown, into a thouſand contradiɛtions. Does the theologian contemplate the curves deſcribed by the heavenly bodies, and conclude from thence that there is a power who moves them ? Cæli enarrant gloriam Dei ! The theologian is then nothing more than an aſtronomer, or natural philoſopher †.

No one doubts, ſay the Chineſe Letters, that there is in nature, *a ruling Power, though he is ignorant what it is:* but when we conjeɛture the nature of this unknown power, *the creation of a God is then nothing more than the deification of human ignorance.* I do not entirely agree with theſe Letters, though I am forced to own with them, that theology, that is to ſay, the ſcience of God, or the incomprehenſible, is not a ſeparate ſcience. What is then theology ? I do not know.

† *It is ſurely much better to be a rational aſtronomer, or philoſopher, than a metaphyſical quibler, or atheiſt, for an atheiſt is nothing elſe: one of thoſe ſublime inveſtigators. who, as Pope ſays,*

> *Nobly take the high priori road,*
> *And reaſon downward till they doubt of God.*

If any one ſhould aſk what was the cauſe of thought, I might reply the aɛtion of the ſoul upon the nerves of the brain. But is the ſoul material or immaterial ? If the latter, how can immateriality aɛt on matter ; and if the former, in what manner does it aɛt ? I

Vol. I.   H   *cannot*

But why has not human reaſon, elucidated by obſervation, yet given a clear definition, or to ſpeak more properly, an adequate and minute deſcription of the principle of life? Becauſe that principle has ſtill eſcaped the moſt accurate obſervation. With the mind it is better acquainted. We can moreover examine this principle, and think on this ſubject without dread of the ignorance and fanatiſm of the bigots. I ſhall therefore here conſider ſome of the remarkable differences between the mind and the ſoul.

FIRST DIFFERENCE.

The ſoul exiſts intire in the infant as well as in the adult, The infant, as well as the man, is ſenſible of pleaſure and pain, but he has not ſo many ideas, nor conſequently ſo much mind or underſtanding as the adult. Now if the infant have as much ſoul without having as much mind, the ſoul is not the mind *. In fact, if the ſoul

---

* They deny a child the power of ſinning before it is ſeven years old. Why? becauſe before that age it is ſuppoſed to have no juſt idea of good or evil. That age paſſed, it is reputed a ſinner, becauſe it is then ſuppoſed to have acquired adequate

cannot anſwer theſe queſtions. I do not know in what manner gravity acts. But what of that, will any one tell me there is no gravity in nature, becauſe I do not know how it is produced? or, becauſe I cannot give a clear explication of the manner in which thought is produced, that therefore I do not think at all? and with juſt as much reaſon do ſome men doubt, or affect to doubt, the exiſtence of a firſt creating cauſe, becauſe they cannot comprehend its manner of exiſtence, that is, becauſe they cannot comprehend what is by its nature incomprehenſible.

and the mind were one and the fame thing, to explain the fuperiority of the adult over the infant, we muft admit more foul in the former, and agree that his foul has encreafed with his body : a fuppofition abfolutely gratuitous, and infignificant, when we diftinguifh the mind from the foul or principle of life.

SECOND DIFFERENCE.

The foul does not leave us till death. As long as I live I have a foul. Is it the fame of the mind? no. I can lofe it during my life : becaufe, while I yet live I can lofe my memory; and the mind is almoft entirely the effect of that faculty. The Greeks gave the name of Mnemofyne to the Mother of the Mufes, becaufe, being attentive obfervers of man, they perceived that his judgment, wit, &c. were in great part the produce of his memory, *

adequate ideas of juft and unjuft   The mind or underftanding is therefore regarded by the church itfelf as an acquifition, and confequently as quite different from the foul.

* Underftanding, or intelligence is alfo in brutes the effect of memory. If a dog comes at my call, it is becaufe he remembers his name. If he obey me when I pronounce thefe words, Softly; take care; dont touch that; it is becaufe he remembers that I am ftrong, and that I have beat him.

What makes animals perform fo many tricks in the public fpectacles? The fear of the whip; of which the look, the fpeech, and gefture of the mafter puts them continually in mind. If my dog ftop and look at me, it is becaufe he would read in my eyes, whether I am pleafed or angry, and confequently know if he fhall approach or fly me. My dog, therefore, owes his intelligence to his memory.

If

If a man be deprived of this faculty, of what can he judge? of fenfations paft? No: he has forgot them; and of fenfations prefent, it is neceffary to have at leaft as much memory as will give him an opportunity of comparing them together, that is, of obferving alternatively the different impreffions he feels at the prefence of two objects. Now, without a memory to preferve impreffions, how perceive the difference between thofe of this inftant, and thofe that the inftant before were perceived and forgotten? There is then no comparifon of ideas, no judgment, no mind, without memory. An ideot, who fets on the bench at his door, is only a man who has little or no memory. If he do not anfwer to queftions that are afked him, it is becaufe he does not remember the ideas affixed to the words, or that he forgets the firft words of a fentence before he hears the laft. If we confult experience, we fhall find that it is to the memory (whofe exiftence fuppofes the faculty of perception) that man owes his ideas and his underftanding. There can be no fenfations without a foul; but without a memory there can be no experience, no comparifon of objects, no ideas: a man would be the fame in his old age that he was in his infancy *. A man is reputed an ideot when he is ignorant;

* If the theologians agree that the infant and the ideot cannot fin, and that they have each of them a foul, it follows that in man fin does not effentially belong to the foul.

but

but he is only really so when his memory no longer exerts its functions *. Now, without losing our soul, we can lose our memory ; as by a fall, an apoplexy, or other accident of the like nature. The mind, therefore, differs essentially from the soul, as we can lose the one and still live, and the other is not lost but with life itself.

THIRD DIFFERENCE.

I have said, that the mind of man is composed of an assemblage of ideas. There is no mind without ideas.

Is it the same with the soul? No : neither thought nor understanding are necessary to its existence. As long as man is sensible, he has a soul. It is therefore the faculty of perception that forms its essence. Deprive the soul of what does not properly belong to it, that is of the faculty of remembrance, and what faculty is left it? That of perception. It then does not even preserve a consciousness of its own existence, because that consciousness supposes a concatenation of ideas, and consequently a memory. Such is the state of

---

* The famous M. Ernaud, the instructor of the deaf and dumb, says, in a memoir presented to the Academy of Sciences at Paris, that if the deaf and dumb have only short intervals of judgment, and reflect but little; if their minds be weak, and their reasoning instantaneous; it is because their memories are almost always stupified, and consequently their ideas and their actions are, and must be, without consequence.

the

the foul, when it has yet no ufe of the faculty of remembrance.

We may lofe our memory by a blow, a fall, or a difeafe. Is the foul deprived of this faculty ? It muft then, without a miracle, or the exprefs will of God, find itfelf in the fame ftate of imbecility it was in the human animal-cule. Thought, therefore, is not abfolutely ne-ceffary to the exiftence of the foul. The foul then, is in us nothing but the faculty of perceiv-ing, and this is the reafon why, as Locke and ex-perience prove, all our ideas come to us by the fenfes.

It is to my memory I owe the comparifon of my ideas and my judgments, and to my foul I owe my fenfations. It is therefore properly * my fenfations, and not my thoughts, as Defcartes af-ferts, that prove to me the exiftence of my foul. But what is the faculty of perception in man ? is it immortal and immaterial ? Of this human rea-fon is ignorant, and revelation inftructs us. Per-haps it will be objected, that if the foul be no-thing more than the faculty of perception, its action,

---

* M. Marion, regent of philofophy in the college of Na-varre, and feveral profeffors, after his example, have maintain-ed that all the operations of the mind may be explained folely by the motion of the animal fpirits, and the traces impreffed on the memory. From whence it follows, that the animal fpi-rits put in motion by exterior objects, can produce in us ideas independent of what we call the foul. The mind, therefore, according to thefe profeffors, is quite diftinct from the foul.

like,

like that of one body's ftriking another, is conftantly neceffary, and that the foul in this cafe
muft be regarded as merely paffive. So Mallebranche believed *, and his fyftem has been
publicly taught. If the theologians of the prefent day condemn it, they will fall into a contradiction with themfelves that will certainly fome-
what embarrafs them. For the reft, as men are
born without ideas of virtue, vice, &c. whatever
fyftem the theologians adopt, they will never
prove that thought is the effence of the foul; and
that the foul, or the faculty of fenfation, cannot exift
in us, without its being put in action, that is to fay,
without our having either ideas or fenfations.

The organ exifts, when it does not found.
Man is in the fame ftate with the organ, when in
his mother's womb; or when overcome with labour, and not troubled by dreams, he is buried in
a profound fleep. If all our ideas moreover, can
be ranged under fome of the claffes of our knowledge, and we can live without having any ideas
of mathematics, phyfics, morality, mechanics, &c.
it is then not metaphyfically impoffible to have a
foul without having any ideas.

---

* According to Mallebranche, it is God that manifefts
himfelf to our underftanding: it is to him we owe all our ideas.
Mallebranche, therefore, did not believe that the foul could produce them of itfelf: he confequently thought it merely paffive.
The Catholic church hath not condemned this doctrine.

The

The favages have little knowledge, they have neverthelefs fouls. There are fome of them who have no ideas of juftice, nor even words to exprefs that idea. They fay, that a man deaf and dumb, having fuddenly acquired his hearing and fpeech, confeffed, that before his cure, he had no idea of God or of death.

The king of Pruffia, prince Henry, Hume, Voltaire, &c. have no more foul than Bertier, Lignac, Seguy, Gauchat, &c. The former, however, have minds as fuperior to the latter, as they have to monkeys, and other animals that are exhibited in public fhews.

Pompignan, Chaumeix, Caveirac *, &c. have certainly very little underftanding, however, we always fay of them, he fpeaks, he writes, and even he has a foul. Now, if by having very little underftanding, a man has not the lefs foul; ideas make no part of it: they are not effential to its being. The foul, therefore, may exift independent of all ideas, and of all underftanding.

Let us here recapitulate the moft remarkable differences between the foul and the mind.

The firft is, that we are born with a perfect foul, but not with a perfect mind.

---

* The names of thefe defpicable mortals are not known in Germany, or in any part of Europe, except by the diminutive parts of M. Voltaire's writings. But for him their exiftence would never have been known.

The

The fecond, that we can lofe our mind, or underftanding, while we yet live, but that we cannot lofe the foul but with life itfelf.

The third, that thought is not neceffary to the foul's exiftence.

Such was doubtlefs the opinion of the theologians, when they maintained, after Ariftotle, that it was to the fenfes the foul owed its ideas. Let it not be imagined, however, that the mind can be confidered as entirely independent of the foul. Without the faculty of fenfation, memory, the productive power of the mind, would be without functions, it would be of no effect *. The exiftence of our ideas and our mind, fuppofes that of the faculty of fenfation. This faculty is the foul itfelf: from whence I conclude, that if the foul be not the mind, the mind is the effect of the foul, or the faculty of fenfation †.

---

* The Treatife on the Mind, fays, that memory is nothing more than a continued, but weakened fenfation. In fact, the memory is nothing more than the effect of the faculty of fenfation.

† I fhall be afked, perhaps, what is the faculty of fenfation, and what produces this phenomenon in us? The following is the opinion of a celebrated Englifh chymift, on the foul of animals: " We find, fays he, in bodies, two forts of pro-
" perties, the exiftence of one of which is permanent and un-
" alterable; fuch are its its impenetrability, gravity, mobility,
" &c. Thefe qualities appertain to phyfics in general."
There are in the fame bodies other properties, whofe tranfient and fugitive exiftence is by turns produced and deftroyed by certain combinations, analyfes, or motions in their interior parts. Thefe forts of properties form the different branches of
natural

C H A P.   III.

Of the objects on which the mind acts.

WHAT is nature? The assemblage of all beings. What can be the employment of the mind in the universe? That of an observer

natural history, chymistry, &c. and belong to particular parts of physics.

Iron, for example, is a composition of a phlogiston and a particular earth. In this composite state it is subject to the attractive power of the magnet. When this iron is decomposed, that property vanishes: the magnet has no influence over a ferruginous earth deprived of its phlogiston.

When a metal is combined with another substance, as a vitriolic acid, this union destroys in like manner in iron the property of being attracted by the magnet.

Fixed alkali, and a nitrous acid have each of them separately an infinity of different qualities; but when they are united, there does not remain any vestige of those qualities, they each of them then ferment with nitre.

In the common heat of the atmosphere, a nitrous acid will disengage itself from all other bodies, to combine with a fixed alkali.

If this combination be exposed to a degree of heat, proper to put the nitre into a red fusion, and any inflammable matter be added to it, the nitrous acid will abandon the fixed alkali, to unite with the inflammable substance, and in the act of this union arises the elastic force whose effects are so surprising in gunpowder.

All the properties of fixed alkali are destroyed, when it is combined with sand, and formed into glass, whose transparency, indissolubility, electric power, &c. are, if I may be allowed the expression, so many new creations, that are produced by this mixture, and destroyed by the decomposition of glass.

Now

of the relations objects have to each other, and to us: the relations that objects have to me are fmall in number. I am prefented with a rofe: its colour, its form, and fmell pleafe, or difpleafe me. Thefe are the relations it has to me. Every relation of this kind is reducible to the agreeable or difagreeable manner in which an object affects me. It is the conclufive obfervation on fuch relations that conftitutes tafte, and its rules.

With regard to the relations objects have to each other, they are as numerous as are, for example, the diverfe objects to which I can compare the form, the colour, and fmell of my rofe. The relations of this fort are immenfe, and their obfervation belongs more directly to the fciences.

Now in the animal kingdom, why may not organifation produce in like manner that fingular quality we call the faculty of fenfation? All the phenomena that relate to medicine and natural hiftory, evidently prove that this power is in animals nothing more than the refult of the ftructure of their bodies; that this power begins with the formation of their organs, lafts as long as they fubfift, and is at laft deftroyed by the diffolution of the fame organs.

If the metaphyficians afk me, what then becomes of the *faculty of fenfation in an animal?* That which becomes, I fhould anfwer them, of the quality of attracting the magnet in iron that is decompofed.

See *Treatife on the Principles of Chymiftry.*

CHAP.

CHAP. IV.

How the Mind acts.

ALL the operations of the mind are reducible to the obferving of the refemblances and differences, the agreements and difagreements that objects have among themfelves and with us. The juftnefs of the mind or judgment depends on the greater or lefs attention with which its obfervations are made.

Would I know the relations certain objects have to each other? What do I do? I place before my eyes, or prefent to my memory two or more of thefe objects; and then I compare them. But what is this comparifon? *It is an alternate and attentive obfervation of the different impreffions thefe objects, prefent or abfent, make on me* *. This obfervation made, I judge, that is, I make an exact report of the impreffions I have received.

Am I, for example, much interefted to diftinguifh between two fhades of the fame colour, that are almoft indiftinguifhable; I examine a long time and fucceffively, two pieces of cloth tinged with thofe two fhades. *I compare them,*

---

* If the memory, the preferver of impreffions received, makes me perceive, in the abfence of the objects, nearly the fame fenfations that they excite in me when prefent, it is indifferent, with regard to the queftion here difcuffed, whether the objects of which I form a judgment, be prefented to my eyes, or my memory.

that

that is, *I regard them alternatively*. I am very attentive to the different impreſſions the reflected rays of theſe two patterns make on my eyes, and I at laſt determine, that one of them is of a deeper colour than the other; that is to ſay, I make an exact report of the impreſſions I have received. Every other judgment would be falſe. All judgment therefore is nothing more than a *recital of the two ſenſations, either actually proved, or preſerved in my memory* *.

When I obſerve the relation objects have to me, I am in like manner attentive to the impreſſions I receive. Theſe impreſſions are either agreeable or diſagreeable. Now in either caſe what it is to judge? *To tell what I feel*. Am I ſtruck on the head? Is the pain violent? The ſimple recital of what I feel forms my judgment.

I ſhall only add one word to what I have here ſaid, which is, that with regard to the judgments formed on the relations objects have to each other, or to us, there is a difference, which though of little importance in appearance, deſerves however to be remarked.

When we are to judge of the relation objects have to each other, we muſt have at leaſt two of them before our eyes. But when we judge of the relation an object has to ourſelves, it is evident,

---

* There can be no judgment without memory; as I have proved in the preceding chapter.

as

as every object can excite a fenfation, one alone
is fufficient to produce a judgment.

From this obfervation I conclude, that every
affertion concerning the relation of objects to each
other, fuppofes a comparifon of thofe objects;
every comparifon a trouble ; every trouble, an efficacious motive to take it.   But on the contrary,
when we are to obferve the relation of an object
to ourfelves, that is to fay, a fenfation, that fenfation, if it be lively, becomes itfelf the efficacious motive to excite our attention.

Every fenfation of this kind carries therefore
conftantly with it a judgment.   I fhall not ftop
longer at this obfervation, but repeat, agreeable
to what I have faid above, that in every cafe to
judge, is to *feel*.

This being fettled, all the operations of the
mind are reduced to mere fenfations.   Why then
admit in man a faculty of judging diftinct from
the faculty of fenfation.   But this is the general
opinion : I own it ; and it even ought to be fo.
We fay, I perceive, and I compare; there is therefore in man a faculty of judging and comparing,
diftinct from the faculty of fenfation. This method
of reafoning is fufficient to impofe on the greateft
part of mankind.   However, to fhew its fallacy,
it is only neceffary to fix a clear idea to the word
compare. When this word is properly elucidated,
it will be found to exprefs no one real operation
of the mind ; that the bufinefs of comparing, as
                                                I have

I have before faid, is nothing elfe than *rendering
ourfelves attentive to the different impreffions excited
in us by objeƐts aƐually before our eyes, or prefent
to our memory* ; and confequently that all judgment is nothing more *than pronouncing of fenfations felt*.

But if the judgment made from the comparifon of material objeƐts be nothing more than
mere fenfations, is it the fame with every other
fort of judgment.

C H A P. V.

*Of fuch judgments as refult from the comparifon of
ideas that are abftraƐted, colleƐive, &c.*

THE words weaknefs, ftrength, fmallnefs,
greatnefs, crime, &c. do not reprefent any
fubftance, that is, any body : how then can the
judgments refulting from the comparifon of fuch
words, or ideas, be reduced to mere fenfations?
I anfwer, that as thefe words do not reprefent any
ideas, it is impoffible, fo long as we do not apply them to any fenfible and particular objeƐt, to
form any judgment about them. But when they
are applied by defign, or imperceptibly, to fome
determinate objeƐt, then the word *great* will exprefs a relation, that is, a certain difference or refemblance obferved between objeƐts prefent to our
fight, or to our memory. Now the judgment
formed

formed of ideas, that by this application become material, will be, as I have repeatedly said, nothing more than the pronouncing of sensations felt.

I shall be asked perhaps, from what motives men have invented and introduced these algebraical expressions, if I may be allowed the term, which till they are applied to sensible objects, have no real signification, nor represent any determinate idea? I answer, that men thought they should by this method be able to communicate their ideas more easily, readily, and even more clearly. It is for this reason that they have in all languages created so many adjectives and substantives that are at once so vague * and so useful.

* In the composition of the language of a polished people, there constantly enters an infinity of pronouns, conjunctions, in short, of words that being void of meaning themselves, borrow their different significations from the expressions with which they are connected, or the phrases in which they are used. The invention of most of these words is owing to the fear that men had of too much increasing the signs of their languages, and a desire of communicating their ideas more easily. If they had in fact been obliged to create as many words as there are things to which they might be applied ; for example, the adjectives *white, strong, great,* as *a great cable, a great ox, a great tree,* &c. it is evident that the multiplicity of words necessary to express their ideas would have been too weighty for their memory. It appeared necessary therefore to invent such words, as representing no real idea themselves, having only a local signification, and expressing merely the relations objects have to each other, should however recall to the mind distinct ideas, the moment these words were connected with the objects whose relation they expressed.

Let

Let us take for example, among thefe infignificant expreffions, that of the word *line*, confidered
in geometry as having length without breadth or
thicknefs; in this fenfe it recalls no idea to the
mind. No fuch line exifts in nature, nor can any
idea be formed of it. What does the mafter defign therefore by ufing it? Merely to induce his
pupil to give all his attention to the length of a
body, without confidering its other dimenfions.

When, for the facility of algebraical cal-
claution, we fubftitute the letters A and B for
fixt quantities, do thefe letters prefent any ideas?
Do they exprefs any real dimenfion? No.
Now what is expreffed in the algebraical language
by A and B, is expreffed in the common language by the words weaknefs, ftrength, fmallnefs, greatnefs, &c. Thofe words exprefs only
a vague relation of things to each other, and do
not exprefs any real and clear idea till the moment they are applied to a determinate object,
and that object be compared with another. It is
then that thefe words being put, if I may fo fay,
in equation or comparifon, exprefs very precifely
the relation of objects to each other. Till that
moment the word greatnefs, for example, recalls
to the mind very different ideas, according as it
is applied to a fly or an elephant. It is the fame
with regard to what is called in man idea or
thought. Thefe expreffions are in themfelves infignificant; yet to how many errors have they

given birth : how often have they maintained in the schools, that *as thought does not belong to extension and matter*, it is evident, that the soul is spiritual. I confess I could never make any thing of this learned jargon. What in fact is the meaning of the word *thought ?* Either it is void of meaning, or like the word *motion* it merely expresses a mode of a man's existence. Now to say that a mode or manner of being, is not a body, or has no extension, nothing can be more clear. But to make of this mode a being, and even a spiritual being, nothing, in my mind, is more absurd.   What again can be more vague than the word *crime ?* That this collective term may convey to my mind a clear and determinate idea, I must apply it to a theft, a murder, or some such action.   Men have invented words of this sort merely to communicate their ideas more easily, or at least more readily.   Suppose a society was instituted into which none but honest men were to be admitted ; in order to avoid the trouble of transcribing a long catalogue of the actions for which any one was to be excluded, they would say in one word, that no man guilty of a crime was to be admitted.   But of what precise idea would the word crime be here the representative ? Of no one. This word could be solely intended to call to the mind of the society those pernicious actions of which its members might become culpable, and to caution them to take heed to their conduct.

In

In fhort, this word would be properly nothing more than a found, and a more concife method of exciting the attention of the fociety.

If like manner, if we are forced to determine the punifhment due to a crime, we muft firft form clear and precife ideas of it, and then recall to our memories, fucceffively, the reprefentation of the different crimes a man may commit : then examine which of thofe offences are moft detrimental to fociety, and laftly, form a judgment which would be, as I have fo often faid, nothing more than *pronouncing the fenfations felt at the prefence of the feveral reprefentations of thofe crimes.*

Every idea whatever may therefore, in its ultimate analyfis, be always reduced to material facts or fenfations. Some obfcurity is thrown on difcuffions of this kind by the vague fignifications of a certain number of words, and the trouble that is fometimes neceffary to deduce clear ideas from them. Perhaps it is as difficult to analyze fome of thefe expreffions, and to reduce them, if I may fo fay, to their conftituent ideas, as it is in chymiftry to decompofe certain bodies. However, let us but apply the method and attention neceffary in this decompofition, and we fhall not fail of fuccefs.

What is here faid will be fufficient to convince the difcerning reader, that every idea and every judgment may be reduced to a fenfation. It would be therefore unneceffary, in order to explain the different

operations

operations of the mind, to admit a faculty of
judging and comparing diftinct from the faculty
of fenfation : but what is, it may be faid, the
principle or motive that makes us compare objects
with each other, and gives us the neceffary attention to obferve their relations ? Intereft, which
is in like manner, as I am going to fhew, an effect of corporeal fenfibility.

C H A P.   VI.

*Where there is no intereft, there is no comparifon
of objects with each other.*

ALL comparifon of objects with each other
fuppofes attention, all attention a trouble, and all trouble a motive for exerting it.
If there could exift a man without defire, he would
not compare any objects, or pronounce any judgment; but he might ftill judge of the immediate
impreffions of objects on himfelf, fuppofing
their impreffions to be ftrong. Their ftrength becoming a motive to attention, would carry with it
a judgment. It would not be the fame if the
fenfation were weak ; he would then have no
knowledge or remembrance of the judgment it
had occafioned. A man furrounded by an infinity of objects, muft neceffarily be affected by an
infinity of fenfations, and confequently form an
infinity of judgments; but he forms them unknown

known to himfelf. Why? Becaufe thefe judgments are of the fame nature with the fenfations. If
they make an impreffion that is effaced as foon
as made, the judgments formed on thefe impreffions are of the fame fort; they leave no remembrance. There is in fact no man who does not,
without perceiving it, make every day an infinity
of reafonings, of which he has no confcioufnefs.
I will take, for example, thofe that attend almoft
all the rapid motions of our bodies.

When in the dance, Veftris makes a cabriole
rather than a entrechat, when Moté in the fen-
cing fchool thrufts tierce rather than quart, if
there be no effect without a caufe, Veftris and Moté
muft be determined by reafons too rapid, if I
may fo fay, to be perceived. So the motion I
make with my hand when a body is going to
ftrike my eye, may be reduced to nearly the fame;
experience tells me, that my hand can refift
without pain the blow of a body that would deprive me of fight: my eyes moreover are dearer
to me than my hand: I ought therefore to expofe my hand to fave my eyes. There is no perfon that would not ufe the fame reafoning in the
fame fituation; but this habitual reafoning is not
fo rapid, but that we perceive the moment we
have put the hand before the eye, the action, and
the caufe of the action? Now how many fenfations are there of the nature of thefe habitual reafonings? How many weak fenfations that do not

fix

fix our attention, or produce in us either confcioufnefs or remembrance ?

There are moments when the ftrongeft fenfations are, fo to fay, imperceptible. I fight, and
am wounded, I continue the combat, and perceive not my wound. Why ? Becaufe the love
of prefervation, rage, and the motion given to
my blood, render me infenfible to the ftroke that
at another time would have fixed all my attention.

There are moments on the contrary, when we
are fenfible of the flighteft impreffions ; that is,
when the paffions of fear, ambition, avarice, envy,
&c. concenter all our attention on an object. Am
I concerned in a confpiracy ? There is no gefture,
no look that can efcape the reftlefs and fufpicious
eyes of my confederates. Am I a painter ? Every
remarkable effect of the light ftrikes me. Am I a
jeweller ? There is no flaw in a diamond that I
do not perceive. Am I envious ? There is no defect in a great character that my piercing eye does
not difcern. In like manner thofe paffions that
by concentering all my attention on certain objects, render me fufceptible of the keeneft fenfations, with regard to them, make me at the fame
time infenfible to every other fort of fenfation.

If I be in love, jealous, ambitious, or difcontented, and in this fituation of my mind I traverfe
the magnificent palace of a monarch, in vain do
the rays reflected from marbles, ftatues, and
paintings,

paintings, strike my eyes : to awaken my attention, some new, unknown object must suddenly
and forcibly strike my sight. Unless such an
impression occur, I walk on without perceiving the
sensations that strike me.

If, on the contrary, in the calm of my desires,
I range through the same place, then, sensible to
all the beauties of nature and art by which it is
embellished, my soul being open to every impression will participate of all it receives. I shall
not indeed be endowed with that keen and piercing
ing look with which the lover, and the ambitious behold every object that affects them. I
shall not like them see what is only visible to the
eyes of the passions. I shall be less acutely, but
more generally sensible. Let a man of pleasure
and a botanist walk by the side of a river, shaded
by stately oaks, and bordered by shrubs and odo-
riferous flowers. The first of them affected merely by the limpidity of the stream, the beauty of
the oaks, the variety of the shrubs, and the fra-
gancy of the flowers, will not see them with the
eyes of the botanist : he will not observe the
uniformity and variety among these shrubs and
flowers. Having no interest to remark them, he
will want the attention to perceive them ; he will
receive the sensations from his judgment, but have
no remembrance of them. It is the botanist,
anxious for his reputation, the scrupulous observer of these various flowers and shrubs, that

I 4   can

can alone make himſelf attentive to the different ſenſations he feels, and the different judgments he forms,*

For the reſt, the conſciouſneſs or unconſciouſneſs of ſuch impreſſions, change not their nature ; it is therefore true, as I have already ſaid, that all our ſenſations carry with them a judgment, whoſe exiſtence, though unnoticed when they fix not our attention, is however not the leſs real.

It reſults from the contents of this chapter, that all judgments formed by comparing objects with each other, ſuppoſes an intereſt in us to compare them. Now that intereſt, neceſſarily founded on our love of happineſs, cannot be any thing elſe than the effect of bodily ſenſibility ; becauſe all our pleaſures, and all our pains have their ſource from thence. This queſtion being diſcuſſed, I conclude that corporeal pains and pleaſures are the unknown principles of all human actions †.

* There is in fact no remembrance without attention, nor any attention without intereſt.

† Mr. Rouſſeau, in ſeveral parts of his Emilius, denies that bodily ſenſibility is the principle of all human actions, but the reaſons on which he founds his denial, ſhew that he has not ſeriouſly reflected on the queſtion.

CHAP.

C H A P. VII.

Corporeal fenfibility is the fole caufe of our actions, our thoughts, our paffions, and our fociability.

A C T I O N.

It is to clothe himfelf, and adorn his miftrefs, or his wife, to procure them amufements, nourifh himfelf and his family, in a word to enjoy the pleafures attached to the gratification of bodily defires that the artizan and the peafant thinks, contrives, and labours. Corporeal fenfibility is therefore the fole mover of man *, he is confe-

---

* What they call intellectual pain, or pleafure, may be always referred to fome bodily pain or pleafure. Two examples will make this evident.

What makes us fond of gaming, even for trifles? Is it the agreeable fenfations we then feel? No: we love it becaufe it relieves us from the difguftful ftate of being weary of ourfelves, and delivers us from that abfence of impreffion which always produces difcontent, and a bodily uneafinefs. What makes us love high play? The love of money. Why do we love money? From a tafte for conveniences, the want of amufements, the defire of avoiding bodily pains and procuring bodily pleafures. Do we not befide love the emotion that high gaming produces in us? Without doubt. But the emotion felt at the moment I lofe or gain a thoufand, two, or if you will, ten thoufand guineas, takes its fource, either from the fear of being deprived of the pleafures I poffefs, or the hope of enjoying thofe that the increafe of my fortune will procure me. Is not this emotion in fome men the effect of pride alfo? There are men fufficiently proud to be mortified when fortune forfakes them, though they play but for pins: but this fort of pride is rare. Befide, this fame pride, as is proved in the Treatife of the Mind, ch. 13. difc.

quently fufceptible, as I am going to prove, but of two forts of pleafures and pains, the one

3. is no other than one of the effects of bodily fenfibility. The principle of the love of play is therefore either the fear of difguft, and confequently pain, or the hope of bodily pleafure.

Is it the fame with regard to the internal pleafure we feel in fuccouring the diftreffed, by performing an act of liberality? This is certainly a very lively pleafure. Every action of this kind fhould be praifed by all, becaufe it is ufeful to all. But what is a benevolent man? One in whom a fpectacle of mifery produces a painful fenfation.

Born without ideas, without vice, and without virtue, every thing in man, even his humanity, is an acquifition: it is to his education he owes this fentiment. Among all the various ways of infpiring him with it, the moft efficacious is to accuftom him from childhood, in a manner from the cradle, to afk himfelf when he beholds a miferable object, by what chance he is not expofed in like manner to the inclemency of the feafons, to hunger, cold, poverty, &c. when the child has been ufed to put himfelf in the place of the wretched; that habit gained, he becomes the more touched with their mifery, as in deploring their fate it is for human nature in general, and for himfelf in particular, that he is concerned. An infinity of different fentiments then mix with the firft fentiment, and their affemblage compofes the total of the fentiment of pleafure felt by a noble foul in fuccouring the diftreffed: a fentiment that he is not always in a fituation to analyze.

We relieve the unfortunate,

1. To avoid the bodily pain of feeing them fuffer.
2. To enjoy an example of gratitude, which produces in us at leaft a confufed hope of diftant utility.
3. To exhibit an act of power, whofe exercife is always agreeable to us, becaufe it always recalls to the mind the images of pleafures attached to that power.
4. Becaufe the idea of happinefs is conftantly connected, in a good education, with the idea of beneficence, and this beneficence in us conciliating the efteem and affection of men, may, like riches, be regarded as a power, or means of avoiding pains and procuring pleafures.

In

are prefent bodily pains and pleafures, the other are the pains and pleafures of forefight or memory.

P A I N.

I know but two forts of pain, that we feel, and that we forefee. I die of hunger; I feel a prefent pain. I forefee that I fhall foon die of hunger. I feel a pain by forefight, the ftrength of whofe impreffion is in proportion to the prox-imity and feverity of the pain. The criminal who is going to the fcaffold, feels yet no torment, but the forefight that makes his prefent punifh-ment, is begun *.

In this manner, as from an affinity of different fentiments, is made up the total fentiment of the pleafure we feel in the exercife of beneficence.

I have here faid enough, to furnifh a man of difcernment with the means of decompofing, in like manner, every other kind of pleafure, called intellectual, and reducing it to mere fenfation.

* There is no doubt but the forefight in thofe dreadful moments, makes men feel a painful bodily fenfation. What is this forefight? An effect of the memory. Now it is the property of the memory to put the organs, to a certain de-gree, into thofe contractions that they would be more forcibly put, by the punifhment itfelf. It is evident, therefore, that all pains and pleafures efteemed interior, are fo many bodily fenfations, and that we cannot underftand by the words in-terior and exterior, any thing but impreffions excited by the memory, or by the actual prefence of objects.

R E M O R S E.

R E M O R S E.

Remorfe is nothing more than a forefight of bodily pain, to which fome crime has expofed us: and is confequently the effect of bodily fenfibility.   We tremble at the defcription of the flames, the wheels, the fiery fcourges, that the heated imagination of the painter or the poet reprefents.   Is a man without fear, and above the law ? he feels no remorfe from the commiffion of a wicked action ; provided, however, that he have not previoufly contracted a virtuous habit ; for then he will not purfue a contrary conduct, without feeling an uneafinefs, a fecret inquietude, to which is alfo given the name of remorfe.   Experience tell us, that every action which does not expofe us to legal punifhment, or to difhonour, is an action performed in general without remorfe *. Solon and Plato loved women and even boys, and avowed it †.   Theft was not punifhed in Sparta :

---

* If difhonour, or the contempt of mankind be infupportable, it is becaufe it prefages evils, as it in part deprives us of the advantages that arife from the union of men in fociety : for contempt implies a want of attention in mankind to ferve us, and prefents the time to come as void of pleafures, and filled with pains ; which are all reducible to bodily fenfation.

† The Gauls were anciently divided into a great number of clubs, or particular focieties, that were compofed of about a dozen families, the women of which were in common. They lived among themfelves without remorfe, but no one dared to have a paffion for a woman belonging to another
club ;

and the Lacedæmonians robbed without remorfe.
The princes of the Eaft can, with impunity, load
their fubjects with taxes, and they do it effec-
tually.   The inquifitor can with impunity, burn
whoever does not think as he does, on certain metaphyfical points, and it is without remorfe that he
gluts his vengeance by hideous torments, for the
flight offence that is given to his vanity by the
contradiction of a Jew or an Infidel.   Remorfe,
therefore owes its exiftence to the fear of punifhment or of fhame, which is always reducible, as I
have already faid, to a bodily fenfation.

F R I E N D S H I P.

It is in like manner, from bodily fenfibility, the
tears flow that bathe the urn of my friend.   I la-
ment the lofs of the man whofe converfation relieved
me from difquietude, from that difagreeable fenfation of the foul, which actually produces a bodily pain : I deplore him who expofed his life
and fortune to fave me from forrow and deftruction ; who was inceffantly employed in promoting
my felicity, and increafing it by every fort of
pleafure.   When a man enters into himfelf, when
he examines the bottom of his foul, he perceives
nothing in all thefe fentiments but the develop-

club: the law forbade it, and remorfe begins where impunity ends.

                                        ment

ment of bodily pain and pleasure. What cannot this pain produce? It is by this mean the magiftrate enchains vice, and difarms the affaffin.

P L E A S U R E.

There are two forts of pleasures, as there are two forts of pains: the one is the prefent bodily pleasure, the other is that of forefight. Does a man love fine flaves and beautiful paintings? If he difcover a treasure he is tranfported. He does not, however, yet feel any bodily pleasure, you will fay: it is true; but he gains at that moment, the means of procuring the objects of his defires. Now this forefight of an approaching pleasure, is in fact an actual pleasure: for without the love of fine flaves and paintings, he would have been entirely unconcerned at the difcovery of the treasure.

The pleasures of forefight, therefore, conftantly fuppofe the exiftence of the pleasures of the fenfes. It is the hopes of enjoying my miftrefs to-morrow that makes me happy to-day. Forefight or memory convert into an actual enjoyment the acquifition of every means proper to procure pleasure. From what motive in fact do I feel an agreeable fenfation every time I obtain a new degree of efteem, of importance, riches, and above all, of power? It is becaufe I efteem power as the moft fure means of increafing my happinefs.

P O W E R.

POWER.

Men love themfelves: they all defire to be happy, and think their happinefs would be complete, if they were invefted with a degree of power fufficient to procure them every fort of pleafure. The love of power therefore takes its fource from the love of pleafure.

Suppofe a man abfolutely infenfible. But, it will be faid, he muft then be without ideas, and confequently a mere ftatue. Be it fo: but allow that he may exift, and even think. Of what confequence would the fcepter of a monarch be to him? None. In fact, what could the moft immenfe power add to the felicity of a man without feeling.

If power be fo coveted by the ambitious, it is as the mean of acquiring pleafure. Power is like gold, a money. The effect of power, and of a bill of exchange is the fame. If I be in poffeffion of fuch a bill, I receive at London or Paris a hundred thoufand crowns, and confequently all the pleafures that fum can procure. Am I in poffeffion of a letter of authority or command? I draw in like manner from my fellow-citizens, a like quantity of provifions or pleafures. The effects of riches and power are in a manner the fame: for riches are power.

In

In a country where money is unknown, in what manner can taxes be paid? In the natural ftate, that is, in corn, wine, cattle, fowls, &c.—How can commerce be carried on? By exchange. Money therefore is to be regarded as a portative merchandife, which it is agreed on, for the facility of commerce, to take in exchange for all other forts of merchandife. Can it be the fame with the dignities and honours with which polifhed nations recompenfe the fervices rendered their country? Why not? What are honours? A money that is in like manner the reprefentative of every kind of provifion and pleafure. Suppofe a country where the honorary money is not current; fuppofe the people to be too free, and too haughty, to fuffer a very great inequality in the ranks and authority of the people: in what manner muft that nation recompenfe great actions, and fuch as are ufeful to the nation? By natural riches and pleafures, that is, by transferring a certain quantity of corn, beer, hay, wine, &c. to the granary and cellar of the hero: by giving him fo many acres of land to till, or fo many handfome flaves. It was by the poffeffion of Brifeis*, that the

* In the ifland of Rimini, no man can marry that has not killed an enemy, and borne away his head. The conqueror of two enemies has a right to marry two wives, and fo on to fifty. What could be the caufe of fuch an eftablifhment? The fituation of thefe iflanders, who being furrounded by nations that were their enemies, would not have been able to refift them,

Greeks recompenced the valour of Achilles. What among the Scandinavians, the Saxons, the Scythians, the Celts, the Samnites, and the Arabs *, was the recompence of courage, of talents and virtues? Sometimes a fine woman, and sometimes a banquet, where feasting on delicate viands, and carousing delightful liquors, the warriors with transport liftened to the carols of the bards.

It is therefore evident, that if money and honours be, among most polished nations, the rewards of virtuous actions, they are in that cafe the representative of the fame possessions, and the fame pleasures that poor and free nations grant to their heroes, and for the acquisition of which those heroes expose themselves to the greatest dangers. Therefore, on the supposition, that these dignities and honours were not the representatives of wealth or pleasures, that they were nothing more than empty titles †; those titles being eftimated accord-

them, if they had not perpetually excited the courage of their people by the highest rewards.

* Among the presents the caravans at this day make to the Arabs of the Desert, the most agreeable are nubile virgins. This was the tribute the victorious Saracens formerly demanded of the conquered. Abderama, after the conquest of the Spaniards, exacted of the petty prince of the Asturias, the annual tribute of a hundred beautiful virgins.

† If in despotic nations the spring of glory be commonly very weak, it is, because glory there does not confer any fort of power, because all power is absorbed in despotism; because in those countries a hero, covered with glory, is not secure from the intrigues of a villanous courtier; because he has no certain property in his effects, or his liberty; because,

ing to their real value, would prefently ceafe to be the objects of defire.   To enter a breach, a crown piece, the reprefentative of a pint of brandy, and the enjoyment of a futlerefs, muft be given to the foldier. The warriors of antiquity, and thofe of the prefent day are the fame *.   Men have not changed their nature, and they will always perform nearly the fame actions for the fame rewards.   If a man be fuppofed indifferent to pleafure and pain, he will be without action : unfufceptible of remorfe, or friendfhip, or, in fhort, of the love of riches or of power : for when we are infenfible to pleafure itfelf, we muft be infenfible

in fhort, he is liable, at the pleafure of his fovereign, to be thrown into a prifon, be deprived of his wealth and honours, and even of life itfelf.

Why does the Englifhman behold, in the greateft part of foreign noblemen, nothing more than gaudy valets and victims adorned with garlands?   Becaufe a peafant in England, is in fact greater than an officer of ftate in another country : the peafant is free ; he can be virtuous with impunity ; and fees nothing above him but the law.

It is the defire of glory that muft be the moft powerful principle of action in poor-republics : and it is the love of money, founded on the love of luxury, that in defpotic countries is the principle of action, and the moving power in nations fubject to that fort of government.

* The eruption of Brennus into Italy, it is well known, was not the firft, but the fifth made by the Gauls.   Bellovefus had made a defcent there before him ; and how did this chief perfuade his countrymen to follow him over the Alps?   By fhowing them the wine of Italy.   " Tafte this wine, he cried, " and fee if you like it ? if you do, follow me, and conquer the " country that produced it."

to

to the means of acquiring it.   What we fearch for in riches and power, is the means of avoiding bodily pains, and procuring bodily pleafures.   If the acquifition of gold and power be always a plea-fure, it is becaufe forefight and memory convert into an actual pleafure all the means of obtain-ing it.

The general conclufion of this chapter, is, that in man all is fenfation : a truth of which I fhall ftill give a frefh proof, by fhowing that his foci-ability is nothing more than a confequence of the fame fenfations.

C H A P. VIII.

Of Sociability.

MAN is by nature a devourer of fruits and of flefh ; but he is weak, unarmed, and confequently expofed to the voracity of animals ftronger than himfelf.   Man, therefore, to avoid the fury of the tyger and the lion, was forced to unite with man.   The object of this union was to attack and kill other animals *, either to feed on them, or to prevent their confuming the fruits and herbs that ferved him for nourifhment.

---

* There is, they fay, in Africa, a fort of wild dogs, that go in packs to make war on animals that are ftronger than themfelves.

In the mean time mankind multiplied, and to fupport themfelves, they were obliged to cultivate
the earth; but to induce them to this, it became
neceffary to ftipulate, that the harveft fhould belong to the hufbandman.   For this purpofe the
inhabitants made agreements or laws among
themfelves.   Thefe laws made ftrong the bonds
of a union, that, founded on their wants, was the
immediate effect of corporeal fenfibility *.   But
cannot this fociability be regarded as an innate
quality †, a fpecies of amiable morality?   All that
we learn from experience on this head, is, that in
man, as in other animals, fociability is the effect
of want.   If the defire of defending themfelves

* Becaufe man is fociable, they have concluded that he is
good.   But they have deceived themfelves.   Wolves form focieties, but they are not good.   We may add, that if man,
as M. Fonteneile fays, has made God after his own image,
the horrible portrait he has drawn of the Divinity ought to
make the goodnefs of man very equivocal.   Hobbes has been
reproached with this maxim : *The ftrong child is a bad child*,
he has however only repeated in other terms, this admired
verfe of Corneille,

Qui peut tout ce qu'il veut, veut plus que ce qu'il doit.

He that can do whatever he will, wills more than he ought.

And this other verfe of Fontaine,

La raifon du plus fort eft toujours la meilleure.

The ftrongeft always reafon beft.

They who write the romance of man, condemn this maxim
of Hobbes ; they that write his hiftory, admire it ; and the
neceffity of laws proves it to be true.

† That curiofity, which certain writers regard as an innate
principle, is the defire in us of being happy, and of improving

makes the grazing animals, as horfes, bulls, &c. affemble in herds; that of chafing, attacking, and conquering their prey, forms in like manner a fociety of carnivorous animals, fuch as foxes and wolves.

Intereft and want are the principles of all fociability. It is, therefore, thefe principles alone (of which few writers have given clear ideas) that unite men among themfelves: and the force of their union is always in proportion to that of habitude and want. From the moment the young favage *, or the young bear, is able to provide for his nourifhment and his defence, the one quits the hut, and the other the den of his parents †. The

ing our condition: it is no other than the development of corporeal fenfibility.

* The greateft part of travellers, fay, that the attachment of the Negroes to their children, is fimilar to that of brute animals to their offspring: this attachment ceafes when they are able to provide for themfelves. See Melanges intereffans des Voyages d'Afia, d'Amérique, &c.

The Anxicos, fays Draper on this head, in his voyage to Africa, eat their flaves: human flefh is as common in their markets, as that of beef in ours. The father feafts on the flefh of his fon, and the fon on the flefh of his father; brothers and fifters eat each other, and the mother without remorfe, feeds on the child fhe has juft brought into the world. In fhort, the Negroes, fays F. Labbat, have neither gratitude nor affection for their relations, or compaffion for the fick. Among thefe people, he adds, mothers are feen inhuman enough to abandon their children to the voracity of the tygers of the woods.

† Nothing is more common in Europe, than to fee children defert their parents, when they become old, infirm,

K 3   incapable

eagle, in like manner, drives away her young ones from the neft, the moment they have fufficient ftrength to dart upon their prey, and live without her aid.

The bond that ties children to their parents, and parents to their children, is lefs ftrong than commonly imagined. A too great ftrength in this bond would be even fatal to focieties. The firft regard of a citizen fhould be to the laws, and the public profperity. I fpeak it with regret, filial affection fhould be in man fubordinate to the love of patriotifm. If this laft affection do not take place of all others, where fhall we find a meafure of virtue and vice? It would then be no more, and all morality would be abolifhed.

For what reafon, in fact, has juftice and the love of God been recommended to men, above all things? Becaufe of the danger to which a too great love of their parents would expofe them, has been in part perceived. If the excefs of this paffion be legitimated, if it be declared the principal attachment, a fon would then have a right to rob his neighbour, or plunder the public trea-

---

incapable of labour, and forced to fubfift by beggary. We fee, in the country, one father nourifh feven or eight children, but feven or eight children are not fufficient to nourifh one father. If all children be not fo unnatural, if fome of them have affection and humanity, it is to education and example they owe that humanity. Nature has made them diminutive bears.

fure-

fure, to fupply the wants, and promote the com-
forts of his father. Every family would form a
little nation, and thefe nations having oppofite
interefts, would be continually at war with each
other.

Every writer, who to give us a good opinion
of his own heart, founds the fociability of man on
any other principle than that of bodily and habitual wants, deceives weak minds, and gives them
a falfe idea of morality.

Nature, no doubt, defigned that gratitude and
habit fhould form in man a fort of gravitation,
by which they fhould be impelled to a love of their
parents : but it has alfo defigned that man fhould
have, in the natural defire of independence, a re-
pulfive power, which fhould dinimifh the too
great force of that gravitation *. Thus the
daughter joyfully leaves the houfe of her mother
to go to that of her hufband ; and the fon quits
with pleafure his native fpot, for an employment
in India, an office in a diftant country, or merely
for the pleafure of travelling.

Notwithftanding the pretended force of fentiment, friendfhip, and habit, mankind change at
Paris, every day, the part of the town, their acquaintance and their friends. Do men feek to

---

* Man hates dependence : from whence, perhaps, comes the
hatred of his father and mother ; and the proverb, founded on
common and conftant obfervation, that *the love of parents
defcends, and does not remount.*

make

make dupes ? They exaggerate the force of fentiment and friendfhip, they reprefent fociability as
an innate affection or principle. Can they, in reality,
forget that there is but one principle of this kind,
which is corporeal fenfibility ? It is to this principle alone, that we owe our felf-love, and the powerful love of independency : if men were, as they
fay, carried toward each other by a ftrong and
mutual attraction, would the heavenly Legiflator
have commanded them to love each other, and to
honour their parents * ? Would it not have left
the care of it to nature, which without the aid of
any law, obliges men to eat and drink when they
are hungry and dry, to open their eyes to the
light, and keep their hands out of the fire ?

Travellers do not inform us that the love
mankind have for their fellows, is fo common
as pretended. The failor, efcaped from a wreck,
and caft on an unknown coaft, does not run with
open arms to embrace the firft man he meets.
On the contrary, he hides himfelf in a thicket,
where he obferves the manners of the inhabitants,
and then prefents himfelf trembling before them.

But if an European veffel chance to approach
an unknown ifland, do not the favages, it is faid,
run in crowds towards the fhip ? They are, with-

---

* The command to love our fathers and mothers, proves
that the love of our parents is more the work of habit and
education, than of nature.

out doubt, amazed at the fight, they are ftruck with the novelty of our drefs, our arms and implements. The appearance excites their curiofity. But what defire fucceeds to this firft fenfation? That of poffeffing the objects of their admiration. They become lefs gay and more thoughtful; are bufied in contriving means to obtain, by force or fraud, the objects of their defires: for that purpofe they watch the favourable opportunity to rob, plunder, and maffacre the Europeans, who, in their conquefts of Mexico and Peru, gave them early examples of fimilar injuftice and cruelty.

The conclufion of this chapter is, that the principles of morality and politics, like thofe of all other fciences, ought to be eftablifhed on a great number of facts and obfervations. Now, what is the refult of the obfervations hitherto made on morality? That the love of men for their brethren, is the effect of the neceffity of mutual affiftance, and of an affinity of wants, dependent on that corporeal fenfibility, which I regard as the principle of our actions, our virtues, and our vices.

In perfevering in my opinion on this point, I think I ought to defend the Treatife on the Mind againft the odious imputations of hypocrify and ignorance.

CHAP.

C H A P.   IX.

A justification of the principles admitted in the Trea-
tise on the Mind.

WHEN the Treatise on the Mind appeared, the theologians regarded me as a
corruptor of morals.   They reproached me with
having maintained, after Plato, Plutarch, and experience, that the love of women had sometimes
excited virtue in men.

The fact, however, is notorious : their reproach,
therefore, is ridiculous.   If bread, it has been said
to them, be a recompence for labour and industry,
why not women * ?   Every object of desire
may become an encouragement to virtue, when it
is not to be obtained but by services done to our
country.

---

* If hunger for bread be the principle of so many actions, and
has so much power over men, how can we imagine that the
desire for women can have no effect on them ? At the moment
a youth is heated with the first fires of love, let its enjoyments
be proposed to him as the recompence of his application : let
him be reminded, even in the arms of his mistress, that it is to
his talents and his virtues he owes her favours.   The young
man, docile, assiduous, virtuous, will then enjoy in a manner
agreeable to his health, to his soul, and to the public good,
the same delight that he would not enjoy, in another situation,
without exhausting his strength, debasing his mind, and dissi-
pating his fortune, by living in a state of stupid ebriety.

In

In thofe ages, when the invafions of the Nor-thern nations, and the incurfions of an infinity of plunderers, held the inhabitants always in arms, when the women being frequently expofed to the infults of the ravagers, were in continual want of protectors, the virtue then the moft in efteem was valour. The favours of the women, therefore, were the recompences of the moft valiant, and con-fequently every man ambitious of thofe favours, endeavoured to elevate himfelf to that enthufiaftic courage, which about four centuries fince animat-ed the renowned knight-errants.

The love of pleafure was therefore in thofe ages the productive principle of the only virtue then known; that is, valour. When the man-ners changed, and a more improved policy fet the timid virgin free from infult, then beauty (for in government all things depend on each other) lefs expofed to the outrages of the ravagers, held its defenders in lefs efteem. If the enthufiafm of women for valour decreafed then in proportion to their fear; if the efteem preferved to this day, for that fort of courage be only the efteem of tradi-tion; if in this age the moft young, affiduous, ob-fequious, and above all, the moft opulent lover is commonly preferred, it is not furprifing; all is as it ought to be.

The favours of women, therefore, according to the changes that happen in manners and govern-ments, either are, or ceafe to be, the encourage-

ments

ments to certain virtues. Love in itfelf is no evil. Why fhould we regard the pleafures as the caufe of the political corruption of manners? Men have had in all ages nearly the fame wants, and in all ages have fatisfied thofe wants. The ages, or the nations moft addicted to love, have been thofe in which men were the ftrongeft and moft robuft. Edda, the Erfe poets, in fhort, all hiftory informs us, that the ages efteemed heroic and virtuous, have not been the moft temperate.

Youth are ftrongly attracted by women: they are more eager after pleafure than thofe of riper years; they are, however, commonly more humane and virtuous, at leaft more active, and activity is a virtue.

It was neither love nor pleafures that corrupted Afia, enervated the manners of the Medes, the Affyrians, Indians, &c. The Greeks, the Saracens, and Scandanavians, were neither more referved nor more chafte than the Perfians and Medes, and yet the former have never been cited among effeminate nations.

If there be a time when the favours of women can become a principle of corruption, it is when they are venal *; when money, far from being the recompence of merit and talents, becomes that of intrigue and flattery; in fhort, when a fatrap or a

---

* It may be afked by fome, perhaps, when the time was that the favours of women were not venal?

nabob

nabob can, by means of injuftice and crimes, obtain from the fovereign the right of pillaging the people, and applying the fpoil to his own emolument.

It is with women as with honours, they are the common objects of the defire of men : if honours be the price of iniquity ; if to attain them the great muft be flattered ; if the weak muft be facrificed to the powerful, and the intereft of a nation to that of a fultan ; then honours, fo juftly invented as a recompence and decoration of merit and talents, become the fource of corruption. Women, like honours, may, therefore, according to times and the manners, become the alternate encouragements to vice or virtue.

The political corruption of manners therefore confifts only in the depravation of the means employed to procure pleafures. The rigid moralift who preaches inceffantly againft pleafures, is nothing more than the echo of his ghoftly father. How can we extinguifh every defire in man without deftroying every principle of action ? He who is affected by no intereft, can have no motive to produce any action worthy a man.

CHAP.

C H A P.   X.

The pleasures of the senses are, in a manner even un-
known to nations themselves, their most powerful
motives.

THE springs of action in man are corporeal pains and pleasures. Why is hunger
the most habitual principle of his activity? Because among all his wants it is that which returns
the most frequently and commands the most im-
periously. It is hunger and the difficulty of appeasing it, that give to the carniverous animals
of the forest so much superiority of intellect over
the grazing herds. It is hunger that furnishes the
former with a hundred ingenious methods of attacking and surprising their game. It is hunger
that keeps the savages for six months together on
the lakes, and in the woods : teaches them to
bend the bow, to weave their nets, and set the
snares for their prey. It is hunger also that
among the polished nations puts the people in action, teaches them to cultivate the land, learn
an artful trade, and fill a difficult employ. But
in the exercise of these employs each one forgets
the motive that made him undertake it ; for the
mind is occupied, not with the want, but with the
means of appeasing it. The difficulty is not to
eat, but to provide the repast.

Pleasure

Pleafure and pain are, and always will be, the only principles of action in man.* If heaven had provided for all his wants ; if nourifhment proper for the body had been, like air and water, an element of nature, man would have been for ever wrapt up in floth.

Hunger, and confequently pain, is the principle of activity in the poor, that is of the greateft number : and pleafure is the principle of activity in thofe who are above indigence, that is, the rich. Now, among all the pleafures, that which without doubt acts the moft forcibly on us, and communicates the greateft energy to the foul, is the love of women. Nature, by attaching the greateft intoxication to the enjoyment of them, intended

---

* If wants be our only motives, it muft then be to them we owe the invention of arts and fciences. It is to that of hunger we are indebted for the art of tilling the foil, of forging the plow-fhare, &c. It is to the neceffity of defending ourfelves againft the rigour of the feafons we owe the art of building, of providing ourfelves with apparel, &c.

As to what concerns the magnificence of equipages, drefs, and furniture, with regard to mufic, theatres, in a word, all the arts of luxury, it is to love, to the defire of pleafing, and the fear of difguft, that we are in like manner to attribute the invention. Without love what arts would have yet been unknown ! What a ftupidity would there be in nature ! Men without wants would be without the principle of action : it is to the want of pleafure that youth owe, in part, their activity, and the fuperiority they have, in that refpect, over thofe of a more advanced age.

to

to make them one of the moſt powerful principles of our activity *.

* There are among the learned, they ſay, thoſe who condemn themſelves to live in a retreat, far from the world. Now,
how can we perſuade ourſelves, that in theſe the love of talents
is founded on the love of corporeal pleaſures, and above all
that of women? How can we reconcile theſe contradictions?
By ſuppoſing it may be with a man of talents as with a miſer :
if he deprive himſelf of neceſſaries to-day, it is with the hope
of enjoying ſuperfluities to-morrow. Does the miſer wiſh for
a fine ſeat, and the man of talents for a fine woman? If to
attain theſe be required great riches, and a great reputation, theſe two men will labour to increaſe, the one his riches,
and the other his renown. Now, if during the time employed
in the acquiſition of the money and the fame, they ſhould grow
old, and contract habits that they cannot break, without efforts of which age has rendered them incapable : the miſer and
the man of talents will then die, the one without his houſe, and
the other without his miſtreſs.

It is not only between theſe two men, but alſo between the
coquet, and the ſame miſer, that we find an infinity of ſimili-
tudes. Each of them are more happy than is imagined, and
each in the ſame manner. The miſer, when counting his
money, enjoys the approaching poſſeſſion of every object that
may be had in exchange for gold : and the coquet admiring
herſelf in her glaſs, enjoys in like manner by anticipation all
the homage that her beauty and graces can procure. I would
adviſe theſe two to ſtop where they are, and not procure either
a ſeat or lovers; for they will find, in the enjoyments of thoſe
objects of their deſires, a diſguſt of which they are at preſent
ignorant.

The ſtate of deſire is a ſtate of pleaſure. Houſes, lovers,
and women, that riches, beauty and talents can procure, are
pleaſures of foreſight, certainly leſs poignant, but more durable
than real and corporeal pleaſures. The body ſoon becomes ex-
hauſted : the imagination never. So that of all our pleaſures,
the latter are thoſe, in general, that give us, in the total of life,
the greateſt ſum of happineſs.

No

No paſſion produces greater changes in man : its empire extends even to brutes. The timid animal that trembles at the approach of another that is even weaker than itſelf, becomes animated by love. At the command of love he ſtops, ſhakes off every fear, attacks and defeats his equals, or even his ſuperiors in ſtrength. There are no dangers, no labours by which love can be diſmayed. It is the ſpring of life. In proportion as its deſires die away, man loſes his activity ; and by degrees, death deprives him of every other ſenſation.

Corporeal pleaſure and pain are the real and only ſprings of all government. We do not properly deſire glory, riches and honours, but the pleaſures only of which glory, riches, and honours are the repreſentatives ; and whatever men may ſay, while we give the workman money that he may drink, to excite him to labour, we muſt acknowledge the power that the pleaſures of the ſenſes have over us.

When I ſaid, in the Treatiſe of the Mind, that it is from the ſtalk of corporeal pleaſure and pain, that we gather all our joys and our pains, I publiſhed an important truth.——What follows ? That it is not in the enjoyment of theſe ſame pleaſures the political depravation of manners can conſiſt. Who in fact are a corrupted and effeminate people ? They who acquire by vicious means the fame pleafures that illuftrious nations acquire by virtuous means.

The declamations of certain moralifts will never prove any thing againft an author, whofe principles are juftified and confirmed by experience.

Let not this difcuffion of corporeal fenfibility be regarded as foreign to my fubject. What have I propofed ? To fhow that all men, equally well organifed, have an equal difpofition for underftanding. What have I done toward it ? I have diftinguifhed between the mind or underftanding, and the foul : I have proved, that the foul is in us nothing but the faculty of fenfation ; that the mind is the effect of it : that in man all is fenfation ; that, confequently, corporeal fenfibility is the principle of his wants, his paffions, his fociability, his ideas, his judgments, his defires, and his actions ; and that, in fhort, if all things can be explained by corporeal fenfibility, it is ufelefs to admit of any other faculty in us *.

Man is a machine, that being put in motion by corporeal fenfibility, ought to perform all that it executes. It is the wheel, that moved by a tor-

---

* Befide the faculty of fenfation, man, they fay, is endowed with that of remembrance. I know it : but as the organ of the memory is corporeal, as its office confifts in recalling impreffions that are paft, and as for that effect it muft excite in us actual fenfations, I am not the lefs authorifed to affert, that in man all is fenfation.

rent, raifes the piftons, and with them the water
defigned to be thrown into the bafon prepared to
receive it.

After having thus fhown that all in us is reducible to fenfation and remembrance, and that our
fenfations are produced by the five fenfes only ; to
difcover next if a greater or lefs underftanding
be the effect of a greater or lefs perfection of the
organs, we muft examine, if in fact, the fuperiority of the mind or underftanding be always in proportion to the acutenefs of the fenfes, and the extent of the memory. If experience prove the
contrary, there is no doubt but that the ufual inequality of minds muft proceed from another
caufe.

It is, therefore, to the fole examination of
this fact, the queftion propofed is now reduced,
and it is to this examination we fhall owe its
folution.

CHAP.

C H A P. XI.

Of the unequal extent of the memory.

I SHALL here only repeat what I have faid in the book on the Mind, and fhall obferve :

1. That the Hardouins, the Longuerues, the Scaligers, in fhort all the prodigies of memory, have commonly had but little genius, and that they are never placed in the fame rank with Machiavel, Newton, and Tacitus *.

2. That to make difcoveries of any kind, and deferve the title of inventor, or man of genius ; if we muft, as Defcartes has proved, meditate more than learn, a man may have a great memory, without a great underftanding †.

---

* *So Pope in his Effay on Criticifm,*

    As on the land while here the ocean gains,
    In other parts it leaves wide fandy plains ;
    Thus in the foul while memory prevails,
    The folid pow'r of underftanding fails ;
    Where beams of warm imagination play,
    The memory's foft figures malt away.

This feems to be a vulgar error ; a ftrong memory and a fertil invention frequently go together, the former being of the utmoft utility to the latter. If a man fhall fit down to invent, he will find that a complete retrofpect of all he has feen, heard or read, relative to any fcience, will afford him the greateft affiftance in his further inventions or improvements in that fcience.

† A great memory makes a great fcholar ; meditation makes the man of genius. The original mind, the mind of a peculiar

He who would acquire a great memory, fhould improve it by daily practice. He that would acquire a certain habit of meditation, fhould in like manner improve it by daily exercife. Now the time fpent in meditation, is not employed in ftoring up facts in the memory. The man who compares and meditates much, has therefore commonly the lefs memory, as he makes the lefs ufe of it. Of what ufe, moreover, is a great memory? The moft common will anfwer the purpofe of a great man. He who underftands his own language, has already a great number of ideas. To merit the title of a man of underftanding, what is he to do? Compare his ideas with each other, and by that mean obtain fome conclufion new and intereſting, either by being ufeful or agreeable. The memory charged with all the words of a language,

---

liar turn, fuppofes a comparifon of objects with each other, and a difcernment of relations unknown to ordinary men. It is not fo with the man of the world: his mind is compofed of tafte and memory. He who knows the moft remarkable paffages in hiftory, the moft bons mots, and curious anecdotes, is the moft agreeable companion. Newton, Locke, and Corneille, were underftood by few. The man of profound penetration is not adapted to the multitude. If the man of the world be not a fublime poet, a fine painter, a profound philofopher, or great general, he is at leaft quite amiable. If his reputation do not extend beyond the circle of his acquaintance, it is becaufe he does not write, does not improve any fcience, and render himfelf ufeful to mankind, and therefore ought not to expect much efteem.

L 3   and

and confequently with all the ideas of a people, is like a palet charged with a certain number of colours : the painter has on that palet the matter of an excellent picture ; it is for him fo to ufe and difpofe them, that they may produce a great truth in the fhades, and a great force of colouring, in a word, a beautiful painting.

A common memory has even more extent than is imagined.   In Germany and England there is fcarce a man of education, who does not under- ftand three or four languages *.   Now if the ftudy of thofe languages be comprifed in the common plan of education, it cannot fuppofe any thing more than a common organifation : all men are therefore endowed by nature with more memory than is re- quifite to inveftigate the greateft truths †.   From

---

* If the French underftand no language but their own, it is the effect of their education, and not their organifation ; let them pafs fome years at London or Florence, and they will eafily underftand Englifh or Italian.

† Nature, they fay, has given to every nation fome pecu- liar quality or genius.   There is no nation in Europe that has not made fome fuccefsful alterations in their military exercifes and evolutions, after the Pruffians.   But too much ftruck with the brilliancy of thefe evolutions, have thefe nations cultivated the means of exciting courage in their foldiers ?   I doubt it. The Europeans have not the fame motives to expofe their lives in battle, that the Greeks and Romans had : and confequent- ly, the courage of armies does not fhow itfelf in enterprizes equally hazardous ; and may be reduced, perhaps, in every warrior, to the fole principle of not being the firft to run away.

whence

whence I infer, that if the superiority of the mind confifts principally, as Mr. Hobbes remarked, in the knowledge of the true fignification of words, and if there be no man who in reflecting on thofe of his own language only, would not find more queftions to difcufs than he could refolve in the courfe of a long life, no man can complain of his memory. There are, they fay, quick and flow memories : we have in fact, a quick remembrance of the words of our own language, and a more flow remembrance of thofe of a foreign tongue; efpecially, if we fpeak it but feldom. But what can we conclude from hence ? Only that we have a remembrance of objects more or lefs prompt, according as they are more or lefs familiar to us. There is but one real and remarkable difference in memories, which is the inequality of their extent. Now, if all men equally well organifed, are, as I have proved, endowed with a memory fufficient to exalt them to the higheft ideas, genius is then not the product of a great memory. Confult on this fubject, chap. iii. difc. iii. of the Treatife on the Mind. I have there confidered this queftion in every light. My opinion appears to have been generally adopted, becaufe experience has confirmed its truth, and proved, that in general, it is not to the defect of the memory we ought to refer the imperfection of the mind or underftanding.

L 4

Does

Does it proceed from the unequal perfection of the other organs? I shall now examine that question.————

C H A P. XII.

Of the unequal perfection of the organs of the senses.

IF in men all be corporeal sensation, they do not then differ among themselves, but in the degrees of their sensations. The five senses are the organs of those sensations; they are the passages by which ideas penetrate even to the soul. But are these passages equally open in all; and according to the different structure of the organs of sight, hearing, touching, taste, and smell *, does not each man ought to smell, taste, touch, see, and hear differently? Lastly, should not those men who have the finest organs have the greatest discernment †, and be, perhaps, the only men that can have it in any remarkable degree?

* Let it not be supposed, however, that there is an extreme difference in the common organisation of men. All have not the same ear, yet in a concert, at certain tunes, all the musicians, all the dancers in an opera, and all the soldiers of a battalion move equally in measure.

† Among men the most perfectly organised, if there be few of remarkable acuteness, it is, they say, because the understanding is the conjunct effect of the fineness of the senses, and of a good education. Be it so: but on this supposition it would be at least impossible that a good education, without a peculiar and remarkable perfection of the senses, could form a great man. Now this fact is disproved by experience.

Experience

Experience, I anfwer, does not here agree with reafon : it demonftrates clearly that it is to the fenfes we owe our ideas, but it does not demon-ftrate that our difcernment is always in propor-tion to the greater or lefs perfection of the fenfes. Women, for example, who are of a more delicate texture than men, have more fenfibility in the touch, but have not more underftanding * than Voltaire, the man, perhaps, the moft furprifing of all others, for the fecundity, extent, and diverfity of his talents.

Homer and Milton were early blind. A blindnefs fo premature fhould imply fome imper-fection in the organ of fight : yet how ftrong and brilliant were their imaginations ? A fimilar ob-fervation may be made on M. Buffon ; he is fhort-fighted : yet what mind more comprehenfive, and

---

* The organifation of the two fexes, is without doubt, in fome refpects very different : but is this difference to be regard-ed as the caufe of the inferiority of the minds of women ? No : on the contrary, it is evident, that no woman being organifed as a man †, none of them confequently fhould have as much underftanding. Now, can the genius of Sappho, Hyppathia, Elizabeth, Catherine II. &c. be efteemed inferior to that of men ? If women be in general inferior, it is becaufe in general they receive a ftill worfe education. Compare together wo-men of very different conditions, fuch as princeffes and cham-bermaids ; I fay, that thefe two ranks of women have com-monly as much underftanding as their hufbands. Why ? Be-caufe the two fexes have here received an education equally bad.

† *Will this be allowed, as to what regards the fenfibility of the organs ? Are there not many women of a more robuft organifa-tion than the generality of men ?*

what

what ſtyle more beautiful *.   Among thoſe who
have the ſenſe of hearing in the greateſt perfection, are there any ſuperior to the St. Lamberts,
the Saurins, the Nivernois, &c.   Of thoſe who
have the ſenſes of taſting and ſmelling in the greateſt perfection, are there any who have more genius
than Diderot, Rouſſeau, Marmontel, Duclos, &c. ?
In whatever manner we interrogate experience, it
will conſtantly anſwer, that the greater or leſs ſuperiority of mind is independent of the greater or
leſs perfection of the organs of the ſenſes, and that
all men equally well organiſed, are endowed by
nature with a fineneſs of the ſenſes ſufficient to
lead them to the greateſt diſcoveries in mathematics, chymiſtry, politics, phyſics, &c. †.

* It has not been remarked, that in the greateſt painters,
the ſenſe of ſeeing is much more acute than that of other
men.

† If a greater or leſs underſtanding depends on the greater
or leſs fineneſs of the ſenſes, it is probable that the different
temperatures of the air, the difference of latitudes and aliments,
muſt have ſome influence on minds, and conſequently that the
country moſt favoured by heaven ſhould produce the moſt ingenious inhabitants.   Now, how can we imagine, that from
the beginning of time to the preſent day, the inhabitants
of ſuch country muſt not have acquired a remarkable ſuperiority over other nations ?   That they muſt not have invented
the beſt laws, and conſequently have been the beſt governed ?
That they muſt not in the courſe of time have ſubdued the
other nations, and in ſhort, have produced, in every claſs, the
greateſt number of renowned men ?

    The generating climate of ſuch a people is hitherto unknown.
Hiſtory does not point out any one among the nations endowed with a conſtant ſuperiority of underſtanding above all others :

If the fublimity of the mind fuppofed fo great a perfection in the organs, before a man is engaged in difficult ftudies, before he entered, for example, in the career of letters or of politics, we fhould examine if he have the eye of an eagle, the feeling of the fenfitive plant, the nofe of the fox, and the ear of the mole.

Dogs and horfes, they fay, are efteemed more or lefs, according as they fpring from this or that race. Therefore, before employing a man, we fhould afk if he fprang from an ingenious or ftupid father. Now thefe queftions are never afked; Why? Becaufe the moft ingenious fathers frequently beget foolifh children; becaufe men the beft organifed, have frequently but little underftanding, and in fhort, becaufe experience proves the inutility of fuch queftions: all it teaches us, is, that there are men of genius of every make, and every temperament, that neither the fanguine,

it fhows, on the contrary, that from Deli to Peterfburg, all nations have been fucceffively ignorant and enlightened: that in the fame fituations every people, as M. Robertfon remarks, have the fame laws, and the fame fagacity, and that we find, for this reafon, the manner of the ancient Germans among the modern Americans.

The difference of latitude and nourifhment has therefore no influence on the minds of men, and perhaps it has lefs than is imagined on their bodies. In fact, the greateft part of politicians in calculating the population of cities and empires from the number of deaths, have from thence obferved, that, at leaft in the greateft part of Europe, the duration of life is nearly the fame.

the

the bilious, or phlegmatic, the great or little, the fat, the lean, the robuft, the tender, the melancholic (2.) or the moft ftrong and vigorous, are always the moft ingenious *.

But fuppofe a man to have extreme fenfibility, what follows ? That he will fometimes have fen-fations unknown to the common rank of men : that he will feel what a lefs delicacy of organifation will not permit another man to feel. But will he have more difcernment ? No : becaufe thofe fen-fations, always fruitlefs till the moment they are compared with each other, will conftantly preferve the fame relation to each other †. But, fuppofe the underftanding to be proportionate to the fine-nefs of the fenfes; and that there are truths which cannot be comprehended but by ten or twelve men of the firft organifation. In this cafe the human mind would not be capable of perfectibility.

* M. Roufſeau, p. 300 and 323 of his Emilius, fays, " The " more hearty and robuft a child grows the more judicious and " refpectable he becomes. To enjoy the inftruments of our in- " telligence, the body muft be beathful and robuft." A good conftitution of body renders the operations of the mind eafy and efficacious. But if M. Roufſeau confult experience, he will find, that the fickly, the delicate, and the deformed, have as much underftanding as the moft vigorous, and well made. Witnefs Pafcal, Pope, Boilleau, and Scarron.

† A fenfation of the memory is nothing but a fact the more, that may be replaced by another. Now a fact adds nothing to the aptitude men have to underftanding, becaufe that ap-titude is nothing elfe than the power of obferving the relations that diverfe objects have to each other.

I may

I may alfo add, that thefe men fo finely organifed, would neceffarily attain a degree of knowledge in the fciences, that would be incommunicable to the common rank of men. Now, fuch degree of knowledge has never been perceived.

There are no truths contained in the works of Locke and Newton, that are not now compre-henfible by all men of a common organifation, and that have not any extraordinary excellence of tafting, fmelling, feeing, hearing, and feeling.

I may alfo add, that as there is nothing fimilar in nature *, among thofe men who have the fineft organifation, each of them muft be, in fome re-fpects, fuperior to the reft. Every man, therefore, muft feel fenfations, and acquire ideas that are incommunicable to his fellows. Now there are no ideas of this kind : whoever has fuch as are clear, can eafily communicate them to others.

---

* Does the diffimilitude of beings exift in their principles, or in their developments ? I know not : Of this we are cer-tain, that the race of cattle become ftronger or weaker, improve or degenerate, according to the goodnefs and abundance of their pafture, and the fame we obferve in oaks : when we fee fome fhort, fome tall, fome ftrait, and others crooked ; in fhort, no two trees that are abfolutely fimilar, it is, perhaps, becaufe no two of them have received precifely the fame culture, or are placed in a fimilar fituation, are expofed to the fame wind, or planted in the fame foil. Now, among inanimate beings, the time of their development anfwers to that of the education of man, which is, perhaps, never the fame, becaufe, no two of them, as I have proved in the firft fection, can receive precifely the fame inftructions.

There

There are, therefore, no ideas that men, commonly well organifed, cannot attain.

The caufes that would operate moft efficacioufly on minds, would be, without doubt, the differences of latitudes and nourifhments. Now, as I have already faid, the grofs Englifhman who feeds on butter and flefh, and breathes a foggy air, has not certainly lefs underftanding than the lean Spaniard, who lives on garlic and onions, in a very dry air. M. Shaw, an Englifh phyfician, who from the fidelity and accuracy of his obfervations, as well as from the late date of his voyage into Barbary, deferves our confidence, fays, when fpeaking of the Moors, "The fmall progrefs this people "have made in the arts and fciences, is not the "effect of incapacity or natural ftupidity. The "Moors have an acute underftanding, and even "genius. If they do not apply themfelves to the "ftudy of the fciences, it is becaufe being with- "out motives to emulation, their government "does not leave them either liberty or leifure fuf- "ficient to cultivate and improve them. The "Moors, like the greateft part of the Orientals, "being born flaves, are naturally enemies to all "labour that does not directly promote their pre- "fent and perfonal intereft."

It is liberty alone that can kindle among a people the facred fire of glory and emulation. If there be periods when, like thofe rare birds brought into a country by a ftorm of wind, great men appear

appear on a fudden in an empire, this apparition is not to be regarded as the effect of a phyfical, but a moral caufe. In every government, where talents are rewarded, thofe rewards, like the teeth of the ferpent, planted by Cadmus, will produce men. If Defcartes, Corneille, &c. rendered the reign of Lewis XIII. illuftrious; Racine, Bayle, &c. that of Lewis XIV. Voltaire, Montefquieu, Fontenelle, &c. that of Lewis XV. it is, becaufe the arts and fciences were under thefe different reigns, fucceffively protected by Richelieu, Colbert, and the late duke of Orleans the regent. Great men, whatever has been faid, belong not to the reign of Auguftus or Lewis XIV. but to the reign that protects them.

If any imagine that it is to the firft fire of youth, to the frefhnefs of the organs, if I may fo fay, that we owe the fine compofitions of great men; they deceive themfelves. Racine was but thirty, when he produced his Alexander, and his Andromache; but he was fifty, when he wrote Athalia, and the latter piece is certainly not inferior to the former *. It is not, moreover, a flight

* At the end of a certain number of years, a man is, they fay, no longer the fame compofer. Voltaire at fixty was no longer the Voltaire of thirty. Be it fo: yet he was equally fagacious. If two men, without being exactly fimilar, can run as faft, leap as high, fhoot as true, and ftrike a ball as far, the one as the other, they may, without being precifely the fame, have an equal underftanding,

indif-

indifpofition, which may occafion a ftate of health more or lefs delicate, that can extinguifh genius.

We do not enjoy every year the fame health ; yet the lawyer gains or lofes every year nearly the fame number of caufes; the phyfician kills or cures nearly the fame number of patients ; and the man of genius, diftracted neither by bufinefs nor plea-fure, by violent paffions nor grievous maladies, produces every year nearly the fame number of compofitions.

Whatever difference there may be in the diet of nations, or the climate they inhabit ; in a word, whatever difference there may be in their tempe-rament *, it will not augment or diminifh the ap-titude that men have to underftanding.   It is not,

* The aptitude or difpofition for underftanding or difcern-ment, as I fhall fhow hereafter, is only an aptitude to difcern the refemblance or difference, the agreement or difagreement between different objects. That the diverfity of temperaments and climates may occafion a difference in the manners and in-clinations of a people; that the favage hunters in the woody countries, would be herdfmen in a grazing country, may very well be: but it is not lefs true, that in every country the inha-bitants conftantly perceive the fame relations between the fame objects. So, from the moment that thefe wandering natives unite into nations, when the marfhes are dried up, and forefts cut down, the diverfity of climates has had no fenfible influ-ence on their minds; and we, therefore, find in Sweden and Denmark, as accomplifhed geometricians, chymifts, natural philofophers, moralifts, &c. as in Greece or Italy. " The " climate of Perfia, fays Chardin, is the moft proper to pro-" mote the vigour both of body and mind." Their climate, however, gives the Perfians no more genius than the French.

there-

therefore, on the ftrength of the body *, or the juvenility of the organs, or the greater or lefs perfection of the fenfes, that depends the greater or lefs fuperiority of the underftanding. To conclude, that experience demonftrates the truth of this fact, is no great matter; I can alfo prove, that if this fact exifts, it is becaufe it cannot exift otherwife, and alfo, that it is a caufe hitherto unknown, that we muft look for the explication of the phenomenon of the inequality of underftandings.

To confirm the truth of this opinion, I think, that after having demonftrated that in men all is fenfation, we muft conclude, that if they differ among themfelves, it conftantly proceeds from the different degrees of their fenfations only.

* If the fuperiority of the mind be independent of the greater or lefs vigour of temperaments, and the greater or lefs finenefs of the fenfes, where fhall we fearch the caufe of this fuperiority ? In the perfection of the interior organifation they will fay : but, I anfwer, if in a clock its interior perfection be fhown by the precifion with which it marks the hour, in man the perfection of his interior organifation fhows itfelf, in like manner, (at leaft, fo far as regards the underftanding) by that of the five fenfes, to which it owes all its ideas. The perfection of the exterior organifation, fuppofes, therefore, that of the interior. But to prove that this laft fort of perfection can have no influence on the underftanding, it will fuffice to fhow, (in conformity to experience) that its fuperiority is intirely independent of the greater or lefs perfection of the five fenfes.

C H A P.   XIII.

On the different manner of receiving sensations.

MEN have different tastes : but this difference may be either the effect of habit
and education, or of the unequal sensibility of their
organisation.   That the Negro, for example,
feels more pleasure in beholding the sooty complexion of an African beauty, than in the roses
and lilies of an European, is in him the effect of
habit.   That men, according to the country they
inhabit, are more affected with this or that sort
of music *, and become in consequence susceptie-
ble of particular impressions, is also the effect of
habit.   All tastes that are factitious, and produced by the difference of education, are not here
the objects of my inquiry ; I here treat only of the

* *M. Rousseau in his Musical Dictionary, relates a remarkable
instance of this kind. There is, says he, among the Swiss a tune
they call Rans-des-Vaches, which was held so dear by them,
that it was forbid, under pain of death, to play it among the
Swiss troops : for it made those that heard it burst into tears,
desert, or die, by exciting in them an ardent desire again to see
their native country.   It is in vain to search in this tune for such
energetic accents as are capable of producing such wonderful effects. These effects are never produced on strangers, but proceed from habit, and by recalling to the minds of those who hear
this tune, their country, their youth, their former pleasure, and ancient manner of living, from whence arises a piercing grief on reflecting that all these are no more.*

different

different taftes produced by the mere different fenfations felt at the prefence of the fame object.

To know exactly what this difference is, we
muft have been fucceffively ourfelves and others.
Now as this can never be, it is only by confidering, with a very great attention, the diverfe impreffions that the fame objects appear to make on
different men, that we can attain fome difcovery
relative to this matter. If we examine this point
clofely we fhall find, that if one faw fquare what
another faw round ; that milk appeared white to
one and red to another ; that to fome men· a rofe
feemed a thiftle, and a well-proportioned man
appeared a monfter, it would be impoffible that
men fhould communicate their ideas, and underftand each other : but they do underftand each
other ; the fame objects therefore excite in them
nearly the fame impreffions.

To make this matter more clear, let us fee in
one and the fame inftance, in what men differ and
refemble each other.

They all refemble each other in one point ; and
that is, they would all free themfelves from difquietude : confequently they would all be employed, and the more lively that employment,
the more agreeable it is to them ; provided, however, the impreffion be not fo pungent as to excite pain.

Men differ in this, that the degree of emotion
which one regards as an excefs of pleafure, is

fometimes

sometimes in another the beginning of pain. The eye of my friend may be pained by a degree of light that gives me pleasure; and yet we both agree that light is the most pleasing object in nature. Now from whence proceeds this uniformity of judgment, with this difference of sensation? From the insignificance in the degree of difference, and because a tender sight finds the same pleasure in a small degree of light, that a strong sight does in the blaze of a mid-day sun. Let us pass from physics to morality, and we shall see still less difference in the manner men are affected by the same objects, and shall find, in consequence, among the Chinese * all our European proverbs: from whence I conclude, that the trivial differences in the organisation of different people, ought not to be regarded; for in comparing the same objects every nation forms the same conclusions.

The invention of the same arts wherever there are the same wants, and where the arts have been equally encouraged by government, is another proof of the essential equality of minds. To confirm this truth, I may also cite the resemblance observed in the laws and governments of different people. Asia, says M. Poivre, peopled in a great

---

* Except in what has an immediate and peculiar relation to the oriental customs and government, there are no proverbs more similar than those of the Germans and the Chinese.

part by the Malaccans, is governed by our ancient feudal laws. The inhabitants of Malacca,
like our anceſtors, are not agricultors, but have
like them a courage the moſt raſh and determined*.
Courage, therefore, is not, as ſome ſtill aſſert,
the effect of a particular organiſation in the Europeans. Men reſemble each other more than is
commonly imagined. Where they differ it is in
the degrees of their ſenſations. Poetry, for example, makes an agreeable impreſſion on almoſt
every one. Every one repeats with almoſt equal
enthuſiaſm, the hymn to light, that begins the
third book of Paradiſe Loſt ; but, they will ſay,
if this paſſage admired by all is equally pleaſing
to all, it is becauſe in painting the magnificent ef-

---

* If the Malaccans, ſays M. Poivre, had been nearer
neighbours to China, that empire would have been ſoon
conquered, and the form of its government changed. Nothing, ſays that author, equals the paſſions of the Malaccans
for theft and plunder : but are they the only nation of
thieves ? Whoever reads hiſtory, finds, that this love of rapine is unhappily common to all men, and is founded on
their idleneſs. They are better pleaſed, in general, to live
by plunder and incurſions, and by expoſing themſelves three
or four months in the year to the greateſt dangers, than be
ſubject to the daily labour of agriculture. But why then are
not all nations thieves ? Becauſe to plunder it is neceſſary to
be ſituate near nations that have ſomething to loſe, that is
ſuch as are agricultors and rich : if not, they have no choice
but to labour or ſtarve.

Every country has it Malaccans. In the Roman catholic
countries the clergy pillage, like them, the tenth of the harveſt : and what the Malaccans take by violence, the prieſts
get by cunning, and by a panic terror.

fects

fects of light, the poet makes ufe of a word, that
by not expreffing any particular degree of light,
leaves every one at liberty to colour the objects
with that tint of light which is moft agreeable to
his fight.   Be it fo : but if light did not make a
ftrong and lively impreffion on all, would it be
univerfally regarded as 'the moft admirable object
in nature? Does not that vortex of fire in which
almoft all nations have placed the throne of the
Divinity, prove the uniformity of impreffions received at the prefence of the fame objects *.
Without this uniformity (which fome philofophers, not very accurate, have taken from the
notion of the abfolute good and beautiful) on
what foundation could the rules of tafte have been
eftablifhed?

The fimple and magnificent pictures of nature
ftrike all men.   But do thofe pictures make precifely the fame impreffion on each of them? No:
we learn, however, from experience, that the impreffions are nearly fimilar ; fo that objects extremely pleafing to fome are always more or lefs
pleafing to others.   It is in vain to repeat here

* To prove the difference of fenfations produced by the
fight of the fame objects, they cite the inftance of painters,
who give a tinge of yellow or grey to all their figures ; but
if this defect in their colouring were an imperfection in the
organ of fight, and that all objects really appeared to them
tinged with yellow and grey, the white on their palet
would appear fo alfo, and they would paint white though they
faw grey.

that

that the uniformity of impreffions produced by the beautiful defcriptions of poetry, is merely apparent; that it is in part the effect of the uncertain fignifications of words, and of a latitude in the expreffions * that correfponds exactly to the various fenfations felt by the afpect of the fame objects. Admitting the fact, it is ftill true, that there are works generally efteemed, and confequently rules of tafte, the obfervation of which produces in all the fenfation of beauty. If this queftion be thoroughly examined, it will appear from the different manner in which men are affected by the fame objects, that the difference of impreffion arifes more from their moral than their corporeal properties.

The refult of this chapter is, that the diverfity of taftes in men, fuppofes a fmall difference only in the degrees of their fenfations : that the uniformity of their judgments, proved by the uniformity of the proverbs of different nations ; by the

* If I fhould be afked again why there are in every language fo many words of indeterminate fignification, I fhould add to what I have faid on this fubject in the 5th chapter of this fection, that want prefided at the formation of languages; and that in the invention of words, men in endeavouring to communicate their ideas in the moft facile manner, perceived, that if they made as many words as there are, for example, different degrees of magnitude, light, gravity, &c. their multiplicity would furcharge the memory : and that therefore it was neceffary to fuffer certain words to retain that vague fignification, which renders their application more general, and the ftudy of languages more concife:

refemresemblance of their laws and governments; by the taste that all have for poetry, and the simple and magnificent pictures of nature, demonstrate that the same objects make nearly the same impressions on all men ; and that if they differ, it is never but in the degrees of their sensations *.

C H A P. XIV.

That the small difference perceived between our sensations, has no influence on the understanding.

MEN at the presence of the same objects can doubtless feel different sensations ; but can they in consequence perceive different relations between these same objects ? No : and supposing, as I have elsewhere said, that snow should appear to some a degree whiter than to others, they would still all agree that snow is the whitest of all bodies.

* If nature, as has been supposed, gives men such unequal disposition to understanding or discernment, why in the arts of dancing, music, painting, do the disciples scarce ever equal their masters ‡, and why does not the unequal disposition in nature overbalance in the pupils the small superior degree of attention that the masters perhaps exercise in the study of their art.

‡ *This will scarce be allowed. Raphael was the disciple of Perugino, a name that would have been long since forgot, but for the transcendant accomplishments of the scholar. Many similar instances might be produced.*

In

•In order that men fhould perceive different relations between the fame objects, thofe objects
muft excite in them impreffions of a nature altogether peculiar : that wood on fire fhould
freeze fome, and that water condenfed by cold
fhould burn others ; that all the objects of nature
fhould offer to each individual a chain of relations
altogether different ; and in fhort, that men fhould
be with regard to each other what they are with
regard to thofe infects whofe eyes being con-
ftructed in a different manner, doubtlefs fee objects under very different forms.

On this fuppofition individuals would have no
analogy in their ideas and fentiments. Men could
neither communicate their, knowledge, nor improve their reafon, nor labour in common on the
immenfe edifice of arts and fciences. Now experience proves, that men make every day difcoveries, and improve the arts and fciences ; therefore they perceive the fame relations between objects.

The enjoyment of a fine woman may excite in
the foul of my friend an intoxication of delight
that it does not produce in mine ; but that enjoyment is in both him and me the moft poignant
of all pleafures. When two men receive a ftroke
of the fame force, they feel perhaps two diftinct
impreffions ; but if the violence of the blow be
doubled, tripled, quadrupled, the pain that each
of

of them feels will in like manner be doubled, tripled, quadrupled.

Suppose the difference of our sensations at the sight of the same object to be more considerable than it really is; it is evident, that the objects preserving the same relation to each other, would strike us with a constant and uniform proportion. But, they will say, cannot this difference in our sensations change our moral affections, and cannot this change produce the difference and inequality in minds? I answer, that all diversity of affection * caused by any difference in the bodily organisation, has not, as experience proves, any influence on the mind. We may therefore prefer either red or yellow, and still be, like Delambert and Clairaut, an equally great geometrician: our palates may be unequally delicate, and we may be equally good poets, painters, or philosophers. In short we may with a taste for sour or sweet, for milk or anchovies, be an equally great orator, physician, &c. All these tastes in us are nothing more than unconnected and sterile facts. It is the same with regard to our ideas, till the moment they are compared with each other. Now to give ourselves the trouble of comparing them, we must be excited by some interest. But when men have this interest, and compare these ideas,

* The only affections that have any sensible effect on the mind, are those that depend on education and prejudice.

why

why do they draw the fame conclufions? Becaufe, notwithftanding the difference of their affections, and the unequal perfection of their organs, they can all attain the fame ideas. In fact, while the fcale of proportions in which objects ftrike us, is not broken, our fenfations conftantly preferve the fame relation to each other. A rofe of a very deep colour, when compared with another rofe, ftill appears deep to every eye. We make the fame judgments of the fame objects. We can therefore always acquire the fame number of ideas, and confequently the fame extent of underftanding.

Men that are commonly well organized, are like certain fonorous bodies, that without being exactly the fame, ftill yield the fame number of founds *. It refults from what has been here

* Certain bodies yield the fame number of founds, but not thofe of the fame kind. It is the fame with the mind. It prefents ideas or images equally fair, but different, according to the various objects with which chance has filled the memories.

Does my memory reprefent nothing but fnow and ice, the tempefts of the north, and the flames of Vefuvius or Ecla? With thefe materials what picture can I compofe? That of the mountains that defend the entrance of the garden of Armida. But if my memory, on the contrary, prefents none but fmiling images, the flowers of fpring, the filver waves, the moffy ground, and fragrant orange groves, what fhall I compofe with thefe delightful objects? The bower to which love carried off Renaud. The fpecies therefore of our ideas, and our imaginations, does not depend on the nature of our mind, which is the fame in all men, but on the fort of ob-

objects

faid, that men always perceiving the fame relations between the fame objects, the unequal perfection of their fenfes has no influence on their underftanding. Let us make this truth more ftriking
by annexing a precife idea to the word Underftanding.

C H A P. XV.

Of the Underftanding or Judgment.

WHAT is the underftanding in itfelf?
An ability to difcern the refemblances
and differences, the agreements and difagreements
that different objects have to each other. But
what is in man the productive principle of his underftanding? His corporeal fenfibility, his memory, and efpecially the intereft he has to combine his fenfations with each other *. The un-

___

jects that chance has engraved on our memories, and the intereft we have to combine them.

* Suppofe that in each fcience and art, men had compared
with each other all objects and all facts hitherto known, and
that they had at laft arrived at the difcovery of all their feveral relations : men having then no new combinations to
form, what we call judgment would no longer exift. Then
all would be fcience, and the human judgment being obliged
to remain inactive, till the difcovery of new facts gave it opportunity of comparing and combining them with each other,
would be like an exhaufted mine that is fuffered to repofe till
new veins are formed.

derftanding

derftanding or judgment is therefore in him nothing more than the refult of the comparifon of his
fenfations ; and a good judgment or underftanding confift in the juftnefs of comparing them.

All men, it is true, do not feel precifely the
fame fenfations, but all perceive objects in a proportion conftantly the fame : all therefore have
an equal aptitude to underftanding or judgment*.

In fact, if, as experience proves, every man perceives the fame relations between the fame objects ; if all of them agree in the truths of geometry ; if, moreover, no difference in the degrees
of their fenfations change their manner of behold-

---

* It follows from this definition of the underftanding, that
if all its operations may be reduced to the obferving the refemblances and differences, the agreements and difagreements
that different objects have to each other, men are not, as has
been often repeated, born with this or that particular genius.

The acquifition of various talents is in men the effect of
the fame caufe ; that is to fay, the defire of glory, and the
attention with which this defire endows them. Now attention can be equally applied to all matters, to poetry, geometry, phyfics, painting, &c. as the hand of the organift can be
indifferently applied to each ftop of the organ. If it be
afked, why men have feldom different forts of genius? I anfwer, it is becaufe fcience is in each kind, the firft matter
of the judgment ; as ignorance is, if I may fo fay, the firft
matter of folly ; and that men have rarely two forts of learning. There are few who join, like Buffon and Delambert,
with the fcience of a Newton or an Euler, the difficult art
of a good writer. I fhall not therefore fay, with the old
proverb, man is born a poet, and becomes an orator ; but
I affert, on the contrary, fince all our ideas come by the
fenfes, that man is not born, but becomes what he is.

ing

ing objects ; if (to give a corporeal example) the
moment the sun rises out of the bosom of the sea,
all the inhabitants of the same coast, struck at the
same instant by the brilliancy of its rays, acknowledge it to be the most resplendent object in nature; it must be confessed, that all men form, or
may form, the same judgments on the same objects ; that they may acquire the same truths *,
and, in short, that if all have not in fact equal
judgment †, all have at least an equal capacity
for it, that is, an aptitude to acquire it ‡.——

* To acquire certain ideas, we must meditate. Is every
one capable of it ? Yes ; when animated by a powerful interest. That interest then endows him with a force of attention,
without which he may, as I have already said, be a learned
man, but never a man of judgment. It is meditation alone
that can reveal to us those first and general truths ; the keys
and principles of sciences. It is to the discovery of these truths,
that we always give the title of great philosopher ; because, in
every sort of science, it is always the universality of principles,
the extent of their application, in a word, the greatness of the
whole, that constitutes a philosophic genius.

† There are some, as I have before said, who attribute to
the physical cause of the difference of latitudes, the difference in
judgments. But to prove this fact, they must, after the definition here given of the judgment, be able to name a country,
where the inhabitants do not perceive either the difference, the
resemblance, the agreement, or disagreement of objects with
each other, and with themselves. Now, such country is hitherto
unknown.

‡ It is because discernment is rare, that it is taken for a particular gift of nature. An alchymist, or a juggler, were extraordinary men, in the ages of ignorance : they were, therefore,
taken for sorcerers, and supernatural beings. It was not,
however, from the great difficulty of surprising and duping foo
an

I shall not insist any longer on this question, but content myself with repeating, on this head, an observation I have already made in the Treatise on the Mind. Which is just.

If you present, I say, to several men a question that is simple and clear, and concerning the truth of which they are indifferent ; they will all form the same judgment *. Because, they all perceive the same relations, between the same objects. All are, therefore, born with a just judgment. Now, it is with the term Just Judgment, as with that of Enlightened Humanity. Does this sort of humanity

by illusion and dexterity. The astonishment in this matter, is, that men can make a serious occupation of such futile arts and illusions. Now, it is the same with the judgment ; if the aptitude to have it be common, nothing is so rare as a strong and constant desire to attain it. There are, they say, few men of genius : why ? because there are few governments that proportion the reward to the labour that the acquisition of great talents is supposed to require.

In comparing alchymists and jugglers to men of discernment, my intention is not to degrade the latter by a humiliating comparison : I mean only to show the cause that has for such a long time past, made discernment be regarded as a gift of nature. I would destroy the marvellous, and not the merit of sagacity : to it we owe the improvements in medicine, surgery, and in every art and science that is useful. Nothing therefore, on the earth is more respectable than a sound judgment ; and, in consequence, there is no nation rightly informed of its interest, that has not an esteem for judgment, in proportion to the utility of the art or science it improves.

* If men differ in opinion concerning the same question, that difference is always the effect, either of their not understanding each other, or of their not having the same object present to their eyes, or their remembrance, or, because being

indifferent

condemn an affaffin to punifhment? It is only occupied at that inftant, with the prefervation of an
infinity of honeft citizens. The idea of juftice,
and, confequently, of almoft all the virtues, is,
therefore, comprifed in the extended fignification
of the word Humanity. It is the fame with the
words Juft Judgment. This expreffion, taken in
its extended fignification, includes, in like manner,
all the different forts of judgments. Of this, at
leaft, we may be affured, that if all in us be fenfation and comparifon of our fenfations, there is
no other fort of judgment than that which compares, and compares juftly.

The general conclufion of what I have faid of
the equal aptitude, that men, commonly well organifed, have to judgment, is that being once
agreed,

That in men all is fenfation;

That they do not think, or acquire ideas, but
by the five fenfes;

That the greater or lefs perfection in the five
fenfes, in changing the degrees of their fenfations,

___

indifferent to the queftion itfeif, they employ but little attention in its inveftigation, and have but little regard to their
judgment.

Now, fuppofing them compelled to attention, by a powerful and common motive, and that they underftand each other,
and have, moreover, the fame object prefent to their eyes, or
their memories: I fay, that perceiving the fame relations between the objects, they will form the fame judgment: from
whence I conclude, that all have the fame capacity of judgment, that is, an equal aptitude to it.

does

does not change the relations objects have to each other.

It is evident, since the judgment consists in the knowledge of these same relations, that the greater or less superiority of the judgment is independent of the greater or less perfection in the organisation. For which reason, women, whose sense of feeling is more delicate than that of men, are not of superior intelligence. It is, I think, difficult to deny this conclusion.

But, they will say, if we regard the universal suffrage rendered to geometric propositions, as a demonstrative proof, that all men, commonly well organised, perceive the same relations between the same objects; why not in like manner regard the difference of opinion in matters of morality, politics, and metaphysics, as a proof, that at least in the latter sciences, men do not perceive the same relations between the same objects.

C H A P.   XVI.

The cause of the difference of opinions in morality,
politics, and metaphysics.

THE progression of the human judgment is
always the same.   The application of the
judgment, to this or that particular study, does
not change that progression.   If men perceive in
certain sciences, the same relations, between
the same objects they compare with each other,
they ought necessarily to perceive the same relations in all.   Observation however does not
agree with this reasoning.   But this contradiction is only apparent.   Its true cause is easy
to discover.   In inquiring after it, we see for example, that if all men agree in the truth of geometric demonstrations ; it is, because they are indifferent to the truth or falsity of those demonstrations ;

Or because they not only annex clear ideas,
but also the same ideas to the words employed in
that science.

Or, lastly, because they have the same conception of a circle, a square, a triangle, &c.

On the contrary, in morality, politics, and
metaphysics, if the opinions of men be very different,

It

It is, becaufe, in thefe matters, they have not always an intereft to fee objects as they really are.

Or, becaufe they have frequently only obfcure and confufed ideas, of the queftions on which they treat;

Or, that they more frequently follow the opinions of others, than their own ;

Or, laftly, that they do not annex the fame ideas to the fame terms. I fhall choofe, for example, thofe of *good*, *intereft*, and *virtue*.

Of the Term GOOD.

Let us take this term in its utmoft extent. To be fatisfied if men can form the fame idea of it, let us fee how the child acquires it.

To fix his attention on this word, fomething fweet * is given him. The word taken in this moft fimple fignification, is applied only to what pleafes the child's tafte, by exciting an agreeable fenfation on his palate.

When a more extenfive fenfe is given to the term, it is employed indifferently, to all that pleafes the child, that is to an animal, a man or his play-fellows. In general, fo long as the expreffion is confined to corporeal objects, as, for example, a ftuff, a tool, or provifion, men form nearly the fame idea of it; and the term recalls to the me-

* *Sweetmeats are called in French, bons bons, that is, good good.*

mory,

mory, at leaft in a confined manner, the idea of
what can be immediately good for them *.

When, in the laft place, this term is taken in a
ftill more extenfive fenfe, and applied to morality,
and the actions of men ; we find, that it then neceffarily includes the idea of fome public utility,
and to agree here about what is good, we muft
previoufly agree about what is ufeful.   Now, the
greateft part of mankind, do not even know that
the general utility is the meafure of the goodnefs
of human actions.

For want of a found education, men have nothing but confufed ideas of moral goodnefs. The
word Goodnefs, employed by them in an arbitrary
manner, recalls to their remembrance, only the
various applications they have heard made of it (3).
Applications always different and contradictory,
according to the diverfity of interefts and pofitions of thofe with whom they live.   To come
to a univerfal agreement in the fignification of the
word Good, when applied to morals, it would be
neceffary to have a very judicious dictionary to

* It is from the adjective *good,* that is formed the fubftan-
tive *goodnefs,* which is taken by fo many people for a real being, or, at leaft, for an inherent quality in certain objects.
Can men be ftill fo ignorant, as not to know that there is no
being in nature named Goodnefs : that it is nothing more than
a name given by man to what each one regards as good for
himfelf, and, in fhort, that the word Goodnefs, like that of
Greatnefs, is a vague expreffion, void of meaning, and that it
prefents no diftinct idea, till the moment we neceffarily, and
without perceiving it, apply it to fome particular object.

fix

fix the precife fenfe of it. Till fuch a work be digefted, all difputes on this fubject will be undeterminable. It is the fame with the word Intereft.

INTEREST.

Among mankind few are honeft; the word In-tereft, muft in confequence excite in moft of them the idea of a pecuniary intereft, or of fome object equally mean and contemptible. Has a noble and elevated foul the fame idea? No: this term recalls to his mind nothing but the fentiment of felf-love. Virtue perceives nothing in intereft, but the powerful and general fpring, that fource of action in all men, which carries them fometimes to vice, and fometimes to virtue. But did the jefuits annex to this word, an idea equally exten-five, when they oppofed my opinion? I know not: but this I know, that being then bankers, merchants, and bankrupts, they ought to have loft fight of every idea of a noble intereft; that this word could not excite in them any other idea, but that of intrigue and pecuniary intereft.

Now fo vile an intereft compelled them to perfue a perfecuted man. Perhaps they in fecret adopt his opinions. As a proof of which they gave at Rouen, in 1750, an entertainment, whofe defign was to fhow, "that pleafure forms youth " to true virtue." The firft act difplayed the civil virtues; the fecond, the warlike virtues; and

the

the third, the virtues proper to religion. In this entertainment they proved this truth by dances. Religion there perfonified, danced with Pleaſure, for her partner ; and to render Pleaſure more endearing, ſaid the Janſeniſt, the jeſuits have put her on breeches *. Now, if pleaſure, according to them, can operate all things on man, what cannot intereſt do with him! Is not all intereſt reducible in us to the ſearch of pleaſure † ?

* We muſt do juſtice to the jeſuits : this accuſation is falſe. They are rarely libertines. The jeſuit, held in by his rules, and indifferent to pleaſures, is totally devoted to ambition. His deſire is to ſubdue the rich and powerful of the earth, either by force or fraud. Born to command, the great men of the earth are in his eyes but puppets, whom he moves at his pleaſure, by the ſtrings of direction and confeſſion. He conceals his interior contempt of them by an outward reſpect. The great are contented with this, and are, without perceiving it, reduced to mere machines. What the jeſuits cannot obtain by ſeduction, they accompliſh by force. Look into the annals of hiſtory, and there you will ſee theſe ſame jeſuits light up the torch of ſedition in China, in Japan, in Ethiopia, and in every country where they have preached the goſpel of peace. In England, we find, that they charged the mine which was to have blown up the parliament: that in Holland they aſſaſſinated the prince of Orange, and in France, Henry IV. that at Geneva they gave the ſignal for ſtorming the city: that their hands are frequently armed with daggers, and but rarely employed in ſelecting pleaſures, and, in a word, that their faults are not thoſe of weakneſs, but of villainy.

† Why did the jeſuits then riſe up with ſuch fury againſt me ? Why do they go into all the great houſes, exclaiming againſt the Treatiſe on the Mind, and forbid any one to read it, repeating inceſſantly, like the father Cañaye to marſhal Hocquincourt, No Mind, Gentlemen, no Mind? It is becauſe, being ſolely zealous of command, the jeſuits always deſire to blind the people? In fact, were men rightly informed of the principle

Pleasures and pains are the moving powers of the universe. God has declared them to be so to the earth, by creating heaven for the virtuous, and hell for the wicked. The Catholic church itself has agreed to this opinion, when, in the dispute between Mess. Bossuet and Fenelon, it decided, that we do not love God (4) for himself, that is, independent of those rewards and punishments, of which he is the disposer. They have, therefore, been always convinced, that man, actuated by the sentiment of self-love, constantly obeys the law of his interest *.

ciple that holds them silent, did they knew that constantly directed in their conduct by an interest, either mean or noble, they always obey that interest : that it is to their laws, and not to their opinions, they owe their genius and their virtue : that with the forms of government of Rome and Sparta, Romans and Spartans might still be produced ; and, in short, by a sagacious distribution of rewards and punishments, of glory and infamy, the interest of particulars may be always united with that of the public, and the people compelled to be virtuous. What method could then be taken to hide from the people the inutility, and even the danger of a sacerdotal power? Could they be long ignorant that the object, really important to the happiness of a nation, is not the creation of priests, but sagacious laws and judicious magistrates. The more clearly the jesuits have seen this principle, the more they have feared for their authority, and the more solicitous they have been to obscure the evidence of such a principle.

* Does the commander desire to advance himself? He wishes for a war. But what in a war are the objects of the subaltern officer? An augmentation of 30l. or 40l. per annum, to his pay, the desire of laying empires waste, and of the death of those friends with whom he lives in intimacy, but who are superior in rank.

N 4

What

What do the diverfity of opinions of this fubject prove? Nothing: except that men do not
underftand each other. They underftand each
other very little better when they talk about
virtue.

VIRTUE.

This word frequently excites in the mind very
different ideas, according to our ftate and fituation,
the fociety with which we live, and the age or
the country in which we were born. If a younger brother, according to the cuftom of Nor-
mandy, fhould avail himfelf, like Jacob, of the
hunger or thirft of the elder, to diveft him of his
right of primogeniture, he would be declared a
cheat by all the tribunals. If a man, by the
example of David, fhould caufe the hufband of
his miftrefs to be facrificed, he would be reckoned, not among the number of the virtuous, but
of villains. It would be to little purpofe, to fay
he made a good end; affaffins fometimes do the
fame, but are never propofed as models of virtue.

Till precife ideas are fixed to this word, we
may always fay of virtue, as the Pirronians faid
of the truth, " it is like the Eaft, different, ac-
" cording to the fituation from whence we re-
" gard it."

In the firft ages of the church, the Chriftians
were in dread of other fects; they were afraid of
not being tolerated; what did they then preach?
Indulgence

Indulgence and love of our neighbour. The word Virtue, then recalled to their minds the idea of humanity and gentleneſs. The conduct of their maſter confirmed them in this idea. Jeſus was gentle with the Eſſenes, the Jews, and the Pagans; he bore no hatred to the Romans. He pardoned the Jews their injuries, and Pilate his injuſtice : he recommended charity to all. Is it ſo at this day ? No : the hatred of our neighbours, and barbarity under the name of zeal and policy, are in France, Spain, and Portugal, now compriſed in the idea of virtue.

The church in its infancy, whatever a man's religion might be, honoured his probity, and was little concerned about his belief. " He that is virtuous, is a Chriſtian, ſaid St. Juſtin, though he be otherwiſe an Atheiſt." *Et quicumque ſecundum rationem et verbum vixere Chriſtiani ſunt, quamvis athei.*

Jeſus, in his parables, preferred * the incredulous Samaritan to the devout Phariſee. St. Paul was ſcarce more difficult than Jeſus, and St. Juſtin. Cornelius is cited as a religious man, becauſe he was honeſt (5). Ch. x. ver. 2. of the

---

* Jeſus declares himſelf every where an enemy to the prieſts. He reproaches them every where with avarice and cruelty. Jeſus was puniſhed for his veracity. O Catholic prieſts, have you ſhowed yourſelves leſs barbarous than the prieſts of the Jews, and can the ſincere adorer of Jeſus have leſs hatred for you ?

Acts

Acts of the Apostles, though he was not yet a
Christian. It is said in like manner of one named
Lydia. Ch. xvi. ver. 14. of the same Acts, that
she served God; though she had not then heard
St. Paul, and was not converted.

In the days of Jesus, ambition and vanity were
not reckoned among the virtues. The kingdom
of God was not of this world. Jesus desired neither riches, nor titles, nor authority in Judea. He
commanded his disciples to forsake their goods,
and follow him. What ideas have they now of
virtue? There is no Catholic Prelate that does
not cabal for titles and honours. No religious
order that has not intrigues at court, that does not
carry on commerce, and grow rich by its bank.
Jesus and his apostles had no such ideas of
honesty.

In the time of the latter, persecution did not
bear the name of charity. The apostles did not
instigate Tiberius to imprison the Gentiles or unbelievers. He who in that age would have compelled others to embrace his opinions, would have
reigned by terror, erected a tribunal of inquisition,
burned his brethren, and seized on their property,
would have been held infamous. The sentences
dictated by sacerdotal pride, avarice, and cruelty,
would have been read with horror. In these
days, pride, avarice, and cruelty, in the countries
of inquisition, are placed in the rank of virtues.

Jesus hated falshood. He would not, therefore,

fore, like the church, have obliged Galileo, with a torch in his hand, to have retracted before the altar of the God of truth, thofe he had difco- vered. The church is no longer an enemy to falfhood : pious frauds are canonifed by it (6).

Jefus, the fon of God, was humble (7), and his haughty vicar pretends to command over fo- vereigns, to legitimate vice at his pleafure, and render affaffins meritorious. He has beatified Clement. His virtue, therefore, is not that of Jefus.

Friendfhip, honoured as a virtue among the Scythians, is not regarded as fuch in a mo- naftery. Their rules even render it criminal (8). The old man fick and languifhing in his cell, is deferted by friendfhip and humanity. If monks were enjoined a mutual hatred, they could not more faithfully obferve it than in a cloifter.

Jefus ordained that they fhould render to Cæfar what was Cæfar's ; he forbid to feize, by force or fraud, the property of another. But the word Virtue, which then implied juftice, had no longer that fignification, in the time of St. Bernard, when he ordained, at the head of the Croifades, that nations fhould forfake Europe to ravage Afia, to dethrone the Sultans, and break in pieces crowns, over which thofe nations had no fort of right.

When, to enrich his order, that Saint promifed a hundred acres in heaven, to thofe who would give ten upon earth : when, by that ridiculous and fraudulent promife, he obtained the lawful

patrimony

patrimony of a great number of heirs ; the idea
of theft and injuſtice, muſt have been then included in the notion of virtue (9).

What other idea could the Spaniards form of
virtue, when the church permitted them to attack
Montezuma, and the Incas, to deſpoil them of their
riches, and ſeat themſelves on the thrones of
Mexico and Peru ? The monks, then maſters of
Spain, could have forced them to reſtore the
Mexicans and Peruvians (10) their gold, their liberty, their country, and their prince : they might at
leaſt have loudly condemned the conduct of the
Spaniards.   What did the theologians ? remain
ſilent.   Have they at other times ſhown more
juſtice ? No : father Hennepin, the recollect, reports inceſſantly, that the only way to convert the
ſavages is to reduce them to ſlavery *.   Could
a method ſo unjuſt and barbarous have been imagined by the recollect Hennepin, if the theologians of the preſent day had the ſame idea of virtue as Jeſus ? St. Paul ſays expreſly, that per-
ſuaſion is the only method to be uſed in convert-
ing of the Gentiles.   Who has recourſe to violence to prove the truths of geometry ? Who
does not know that virtue recommends itſelf ?
In what caſe, therefore, ought priſons, tortures, and
butcheries to be uſed ? When they preach crimes,
errors, and abſurdities.

* See Deſcription of the Manners of the Savages of Louiſa-
na, page 105.

It

It was with sword in hand, that Mahomet proved the truth of his dogmas. A religion, said then the Christians, that permits man to force the belief of man, is a false religion. They condemned Mahomet in their discourses, and justified him by their conduct. What they called vice in him, they call virtue in themselves. Could they believe that the Muffulman, fo fevere in his principles, was more gentle in his manners than the Catholics. Must the Turk be tolerant toward the Christian (11), the infidel, the Jew, and gentile, and the monk; whose religion makes a duty of humanity, burn in Spain his brethren, and in France throw into prisons the Janfenist and the Deist?

Could the Christian commit so many abominations, if he had the same idea of virtue, as the son of God; and if the priest, obedient to the advice of his ambition only, were not deaf to that of the gospel? If to the word Virtue there had been annexed a clear, precise, and invariable idea (12), men could not have always had such different and extravagant ideas concerning it.

CHAP.

C H A P. XVII.

The word Virtue, excites in the Catholic clergy, no other idea than that of their own advantage.

IF almoſt all religious bodies, ſaid the illuſtrious and unfortunate attorney-general of the parliament of Brittany, are by their inſtitution animated with an intereſt, contrary to that of the public welfare, how can they form ſound ideas of virtue ? Among the prelates, there are few Fenelons (13), few that have his virtues, his humanity, and his diſintereſted ſpirit. Among the monks, they may count, perhaps, a great many ſaints, but few honeſt men. Every religious body is greedy of riches and power : no bounds are ſet to their ambition *. A hundred ridiculous bulls,

---

* The humble clergy declare themſelves to be the firſt body in the ſtate: however, (as is obſerved by a man of much diſcernment) there are but three bodies abſolutely eſſential to the adminiſtration : the firſt, is the body of magiſtrates, who are to defend my property againſt the uſurpation of my neighbour. The ſecond, is the body of the army, charged in like manner to defend my property againſt the invaſion of foreigners. The third, is the body of the citizens, who appointed to receive the revenues, furniſh a maintenance for the two others. Now, to what purpoſe ſerves the order of the clery, more expenſive to the ſtate, than the three others together ? To maintain the morals of the people. But there are morals in Penſylvania, and no clergy.

iſſued

iffued by the popes, in favour of the jefuits, prove
this fact.   But if the jefuits are ambitious, is the
church lefs fo ?   Let any one open its hiftory :
that is, the hiftory of the errors and difputes of
the fathers, the enterprizes of the clergy, and the
crimes of the popes : he will every where find the
fpiritual power, an enemy to the temporal *,
forget that its kingdom is not of this world, and
endeavours continually, by frefh efforts, to poffefs
itfelf of the riches and power of the earth, and not
only to take from Cæfar that which is Cæfar's,
but would attack him with impunity.   If it were

---

* The church by declaring itfelf the fole judge of what is,
and what is not fin, has thought under that title to be
able to affume the fupreme jurifdiction.   In fact, if no one has
a right to punifh a good action, and recompenfe one that is bad ;
the judge of their goodnefs or badnefs is the fole lawful judge
of a nation : princes and magiftrates are nothing more than the
executioners of the fentences of others ; their function is reduced to that of the hangman's.   The project was great ; it
was covered with the veil of religion : it did not at firft alarm
the magiftracy.   The church was, in appearance, fubject to
their authority, and waited to deprive them of it, when it
fhould be acknowledged the fole judge of the merit of human
actions, that acknowledgment would univerfally legitimate its
pretenfions.   What power could fovereigns have oppofed to
that of the church ?   No other than the force of arms.   The
people, then flaves to two powers, whofe will and laws would
have been frequently contradictory, muft have waited till force
had decided between them, which fhould be obeyed.
    This project, I confefs, has not been fully executed.   But
it is conftantly true, notwithftanding the infignificant diftinction
of temporal and fpiritual, that in every Catholic State there
are really two kingdoms, and two abfolute mafters over every
inhabitant.

poffible,

possible, that the superstitious Catholics could preserve any idea of just and unjust, they would be shocked, on reading such a history, and hold the sacerdotal power in horror.

Does a prince promise, in such a year, to suppress such a tax? Does the year pass over, and he boldly break his word? Why does not the church reproach him publicly, with the violation of his promise? Because, indifferent to the public welfare, to justice, and humanity, it is solely employed in promoting its own interest. If the prince be a tyrant, it absolves him. But if he be what they call a heretic, it anathematises, deposes, assassinates him. What, however, is this crime of heresy: the word, when pronounced by judicious and dispassionate men, signifies nothing more than a *particular opinion*. It is not from such a church that we must expect clear ideas of equity. The clergy will never give the title of virtuous, but to such actions as tend to the increase of its power and revenues. To what cause, but that of the interest of the priesthood, can we attribute the contradictory decisions of the Sorbonne *? Without this interest would they have maintained at one time, and tolerated at all times, the regicide doctrine of the jesuits? Would they have concealed its odious nature?

---

* It would be a striking collection, that of the contradictory condemnations made by the Sorbonne, before and since Descartes, against almost every work of genius.——

Would

Would they have waited for the magiftrate to point it out?

But in receiving that doctrine, they have fhown more folly than villany. That they are dolts, I agree: but can we fuppofe them to be honeft, when we confider the fury with which they attack philofophical writings, and the filence they obferve on thofe of the jefuits? By approving in their affembly, the morality of thofe religious *, either the doctors of the Sorbonne judge them to be found (14), without examining them, (and, in that cafe, what opinion can we have of fuch ftupid judges?) or, they judge them found, after having examined them, and acknowledge them for fuch, (and, in that cafe, what opinion can we have of fuch ignorant judges?) or, laftly, thefe doctors, after having examined them, and found them bad, approve them through fear (15), intereft, or ambition, (and, in this laft cafe, what opinion can we have of fuch knavifh judges?)

In a journal, entitled "Chriftianity, or, Religion avenged," if the theologian Gauchat, a hired declaimer againft the moft efteemed philofophers and writers of Europe, is always filent about what regards the jefuits, it is, becaufe he expects protection and preferment from them.

---

* There are among thefe doctors men of learning and probity: but they rarely make part of their affemblies; which are, as M. Voltaire obferves, commonly compofed of the dregs of the college.

That intereft conftantly dictates the judgments of the theologians, is well known.   The
Sorbonnifts have therefore no longer any pretenfions
to the title of moralifts ; they are even ignorant of
its principles. The infcription on fome dials, *Quod
ignoro, doceo, I teach what I don't know,* fhould
be the motto of the Sorbonne.   Would they
otherwife take for their guides to heaven, and to
virtue, the fautors of jefuitical morality ? Let
thefe doctors ftill exalt the excellence of the theological virtues.   Thofe virtues are local ; true
virtue is reputed fuch in all ages, and all countries (16).   The name of virtue fhould be given
to fuch actions only, as are ufeful to the public,
and conformable to the general intereft.   Has
theology conftantly kept the people from the
knowledge of this fort of virtue ? and has it always obfcured in them the ideas of it ? It is the
effect of the intereft of theology ; and it is in conformity to this intereft, that the prieft has every
where folicited the exclufive privilege of public
inftruction. The French comedians built a theatre
at Seville ; the chapter and vicar made them de-
molifh it : Here, faid one of the canons, our company will fuffer no actors, but their own.

O man ! cried an ancient fage, who can ever
fay how far thy folly and ftupidity will carry
thee ? The theologian knows, laughs at it, and
profits by it.———

It

It was ever the increase of their wealth and power that the theologians pursued under the name of religion *. We cannot be astonished therefore that their maxims change with their situation, that they have not now the same ideas of virtue they formerly had, and that the morality of Jesus is not that of his ministers. It is not the Catholics only, but every sect and every people, that, for want of determinate ideas of probity, have had very different notions concerning it, according to the diversity of ages and countries (17).

CHAP. XVIII.

Of the different ideas that different nations form of virtue.

IN the East, and especially in Persia, celibacy is a crime. Nothing, say the Persians, is more opposite to the design of nature, and of the Creator, than celibacy †. Love is a corporeal want, a necessary secretion. Should any one by a vow of continence oppose the vow of nature?

---

* Why does every monk, who defends with a ridiculous zeal the false miracles of his founder, laugh at the attested existence of spectres? Because he has no interest to believe them. Take away interest, and there remains nothing but reason, and reason is not credulous.

† In Persia a lad no sooner attains the age of puberty than they give him a concubine.

God,

God, who gave us organs, does nothing in vain :
its his pleafure that we fhould ufe them.

Solon, the fagacious legiflator of Athens,
made little account of this monkifh chaftity (18).
If in his laws, fays Plutarch, he exprefly forbids
flaves to perfume themfelves, and the love of
young people, it is, adds the hiftorian, that even
in the Greek amours Solon did not fee any thing
difhoneft. But thofe haughty republicans, who
purfued without fhame all forts of amours, would
not debafe themfelves by the vile profeffion of a
fpy or informer : they did not betray the intereft
of their country, nor violate the property or liberty of their fellow-citizens. A Greek or a Roman would not, without confufion, have received
the fetters of flavery. The true Roman could
not bear, without horror, even the fight of an Afiatic tyrant.

In the time of Cato the Cenfor, Eumenes came
to Rome. At his arrival all the young people
crowded round him : Cato alone fhunned him (19).
Why Cato, they faid, do you fly a fovereign fo
courted, fo good a king, fuch a friend to the Romans ? Let him be as good as you pleafe, replied
Cato, *Every defpotic prince is a devourer of human
flefh* (20), *that all virtuous men fhould avoid.*

It is in vain to attempt the enumeration of all
the different ideas that different nations (21) and
private perfons (22) have had of virtue. We
can only fay, that a catholic who has more veneration

ration for the founder of an order of drones, than for a Minos, a Mercury, a Lycurgus, &c. has certainly no juſt idea of virtue. Now till precife ideas be annexed to this word, every man muſt, according to the education chance has given him, form thoſe that are different.

A young girl is brought up by a ſtupid and bigoted mother. This girl can underſtand by the word Virtue nothing but the exactitude with which the nuns faſt, and recite their prayers. The word therefore excites no ideas in her but thoſe of diſcipline, hair-cloth, and pater-noſters.

Another daughter is brought up, on the contrary, by judicious and patriotic parents, who never give her any examples as virtuous but ſuch as are uſeful to our country ; nor ever extol any character but ſuch as Arria, Porcia, &c. this girl will neceſſarily have ideas of virtue very different from the former. The one will admire in Arria the force of virtue, and the example of conjugal love ; the other will regard the ſame Arria as a Pagan, a woman of the world, a ſuicide, and devoted to damnation ; one who ought to be ſhunned and deteſted.

Make the ſame experiment on two young men as on the two daughters : let one of them be an aſſiduous reader of the lives of ſaints, and a witneſs, ſo to ſay, of the torments the demon of the fleſh makes them ſuffer ; ſee them continually flogging themſelves, rolling among thorns, feed-

O 3

ing

ing on women of fnow, &c. He will have very different ideas of virtue from him who, devoting himfelf to more noble and inftructive ftudies, takes for his models fuch men as Socrates, Scipio, Ariftides, Timoleon ; and that I may come home to the age in which I live, Miron, Harley, Pibrac, and Barillon (23), " thofe refpectable magi-" ftrates, thofe illuftrious victims of a love for " their country, who by their wife and juft max-" ims, diffipated, fays cardinal de Retz, more fac-" tions than all the gold of Spain and England " could kindle." It is therefore impoffible that the word Virtue fhould not excite in us different ideas (24), according as we read Plutarch, or the Golden Legend. Thus, fays Mr. Hume, they have, in every age and every country, erected altars to men of characters totally different.

Among the Pagans it was to Hercules, Caftor, Ceres, Bacchus, and Romulus, that they rendered divine honours ; but among the Muffulmans, as among the Catholics, it is to an obfcure dervis, or a vile monk, in a word to a Dominic or an Antony, they decree the fame honors.

It was after having deftroyed monfters and punifhed tyrants ; it was by their courage, their talents, their beneficence, and humanity, that the ancient heroes opened the gates of Olympus. But at this day it is by fafting, caftigation, and poltroonery, by a blind fubmiffion and a vile obedience, that the monk opens the gate of Heaven.

This

This revolution in human minds, no doubt, ſtruck Machiavel, ſo that he ſays in his fourth Diſcourſe, " Every religion that makes a duty of " ſufferings and humility, that inſpires a people with " a mere paſſive courage ; enervates their minds, " debaſes their ſpirit, and prepares them for ſla- " very." The effect would doubtleſs have nearly followed the prediction, if, as Mr. Hume obſerves, the cuſtoms and laws of ſociety had not modified the character and genius of religions.

We have ſeen in theſe two chapters, what indeterminate ideas are annexed to the words *good*, *intereſt*, and *virtue*. I have ſhown that theſe words, conſtantly employed in an arbitrary manner, excite, and ought to excite, different ideas according to the ſociety with which we live, and the application we propoſe to make of them. Whoever would diſcuſs a queſtion of this kind, ſhould therefore firſt ſettle the ſignification of the words. Without this preliminary, every diſpute of this nature will be indeterminable. Thus men on almoſt all queſtions in morality, politics, and metaphyſics, underſtand each other the leſs, the more they reaſon about them.

The words once defined, a queſtion is reſolved almoſt as ſoon as propoſed ; which proves, that all minds are juſt, and all perceive the ſame relations between the ſame objects ; a proof that in morality, politics, and metaphyſics (25),

O 4 the

the diverfity of opinions is the mere effect of the uncertain fignification of words, of the abufe that is made of them, and perhaps of the imperfection of languages. But what remedy is there for this evil?

C H A P. XIX.

There is but one method of fixing the uncertain fignification of words; and but one nation that can make ufe of it.

TO determine the uncertain fignification of words, a dictionary fhould be compofed, in which determinate ideas muft be annexed to different expreffions (26). This difficult work can be performed only among a free people. England is perhaps the only country in Europe from which the univerfe can expect and obtain this benefaction. But is ignorance there without a protector? There is no nation where fome individuals have not an intereft in mixing the darknefs of falfhood with the light of the truth. The defire of the blind is that blindnefs fhould be univerfal; the defire of knaves, that ftupidity fhould be extended, and dupes be multiplied. In England, as in Portugal, there are men great and unjuft; but what can they do at London againft a writer? There is no Englifhman who, behind the rampart of his laws, cannot brave the power of the great, and laugh at their ignorance, fuperftition, and

ftu=

ftupidity *. The Englifhman is born free; let him therefore profit by that liberty to enlighten the world; let him contemplate in the homage that is at this day rendered to the men of genius among the Greeks, what pofterity will render to him; and let the profpect animate his endeavours.

This age, they fay, is the age of philofophy: all the nations of Europe have produced men of genius in this fcience; all now feem occupied in the fearch after truth. But in what country can it be publifhed with impunity? There is but one; which is England.

Englifhman †, make ufe of thy liberty; of that gift which diftinguifhes the man from the vile flave and domeftic animal, to difpenfe light to the nations of the earth! Such a benefaction will infure you their eternal acknowledgment. What applaufe can be refufed to people virtuous enough to permit their writers to fix in a dictionary the precife fignification of each word, and by that mean to diffipate the myfterious obfcurity that ftill envelopes morality, politics, metaphy-

* *The liberty of the Englifh appears to foreigners, as moft things do at a diftance, greater than it really is. But a few years fince a man named Annett was confined feveral months in a common geal with felons, and fuffered the infamous punifhment of the pillory, for publifhing fome thing that was difagreeable to my lords the bifhops.*

† Every government, fay the Englifh, that forbids to think and to write on the objects of adminiftration, is without difpute, a government of which no good can be faid.

fics,

fics, theology, &c. (27). It is referved for the authors of fuch a dictionary to terminate fo many difputes, eternifed by the abufe of words (28); they alone can reduce the fcience of men to what they really know.

This dictionary, tranflated into all languages, would be the general collection of almoft all the ideas of mankind. Let precife ideas be annexed to each expreffion, and the fchool divine, who by the magic of words, has often thrown the world into confufion, will be a magician without power. The talifman, in the poffeffion of which his ability confifted, will be broken. Then all thofe fools, who under the name of metaphyficians, have for fo long a time wandered in the land of chimeras, and who, on bladders blown up by wind, traverfe, in every direction, all the depths of infinity, will no longer fay they fee what they fee not, and know what they know not; they will no longer impofe on mankind. Then the propofitions in morality, politics, and metaphyfics, becoming as fufceptible of demonftration as the propofitions of geometry, men will all have the fame ideas of thofe fciences, becaufe all of them, (as I have fhewn), will neceffarily perceive the fame relations between the fame objects.

A new proof of this truth is, that in combining nearly the fame facts, either in the material world as is demonftrated by geometry, or in the intellectual world, as is proved by metaphyfics, all men have,

have, in all times, come to nearly the fame conclufion,

C H A P. XX.

The excurfions of men, and their difcoveries in the in-
tellectual kingdoms, have been always nearly the
fame.

AMONG the imaginary countries that the
human mind runs over, that of the fairies,
the genii, and enchanters, is the firft where I fhall
ftop. Mankind love fables : every one reads
them, hears them, and makes them. A confufed
defire of happinefs attends us with pleafure through
the land of prodigies and chimeras.

With regard to chimeras, they are always of the
fame kind. All men defire riches without number, power without bounds, and pleafure without
end ; and this defire always flies before the poffeffion.

How happy fhould we be, fay the greateft part
of mankind, if our wifhes were fulfilled as foon as
formed ? O thoughtlefs man! can you be always
ignorant, that a part of your felicity confifts in the
defire itfelf ? It is with happinefs, as with the
golden bird fent by the fairies to a young princefs :
the bird fettles at thirty paces from her ; fhe goes
to catch it, advances foftly, is ready to feize it ;
the bird flies thirty paces further ; fhe paffes feveral

months

months in the purfuit, and is happy. If the bird had fuffered itfelf to be taken at firft, the princefs would have put it in a cage, and in one week would have been tired of it. This is the bird of happinefs, that the mifer and the coquette inceffantly purfue. They catch it not, and are happy in their purfuit, becaufe they are fecure from difguft. If our defires were to be every inftant gratified, the mind would languifh in inaction, and fink under difquietude. Man muft have defires ; a defire new and eafy to be gratified muft conftantly fucceed to a defire fulfilled (29). Few men acknowledge they have this want ; it is however to a fucceffion of their defires they owe their felicity.

Continually impatient to gratify their wifhes, men built inceffantly caftles in Spain ; they would intereft all nature in their happinefs ; but not being able to effect it, they addreffed themfelves to imaginary beings, to fairies and genii. If they fuppofe the exiftence of thofe beings, it is from a confufed hope that by the favour of an enchanter they may become, as in the Thoufand and One Nights, poffeffed of the marvellous lamp, and nothing will then be wanting to their felicity.

It is therefore a defire of happinefs that produces a greedy curiofity, and the love of the marvellous, that amongft divers people has created fupernatural beings, which under the names of fairies, genii, fylphs, enchanters, &c. have always been the fame beings, and by whom prodigies
nearly

nearly the fame have been every where performed ; which proves that in this kind the difcoveries have been nearly fimilar.

PHILOSOPHICAL TALES.

The tales of this fort, more grave and important, though fometimes equally frivolous and lefs entertaining than the foregoing, have preferved among themfelves the fame refemblance. In the number of thefe tales, that are at once fo ingenious and difgufting, I place the beauty of morality *, the natural goodnefs of men, and the feveral fyftems of the material world ; of which experience alone ought to be the architect : if the philofopher confults it not, or has not the courage to ftop where obfervation fails, when he thinks to make a fyftem he makes nothing but a romance.

This philofopher, for the want of experiments, is forced to fubftitute hypothefes, and to fill up with conjectures the immenfe interval, that the prefent, and what is ftill more, paft ignorance, have left in all parts of his fyftem. With regard to hypothefes, they are almoft all of the fame kind. Whoever reads ancient philofophers, will fee that they almoft all adopt nearly the fame

* The beauty of morality is only to be found in the paradife of fools, where Milton makes agni, fcapularies, chaplets, and indulgences, inceffantly whirl about.

plan,

plan, and that where they differ, it is in the choice of the materials employed in the conftruction of the univerfe.

Thales faw but one element in all nature, which was the aqueous fluid. Proteus, the marine god, who metamorphofed himfelf into fire, a tree, water, and an animal, was the emblem of his fyftem. Heraclitus difcovered the fame Proteus in the element of light : the earth appeared to him to be a globe of fire reduced to a ftate of fixity. Anaximines made of the air an indefinite agent ; it was the common parent of all the elements. The air condenfed, formed water ; ftill more denfe, formed earth. It was to the different degrees of the air's denfity that all beings owed their exiftence. They who after the firft philofophers affumed like them the office of architects of the palace of the univerfe, and laboured at its conftruction, fell into the fame errors : Defcartes is a proof.

It is by proceeding from fact to fact that we attain to great difcoveries. We muft advance in the train of experience, and never go before it. The impatience natural to the human mind, and efpecially to men of genius, cannot accommodate itfelf to a progrefs fo flow (30), but always fo fure ; they would guefs at what experience alone can reveal. They forget that it is on the knowledge of a firft fact, from which all thofe of nature may be deduced, that the difcovery of the fyftem of the world depends ; and that it is only by
chance,

chance, analyfis, and obfervation that the firft fact can lead to the general principle *.

Before men undertake to conftruct the palace of the univerfe, what materials fhould they draw from the mines of experience? It is at length time that all fhould labour in the ftructure of this fabric ; and happy will they be to conftruct fome detached parts of the projected edifice : the moft affiduous difciples of experiments are fenfible that without it they wander in the land of chimeras, where men in all ages have feen nearly the fame phantoms, and have always embraced thofe errors, whofe refemblance proves at once the uniform manner in which men of all countries combine the fame objects, and the equal aptitude they have to difcernment.

RELIGIOUS TALES.

Thefe fort of tales, lefs amufing than the firft, lefs ingenious than the fecond, and yet more refpected, have armed nations againft each other, have made rivers of human blood to flow, and have filled the world with defolation. Under the title of Religious Tales, I comprehend in general all the falfe religions ; thefe have always preferved among themfelves the ftrongeft refemblance.

* Our author talks here as if he were ignorant of the Newtonian fyftem of the univerfe, founded on clear undeniable experiments. But can that be poffible?

Among

Among the many various caufes to which we
may afcribe the invention of thefe tales (31), I
cite the defire of immortality for the firft. The
proof, if we believe Warburton and fome other
learned men, that God was the author of the Jewifh law, is, fay they, that in the law of Mofes there
is no mention of rewards or punifhments, or the
life to come, nor confequently of the immortality
of the foul. Now, they add, if the religion of the
Jews had been of human inftitution, men would
have made the foul immortal ; a lively and powerful intereft would have induced them to believe it
fuch (32): this intereft is their horror for death and
annihilation. This horror would have been fufficient, without the aid of revelation, to have made
them invent that dogma. Man would be immortal in his prefent ftate, and would believe himfelf
fo, if all the bodies that furround him did not
every inftant prove the contrary. Forced to yield
to this truth, he has ftill the fame defire of immortality. Efon's cauldron of rejuvinefcence
proves the antiquity of this defire. To make it
perpetual, it was neceffary to found it on fome
probability at leaft ; to effect this, they made the
foul of a matter extremely fubtle ; they fuppofed it
an indeftructible atom, that furvived the diffolution of all the other parts, in a word, a principle of life *.

* *The opinions of men, uninfluenced by revelation, concerning a
future ftate, will ever be different, according to their different circumftances.*

This being, under the name of foul *, was to preferve after death all the affections of which it was fufceptible during its union with the body. This fyftem fuppofed men doubted the lefs of the immortality of the foul, as neither experience nor obfervation could contradict fuch belief, for neither of them can form any judgment of an imperceptible atom. Its exiftence indeed was not demonftrated ; but what proof do we want of what we wifh to believe, and what demonftration is ftrong enough to prove the falfity of a favourite opinion ? It is true we never meet with any fouls in our walks, and it is to fhew the reafon of this, that men, after having created fouls, thought them-felves obliged to create a country for their habita-tion. Each nation, and even each individual, ac-cording to his inclinations, and the particular nature of his wants, has formed a particular

cumftances. *The good man will readily believe it, for it is his in-tereft there fhould be a future ftate. The bad man will ftrive hard to difbelieve it, for he will think it his intereft there fhould not be a future ftate ; but after many unfuccefsful ftruggles his mind muft remain in doubt and confufion ; for it is impoffible he fhould ever be certain there is no future exiftence.*

As a frequent reflection on a futurity, attended with a firm belief of it, makes one of the moft valuable enjoyments of the prefent life, ought not a man to rank thofe who would deprive him of that enjoyment, among the moft pernicious of his enemies?

* The favages do not refufe a foul to any thing ; their guns, their caldrons, or the materials of their buildings. See P. Hennepin, Voyage de la Louifiane, p. 94.

plan *. Sometimes the savage nations placed this habitation in a vast forest, full of wild fowl, and watered with rivers stocked with fish : sometimes they placed it in an open level country, abounding in pasture ; in the middle of which rose a bed of strawberries as large as a mountain, different parts of which they portioned off, for the nourishment of themselves and their families.

People less exposed to hunger, and beside more numerous and better instructed, placed on this spot all that is delightful in nature, and gave it the name of Elysium. Covetous mortals formed it after the plan of the garden of Hesperides, and stocked it with trees, whose golden branches were loaded with fruits of diamonds. The more voluptuous nations placed in it trees of sugar and rivers of milk, and furnished it with delicious animals. Each people in this manner furnished the country of souls with what was on earth the object of their desires. Imagination, directed by different wants and inclinations, operated every where in the same manner, and consequently made but little variation in the invention of false religions.

If we believe the president de Brosse, in his excellent history of Fetichism, or the worship ren-

---

* *The cursory reader will do well to remember, that all here said about a future state, relates merely to the different conjectures of different nations, and has nothing to do with what we are taught by revelation ; but is brought to shew, that in works of imagination the human mind operates nearly in the same manner in all ages and all nations.*

                                                                     dered

dered to terreſtrial objects, it was not only the firſt
of religions, but its worſhip preſerved to the preſent day in almoſt all Africa, and eſpecially in Ni-
gritia, was formerly the univerſal religion *. It is
known, he adds, that in the Pierres Bœtites, it
was Venus Urania they worſhipped. That in the
foreſt of Dodona the Greeks adored the oaks. It
is alſo known that dogs, cats, crocodiles, ſerpents,
elephants, lions, eagles, flies, monkies, &c. have
had altars erected to them as gods, not only in
Egypt but in Syria, Phœnicia, and almoſt all
Aſia. We know alſo that lakes, trees, the ſea,
and the unformed rocks have in like manner been
the objects of adoration of nations of Europe and
America. Now ſuch an uniformity in the firſt religions, proves one ſtill greater in the minds of
men, as we ſtill find the ſame uniformity in religions more modern or leſs groſs. Such was the
Celtic religion : the Mitras of the Perſes we find in
the god Thor ; Ariman in the Wolf ; Feuris, the
Apollo of the Greeks, in Baldar ; Venus in Freia ;
and the Deſtinies in the three ſiſters Urda, Veran-
di and Skulda : theſe three ſiſters are ſeated by
the ſource of a fountain, whoſe waters lave the
roots of a famous aſh named Yaraſel ; its branches

---

* If by catholic is to be underſtood univerſal, papiſm
does wrong to pretend to the title. The religion of Feti-
chiſm, and that of the Pagans are thoſe only that have been
truly catholic.

P 2 ſhadow

fhadow the earth, and its fummit, that reached
above the clouds, formed its canopy.

The falfe religions have therefore been almoft
every where the fame. From whence arifes this
uniformity? From men's being animated by nearly
the fame intereft, having nearly the fame objects to
compare together, and the fame inftrument, that
is, the fame judgment to combine them; they
have therefore neceffarily formed the fame conclufions: it is, becaufe, in general, all are proud;
that, without any particular revelation, and confequently without proof, all regard man as the only
favourite of heaven, and the principal object of its
cares. May we not, after a certain monk, fometimes repeat, " What is a capuchin compared to
" a planet ?"

Muft we, to found the haughty pretenfions of
man on facts, fuppofe, as in certain religions, that
the Divinity, forfaking heaven for earth, formerly
came down to converfe with mortals in the form
of a fifh, a ferpent, or a man? Muft we, to prove
the intereft heaven takes in the inhabitants of
the earth, publifh books, in which, according to
fome impoftures, are included all the precepts and
duties that God requires of man?

Such a book, if we believe the Muffulmans,
compofed in heaven, was brought down to the
earth by the angel Gabriel, and given by that angel to Mahomet. It is called the Koran. When
we open this book, we find it capable of a thoufand
inter-

interpretations : it is obfcure and unintelligible ; yet fuch is human blindnefs, that they ftill regard as divine, a work in which God is painted under the form of a tyrant ; where this fame God is inceffantly employed in punifhing his flaves for not comprehending what is incomprehenfible ; in fhort, where this God, the author of phrafes that are unintelligible without the commentary of an Iman, is properly nothing more than a ftupid legiflator, whofe laws have conftantly need of interpretation. How long will the Muffulmans preferve fo much veneration for a work fo filled with abfurdities and blafphemies ?

To conclude; if the metaphyfics of falfe religions, if the excurfions of human minds in the countries of fouls, and the difcoveries in the intellectual regions, have been every where the fame, let us further fee if the impoftures (33) of the facerdotal bodies for fupporting thefe falfe religions, have not in all countries preferved amongft themfelves the fame refemblances.

P 3

CHAP.

C H A P. XXI.

The impoſtures of the miniſters of falſe religions.

IN every country, the ſame motives of intereſt, and the ſame facts have combined to furniſh ſacerdotal bodies with the ſame means to impoſe on the people; and in every country the prieſts have made uſe of them *.   A private perſon may be moderate in his deſires, and content with what he poſſeſſes; a body is always ambitious: it conſtantly endeavours, with greater or leſs rapidity, to increaſe its power and wealth.   The deſire of the clergy has been in all times to be powerful and opulent †.   By what method can it ſatisfy this deſire ?   By the vending of hope and fear.   The prieſts, wholeſale dealers in theſe commodities, were ſenſible that the ſale would be certain and lucrative; and that if hope ſupported the hawker who ſold in the ſtreets the chance of a great prize, and the quack who ſold on a ſcaffold the chance of a cure,

---

* In the Indies the prieſts annex certain virtues, and indulgences to extinguiſhed fire brands, and ſell them very dear.   At Rome father Peepe, a jeſuit, ſold in like manner little prayers to the Virgin : he made hens ſwallow them, affirming, that they would make them lay their eggs better.

† *What makes all doctrines plain and clear ?*
  About two hundred pounds a year :
  And that which was prov'd true before
  Proved falſe again ?—Two hundred more.
                          HUDIBRAS.

it

it would in like manner maintain the bonze, and talopouin, who fold in their temples the fear of hell and the hope of heaven: and if the quack made a fortune by vending one of thefe commodities only, that is hope, the prieft muft make a greater by felling both hope and fear. Man, faid they, is timid; there will confequently be moft got by the fale of the laft article. But to whom fhall we fell it? To the finners. And to whom fell hope? To the penitents. Convinced of this truth, the priefthood confidered that a great number of buyers fuppofed a great number of finners; and that as the prefents of the fick enriched the phyfician, offerings and expiations of finners would inrich the prieft; and therefore as fick people were neceffary to one, finners were to the other. The finner would be conftantly a flave to the prieft; and by the multiplication of fins, which would promote the fale of indulgences, maffes, &c. the power and riches of the clergy would increafe. But if among the fins the priefts counted thofe actions only that were really preju-dical to fociety, the facerdotal power would be of little confequence; it would only extend to cheats and villains: now the clergy would have it extend to honeft men alfo. To effect which, it was ne-ceffary to create fuch crimes as honeft men might commit. The prieft therefore ordained that the leaft liberties between the two fexes, that the mere defire of pleafure, fhould be a fin. They moreover

infti-

inftituted a great number of fuperftitious ceremonies, and ordered every individual to obey them;
declaring the inobfervation of thofe ceremonies to
be the greateft of all crimes, and that the violation
of the ritual law fhould be, as among the Jews, if
poffible, more feverely punifhed than the moft abominable villainy.

These rites and ceremonies, more or lefs numerous among different nations, were every where
nearly the fame : they were every where held facred, and fecured to the priefthood the greateft authority over the feveral orders of the ftate (34).

There were however among the priefts of different
nations fome, who, more dextrous than others, exacted from the people not only the obfervance of
certain ceremonies, but the belief of certain dogmas alfo. The number of thefe dogmas increafed
infenfibly, and with them increafed infidels and
heretics *. What did the clergy then ? They ordained that herefy fhould be punifhed with a confifcation of property ; and this law augmented the
riches of the church : they decreed moreover,
that infidelity fhould be punifhed with death ; and
this law augmented their power. From the moment the priefts condemned Socrates, genius, virtue, and even kings themfelves trembled before the
facerdotal power; its throne was fupported by
confternation and panic terror ; that fpreading
over the minds of the people the darknefs of igno-

* We fay in Europe, God is in heaven : to fay fo in Bul-
garia is herefy and impiety.

rance, became the unfhaken props of pontifical power. When man is forced to extinguifh the light of reafon within him, and has no knowledge of juft or unjuft, it is then he confults the prieft, and implicitly follows his counfels.

But why does not man rather have recourfe to the natural law ? The falfe religions themfelves are founded on that common bafis. That I allow : but natural religion is nothing more than reafon itfelf (35). Now how can a man believe in his reafon when he is forbid the ufe of it ? Befide, who can perceive the natural law through that myfterious cloud with which the facerdotal power furrounds it ? This law, they fay, is the canvafs of all religions. Be it fo ; but the priefts have embroidered fo many myfteries on this canvafs, that the embroidery entirely covers the ground. Whoever reads hiftory will find that the virtue of the people diminifhes in proportion as their fuperftition increafes *. By what means can a fuperftitious man be inftructed in his duty ? How in the night of error and ignorance can he perceive the path of juftice? In a country where all learning is confined to the priefthood, clear and juft ideas of virtue can never be formed.

---

* Superftition is ftill the religion of the wifeft people. The Englifh neither confefs nor pray to faints ; their devotion confifts in not working or finging on a Sunday. A man who fhould play on a fiddle on that day would be reckoned impious : but he is a good Chriftian if he pafs the day in a public houfe with wenches,

The

The interest of the priests is not that a man act virtuously, but that he do not think. *It is neces-sary,* say they, *that the son of man know little, and believe a great deal* *.

I have thus shewn the uniform means by which the priests acquire their power ; let us now see if the means by which they preserve it are not also uniform.

C H. A P.   XXII.

Of the uniformity in the means by which the ministers of false religions preserve their authority.

IN every religion the first object the priests pro-pose is to stifle the curiosity of mankind, and to prevent the examination of every dogma whose absurdity is too palpable to be concealed.

To attain this end the human passions must be flattered : to perpetuate the blindness of men, they must be made to believe it is their interest, and consequently desire it. Nothing is more easy to a bonze. The practice of virtue is more troublesome than the observance of ceremonies. It is less difficult to kneel before an altar, to offer a sacrifice, to bathe in the Ganges (36), and eat fish on Fridays, than to pardon, like Camillus, the ingratitude of our fellow-citizens ; to spurn

---

* The priests will not allow that God renders to every one according to his works, but according to his faith.

at

at riches like Papirius ; or to inftruct mankind like Socrates : let us therefore flatter, fays the bonze, the human vices, that thofe vices may be our protectors ; let us fubftitute in the place of virtue, offerings and expiations, that we may, by certain fuperftitious ceremonies, cleanfe the foul foul from the blackeft crimes. Such a doctrine could not fail to increafe the riches and authority of the bonzes. They faw all the importance of this doctrine ; they made it public, and the people received it with joy : for the priefts were conftantly more loofe in their morals, and more indulgent to crimes, in proportion as they were more fevere in their difcipline, and more rigid in punifhing the violation of ceremonies *.

Every temple then became an afylum for villains ; incredulity alone found there no refuge. Now as there are in all countries but few unbelievers, and many villains, the intereft of the greateft number was to agree with the priefts.

Between the tropics, fays a navigator, there are two iflands oppofite each other: in the one, no man is reckoned honeft who does not believe in a certain number of abfurdities, and unlefs he be able to indure the greateft itching without fcratching : it is to the patience with which they fupport their

---

* If the catholics be in general without morals, it is becaufe for the practice of real virtues, the priefts of the papiftical religion have conftantly fubftituted that of fuperftitious ceremonies.

prurience

prurience that virtue is principally aſcribed. In the other iſle, no belief is impoſed on the inhabitants, and they may ſcratch where they itch, or even tickle themſelves till they laugh ; but no one is reckoned virtuous who does not perform actions uſeful to ſociety. Muſt not the people diſcern the abſurdity of this religious morality ? I anſwer, a prieſt, wrapt up in a ſolemn veſtment, affecting an auſtere manner, and obſcure language, and ſpeaking only in the name of God and religion, deludes the people by the eyes and the ears ; and though the words Morality and Virtue are in his mouth void of meaning, it imports little : thoſe words, pronounced in a mortified tone, and by a man in the habit of penitence, always impoſe on human imbecillity.

Such were the tricks, and if I may ſo ſay, the ſplendid mummery, under which the prieſts concealed their ambition and perſonal intereſt. Their doctrine was moreover ſevere in certain reſpects, and that ſeverity ſerved ſtill more to deceive the vulgar. It was the box of Pandora that glittered without, but within were fanaticiſm, ignorance, ſuperſtition, and all thoſe evils that have ſucceſſively ravaged the earth. Now I aſk, when we ſee the miniſters of falſe religions in all ages employ the ſame means to increaſe their wealth and power *,

---

* If the prieſts make themſelves every where the depoſitaries and the diſtributors of charities, it is that they may appropriate a part of them, and by the diſtribution of the reſt keep the poor in their pay. Every method of acquiring money
and

to preferve their authority, and multiply the number of their flaves ; when we find in every country the fame abfurdities in falfe religions, the
fame impoftors in their minifters, and the fame
credulity in the people (37), if it be poffible to
imagine that there is effentially between men that
inequality of underftanding fome fuppofe ?

But fuppofing underftanding and talents to
be the effects of a particular caufe, how can we
perfuade ourfelves that men of great abilities, and
confequently endowed with that particular organifation, could have believed the fables of Pagan-
ifm, have adopted the opinions of the vulgar, and
fometimes become martyrs to the moft palpable
errors ? Such facts, which are inexplicable if we
fuppofe the underftanding to be the product of
organifation, become fimple and clear when it is
regarded as an acquifition. We do not then
wonder that men of genius, in certain matters,
fhould have no fuperiority in thofe fciences or
queftions they have never ftudied. On this fuppofition, all the advantage a man of difcernment
can have over others, (and a confiderable advantage it certainly is), refults from a habit of atten-

and authority appears lawful to the priefthood. It is without
blufhing that the catholic clergy charge the reparation of the
churches on thofe very people whofe wealth they have exhaufted. Tne churches are the farms of the clergy ; but, contrary
to opulent landlords, they find the means of making others
fupport them.

tion,

tion, and a knowledge of the best methods to be taken in the examination of a question; an advantage that is useless when not employed in the search of that particular truth.

The uniformity of frauds (38) employed by the ministers of the false religions, the resemblance of the phantoms seen by them in the intellectual regions (39), and the equal credulity of the people, prove therefore that nature has not given to men that unequal portion of judgment which has been supposed; and that in morality, politics, and metaphysics, if they form very different judgments of the same objects, it arises from their prejudices, and the indeterminate significations that are annexed to the same expressions.

I shall only add, that if judgment be reduced to the science or knowledge of the true relations objects have to each other, and that if whatever be the organisation of individuals, that organisation, as is demonstrated by geometry, makes no change in the constant proportions with which objects strike them, it necessarily follows, that the greater or less perfection of the organs of the senses, can have no influence over our ideas, and that all men organised in the common manner will consequently have an equal aptitude to judgment or understanding. The only method remaining to render this truth more evident, if that be possible, is to fortify the proofs by augmenting them. Let us endeavour this by another series of propositions.

CHAP.

C H A P. XXIII.

There is no truth not reducible to a fact.

ALMOST all philofophers agree, that the moft fublime truths once fimplified and reduced to their plaineft terms, may be converted into facts, and in that cafe prefent nothing more to the mind than this propofition, *white is white, and black is black* (40). The aparent obfcurity of certain truths is not therefore in the truths themfelves, but in the confufed manner of reprefenting them, and the impropriety of the words ufed in exprefling them. Can they be reduced to fimple facts? If every fact can be equally well perceived by every man organifed (41) in the common manner, there is no truth they cannot comprehend. Now if all men can conceive the fame truths, they muft have effentially all the fame aptitude to underftanding.

But is it quite certain that every truth may be reduced to thofe clear propofitions abovementioned? I fhall add only one proof to what the philofophers have already given: I deduce it from the perfectibility of the human mind or underftanding; experience demonftrates that the underftanding is capable of it. Now what does this perfectability fuppofe? Two things:

The

The one, that every truth is essentially comprehensible by every mind.

The other, that every truth may be clearly represented.

The capacity that all men have to learn a trade proves this. If the most sublime discoveries of the ancient mathematicians are at this day comprised in the elements of geometry, and are understood by every student in that science, it is because those discoveries are reduced to facts.

Truths being once brought to this point of simplicity, if there be some among them that men of ordinary capacity cannot comprehend, it is then, they may say, that borne up by experience, like the eagle, who alone among the feathered race can soar above the clouds and gaze upon the sun, the man of genius alone can raise himself to the intellectual regions, and there sustain the resplendency of a new truth. Now nothing is more contrary to experience. Does a man of genius discover a truth, and represent it clearly? At the same instant all men of ordinary capacity seize it, and make it their own. The genius is an adventrous chief, that pierces through the regions of discoveries : he lays open the road, and men of common capacity rush in crouds after him. They have therefore the force necessary to follow him, otherwise genius would there penetrate alone.

Now

Now to the prefent day its only privilege is to make the firft track *.

But if there be a period when the higheft truths are attainable by common minds, when is that period? When freed from the obfcurity of words, and reduced to propofitions more or lefs fimple, they pafs from the empire of genius to that of the fciences. Till then, like thofe fouls that they fay wander in the celeftial abodes, waiting till they can animate a body, and appear before the light, the truths yet unknown wander in the regions of difcoveries, waiting for fome genius to feize them, and tranfport them to this terreftrial dwelling. Once defcended on the earth, and perceived by fuperior minds, they be-come a common property.

If in this age, fays M. Voltaire, men commonly write better in profe than in the laft age, to what do the moderns owe this advantage? To the models they have before them. The moderns could not boaft of this fuperiority, if the genius of the laft age, already converted into fcience (42), was not, if I may fo fay, entered into the circulation. When the difcoveries of genius are metamorphofed into fciences, each difcovery depofited in their temple becomes a public property; the temple is open to all. Whoever defires to learn, learns, and is

* It feems to follow from this paragraph, that every man who will, may underftand all the truths in the fublime geometry and the depths of fluxions, provided they be properly explained.

fure

fure to make nearly fo many feet of fcience per
day. The time fixed for apprenticefhip is a proof
of this. If the greateft part of arts, at the degree
of perfection to which they are now carried, may
be regarded as the produce of the difcoveries of a
hundred men of genius placed end to end ; to exercife thofe arts it is neceffary therefore that the
workman unite them in himfelf, and know how
properly to apply the ideas of thofe hundred men
of genius : what can be a ftronger proof of the perfectability of the human mind, and of its aptitude to comprehend every fort of truth ?

If from the arts I pafs to the fciences, it will
be equally apparent that the truths, whofe difcoveries formerly deified their inventor, are now
quite common. The fyftem of Newton is taught
every where.

It is with the author of a new truth as with an
aftronomer, whom curiofity or the defire of glory
calls up to his obfervatory. He points his glafs
to the heavens, and in the immenfity of fpace beholds a new ftar or fatellite. He calls his friends ;
they go up, and looking through the telefcope,
behold the fame ftar : for with organs nearly the
fame, men muft difcover the fame objects.

If there were ideas that ordinary men could not
attain, there would be truths difcovered in the
procefs of ages, that could not be comprehended
but by two or three men equally organifed. The
reft of the human race would be fubject in this refpect

to

to an invincible ignorance. The difcovery of the fquare of the hypothenufe being equal to the fquare of the other two fides of a triangle, could not be known but to another Pythagoras : the human mind could not be fufceptible of perfectibility ; in a word, there would be truths referved to certain men only. Experience, on the contrary, fhews us that the moft fublime difcoveries, clearly reprefented, are conceivable by all. From hence arifes that aftonifhment and fhame we perceive when we fay, *there is nothing more plain than that truth ; how was it poffible I did not perceive it before ?* This is doubtlefs fometimes the language of envy, as in the cafe of Chriftopher Columbus. When he departed for America, the courtiers faid, *nothing is more ridiculous than fuch an enterprize :* and at his return, *nothing was more eafy than fuch a difcovery.* Though this be frequently the language of envy, is it never that of the heart? Is it not with the utmoft fincerity, when fuddenly ftruck by the evidence of a new idea, and prefently accuftomed to regard it as trivial, that we think we always knew it.

If we have a clear idea of the expreffion of a truth, and not only have it in our memory, but have alfo habitually prefent to our remembrance all the ideas of the comparifon from which it refults, and if we be not blinded by any intereft or fuperftition, that truth being prefently reduced to plaineft terms, that is, to this fimple propofition, *that*

Q 2

white

white is white, and black is black, is conceived almoft as foon as propofed.

In fact, if the fyftems of Locke and Newton,
without being yet carried to the laft degree of per-
fpicuity, are neverthelefs generally taught and underftood, men of a common organifation can
therefore comprehend the ideas of thofe of the
greateft genius.   Now to conceive their ideas (43),
is to have the fame aptitude to underftanding.
But if men can attain thofe truths, and if their
knowledge in general be conftantly in proportion
to the defire they have to learn, does it follow that
all can equally attain to truths hitheto unknown ?
This objection deferves to be confidered.

C H A P. XXIV.

*The underftanding neceffary to comprehend the truths
     already known, is fufficient to difcover thofe that
     are unknown.*

A Truth is always the refult of juft compari-
fons made of the refemblances or differences, the agreements or difagreements between
different objects.   When a mafter would explain
to his fcholars the principles of a fcience, and demonftrate the truths already known, he places
before their eyes the objects of the comparifon
from which thofe truths are to be deduced.

But

But when a new truth is to be fought after, the inventor muft in like manner have before his eyes the objects of comparifon from which that truth is to be deduced: But what fhall prefent them to him? Chance; the common mother of all inventions. It appears therefore, that the mind of man, whether it follow the demonftration of a truth, or whether it difcover it, has in both cafes the fame objects to compare, and the fame relations to obferve; in fhort, the fame operations to perform*. The underftanding neceffary to comprehend truths already known, is therefore fufficient to difcover thofe that are unknown. Few men indeed attain the latter; but this is the effect of (1) the different fituations in which they are placed, and that feries of circumftances to which is given the name of chance; or (2) to the defire, more or lefs cogent, that men have to diftinguifh themfelves, and confequently to their greater or lefs paffion for glory.

The paffions can do all things. There is no girl fo ftupid that love will not make witty.

---

* I might even add, that it requires more attention to follow the demonftration of a truth already known, than to difcover one. Suppofe, for example, it be a mathematical propofition; the inventor in this cafe is already acquainted with geometry: he has its figures habitually prefent to his memory; he recollects them, fo to fay, involuntarily; and his attention is folely employed in obferving their relations. With regard to the fcholar, thofe fame figures not being habitually prefent to his memory, his attention is neceffarily divided between the trouble of recollecting the figures, and of obferving their relations.

What

What means does it not furnifh her with, to deceive the vigilance of her parents, to fee and converfe with her lover? The moft ftupid frequently become the moft inventive.

A man without paffions is incapable of that degree of attention to which a fuperior judgment is annexed : a fuperiority that is perhaps lefs the effect of an extraordinary effort than an habitual attention.

But if all men have an equal aptitude to underftanding, what can produce that difference we find between them?

N O T E S.

N O T E S.

1. (page .) IF men, and especially the Europeans, say the Banians, always in fear and mistrust of each other, are ever ready to war together; it is because they are still animated with the spirit of their first parents, *Cutteri* and *Toddicastrée*. This *Cutteri*, who was the second son of *Pourons*, and destined by God to people one of the four quarters of the earth, turned his steps toward the west. The first object he met was a woman named *Toddicastrée*. She was armed with a *chuchery*, and he with a sword. As soon as they perceived each other, they attacked and fought together for two days and a half: the third day, tired with the combat, they parlied, they loved, married, and lay together: they had children, that, like their progenitors, are always ready to attack when they met together.

2. (p. 156.) That the most witty and the most thoughtful are sometimes melancholy, I allow; but they are not witty and thoughtful because they are melancholy, but melancholy because they are thoughtful. In fact, it is not to his melancholy but to his wants that a man owes his discernment: want alone draws him from his natural indolence. If I think, it is not because I am strong or weak, but because I have more or less interest to think. When they say of misfortune that it is the *great teacher of man*, they say nothing more than that misfortune, and the desire to be freed from it, obliges us to think. Why does the desire of glory frequently produce the same effect? Because glory is to some a want. Moreover, neither Rabelais, nor Fontenelle, nor Fontaine, nor Scarron were esteemed melancholic, yet nobody denies their superiority of wit, greater or less.

3. (p. 180.) What I here say of goodness may be equally applied to beauty. The different ideas we form of it arises, almost always, from the explications we have heard made of the word in our infancy. When we have heard a woman of a particular figure constantly extolled, that figure is fixed in our mind as a model of beauty; and we always judge of other women according to the greater or less

resem-

resemblance they have to that model. From hence the diversity of our tastes, and the reason why we prefer a woman of an elegant shape, to one that is gross, and who is preferred by another.

4. (p. 183.) This decision of the church shows the ridicule of a judgment that has been passed on me. How, they have said, can I maintain that friendship is founded on want and a reciprocal interest? But if the church, and the Jesuits themselves agree, that God, though all good and powerful, is not beloved for himself; it is not then without some private reason that I love my friend. Now of what nature can this reason be? It is not of the sort that produces hatred; that is a sentiment of trouble and grief; on the contrary, it is of the nature of those that produce love, that is, a sentiment of pleasure. The judgments that have passed on me relative to this matter are so absurd, that it is not without shame I here reply to them.

5. (p. 185.) The primitive church did not cavil with mankind about their belief: Synesius is a proof of this. He lived in the fifth century; and was a Platonic philosopher. Theophilus, then bishop of Alexandria, desirous of doing himself honour by a conversion, entreated Synesius to be baptized by him. The philosopher consented, on condition that he should preserve his opinions. A short time after, the inhabitants of Ptolomais asked Synesius for their bishop. Synesius refused the episcopacy, and his reasons for it he gives in his hundred and fifth letter to his brother. " The more I ex-
" amine myself, he says, the less I find that I am proper to be
" a bishop. I have hitherto divided my life between the
" study of philosophy and amusement. When I go out of
" my closet, I give myself up to pleasure. Now it is not
" right, they say; that a bishop be joyous: he is a divine
" man. I am beside incapable of all application to civil and
" domestic affairs. I have a wife that I love, and it is equal-
" ly impossible for me, either to quit her, or only see her in
" secret. This Theophilus knows; but this is not all. The
" mind cannot quit the truths that have been demonstrated
" to it. Now the dogmas of philosophy are contrary to those
" a bishop ought to teach. How can I preach the creation of
" the soul after the body, the end of the world, the resur-
                                                    " rection,

" rection, and in fhort things that I do not believe ? I cannot
" bring myfelf to falfify.

" A philofopher, they fay, can accommodate himfelf to the
" weaknefs of the vulgar, and conceal thofe truths he can-
" not believe. Yes ; but in that cafe the diffimulation
" muft be abfolutely neceffary. I would be a bifhop if I
" could preferve my opinions and talk of them with my
" friends; and if, to keep the people in their errors, they would
" not force me to entertain them with fables. But if a bifhop
" muft preach the contrary to what he thinks, and think
" with the people, I fhall refufe the epifcopacy. I do not
" know if there be truths that ought to be held from the vul-
" gar; but I know, that a bifhop ought not to preach the con-
" trary of what he believes. The truth ought to be refpect-
" ed as the Divinity, and I proteft before God that I will ne-
" ver falfify my fentiments in my preachings." Synefius, notwithftanding his repugnance, was ordained a bifhop, and
kept his word. The hymns he compofed are nothing more
than expofitions of the fyftems of Pythagoras, Plato, and the
Stoics, adjufted to the dogmas and worfhip of the Chriftians.

6. (p. 187.) Pious calumny is alfo a virtue of new creation. Rouffeau and I have been its victims. How many
paffages of our works have been falfely cited in the mandates
of the holy bifhops ? There are therefore now holy calumni-
ators. ¸

7. (ibid.) The clergy who call themfelves humble, refemble
Diogenes, whofe pride was feen through the holes in his
cloak.

8. (ibid.) Read on this fubject the laft chapters of the
rules of St. Benedict ; you will there fee that if the monks
be obdurate and wicked, it is what they ought to be.

The generality of men, affured of their fubfiftence, and
without concern on that account, become infenfible : they do
not deplore in others the evils they cannot fuffer. Befide,
the happinefs or mifery of a monk, confined in a cloifter, is
entirely independent of that of his relations and fellow-citizens. The monks therefore muft regard the men of the world
with the fame indifference a traveller regards the beafts he
meets in a foreft. It is the monaftic laws that condemn the
religious orders to inhumanity. In fact, what is it that produces in men the fentiment of benevolence ? The affiftance,
either

either remote or near, that they may afford each other. This is the principle that unites men in fociety. Do the laws eftrange my intereft from that of the public? From that moment I become wicked. From thence the feverity of arbitrary governments, and the reafon why monks and defpots are in general the moft inhuman of men.

9 (p. 188) They formerly believed that God, according to the difference of times, could have different ideas of virtue; the church has clearly explained this doctrine in the council of Ball, held on account of the Huffites; who having protefted againft admitting any doctrine that was not contained in the fcriptures; the fathers of the council informed them, by the mouth of cardinal Cafan "That the fcriptures were not ab-" folutely neceffary to the prefervation of the church, but " only to its better regulation: that they fhould be always " interpreted according to the prefent ftate of the church, " which by changing its fentiments obliges us to believe that " God changes his alfo."

10. (ibid.) They boaft much of the reftitutions that religion caufes to be made. I have fometimes feen the reftitution of copper, but never of gold. The monks have not yet reftored the heritage, nor the catholic princes the kingdoms that have been ravifhed from the Americans.

11. (p. 189.) It is but juftice to arm intolerance againft an intolerant; as a prince ought to oppofe an army againft the army of his enemy.

12. (ibid.) On opening the Encyclopedia at the article *Virtue*, how was I furprifed to find, not a definition of virtue, but a declamation on the fubject. *O man!* cries the compofer of that article, *wouldft thou know what is virtue? Enter into thyfelf. Its definition is at the bottom of thy heart.* But why was it not in like manner at the bottom of the compofer's heart, and if it were there, why did he not give it us? Few authors, I confefs, think fo highly of their readers, and fo meanly of themfelves. If that writer had reflected more on the word Virtue, he would have perceived, that it confifted in the knowledge of what men owe to each other, and that it confequently fuppofes the formation of focieties. Before this formation, what good or evil could be done to a fociety not yet exifting? A man of the woods, a man naked and with-

out

out language, might eafily acquire a clear idea of ftrength or weaknefs, but not of juftice and equity.

A man born in a defart ifland, and abandoned to himfelf, would live there without vice or virtue. He could not exercife either of them. What then are we to underftand by the words Virtuous and Vicious ? Actions ufeful or detrimental to fociety. This idea, clear and fimple, is, in my opinion, preferable to all obfcure and inflated declamations on virtue.

A preacher, who in his fermons gives no clear definition of virtue ; a moralift, who maintains that all men are good, and does not believe any of them unjuft, is fometimes a fot, but more frequently a knave, that would be thought honeft merely becaufe he is a man.

To pretend to draw a faithful portrait of humanity, perhaps a man fhould be virtuous, and, to a certain point, irreproachable.

What I know of the matter, is, that the moft honeft are not they who fuppofe men to have the moft virtue. If I would be well affured of mine, I would fuppofe myfelf to be a citizen of Rome, or of Greece ; and I would afk myfelf, whether in the fituation of Codrus or Regulus, Brutus or Leonidas, I fhould have done the fame actions. The leaft hefitation in this cafe would teach me that I was but weak in virtue. Of every fort the ftrong are rare, and the lukewarm common.

13. (p. 190.) The humanity of M. Fenelon, is renowned. One day, a vicar boafted, in his prefence, of having abolifhed dancing on a Sunday, in his village. Mafter vicar, faid the archbifhop, let us be lefs fevere towards others ; let us abftain from dancing ourfelves, but let the peafants dance if they like it. Why fhould we not let them for a fhort time forget their mifery ? Fenelon, juft, and always virtuous, lived a part of his days in difgrace. Boffuet, his rival in genius, was lefs honeft, and always in favour.

14. (p. 193.) The morality of Jefus, and that of the Jefuits, have nothing in common ; the one is deftructive of the other. This is evident, by the extracts that the parliaments have given. But why do the clergy inceffantly repeat, that the fame ftroke has deftroyed the Jefuits and religion? It is, becaufe, in the ecclefiaftical language, religion and fuperftition are fynonimous. Now fuperftition, or the papal power, has, perhaps, really fuffered by the banifhment of that order.

For

For the reſt, let not the Jeſuits flatter themſelves, that they will ever be recalled into France and Spain. It is known by what proſcriptions their recall would be followed, and to what exceſs the cruelty of an enraged Jeſuit is carried.

15. (p. 193.) The fear with which the Jeſuits were regarded, ſeemed to have ſet them above all attack. To brave their hatred and their intrigues, ſuch men as Chauvelin were neceſſary, noble ſouls, generous citizens, and friends to the public. To deſtroy ſuch an order, courage alone was not ſufficient; genius was alſo requiſite. It was neceſſary to ſhow the people the poignard of the regicide, wrapped up in the veil of reſpect and devotion: to diſcover the hypocriſy of the Jeſuits through the cloud of incenſe they ſpread around the throne and the altars; to embolden the timid prudence of the parliaments, and make them clearly diſtinguiſh between the extraordinary and the impoſſible.

16. (p. 194.) It is with the judgment as with virtue. The judgment applied to the various ſciences of geometry, phyſics, &c. is judgment in all countries. The judgment, when applied to the falſe ſciences of magic, theology, &c. is local. The firſt of theſe, is to the other what the money of Africa, named the ſhell *Coris*, is to the money of gold and ſilver; the one has circulation among ſome Negro nations, the other over the whole earth.

17. (p. 195.) On what ſhould we eſtabliſh the principles of a good morality? On a great number of facts and obſervations. It is, therefore, to the premature formation of certain principles, that we ought, perhaps, to attribute their obſcurity and falſity. In morality, as in all other ſciences, what ſhould be done before we form a ſyſtem? Collect the materials neceſſary for the conſtruction. We cannot now be ignorant, that an experimental morality, founded on the ſtudy of men, and of things, as far ſurpaſſes a ſpeculative and theological morality, as experimental philoſophy exceeds a vague and uncertain theory. It is becauſe religious morality never had experiment for its baſis, that the theological empire was ever regarded as the region of darkneſs.

18. (p. 196.) The monks, themſelves, have not always held chaſtity in equal eſteem. Some of them, called Mamillaires, have held, that a man might, without ſin, feel the boſom of a nun. There is no act of laſciviouſneſs, that ſuperſtition has not in ſome part made an act of virtue. In Japan, the Bonzes
may

may love men, but not women. In certain cantons of Peru, the acts of the Greek loves were acts of piety; it was an homage to the gods, and rendered publicly in their temples.

19. (p. 196.) Mrs. Macauley, the illustrious author of a History of England, is the Cato of London, " Never, says she, has " the view of a despotic monarch, or prince, foiled the pu- " rity of my looks."

20. (ibid.) It is an absurdity common to all nations, to ex- pect humanity and science in their tyrant. To attempt to make good scholars, without punishing the idle, and rewarding the diligent, is a folly. To abolish the law that punishes theft and murder, and require that men should not steal or murder, is a voluntary contradiction. To desire that a prince should apply himself to the affairs of the state, and that he should have no interest to apply himself to them, that is, that he should not be punished, if he neglect them: to desire, in short, that a man above the law, that is without law, should be always humane and virtuous, is to desire an effect without a cause. Cast men bound into the den of a tyger, and he will devour them. The de- spot is the tyger.

21. (ibid.) The Calmucks marry as many wives as they please; they have beside, as many concubines as they can main- tain. Incest is no crime among them. They see nothing more in a man and a woman, than a male and a female. A father without scruple marries his daughter: no law forbids.

22. (ibid.) Every one says, I have the most just ideas of virtue: whoever does not think as I do, is wrong. Every one laughs at his neighbour. Every one points with his finger, and never laughs at himself but under the name of another. The same inquisitor who condemned Galileo, doubtless, con- demned the wickedness and stupidity of the judges of Socrates: he did not think that he should one day be like them, the scorn of his own age, and of posterity. Does the Sorbonne think itself despicable for having condemned Rousseau, Mar- montel, myself, &c.? No; it is the stranger who thinks so, in its stead.

23. (p. 198.) Barillon was exiled to Amboise, and Riche- lieu, who sent him thither, was the first minister, says cardinal de Retz, who dared to punish in the magistrates, *that noble firm-* *ness with which they represented to the king those truths, for de-* *fence of which their oaths obliged them to expose their lives.*

24. (p. 198.)

24. (p. 198.) If it be true, that virtue is ufeful to a ftate, it muft be alfo ufeful to give clear ideas of it, and to engrave them, in the moft tender infancy, on the memories of men. The definition I have given of virtue in the Treatife on the Mind, Difc. iii. chap. 13. appears to me to be the only one that is juft. " Virtue, I have there faid, is nothing more than " the defire of public happinefs. The general welfare is the " object of virtue; and the actions it enjoins, are the means it " employs to accomplifh that object. The idea of virtue, I " have added, muft therefore be every where the fame."

If in various ages and countries men appear to have formed different ideas of virtue, if philofophers have, in confequence, " treated the idea of virtue as arbitrary, it is becaufe they have " taken for virtue itfelf, the feveral means it makes ufe of to " accomplifh its object, that is to fay, the feveral actions it " enjoins. Thefe actions have certainly been fometimes very " different, becaufe the interefts of nations change, according " to the age and their fituation; and laftly, becaufe the public " good may, to a certain degree, be promoted by different " means."

The entrance of foreign merchandize permitted to-day in Germany, as advantageous to its commerce, and conformable to the good of the ftate, may be to-morrow forbid. To-morrow the purchafer may be declared criminal, if by fome circumftances that purchafe become prejudicial to the national intereft. " The fame actions may therefore become fuccef- " fively ufeful and prejudicial to a nation, and merit by turns " the name of virtuous and vicious, without the idea of vir- " tue's fuffering any change, or ceafing to be the fame." Nothing is more agreeable to the natural law, than this idea. Could it be imagined that principles fo found, and fo conformable to the public good, would have been condemned ? Could it be imagined that a man would be perfecuted, who had defined, " true probity to be the habitude of actions ufeful to " our country, and regarded as vicious every action detrimen- " tal to fociety ?" Is it not evident that fuch a writer could not advance maxims contrary to the public good, without contradicting himfelf. Such, however, was the power of envy and hypocrify, that I was perfecuted by the fame clergy, who, without oppofition, had fuffered the audacious Bellarmin to be

elevated

elevated to the rank of a cardinal, for having maintained, *that if the pope forbids the exercise of virtue, and command that of vice; the Roman church, under pain of a sin, was obliged to abandon virtue for vice, nisi vellet contra conscientiam peccare.* The pope therefore, according to this Jesuit, had the right of destroying the natural law, and of stifling in man every idea of justice and injustice, and, in short, of replunging morality into that chaos, from which philosophy has drawn it with so much pains. Did the church ought to approve such principles? Why did the pope suffer their publication? Because they flattered his pride.

Papal ambition, always greedy of power, is never scrupulous in the choice of the means. In what country has not the maxim the most abominable, the most contrary to the public good, been tolerated by the power to whom it is favourable? In what country have they constantly punished the wretch who has incessantly repeated to the prince, " Thy power over thy " subjects is without bounds: thou mayest at thy will despoil " them of their property, load them with fetters, and deliver " them up to the most cruel tortures." It is always with impunity, that the fox repeats to the lyon, *You do them, Sire, a great deal of honour in making them beggars.*

> *Vous leur faites, Seigneur,*
> *En les croquant beaucoup d' honneur.*

The only expressions that cannot be repeated to princes without danger, are those that fix the bounds, which justice, the public good, and the law of nations, set to their authority.

25. (p. 199.) By metaphysics, I do not mean that jargon transmitted by the Egyptian priests to Pythagoras, by him to Plato, and by Plato to us, and which is still taught in some schools: but I mean, with Bacon, the knowledge of the first principles of any art or science whatever. Poetry, music, and painting, have their first principles, founded on a constant and general observation ; they have, therefore, their metaphysics.

As to the scholastic metaphysics, is it a science? No: but I have just said a jargon ; it is tolerable only to the false mind that can accommodate expressions void of sense : to the ignorant, who take words for things; and to knaves who want to make dupes. By a man of sense it is despised.

All metaphysics, not founded on observation, consist solely in the art of abusing words. It is this metaphysics, that in the
land

land of chimeras, is continually running after bladders of foap; from which it can never get any thing but air.

Now, banifhed to the fchools of theology, it ftill divides them by its fubtilities, and may one day again light up fanaticifm, and again make human blood to ftream.

I compare thefe two forts of metaphyfics to the two different philofophies of Democritus and Plato. The firft raifes it-felf by degrees from earth to heaven, and the other defcends by degrees from heaven to earth. The fyftem of Plato was founded on the clouds, and the breath of reafon has already diffipated the clouds, and the fyftem.

26. (p. 200.) Men have always been governed by words. If half of the weight of the filver in a crown be diminifhed, and its numeral value ftill preferved, the foldier thinks he has near-ly the fame pay. The magiftrate, authorifed to judge defi-nitively to a certain amount, that is, to fuch a weight of filver, muft not judge to the amount of half that fum. In like man-ner are men duped by words, and by their uncertain fignifica-tions. Writers are conftantly talking about *good morals*, with-out attaching any clear ideas to thofe words. Can they be ig-norant, that good morals is one of thofe vague expreffions, of which every nation forms different ideas? If there be univerfal good morals, there are alfo thofe that are local, and confe-quently, I can, without offending good morals, have a feraglio at Conftantinople, and not at Vienna.

27. (p. 202.) Theological difputes never are, and never can be, any thing more than difputes about words. If thefe dif-putes have frequently occafioned great commotions on the earth, it is becaufe princes, faid M. Chalotais, feduced by fome theologians *, have taken a part in thefe quarrels. Let go-vernments defpife their difputes; and the theologians, after rail-ing, and reciprocally accufing each other of herefy, &c. will grow tired of talking, without underftanding each other, and without being underftood. The fear of ridicule will make them filent.

28. (ibid.) It is to the difputes about words, that we are in like manner to refer almoft all the accufations of atheifm.

* *Perhaps it has happened, at leaft as frequently, from the knavery of princes, who by encouraging one party againft the other, have weakened them both, and confequently increafed their own ftrength.*

There

There is no man of underſtanding who does not acknowledge an active power in nature. There is, therefore, no atheiſt.

He is not an atheiſt who ſays, that motion is God; becauſe, in fact, motion is incomprehenſible, as we have no clear idea of it, as it does not manifeſt itſelf but by its effects; and laſtly, becauſe by it all things are performed in the univerſe.

He is not an atheiſt, who ſays, on the contrary, that motion is not God: becauſe, motion is not a Being, but a mode of Being.

They are not atheiſts, who maintain that motion is eſſential to matter, and regard it as the inviſible and motive force that ſpreads itſelf through all its parts. Do we ſee the ſtars continnally changing their places, and rolling perpetually round their centre: do we ſee all bodies deſtroyed and reproduced inceſſantly, under different forms; in ſhort, do we ſee nature in an eternal fermentation and diſſolution? Who then can deny, that motion is, like extenſion, inherent in bodies, and that motion is not the cauſe of what is? In fact, ſays Mr. Hume, if we always give the names of cauſe and effect to the concomitance of two facts, and that wherever there are bodies, there is motion; we ought then to regard motion as the univerſal ſoul of matter, and the divinity that alone penetrates its ſubſtance. But are the philoſophers of this laſt opinion atheiſts? No: they equally acknowledge an unknown force in the univerſe. Are even thoſe who have no ideas of God, atheiſts? No; becauſe then all men would be ſo: becauſe no one has a clear idea of the Divinity: becauſe in this caſe every obſcure idea is equal to none, and laſtly, to acknowledge the incomprehenſibility of God, is, as M. Robinet proves, to ſay by a different turn of expreſſion, that we have no idea of him.

29. (p. 204.) Man, to be happy, muſt have deſires, ſuch as employ him, and ſuch whoſe objects his labour or his talents can procure him. Among the deſires of this ſort, the moſt proper to keep him from diſguſt is that of glory. This ſprings up equally in all countries. It ſometimes happens, that the ſearch after glory expoſes a man to too much danger: what rational motive can excite him to the purſuit of it in a kingdom where they perſecute ſuch men as Voltaire, Monteſquieu, &c. If France, ſay the Engliſh, be reckoned a delicious country, it is for thoſe that are rich, and do not think.

30. (p. 2c6.) Far from condemning a fyftematic fpirit, I admire it in great men. It is to the efforts made to deftroy or defend thofe fyftems that we doubtlefs owe an infinity of difcoveries.

Let men therefore continue to explain, by a fingle principle, if it be poffible, all the phyfical phenomena in nature : but be continually on their guard againft thofe principles; let them be confidered merely as one of the different keys we may fucceffively try, that we may at laft find that which fhall open the fanctuary of nature. But above all, let us not confound tales with fyftems ; the latter muft be fupported by a great number of facts. It is thefe alone that fhould be taught in the public fchools : provided however that we do not ftill maintain them to be true, a hundred years after experience has proved them to be falfe.

31. (p. 2c8.) Whence comes it, it was faid to a certain cardinal, that there have been in all times priefts, religions, and forcerers ? Becaufe, he replied, there have always been bees and hornets, labourers and idlers, knaves and dupes.

32. (ibid.) Without examining if it be the intereft of thepublic to admit the doctrine of the immortality of the foul, I fhall obferve that at leaft this dogma has not always been politically regarded as ufeful. It took its rife in the fchools of Plato; but Ptolemy Philadelphus, king of Egypt, thought it fo dangerous, that he forbid it to be preached in his dominions on pain of death.

33 (p. 213.) It is known that the ancient Druids were animated with the fame fpirit as the Popifh priefts now are ; that they had, before them, invented excommunication ; that like them they would command over people and kings ; and that they pretended to have, like the inquifitors, the power of life and death, among all nations where they were eftablifhed.

34: (p. 216.) I one day attended on a reprefentation the clergy of a German court made to their prince : I bore the marvellous ring, which makes men fay and write, not what they would have others hear and read, but what they really think. Without the virtue of my ring, I fhould doubtlefs never have heard or read the following difcourfe.

When the clergy thought they had convinced the prince that religion was loft in his dominions; that debauchery and impiety boldly ftalked abroad ; that the holy days were profaned by là-
- bour;

bour; that the liberty of the prefs fhook the foundations of his throne and of the altars, and that in confequence the bifhops enjoined the fovereign to arm the laws againft the liberty of thought, to protect the church and deftroy its enemies : the following were the words I feemed to bear in that adrefs

" Prince, your clergy are rich and powerful, and would be
" ftill more fo. It is not the lofs of morality and religon, but
" that of their authority, they deplore. They defire to have the
" greateft authority, and your people are without refpect for the
" facerdotal power. We therefore declare them to be impious;
" we exhort you to reanimate their piety, and for that purpofe
" to give your clergy more authority over them. The mo-
" ment chofen to accufe the people, and irritate you againft
" them, is not perhaps the moft favourable. Your foldiers
" have never been fo brave, your artifans more induftrious,
" your citizens more zealous for the public welfare, and con-
" fequently more virtuous. They will tell you, without doubt,
" that the people moft immediately fubject to the clergy, that
" the modern Romans have neither the fame valour, nor the
" fame love for their country, nor confequently the fame vir-
" tue. They will add, perhaps, that Spain and Portugal,
" where the clergy command fo imperioufly, are ruined and
" laid wafte by ignorance, floth, and fuperftition ; and, in
" fhort, that among all nations, they who are generally ho-
" noured and refpected, are thofe fame enlightened people to
" whom the Catholic church will always give the name of im-
" pious.

" Let your ears, O prince, be for ever clofed againft fuch re-
" prefentations; that, in concert with your clergy, you may
" fpread darknefs over your dominions, and know that a
" people fkilful, rich, and without fuperftition, are, in the eyes
" of the prieft, a people without morals. Is it, in fact, the rich
" and induftrious citizen, who has for example, all the refpect
" for the virtue of continence that it deferves ?

" It is, they will fay, in this refpect with the prefent age, as
" with thofe that are paft. Charlemagne, created a faint for
" liberality toward the priefthood, loved women as well as
" Francis I. and Henry VIII. Henry III. king of France,
" had a tafte lefs decent. Henry IV. Elizabeth, Lewis XIV.
" and queen Anne careffed their miftreffes, or their lovers, with
" the fame hands with which they laid their enemies in the

" duſt. They will add, that the monks themſelves have al-
" moſt always enjoyed in ſecret forbidden pleaſures ; and in
" ſhort, that without changing the natural conſtitutions of the
" inhabitants,it is very difficult to keep them from that damn-
" able diſpoſition that carries them toward women. There is
" however one method to prevent it, and that is to make them
" poor. It is not from a ſound and well fed body that the de-
" mon of the fleſh can be driven : it is to be effected only by
" prayer and faſting.

    " That, by the example of ſome of your neighbours, your
" majeſty therefore will permit us to ſtrip your ſubjects of all
" their ſuperfluities, to tithe their lands, to pillage their pro-
" perty, and to keep them in the ſtricteſt neceſſity. If, touched
" by theſe pious remonſtrances, your majeſty ſhall regard our
" prayers, may benedictions pour down upon you ! No praiſe
" can equal ſo meritorious an action. But in an age when cor-
" ruption infects all minds, when impiety hardens every heart,
" may we hope that your majeſty and your miniſters will
" adopt a counſel ſo ſalutary, a method ſo eaſy to ſecure the
" continence of your ſubjects ?

    " With regard to the profanation of holidays, our remon-
" ſtrances may again appear abſurd. The man who labours
" on Sundays and holidays does not get drunk, or run after
" women ; he injures no one, he ſerves his country and his fa-
" mily, and augments the commerce of his nation.

    " Of two ſtates equally numerous and powerful, let one of
" them make, as in Spain, 130 holidays in the year, and
" ſometimes the day after; and the other, on the contrary,
" keep no ſaints days, the latter of theſe people will have 80
" or 90 days of labour more than the other, and can furniſh
" the articles of its commerce at a lower price : its lands will
" be better cultivated, its harveſt more abundant, and the ba-
" lance of trade will be in its favour. The latter therefore, be-
" ing more rich and powerful than the former, may one day
" give it laws.   There is nothing in common between the na-
" tional intereſt and that of the clergy. The prieſt, ſolely jealous
" of command, what would he do ? Contract the mind of the
" prince, and extinguiſh in him even the lights of nature.   A
" nation governed by ſuch a prince will, ſooner or later, be-
" come a prey to ſome neighbour more rich, more learned, and
" leſs ſuperſtitious. So that the grandeur of the Catholic cler-

                                                    " gy

" gy is always deſtructive of the grandeur of a ſtate. Do the
" prieſts declaim againſt the profanation of holidays ? Be not
" deceived, it is not the love of God, but that of their autho-
" rity, by which they are influenced. We learn from expe-
" rience, that the leſs a man frequents the temples, the leſs
" reſpect he has for their miniſters, and the leſs authority thoſe
" miniſters have over him. Now if power be the ruling paſ-
" ſion of a prieſt, it is of little conſequence to him whether a
" holiday be to the labourer a day of debauch ; whether, on
" going from the temple, he run after wenches and frequent
" public houſes, and paſs the remainder of the day in ebriety.
" The more ſins, the more expiations and offerings ; the more
" riches and power is acquired by the prieſt. What is the in-
" tereſt of the church ? To multiply vices ? What does it aſk
" of men ? To be ſtupid and wicked. Behold, Sire, with
" what we are reproached by the impious. With regard to the
" liberty of the preſs, if your clergy riſe up ſo violently againſt
" it, if they tell you inceſſantly that it ſaps the foundation of
" the law, and renders religion ridiculous, believe it not.

" It is not that your clergy do not perceive, with the ſolid
" and ingenious author of the _Engliſh Inveſtigator_, that truth is
" proof againſt ridicule, and that ridicule is the touchſtone of
" truth. A ridicule caſt on a demonſtration is like mud thrown
" againſt marble : it ſoils it for a moment, it dries ; the rain
" comes, and the ſpot diſappears. To agree that a religion
" cannot ſtand againſt ridicule, is to allow it to be falſe Does
" not the Catholic church repeat inceſſantly that the gates of
" hell ſhall never prevail againſt it ? Yes ; but prieſts are
" not religion. Ridicule may weaken their authority, and
" fetter their ambition ; they therefore conſtantly cry out
" againſt the liberty of the preſs, and entreat your majeſty to
" forbid your ſubjects the practice of writing and thinking,
" that you may deprive them in this reſpect of the privileges
" of men, and conſequently ſhut the mouth of every one that
" can inſtruct mankind.

" If ſo many demands appear indiſcreet, and that, jealous of
" the happineſs of your people, you would, Sire, rule over in-
" telligent inhabitants only, know, that the ſame conduct
" that will render you dear to your ſubjects, and reſpectable to
" ſtrangers, will be imputed to you as a crime by your clergy.
" Dread the vengeance of a powerful body, and for the future

R 3

" re-

" refign to them your fword ; it is then that, affured of the piety
" of your people, the facerdotal power may again affume over
" them its ancient authority, fee from day to day that authority
" increafe, and at laft make ufe of it to bring you into fub-
" jection.

" We defire the more earneftly that your majefty would re-
" gard our fupplication, and authorize our demand, as it will
" deliver us from a fecret inquietude, that is not without foun-
" dation. Quakers may eftablifh themfelves in your domini-
" ons ; they may propofe to communicate, gratis, to the cities,
" towns, and villages, all inftruction, moral and religious, that
" is neceffary : they might moreover form certain companies of
" finance, who might undertake this enterprize of inftruction at
" a difcount, and furnifh it ftill cheaper and cheaper. Who
" can fay whether the magiftrates might not then take it in
" their heads to feize on our revenues, and employ them to
" difcharge a part of the national debt, and by that mean make
" your nation the moft refpectable in Europe. Now it is of
" little confequence to us, Sire, whether your people be happy
" and refpectable, but is of great confequence that the facerdo-
" tal body be rich and powerful."

This is what the reprefentations of the clergy feemed to me
to contain. I fhall not weary myfelf with confidering the
addrefs, the artifice with which the priefts have in all countries
continually afked in the name of heaven, the power and riches
of the earth. I admire the confidence they have always had in
the weaknefs of the people, and efpecially men in power.
But what moft of all furprifes me is, (when I reflect on the ages
of ignorance,) to find that in this refpect moft fovereigns have
always been out of the power of the clergy.

55. (p. 217.) There are fome who fay that at the moment of
our birth God engraves on our hearts the precepts of the natural law. Experience proves the contrary. If God is to be regarded as the author of the laws of nature, it is as being the
author of corporeal fenfibility, which is the mother of human reafon. This fort of fenfibility, at the time of the union
of men in fociety, obliged them, as I have already faid, to
make among themfelves conventions and laws, the affemblage
of which compofes what is called the laws of nature. But have
thofe laws been the fame among different nations ? No : their
greater or lefs perfection was always in proportion to the progrefs

grefs of the human mind ; to the greater or lefs extent of knowledge that focieties acquired, of what was ufeful or prejudicial;
and this knowledge has been in all nations the produce of
time, experience, and reflection.

To make us fee in God the immediate author of the laws of
nature, and confequently of all juftice, ought the theologians
to admit him to have paffions, fuch as love, or vengeance?
Ought they to reprefent him as a Being fufceptible of predi-
lection ; in fhort, as an affemblage of incoherent qualities ? Is
it in fuch a God that we can difcern the author of juftice ? Can
we thus endeavour to reconcile irreconcileables, and confound
truth with falfhcod, without perceiving the impoffibility of
fuch a connection ? It is time that men, deaf to theological
contradictions, liften to nothing but the doctrines of wifdom:
for, St. Paul fays, " It is high time to awake out of fleep ;
" the night (of ignorance) is far fpent, the day (of fcience) is at
" hand; let us therefore put on the armour of light," to deftroy
the phantoms of darknefs, and for that purpofe let us reftore to
men their natural liberty, and the free exercife of reafon.

36. (p. 218.) Can it be, that among almoft all nations the
idea of fanctity is annexed to the obfervance of a ritual cere-
mony, an ablution, &c. Can men be ftill ignorant that the
only citizens conftantly virtuous and humane, are thofe that are
happy in their character. In fact, who among the devout are
the moft eftimable ? They that, full of confidence in God, forget there is a hell Who, on the contrary, among the fame
devout are the moft odious and inhuman ? They that, timid,
difcontented, and unhappy, fee hell continually open before
them Why are the devout in general the torment of their
dwellings, railing inceffantly at their fervants, and making
themfelves hateful ? Becaufe, having the idea of the devil before them, and fearing perpetually to be carried away by him,
their fear and their unhappinefs render them malignant. If
youth be in general more virtuous and more humane than age,
it is becaufe, having more defires and more health, they are
more happy. Nature did wifely, faid an Englifhman, to limit
the life of man to 80 or 100 years. If heaven had prolonged
his old age he would have become too wicked.

37. (p. 221.) If in Tartary, under the name of Dalai Lama,
the grand pontiff be immortal ; in Italy, under the name of
Pope, their pontiff is infallible. If in the country of the

R 4

Mongales the vicar of the grand Lama receive the title of Ku-
tuchta, that is vicar of the living God, in Europe the Pope
bears the same title.   At Bagdat, in Tartary, at Japan, if with
a design to debase and subdue their kings, the pontiffs, under
the name of caliphs, lama, and dairo, have made emperors
kiss their feet ; and if these pontiffs, when mounted on a mule,
have obliged the emperors to take the bridle and lead them
through the streets : has not the pope exacted the same ser-
vility from the monarchs of the West ? The pontiffs in every
country have therefore made the same pretensions, and the
princes the same submission.

If the deputies for the office of caliph have made human
blood to stream in the East, the disputes for the papacy have in
like manner made it stream in the West.   Six popes have af-
fassinated their predecessors, and set themselves in their
place.   The popes, says Baronius, were not then men but
monsters.

Have we not every where seen the name of orthodox given to
the strongest religion, and that of heresy to the weakest ? Every
where has the sacerdotal power been productive of fanaticism,
and fanaticism of murder.   Every where have men suffered
themselves to be burned for theological absurdities, and given
in this manner equal proofs of obstinacy and courage.

But it is not in religious affairs only that men have every
where shewed themselves to be the same : the same resemblance
is to be found among them when some change in their habits
and customs has been in agitation.   The Mantchoux Tartars,
who conquered the Chinese, would have cut off their hair ; but
the latter broke their fetters, routed the terrible Mantchoux,
and triumphed over their conquerors.   The czar would shave
the Russians, and they revolted.   The king of England would
make the Highlanders wear breeches, and they rose in arms.
In the East and the West the people are therefore every where the
same, and every where the same causes have raised up and
pulled down empires.

At the time of the conquest of China, what was the prince
that occupied the throne ? A weak wretch, an idol, whom they
dared not inform of the bad state of his affairs, and to whom in-
cense was continually offered by his favourites, while he was
solely surrounded by intriguing courtiers, without judgment,
without knowledge, and without courage.   Who commanded
over

over the empires of the Eaft and Weft, when Rome and Conftantinople were taken and plundered by Alaric and Mahomet
the fecond ? Princes of the fame fort.   Such perhaps was the
ftate of France in the old age of Lewis XIV. when it was
beaten on every fide.

It appears that men are every where the fame from the dege-
neracy and ignorance into which every people fucceffively fall,
according to the intereft their government has to degrade them.
If a minifter be weak, and fear that the people will open their
eyes, and difcover his incapacity, he keeps them faft clofed,
and the ftupidity of the people is then not the effect of a phyfical, but a moral caufe.

Does not a caufe of the fame kind animate with the fame fpirit thofe whom chance has brought up to the fame employments ? What is in Spain, Germany, and even in England the
firft care of the man in place ? To enrich himfelf.   The public
welfare holds the fecond place only.

If in the inferior offices of government almoft all men have
the fame fupercilious behaviour, and the fame incapacity for
adminiftration ; to what is it to be attributed ? To a defect in
their organifation ? No : but to that of their inftruction.   All
men practifed in the fineffe of chicanery, and accuftomed to
judge only by precedent, remount with difficulty to the firft
principles of laws ; they extend the memory, and contract the
judgment.

In the mind, as in the body, thofe parts only are ftrong that
are exercifed : the legs of chairmen and the arms of labourers
make this evident.   If the mufcles of reafon in the men of the
law are commonly weak, it is becaufe they have little exercife.

Facts without number prove that men are every where effentially the fame ; that the difference of climate has no fenfible
influence over their minds, and even very little over their taftes.
The Illinois and the Icelander fits by his keg of brandy till
he has drank it out. In almoft every country the women have
the fame defire to pleafe as in France, the fame tafte for drefs,
the fame care of their beauty, the fame averfion to the country,
and the fame love for the capital, where, conftantly furrounded
by a number of admirers, they find themfelves really of more
importance.

When we caft our eyes over the univerfe, and perceive
the fame ambition in all hearts, the fame credulity in all
                                                        minds,

minds, the fame duplicity in all priefts, the fame coquetry in all women, and the fame love of riches in all ranks of people, how can we doubt but that men all refembling each other, differ only in the diverfity of their inftruction : that in every country their organs are nearly the fame, and that they make nearly the fame ufe of them ; and that in fhort the hands of the Indians and Chinefe are, for that reafon, equally adroit in the fabric of ftuffs as thofe of the Europeans. Nothing proves therefore what is inceffantly repeated, that it is to the difference of latitudes we ought to attribute the inequality of minds.

38. (p. 222) The frauds of the priefts are every where the fame : they are every where anxious to appropriate the wealth of the laics. The Romifh church for this fells a licence for relations to marry : it engages for fo many maffes, that is for fo many fix-penny pieces, to deliver every year fo many fouls out of purgatory, and confequently to remit them fo many fins. At the Pagoda of Tinagogo, as at Rome, the priefts for the fame fums fell nearly the fame hopes.

"At Tinagogo, (fays the author of l'Hiftoire general des "Voyages, tom. ix. p. 462.) on the third day after a facrifice "that is made to the new moon in December, they place in fix "long and handfome ftreets an infinity of balances fufpended by "brafs rods ; there each devotee, to obtain the remiffion of "his fins, gets into one of the fcales of a balance, and, accord-"ing to the different nature of his crimes, puts into the other "fcale different forts of provifions or monies as a counterpoife. "If his confcience reproach him with gluttony and violation "of a faft, the counterpoife confifts of honey, fugar, eggs, and "butter. If he has been guilty of fenfual pleafures, he weighs "himfelf againft cotton, feathers, cloth, perfumes, and wine. "Has he been uncharitable ? He weighs himfelf againft pieces "of money. Is he idle ? The counterpoife is wood, rice, coal, "cattle, and fruits. Is he, laftly, proud ? He weighs himfelf "againft dry fifh, brooms, cow-dung, &c. Now all that ferves "for counterpoife to the finners belongs to the priefts. All "thefe forts of donations form large piles. Even the poor, "who have nothing to give, are not exempt from thefe alms. "They offer their hair : more than a hundred priefts fit with "fciffars in their hands to cut it off. The hair is alfo formed into "great

" great heaps : more than a thousand priests, ranged in order,
" form of it cords, braids, rings, bracelets, &c. which the de-
" vout souls purchase, and carry away as precious gages of the
" favour of heaven. To form an idea of the sum to which the
" alms to the pagoda of Tinagego only may amount, it will
" suffice, says Pinto, the author of this relation, to mention that
" the ambassador having asked the priests at what sum they
" estimated those alms, they answered without hesitation, that
" only for the hair of the poor they got every year more than a
" hundred thousand pardins, that is, ninety thousand ducats of
" Portugal."

39.(p. 222.)Some philosophers have defined man to be *a monkey
that laughs*; others, *a rational animal*; and others, *a credulous animal*. This animal, they add, is mounted on two legs, has flexible
fingers, and dextrous hands : he has many wants, and consequently great industry. He is moreover as vain and proud as
credulous. He thinks that the whole system of nature was
made for the earth, and the earth made for him. Is not this
definition or description of man extremely just ?

40. (p. 223.) Every one asks, what is truth or evidence ?
The root of the word indicates the idea we ought to annex to
it. *Evidence* is derived from *videre, video*, I see.

What is to me an evident proposition ? It is a fact, of whose
existence I can convince myself by the testimony of my senses,
that never deceive me when I interrogate them with the necessary precaution and attention.

What is an evident proposition to the generality of mankind ? It is, in like manner, a fact of which all may convince
themselves by the testimony of their senses, and whose existence
they may moreover verify every instant. Such are these two
facts, *two and two make four* ; *the whole is greater than a part*.

If I pretend, for example, that there is in the north sea a
polypus named kraken, and that this polypus is as large as a
small island. This fact, though evident to me, if I have seen
and examined it with all the attention necessary to convince
me of its reality, is not even probable to him that has not
seen it; it is more rational in him to doubt my veracity, than to
believe the existence of so extraordinary an animal.

But if after travellers I describe the true form of the buildings in Pekin, this description, evident to those who inhabit
them, is only more or less probable to others : so that the true

is not always evident, and the probable is often true. But in what does evidence differ from probability? I have already said, "Evidence is a fact that is fubject to our fenfes, and " whofe exiftence all men may verify every inftant. As to " probability, it is founded on conjectures, on the teftimony of " men, and on a hundred proofs of the fame kind. Evidence " is a fingle point : there are no degrees of evidence. On the " contrary, there are various degrees of probability according " to the difference, 1. of the people who affert; 2. of the fact " afferted." Five men tell me they have feen a bear in the fo-refts of Poland : this fact not being contradicted by any thing, is to me very probable. But if not five only, but five hundred men fhould affure me they met in the fame forefts ghofts, fai-ries, demons, their united evidence would not be to me at all probable ; for in cafes of this nature, it is more common to meet with five hundred romancers, than to fee fuch pro-digies.

41. (p. 225.) Let us place before our eyes all the facts from the comparifon of which a new truth is to refult ; and let us annex clear ideas to the words that are ufed in its demonftra-tion. Nothing can conceal it from our perception ; and this truth prefently reduced to a fimple fact, will be conceived by every attentive man almoft as foon as propofed. To what then can we attribute the fmall progrefs made in the fciences by a young man ? To two caufes :

The one is, the want of method in the inftructors ;

The other, the want of ardour and attention in the pupil.

42. (p. 225.) The perpetual metamorphofes of genius into fcience has often made me fufpect that all things in nature, of themfelves, prepare and lead to it. Perhaps the perfection of arts and fciences is lefs the work of genius than of time and ne-ceffity. The uniform progrefs of the fciences in all countries confirm this opinion. In fact, if in all nations, as Mr. Hume obferves, *it is not till after having wrote well in verfe, that they come to write well in profe*, fo conftant a progrefs of human rea-fon appears to me the effect of a general fecret caufe : it at leaft fuppofes an equal aptitude to underftanding in all men of all ages and countries.

43. (p. 228.) Since men converfe and difpute with each other, they muft feel themfelves endowed with the faculty of

perceiving

perceiving the fame truths, and confequently an equal aptitude to underftanding. Without this conviction, what could
be more abfurd than the difputes of politicians and philofophers ? To what end fhould they talk when they cannot underftand each other ? But fince they do, it is evident that the
obfcurity of a propofition is never in the things, but in the
words. So that on this fubject one of the moft illuftrious
Englifh writers fays, that if men were agreed about the fignification of words, they would prefently perceive the fame truths,
and all adopt the fame opinions. See Hume on Liberty and
Neceffity, Sect. 8.

This fact, proved by experience, gives the folution to a
problem propofed five or fix years fince by the Academy of
Berlin, which was, *If the truths of metaphyfics in general, and the
firft principles of natural theology and morality, are fufceptible of the
fame evidence as the truths of geometry.* Annex a clear idea to
the word *probity*, and regard it with me as *the practice of actions
ufeful to our country.* What is then to be done to determine
demonftratively what actions are virtuous, and what vicious ?
Name thofe that are ufeful or prejudicial to fociety. Now in
general nothing is more eafy. It is therefore certain, if the
public good be the object of morality, that its precepts being
founded on principles as certain as thofe of geometry, are like
the propofitions of that fcience, fufceptible of the moft rigorous
demonftration. It is the fame of metaphyfics ; which is a real
fcience, when diftinguifhed from that of the fchools, it is kept
within the bounds affigned it by the definition of the illuftrious
Bacon.

SECTION III.

Of the general caufes of the inequality of
underftandings.

C H A P. I.

What thefe caufes are?

THEY are reducible to two.
The one is the different feries of events,
circumftances, and fituations that attend different men ; (feries to which I give the name of
chance.)

The other is the defire more or lefs earneft
that they have to inftruct themfelves.

Chance is not favourable to all, in precifely
the fame degree ; and yet it has more fhare than
is imagined in the difcoveries with which we honour genius.   To know all the influence of
chance let us confult experience, which will teach
us that in the arts it is to chance we owe almoft
all our difcoveries.

In chemiftry it is to the procefs in the grand
work that the adepts* owe moft of their fecrets ;
thefe fecrets were not the objects of their fearch ;

---

* Some adepts have fearched for the philofopher's ftone in
Genefis : the ecclefiaftics alone have found it there.

they

they ought not therefore to be regarded as the product of genius. If what I fay of chemiftry be applied to the different forts of fciences, it will be found that in each of them chance has difcovered all. Our memory is the chemift's crucible. It is from the mixture of certain matters thrown into a crucible, without defign, that fometimes refult the moft unexpected and aftonifhing effects; and it is in like manner from the mixture of certain facts, without defign, in our memory, that ideas the moft original and moft fublime refult. All the fciences are equally fubject to the dominion of chance. Its influence is the fame over all, but does not difcover itfelf in a manner equally ftriking.

C H A P.   II.

Every new idea is the gift of chance.

A Truth that is entirely unknown cannot be the object of my meditation; it may be confidered as difcovered when I get a glimpfe of it. The firft furmife is here the ftroke of genius. But to what do I owe the firft furmife? Is it to my underftanding? No: it cannot employ itfelf in the fearch of a truth, of whofe exiftence it it has not even a conception. This furmife is therefore the effect of a word, a lecture, a converfation,

fation *, an accident; in fhort, fomething to which I give the name of chance. Now if we are indebted to chance for our firft furmifes, and confequently for our difcoveries, can we be affured that we do not alfo owe to it the means of extending and completing them ?

The fyren of Comus is the moft proper fubject to exemplify my ideas. If this fyren was for a long time fhewn at the fair †, without any one's gueffing at its mechanifm, it was becaufe chance did not place before the eyes of any one, the objects of comparifon from which the difcovery muft have proceeded. It was more favourable to Comus. But why is he not in France reckoned among men of great genius ? Becaufe his mechanifm is more curious than ufeful. If it were attended with a very extenfive advantage, no doubt but public gratitude would have placed Comus

---

* It is to the heat of converfation and difpute that we frequently owe the moft happy ideas. If thofe ideas once efcaped the memory, are no more reprefented, but loft without recovery; it is becaufe we can fcarce poffibly find ourfelves twice in precifely the fame concourfe of circumftances that gave them birth. Such ideas therefore ought to be regarded as the gifts of chance.

† The fair St. Germains at Paris : it was likewife exhibited by Comus in London a few years fince. The conftruction of this machine may be feen in the third volume of my Rational Recreations. Whatever utility might have attended this performance, it would certainly never have entitled Comus to the appellation of a man of genius, as it is evidently taken from the Onomatomantica Magnetica, defcribed by Kircher in his fecond book De Art. Magnet. printed at Cologn in 1643.

in

in the rank of the moſt illuſtrious men. He would have owed his diſcovery to chance, and the title of a man of genius to the importance of that diſcovery.

What follows from this inſtance ?

1. That every new idea is a gift of chance.

2. If there be ſure methods of forming men of learning and men of underſtanding, there are none for forming men of genius, and inventors. But whether we regard genius as a gift of nature or chance, is it not in either caſe the effect of a cauſe independent of ourſelves ? In this caſe, why re-gard as a matter of ſo much importance the greater or leſs perfection of education ? The rea-ſon is plain. If genius depend on the greater or leſs perfection of the ſenſes, as inſtruction cannot change the natural faculties of man, give hearing to the deaf, or ſpeech to the dumb *, education is abſolutely uſeleſs. On the contrary, if genius be in part the gift of chance, men, after aſſuring themſelves by repeated obſervations of the means employed by chance in forming great talents, may, by making uſe of nearly the ſame means, produce nearly the ſame effects, and immenſely in-creaſe thoſe great talents.

Suppoſe, to produce a man of genius, chance ſhould be combined in him with the love of glo-

* This is not univerſally true ; many dumb perſons have been taught to ſpeak very intelligibly.

ry: fuppofe again, that a man be born under a government that, far from honouring, degrades talents ; in this cafe it is evident that a man of genius muft be entirely the work of chance.

In fact, this man muft have either lived in the
world, and owed his love of glory to the efteem
that was paid to talents by the particular fociety
with which he was connected *, or he muft have
lived in retreat, and owed the fame love of glory
to the ftudy of hiftory, and the remembrance of
the honours anciently paid to virtue and talents ;
or laftly, to an ignorance of the contempt his
fellow-citizens have for each other.

Suppofe, on the contrary, that this man be born
in an age and under a form of government where
merit is honoured : on this hypothefis it is evident
that his love for glory, and his genius, will not be
the work of chance, but of the very conftitution
of the ftate, and confequently of his education, on
which the form of governments has always the
greateft influence.

If we confider underftanding and genius as
lefs the effects of organifation than chance (1),
it is certain, as I have already faid, that by obferving the means made ufe of by chance in forming great men, we might, according to this obfervation, model a plan of education that would, by

* There are fuch focieties among all nations, even the moft
ftupid, if they be civilized.

encreafing

increafing their number in a nation, vaftly retrench the power of this fame chance, and diminifh the immenfe fhare it now has in our inftruction.

Yet if it be always to unforefeen caufes or incidents that we owe the firft furmife, and confequently the difcovery of every new idea, chance, I agree, will ftill conftantly preferve a certain influence over our minds : but this influence has alfo its bounds.

C H A P. III.

Of the limits to be fet to the power of chance.

IF almoft all objects, confidered with attention, did not contain the feed of fome difcovery : if chance did not diftribute its gifts in a manner nearly equal, and did not offer to all, objects of comparifon, from whence new and great ideas may arife, the underftanding would be almoft entirely the gift of chance.

It would be to our education that we owed our knowledge, and to chance that we owed our underftanding, and each one would have more or lefs, according as chance had been more or lefs favourable to him. Now what does experience teach us concerning this matter? That the inequality of underftandings is lefs the effect of the too unequal diftribution of the gifts of chance,

S 2   than

than the indifference with which we receive
them.

The inequality of underftandings ought therefore to be regarded principally as the effect of the
different degree of attention, exerted in obferving
the refemblances and differences, the agreements
and difagreements between diverfe objects. Now
this inequality of attention is in us the neceffary
produce of the unequal force of our paffions.

There is no man animated with an ardent defire of glory that does not always diftinguifh himfelf, more or lefs, in the art or fcience he cultivates. It is true, that between two men equally
defirous of becoming illuftrious, it is chance
that by prefenting to one of them objects of comparifon from whence refult the moft fruitful ideas
and the moft important difcoveries, determines
his fuperiority. Chance, by the influence it always has over the choice of objects that offer
themfelves to us, will therefore always preferve
fome influence over our underftandings. When
we confine its power within thofe narrow limits,
we do all that is poffible. To what ever degree
of perfection the fcience of education may be
carried, we muft never expect to make men of
genius of all the habitants of a nation; all it
can do is to increafe them, and to make the greateft
part of them men of knowledge and difcernment,
and this is all that is within its power. It is fufficient to roufe the attention of a people, and encourage

courage them to cultivate a ſcience whoſe perfection will procure in general ſo much happineſs to humanity, and in particular ſo many advantages to the nations by whom it is cultivated.

A people to whom the public education gave genius to a certain number of citizens, and diſcernment to almoſt all, would be without doubt the firſt people in the univerſe. The only and ſure method to produce this effect is early to habituate children to the fatigue of attention.

The ſeeds of diſcoveries preſented to us by chance will remain barren, if attention do not render them fruitful. The ſcarcity of attention is the cauſe of that of genius. But what muſt be done to force men to application? Inſpire them with the paſſions of emulation, glory, and the love of truth. It is the unequal force of thoſe paſſions that we ought to regard in man as the cauſe of the great inequality of their underſtandings.

S 3 CHAP.

C H A P. IV.

*Of the second cause of the inequality of understand-
ings.*

ALMOST all men are without paffions,
without love of glory (2) : and far from exciting in them this defire, moft governments, by a
mean and falfe policy (3) endeavour on the contrary to extinguifh it ; therefore, indifferent to
glory, the people make little account of public
efteem, and little efforts to deferve it.

I fee among the greateft part of mankind none
but greedy men of commerce. If they fit out a
fhip, it is not with the hope to give their name to
fome new country. Solely fenfible to the love of
gain, all they fear is left their veffel fhould depart
from the frequented tracts ; now thofe tracts lead not
to difcoveries. If the fhip by chance, or a tempeft,
be carried to an unknown land, the pilot compelled to ftop there, makes no inquiry either concerning the country or the habitants ; he takes in
water, fets fail, and hurries to another coaft, to exchange his merchandize: returned at laft to his
own port, he unloads, fills the warehoufes of his
owners with commodities, but brings back no difcoveries,

There

There are but few fuch men as Columbus*.
They who now launch forth on the vaft ocean
are folely anxious for honours, employments,
wealth, and power: few embark to make difcoveries of new fcience. How then can we wonder that fuch difcoveries are rare ?

Truths are fown by the hand of Heaven, here
and there, in an obfcure and pathlefs foreft; a
road bounds that foreft ; it is frequented by an infinity of travellers, among whom are fome curious
men, whom even the thicknefs and obfcurity of
the wood infpires with a defire to penetrate it.
They enter, but embarraffed by the trees, and
torn by the briars, they are difgufted with the entrance, abandon the enterprize, and regain the
beaten path. Others, but their number is fmall,
animated, not by a vague curiofity, but an ardent
and conftant defire of glory, pierce into the thick-
eft part of the foreft, pafs the dangerous bogs,
nor ceafe their courfe till chance prefents them
with the difcovery of fome truth, more or lefs
important. That difcovery made, they turn their
fteps, and make a path from that truth to the
high road, which every traveller then perceives as
he paffes by, becaufe all that have eyes may fee

* It would have been much for the honour of Spain, and much
for the intereft of humanity, if fuch a man as Columbus had never
exifted. What did Spain get by his difcovery? Wealth: and
what did it lofe? Every title to juftice and humanity ; and entailed
a horrid, deteftable, indelible difgrace on the name of Spaniard and
Chriftian.

it ;

it ; and nothing is wanting to the difcovery but an earneft defire to fearch it out, and the patience ne-ceffary to find it.

Does a man, anxious for a great name, fet him-felf in the purfuit of an important truth ? He fhould arm himfelf with the patience of a hunter. It is the fame with the philofopher as with the Indian : the leaft movement of the latter feparates him from his game, and the leaft inattention of the former carries him away from the truth. · Now nothing is more painful than to keep the body or the mind for a long time in the fame immo-bility or attention : it is the confequence of a ftrong paffion. In the Indian it is the neceffity of eating, in the philofopher the defire of glory, that produces this effect.

But what is this defire of glory ? Even the de-fire of pleafure. So that in every country where glory ceafes to be the reprefentative of pleafure, the citizen is indifferent to glory, and the country is fterile in men of genius and difcoveries. There is no nation however that does not from time to time produce illuftrious men ; becaufe there is none where fome individual is not to be found, who, ftruck, as I have faid, with the eulogies lavifhed in hiftory on talents, does not defire to merit the fame applaufe, and does not fet himfelf for that purpofe in fearch of fome new truth. If he obtain the object of his inquiry, and accomplifh his difcovery, he is elated with the acquifition, and

and carries it about his country in triumph. But what is his furprize, when, from the indifference with which mankind receive it, he finds at length the little confequence with which they regard it.

Then convinced, that in exchange for the labour and anxiety the fearch of truth demands, he fhall receive but little renown, and much perfecution, his courage fails; he becomes difgufted, no longer purfues new difcoveries, but delivers himfelf up to indolence, and ftops fhort in the midft of his career.

Our attention is fugitive: ftrong paffions are neceffary to keep it fixed. A man for amufement will calculate a page of figures, but he will not calculate a volume, unlefs urged to it by the powerful motive of glory or wealth. Thofe are the paffions that put in action that equal aptitude men have to underftanding: without them that aptitude is in us no more than a lifelefs power.

What, once more, is the underftanding or judgment? The knowledge of the true relations that a certain number of objects have to each other, and to ourfelves. To what do we owe this knowledge? To meditation and the comparifon of objects? But what does this comparifon fuppofe? An intereft, more or lefs ardent, to compare them. The underftanding is therefore in us the produce of that intereft, and not of the greater or lefs perfection of the fenfes.

But,

But, it will be faid, if the ftrength of our conftitution determines that of our defires ; if man
owes his genius to his paffions, and his paffions to
his temperament, on this fuppofition, genius will
ftill be in us the effect of organifation, and confequently the gift of nature.

It is to the difcuffion of this point that this important queftion is now reduced : it is on the examination of this fact that its complete folution
depends.

N O T E S.

N O T E S.

1. (page 258.) I Have known the ſtupidity and wickedneſs of theologians : every thing is to be feared from them. I am therefore forced to renew, from time to time, the ſame profeſſion of faith, and to repeat that I do not conſider chance as a being ; that I do not make a God of it ; and that by this word I only mean, *a ſeries of effects, of which we do not perceive the cauſes.* It is in this ſenſe that they ſay of chance, *it determines the dice* ; yet all the world knows, that the manner of ſhaking the box and throwing the dice is the cauſe that 3 turns up and not 6.

2. (p. 262.) Let thoughtleſs men declaim inceſſantly againſt the paſſions. We learn however from experience that there is no great artiſt, nor great general, nor great miniſter, nor great poet or philoſopher without them. Philoſophy, as the etymology of the word proves, conſiſts in the love and ſearch after wiſdom. Now all love is a paſſion : it is therefore the paſſions that have ſupported in their labours, Newton, Locke, Bayle, &c, Their diſcoveries were the price of their meditations. Theſe diſcoveries ſuppoſe a lively, conſtant, aſſiduous purſuit of the truth, and that purſuit a paſſion.

He is not a philoſopher who, indifferent to truth or falſehood, delivers himſelf up to that apathy, to that pretended philoſophical repoſe, which holds the mind in a ſtate of inſenſibility, and retards its progreſs toward the truth. That this ſtate is eaſy, free from envy and the fury of bigots, and conſequently that the ſlothful may call himſelf prudent, I allow, but not that he call himſelf a philoſopher. What company is moſt dangerous to youth ? That of thoſe prudent and diſcreet men; and who are the more ſure to ſtifle in youth every kind of emulation, as they point out to him in ignorance a ſecurity from perſecution, and conſequently the happineſs of inaction.

Among the apoſtles of idleneſs there are ſometimes men of much underſtanding ; but theſe are they who owe their indolence to the diſguſts and chagrin met with in their ſearch after truth. The greateſt part of the reſt are men of mediocrity,

who

who would have all men be the fame. It is envy that makes them preach up idlenefs.

What is to be done to efcape the feduction of their reafoning ? Sufpect its fincerity. Remember that an intereft, either mean or noble, always makes men argue : that all fuperiority of underftanding is difguftful to him who difdains glory, and wraps himfelf up in what is called a philofophical indolence ; and that fuch a man has always an intereft in ftifling in the hearts of others an emulation that would give him too many fuperiors.

3. (p 262.) The aim of the greateft part of defpotic princes is to reign over flaves, and to change each man into an automaton. Thefe defpots, feduced by the intereft of the prefent moment, forget that the imbecillity of the fubjects announces the fall of monarchs ; that it is deftructive to their empire, and in fhort, that it is on the whole more eafy to govern an enligtened people, than fuch as are ftupid.

SECTION IV.

Men commonly well organifed are all fufceptible of the fame degree of paffion :
the inequality of their capacities is always
the effect of the difference of fituation in
which chance has placed them. The original character of each man, (as Pafcal has
obferved), is nothing but the produce of
his firft habits.

C H A P. I.

Of the little influence organifation and temperament
have on the paffions and characters of men.

AT the moment the child is delivered from the
womb of its mother, and opens the gates
of life, he enters it without ideas and without
paffions. The only want he feels is that of hunger. It is not therefore in the cradle that we receive the paffions of pride, avarice, ambition, the
defire of efteem and of glory. Thofe factitious
paffions *, generated in the bofoms of towns and

---

* In Europe, to the number of factitious paffions we may add
jealoufy. Men are there jealous becaufe they are vain. Vanity makes a part of almoft all the principal European amours :
it is not fo in Afia ; jealoufy is there the mere effect of corporeal pleafures. It is known by experience, that the more the
defires of the fultanas are reftrained, the more ardent they be-

cities, fuppofe conventions and laws already
eftablifhed among men, and confequently their
union in fociety.   Such paffions would be therefore unknown to him that was borne by a tempeft
at the moment of his birth to a defert coaft, and
like Romulus nourifhed by a wolf; and to him
whom fome fairy ftole in the night from his cradle,
and placed in one of thofe folitary enchanted
caftles where formerly dwelt fo many knights and
princeffes.   Now if we are born without paffions,
we are alfo born without character.   The love of
glory produced in us, is an acquifition, and confequently the effect of inftruction.   But does not
nature endow us, in the moft early infancy, with
the fort of organifation proper to form in us
fuch or fuch a character? On what is this conjecture founded? Has it been remarked that a certain difpofition in the nerves, the fluids, or
mufcles, conftantly produces the fame manner of
thinking ; that nature retrenches certain fibres of
the brain from one, to give them to another ; and
confequently always infpires the latter with a
lively defire of glory? On the fuppofition that
characters are the effect of organifation, what can
education do? Can the moral change the corporeal difpofition? Can the moft juft maxim give

come, and the more pleafure they give and receive. Jealoufy,
daughter of the luxury of fultans and vifirs, makes them build
feraglios, and confine their women.

hearing

hearing to the dumb? Can the moſt ſagacious leſſons of a preceptor level the back of him that is crooked, or ſtraighten the leg of the cripple, or encreaſe the ſtature of a pigmy? What nature has done, ſhe alone can undo.   The only ſentiment that is engraved in our hearts in infancy is the love of ourſelves : this love, founded on cor· poreal ſenſibility, is common to all men ; therefore however different their education may be, this ſentiment is always the ſame in them ; ſo that in all countries, and at all times, men have loved, do love, and will love themſelves in preference to all others. If a man be variable in all other ſentiments, it is becauſe all others are the effect of moral cauſes. Now if theſe cauſes be variable, their effects muſt be ſo likewiſe.   To eſtabliſh this truth by experience at large, I ſhall firſt conſult the hiſtory of nations.

C H A P.

CHAP. II.

Of the alterations that have happened in the cha-
racters of nations, and of the causes by which
they were produced.

EACH nation has its particular manner of
seeing and feeling, which forms its character: and in every nation its character either
changes on a sudden, or alters by degrees, according to the sudden or insensible alterations in
the form of its government, and consequently of
its public education*.

That of the French, which has been for a
long time regarded as gay, was not always so.
The emperor Julian says of the Parisians, "I
"like them, because their character, like mine, is
"austere and serious (1)."

The characters of nations therefore change:
but at what period is the alteration most perceptible? At the moment of revolution, when a people pass on a sudden from liberty to slavery.
Then from bold and haughty they become weak
and pusillanimous: they dare not look on the man
in office: they are inthralled, and it is of little
consequence by whom they are inthralled. This
dejected people say, like the ass in the fable,

---

* The form of government under which we live always
makes a part of our education.

whoever

whoever be my master, I cannot carry a heavier load.
As much as a free citizen is zealous for the glory
of his nation, so much is a slave indifferent to the
public welfare. His heart, deprived of activity
and energy, is without virtue, without spirit, and
without talents ; the faculties of his soul are stupified ; he becomes indifferent to the arts, commerce, agriculture, &c. It is not for servile
hands, say the English, to till and fertilise the
land. Simonides entered the empire of a despotic
sovereign, and found there no traces of men. A
free people are courageous, open, humane, and
loyal (2). A nation of slaves are base, perfidious,
malicious, and barbarous : they push their cruelty
to the greatest excess. If the severe officer has all
to fear from the resentment of the injured soldier
oh the day of battle, that of sedition is in like manner for the slave oppressed, the long expected day
of vengeance ; and he is the more enraged in proportion as fear has held his fury the longer re-
strained *.

What a striking picture of a sudden change in
the character of a nation does the Roman history
present us. What people, before the elevation of
the Cæsars, shewed more force, more virtue, more
love for liberty, and horror for slavery ? And
what people, when the throne of the Cæsars was

* The deposition of Nabob-Jaffier-Ali-Kan, related in the
Leyden Gazette of the 23d of June, 1761, is a proof of this.

established,

eſtabliſhed, ſhewed more weakneſs and depravity? (3) Their baſeneſs diſguſted Tiberius.

Indifferent to liberty, when Trajan offered it,
they refuſed it : they diſdained that liberty their
anceſtors had purchaſed with ſo much blood.
All things were then changed in Rome ; and that
determined and grave character which diſtinguiſhed
its firſt inhabitants, was ſuccéeded by that light
and frivolous diſpoſition with which Juvenal reproaches them in his tenth ſatire.

Let us exemplify this matter by a more recent
change.   Compare the Engliſh of the preſent day
with thoſe under Henry VIII. Edward VI. Mary,
and Elizabeth : this people now ſo humane,
indulgent, learned, free, and induſtrious, ſuch
lovers of the arts and of philoſophy, were then
nothing more than a nation of ſlaves, inhuman
and ſuperſtitious ; without arts and without induſtry.

When a prince uſurps over his people a bound-
leſs authority, he is ſure to change their character,
to enervate their ſouls ; to render them timid and
baſe (4).   From that moment, indifferent to
glory, his ſubjects loſe that character of boldneſs
and conſtancy proper to ſupport all labours and
brave all dangers : the weight of arbitrary power
deſtroys the ſpring of their emulation.

Does a prince, impatient of contradiction (5),
give the name of factious to the man of veracity ?
He ſubſtitutes in his nation the character of falſity
for

for that of franknefs. If in thofe critical moments the prince, giving himfelf up to flatterers, find that he is furrounded by men void of all merit, whom fhould he blame? Himfelf: for it is he that has made them fuch.

Who could believe, when he confiders the evils of fervitude, that there were ftill princes mean enough to wifh to reign over flaves; and ftupid enough to be ignorant of the fatal changes that defpotifm produces in the character of their fubjects?

What is arbitrary power? The feed of calamities, that fown in the bofom of a ftate fprings up to bear the fruit of mifery and devaftation. Let us hear the king of Pruffia: *Nothing is better*, faid he, in a difcourfe pronounced to the academy of Berlin, *than an arbitrary government, under princes juft, humane, and virtuous: nothing worfe, under the common race of kings.* Now how many kings are there of the latter fort! and how many fuch as Titus, Trajan, and Antoninus? Thefe are the thoughts of a great man. What elevation of mind, what knowledge does not fuch a declaration fuppofe in a monarch? What in fact does a defpotic power announce? Often ruin to the defpot, and always to his pofterity (6). The founder of fuch a power, fets his kingdom on a fandy foundation. It is only a tranfient, ill-judged notion of royalty, that is, of pride, idlenefs, or fome fimilar paffion, which prefers

T 2

the

the exercife of an unjuft and cruel defpotifm over wretched flaves, to that of a legitimate and friendly power (7), over a free and
happy people.   Arbitrary power is a thoughtlefs
child, who continually facrifices the future to the
prefent.

The moft redoubtable enemy of the public welfare, is not riot or fedition, but defpotifm (8) : it
changes the character of a nation, and always for
the worfe : it produces nothing but vices. Whatever might be the power of an Indian fultan, he
could never form magnanimous fubjects ; he
would never find among his flaves the virtues of
free men.   Chymiftry can extract no more
gold from a mixed body than it includes ; and
the moft arbitrary power can draw nothing from
a flave but the bafenefs he contains.

Experience then proves that the character and
fpirit of a people change with the form of government ; and that a different government gives by
turns, to the fame nation, a character noble or bafe,
firm or fickle, courageous or cowardly.   Men
therefore are endowed at their birth, either with no
difpofition, or with difpofitions to all vices and all
virtues ; they are therefore nothing more than the
produce of their education.   If the Perfian have
no idea of liberty, and the favage no idea of fervitude, it is the effect of their different inftruction.

Why, fay ftrangers, do we we perceive at once,
in all the French, the fame fpirit, and the fame character,

racter, like the fame phyfiognomy in all Negroes ?
Becaufe the French do not judge or think for
themfelves (9), but after the people in power.
Their manner, of judging for this reafon muft
be fufficiently uniform. It is with Frenchmen as
with their wives : when they paint themfelves, and
go to a public fhow, they all feem of the fame
complexion. I know that with attention we can
always difcover between the charaters and underftandings of individuals ; but to do this requires
time.

The ignorance of the French, the iniquity of
their police, and the influence of their clergy, render them in general more like each other than
men of other countries. Now if fuch be the influence of the form of government on the manners and charater of a people, what alteration in
the ideas and charaters of individuals ought not
to be produced by the alterations that happen in
their fortune and fituation !

CHAP. III.

*Of the alterations that happen in the characters of in-
dividuals.*

THAT which occurs in a great and ftriking manner in nations, occurs in little,
and in a manner lefs fenfible, in individuals. Almoft every change in their fituation produces one
in their charaéters*. A man is fevere, peevifh, im-
perious; menaces and torments his flaves, his children and domeftics. He lofes himfelf by chance in a
foreft, and when night comes on, retires to a cavern, where he perceives a lion is couching.
Does this man preferve his morofe and quarrel-
fome temper? No: he creeps with the utmoft
caution into a corner of the den, left by the fmall-
eft noife he fhould roufe the fury of the beaft.

From the den of the natural lion let us tranfport him to the cavern of a moral lion: let us
place him in the fervice of a cruel and defpotic
tyrant: mild and moderate in the prefence of his
mafter, perhaps this man will become the moft

---

* *Manners with fortunes, humours turn with climes,*
Tenets with books, and principles with times.
Afk mens opinions: Scoto now fhall tell
How trade increafes, and the world goes well;
Strike off his penfion, by the fetting fun,
And Britain, if not Europe, is undone.

POPE.

mean

mean and cringing of all his flaves. But it will be faid, his character is conftrained, not altered: it is a tree that is bent by force, and whofe natural elafticity will foon reftore it to its former figure. But can it be imagined, that after a tree has been for fome years bent into a particular figure, it will ever return to its original form ? Whoever fays that men do not eafily change their characters by conftraint, only fays that habits long eftablifhed are not to be deftroyed in an inftant.

The man of ill humour preferves his character, becaufe he has always fome inferior on whom he can exercife his ill nature. But let him be kept a long time in the prefence of a lion or a tyrant, and there is no doubt but a continued reftraint, transformed into a habit, will foften his character. In general, as long as we are young enough to contract new habits, the fole incurable faults, and vices, are thofe we cannot correct without employing means of which morals, laws, or cuftoms do not allow the practice. There is nothing impoffible to education : it makes the bear dance.

If we reflect on this fubject, we perceive that our firft nature, as Pafcal and experience prove, is nothing elfe than our firft habit *.

---

* If the author of Emilius has denied this maxim, it is be-caufe he did not rightly comprehend the fenfe of Pafcal.

T 4 Man

Man is born without ideas and without paffions, but he is born an imitator and docile to example ; confequently it is to inftruction he owes his habits and his character. Now I afk, why habits contracted during a certain time, cannot at length be effaced by contrary habits. How many people do we fee change their character with their rank, according to the different place they occupy at court, and in the miniftry ; in fhort, according to the change that happens in their fituation. Why does the robber, when tranfported from England to America, frequently become honeft ? Becaufe he becomes a man of property, and has land to cultivate ; in fhort, becaufe his fituation is changed.

The officer in the camp is void of compaffion ; accuftomed to the fight of blood, he beholds it unmoved. But when he returns to London, Paris, or Berlin, he returns to the feelings of humanity. Why fhould we regard each character as the effect of a particular organifation, when we cannot determine what that organifation is ? Why fearch in occult qualities for the caufe of a moral phenomenon, which the developement of the paffion of felf-love fo clearly and readily explains?

C H A P.

C H A P. IV.

Of self-love.

MAN is fenfible of bodily pleafure and pain, confequently he flies from the one, and purfues the other ; and it is to this conftant pur-fuit and flight that is given the name of felf-love.

This fentiment, the immediate effect of corpo-real fenfibility, and confequently common to all, is infeparable from man. As a proof I offer its permanence, impoffibility of deftruction, or even alteration. Of all our fentiments it is the only one that has thefe properties : it is to this we owe all our defires, and all our paffions ; which are nothing more in us than the application of felf-love to particular objects *.

It is therefore to this fentiment, diverfly modi-fied according to the education we receive, the government under which we live, and the different fituations in which we are placed, that we are to

---

* *Modes of felf-love the paffions we may call ;*
'Tis real good, or feeming, moves them all:
But fince not ev'ry good we can divide,
And reafon bids us for our own provide ;
Paffions, tho' felfifh, if their means be fair,
Lift under reafon, and deferve her care.

POPE.

attri-

attribute the amafing difference in the paffions and characters of men.

Self-love makes us totally what we are. Why are we fo covetous of honours and dignities? Becaufe we love ourfelves, and defire our own happinefs, and confequently the power of procuring it. The love of power, and the means of procuring it, is therefore neceffarily connected in man with the love of himfelf (10). Every one would command, becaufe every one would increafe his felicity, and engage all his fellow-citizens to promote it. Now among all the methods to engage them, the moft certain is power or force. The love of power, founded on that of happinefs, is therefore the common object of all our defires (11). Thus riches, honour, glory, envy, importance, juftice, virtue, intolerance, in a word, all the factitious paffions* are in us nothing but the love of power, difguifed under thofe different names.

Power is the only object of man's purfuit. To prove this, I fhall fhew that all the paffions above recited are in us properly nothing more than the love of power ; and I conclude from this love being common to all, that all are fufceptible of the defire of efteem and glory, and confequently of the fort of paffion proper to put in action the equal

---

* All our paffions are factitious, except corporeal wants, pains, and pleafures.

aptitude

aptitude that men, organifed in the common manner, have to underftanding.

C H A P. V.

Of the love of riches and glory.

AT the head of the cardinal virtues are placed
force or power: it is the virtue moft, and
perhaps the only one really, efteemed. The portion of weaknefs is contempt.

From whence arifes our difdain of the Oriental
nations, fome of whom are equal to us in induftry,
as is apparent from the fabric of their ftuffs ; and
feveral of whom furpafs us perhaps in the focial
virtues ? Do we defpife them merely for the meannefs with which they bear the cruel and fhameful
yoke of tyrannical power ? Such a contempt would
be juft : but no ; we defpife them as enervate and
not practifed in arms. It is therefore force that we
refpect (12), and weaknefs that we defpife. The
love of power however is common to all * ; all defire it ; but all do not, like Cæfar and Cromwell,
afpire to fupreme power : few men can conceive
the defign, and ftill fewer are able to execute it.

* The man without defire, who thinks himfelf perfectly
happy, muft be, without doubt, infenfible to the love of
power. Are there men of this fort ? Yes : but their number
is too fmall to deferve regard.

The

The fort of power generally defired is that eafily attained. Every one may become rich, and every one defires wealth : for by that we can gratify all our appetites, fuccour the afflicted, and oblige, confequently command, a boundlefs number of individuals *.

Glory, like riches, procures power ; and we in like manner purfue it. Glory is acquired either by arms or eloquence. We know in what efteem eloquence was held at Rome and in Greece ; it there conducted men to grandeur and power. *Magna vis & magnum nomen*, fays Cicero, *funt unum et idem*. Among thofe people a great name gave great power. The renowned orator commanded a number of clients. Now in every republic, whoever is followed by a croud of clients is always a powerful citizen. The Hercules of the Gauls, from whofe mouth there iffued an infinity of gold threads, was the emblem of the moral force of eloquence. But why is that eloquence, formerly fo refpected, no longer honoured and cultivated, except in England ? Becaufe it is no where elfe the road to honours.

---

* *What nature wants, commodious gold beflows,*
'Tis thus we eat the bread another fows.
Ufeful, I grant, it ferves what life requires,
But dreadful too, the dark affaffin hires :
Trade it may help, fociety extend ;
But lures the pirate, and corrupts the friend.
It raifes armies in a nation's aid ;
But bribes a fenate, and the land's betray'd.
                                        POPE.

The

The love of glory, of esteem, and importance is therefore properly nothing more than a disguised love of power.

Glory, they say, is the mistress of almost all great men : they pursue her through all dangers ; to obtain her they brave the labours of war, the fatigue of study, and the resentment of a thousand rivals (13). That is, in countries where glory gives power ; where it is nothing more than an empty title, where merit has no real importance, the citizen, indifferent about public fame, will make few efforts to obtain it. Why is glory regarded as a plant of a republican soil, that degenerating in a despotic country, never thrives with remarkable vigour ? Because in glory we in reality seek nothing but power, and under an arbitrary government all power vanishes before that of the despot. The man who there passes the night under arms, or in his study, thinks that he is animated by a desire of public esteem : but he deceives himself. Esteem is only the name he gives to the object of his pursuit ; power is the thing itself.

From hence I observe, that the splendor and power with which glory is sometimes surrounded, and that renders it so dear to us, must also frequently render us odious to our fellow-citizens, and from hence proceeds envy.

CHAP.

CHAP. VI.

Of envy.

MERIT, says Pope, produces envy, as the body produces the shadow. Envy infers merit as smoke does fire. Envy, exasperated by merit, respects no place or dignity, not even the throne: it equally pursues a Voltaire, a Catinat, and a Frederic. If we were frequently to recollect how far its fury extends, perhaps, terrified by the persecutions that attend the steps of a man of great talents, we should not have courage to acquire them.

The man of genius who says to himself, while seated by his lamp, this night my work will be finished: to-morrow is the day of recompence. to-morrow the grateful public shall acknowledge the obligation it owes me: to-morrow I shall obtain the crown of immortality. This man forgets the power of envy. To-morrow arrives: the work is published: it is a finished work: the public however does not acknowledge its obligation. Envy drives far from the author the sweet perfume of eulogy *, and in its stead substitutes the

---

* Of all the passions envy is the most detestable ; the portrait drawn of it, by I know not what poet, is horrible.

Compassion, says he, is softened by the misfortunes of men ; envy rejoices in their tortures.

There

ſtench of a malignant criticiſm and injurious calumny. The ſun of glory ſcarce ever ſhines but
on the tomb of a great man. He that deſerves
eſteem ſeldom enjoys it ; and he that plants the
laurel rarely repoſes under its ſhadow *.

But does envy dwell in every heart? There is none
that is not at leaſt penetrated by it. How many great
men are there that cannot ſuffer competitors, that
will not admit a partition of eſteem with any of their
brethren; and forget, that at the banquet of glory,
every one ſhould have, if I may ſo ſay, his portion ?

Even the moſt noble ſouls ſometimes lend an
ear to envy ; they reſiſt its aſperſions, but not without difficulty. Nature has made man envious : to
deſire an alteration in this reſpect, is to deſire he
would ceaſe to love himſelf, that is, to deſire an
impoſſibility. Let not the legiſlature therefore

There is no paſſion that does not propoſe ſome pleaſure for
its object ; the ſole object of envy is the miſeries of others.

Merit contemns the proſperity of the wicked and the ſtupid ; envy, that of the good and learned.

Love and wrath, lighted in the heart, there burn for an
hour, a day, a year ; envy gnaws it to the laſt moment of exiſtence.

Under the banner of envy march hatred, calumny, cabal,
and treachery.

Envy is every where attended by meagre famine ; the ve-
nom of peſtilence, and the devaſtation of war.

* If great writers become the preceptors of mankind after
their death, it muſt be confeſſed, that while they live, the preceptors are ſufficiently chaſtiſed by their pupils.

attempt

attempt to filence jealoufy, but to render its rage impotent, and eftablifh, as in England, laws proper to protect merit againft the refentment of a minifter, and the fanaticifm of a prieft. This is all that fagacity can do in favour of talents. To pretend to more, and flatter ourfelves with annihilating envy, is folly. All ages have declaimed againft this vice : what have their declamations produced ? Nothing. Envy ftill exifts, and has loft nothing of its force, becaufe nothing can change the nature of man.

There is a time however when envy is not felt; and that time is in early youth. Do we propofe to furpafs, or at leaft to equal the merit of men already honoured with public applaufe ; do we afpire to a participation of the applaufe that is decreed them? Then, full of refpect, their prefence excites our emulation; we extol them with tranfport ; becaufe we have an intereft in praifing them, in habituating the public to refpect in them our future talents. Praife is therefore a tribute that youth freely pays to merit, and that is conftantly refufed it by maturer age.

At thirty years the emulation of twenty is changed into envy. When we lofe the hope of equalling thofe we admire, admiration gives place to hatred. The refource of pride is the contempt of talents. The defire of the man of mediocrity is to have no fuperiors. How many envious men repeat foftly after a comic writer,

.

Je

Je t'aime d'autant plus que je l'efteme moins.

The lefs I efteem thee I love thee the more.

If we cannot ftifle the reputation of a celebrated man, we at leaft expect from him the moft fub-miffive modefty. The envious have reproached M. Diderot even with the firft words of his Interpretation of Nature : *Young man, take this and read.* They were not formerly fo difficult: the counfellor Dumoulin faid of himfelf ; *I that have no equal, and am fuperior to all the world.* The many humiliating circumftances now required of authors fuppofes a remarkable increafe of pride in readers ; fuch a pride declares a hatred of merit ; and that hatred is natural. In fact, if anxious for happinefs men court power, and confequently the glory and importance it procures, they muft deteft what in a man too illuftrious deprives them of it. Why do they circulate fo many bad reports of men of genius ? Becaufe they find themfelves inwardly conftrained to think well of them. When they draw for a twelfth-cake, there is a part fet afide for God ; and when they examine the merit of a man of eminence, they always find fome defect: that is the portion of envy.

When a man cannot raife himfelf above the rank of his fellow-citizens, he endeavours to bring them down to him. He who cannot be their fuperior, would at leaft be their equal * (14). Such is man, and such he always will be.

Among virtuous characters, and the most above gross envy, perhaps there is no one not stained with a slight blemish of it. Who in fact can boast of having always heartily commended genius? With having never dissembled his esteem? With having never held a culpable silence, and with praises given to talents not having added one of those perfiduous *buts*, that jealousy so frequently forces from us †.

Every great talent is in general an object of hatred, and from hence that eagerness with which we purchase those pamphlets that lash them so furiously. Why else do we read them? It cannot be a desire to improve our taste (15); for those writers do not pretend to the abilities of a Longinus or Despreaux; not even to enlighten the public. Let him who cannot compose a good work never

* *I have no title to aspire,*
Yet when you sink I seem the higher:
In Pope I cannot read a line,
But with a sigh I wish it mine;
When he can in one couplet fix
More sense than I can do in six,
It gives me such a jealous fit,
I cry, pox take him and his wit!

SWIFT.

† How many men extol the ancients above the moderns, merely that they may not be forced to acknowledge they have among themselves such men as Locke, Seneca, Virgil, &c.

pretend

pretend to amuse himself with criticising those of others.

The impotency of producing any thing good makes a critic ; his profession is humble. If such writers as Desfontaine please, it is as consolators of the stupid *. The bitterness of satire is the proof of genius.

To blame with rancour is the praise of envy. It is the first eulogy an author receives, and the only one he can draw from his rivals. Men applaud with regret : it is themselves only they would find praise worthy. There is scarce any man who cannot persuade himself of his own merit : has he common sense ? he prefers it to genius : has he some diminutive virtues ? he gives them the preference to great talents. We despise all that is not self. There is but one man who can believe himself free from envy ; and it is he that has never examined his own heart.

The protectors and panegyrists of genius are youth (16), and some few learned and virtuous men. But their impotent protection (17) can give a writer neither credit nor consideration. Yet, what is the common nourishments of talents and virtue ? Consideration and eulogy. Deprived of this subsistence, they both languish and die :

---

* Racine and Pradon, each wrote a Phedra. The Desfontains of the age rose against Racine, and their criticisms were applauded : they discharged the sots, for some time, from the insupportable burden of esteem.

the

the activity and energy of the foul is extinguish-ed; as the flame goes out that has nothing to nourish it.

In almost all governments, talents, like the prisoners of the Romans, condemned and given up to wild beasts, become their prey. Is genius despised at court? Envy does the rest, (18) it destroys the very seed of genius. When merit is continually obliged to strive with envy, it becomes fatigued, and quits the ground, if there be no prize ordained for the conqueror. We love neither study nor glory for themselves; but for the pleasures, esteem, and power they procure. Why? Because in general, we are less desirous of being estimable than esteemed. Most writers, anxious only for the glory of the present moment (19), and to flatter the taste of their age and nation (20), present them with nothing but ideas adapted to the present day, and such as are agreeable to men in power, from whom they can expect money and consideration, together with an ephemeral success.

There are men, however, who disdain the glory of a moment; who, transporting their imaginations into futurity, and enjoying in advance the eulogies and respect of posterity, fear to survive their reputation (21). This motive alone makes them sacrifice the glory and consideration of the present moment, to the hope of, sometimes a distant, but greater glory and importance. These

men

men are rare: they defire the applaufe of none but worthy citizens.

What were the cenfures of the Sorbonne to Marmontel (22) ? He would have blufhed at their applaufe. A garland wove by ftupidity, cannot fit eafy on the head of a genius. It is like the new ornament with which they have in Languedoc crowned the fquare houfe. The traveller, as he paffes, fays, "Behold the hat of Harlequin on "the head of Cæfar."

Let it not be imagined, however, that the man moft folicitous for a durable reputation, loves glory and truth themfelves. If fuch be the nature of each individual, that he is neceffitated to love himfelf before all things, the love of truth muft be in him always fubordinate to the love of his happinefs. He can only love in the truth the means of increafing his own felicity. Therefore he will purfue neither glory nor truth in a country and under a government where they are both defpifed.

The refult of this and the preceding chapter, is, that the fury of envy, the defire of riches and talents, the love of importance, glory, and truth, are never in man any thing elfe than the love of power (23), difguifed under thofe different denominations.

U 3 CHAP.

CHAP. VII.

Of justice.

JUSTICE is the confervator of the life and liberty of the citizens. Each one defires to enjoy his feveral properties; each one therefore loves juftice in others, and would have them behave juftly toward him. But who is folicitous to be juft toward others? Do men love juftice for the fake of juftice, or for the confideration it procures? That is the object of my inquiry.

Man is fo often ignorant of himfelf: we perceive fo much contradiction between his conduct and his difcourfe*, that to know him we muft ftudy his actions and his nature itfelf.

---

* In morality, as in religion, there are a few fincere, and a great many hypocrites. A thoufand men adorn themfelves with fentiments not their own, and that they cannot have. When we compare their conduct with their difcourfe, we find none but knaves that would make dupes. We ought in general to miftruft the probity of thofe who pretend to extraordinary probity, and fet themfelves up for ancient Romans. There are who appear really virtuous at the moment the curtain is drawn up, and they are going to perform a great part on the theatre of the world. But behind the fcenes how many are there who preferve the fame character of equity, and are always juft?

What convinces me of the love the ancient Romans had for virtue, is the knowledge of their laws, and their manners; without this knowledge, the virtue of the modern Romans would

C H A P. VIII.

Of justice confidered in the man of nature.

TO judge of man, let us confider him in his primitive state, in that of a ferocious favage. Does the favage love and refpect equity? No: it is force he regards. He has no idea of equity in his heart, nor any word to exprefs it in his language. What idea can he form of it, and what in fact is injuftice? The violation of a convention or law made from the advantage of the majority. Injuftice, therefore, cannot precede the eftablifhment of a convention, a law, and a common intereft. Before law, there is no injuftice. *Si non effet lex, non effet peccatum.* Now what does the eftablifhment of laws fuppofe?

1ft. The union of men in a fociety, greater or lefs.

2d. The formation of a language proper to communicate a certain number of ideas *.

---

would make me fufpect that of the ancient, and I fhould fay with Cardinal Beffarion, on the fubject of miracles, *that the new make the old doubtful.*

The man juft, but intelligent, will not pretend to love juftice for itfelf. Is he without fault? We allow without blufhing, that in all our actions we never have any thing but our happinefs in view; but we always confound it with that of our fellow-citizens. Few place it fo happily.

* According to Mr. Locke, "A law is a rule prefcribed to "the people, with the fanction of fome punifhment or reward,

"proper

Now if there be favages whofe language does not contain above five or fix founds or cries, the formation of a language muft be the work of feveral centuries. Until that work be completed, men without convention and laws, muft live in a ftate of war.

This eftate, they will fay, is a ftate of mifery; and mifery being the creator of laws, muft force men to accept them. Yes; but till this acceptation, men are not the lefs unjuft for being miferable. How can they be faid to ufurp the field or orchard of the prefent poffeffor, and commit a robbery, when there is no property or partition of fields or orchards? Before the public intereft has declared the law of firft poffeffion to be held

---

"proper to determine their wills. All law, according to him, "fuppofe reward or punifhment attached to its obfervation or "infraction."

This definition laid down, the man who violates, among a polifhed people, a convention not attended with this fanction, is not punifhable: he is however unjuft. But could he be unjuft before the eftablifhment of all convention, and the formation of a language proper to exprefs injuftice? No: for in that ftate, man can have no idea of property, nor confequently of juftice.

What does experience teach us about this matter? Experience, to which, in morality as well as in phyfics, we muft fubmit the moft plaufible theories, and which alone can eftablifh their truth or falfity; experience tells us, that man has ideas of force before thofe of juftice; that, in general, he has no love for juftice; that even in polifhed nations, where they are continually talking of equity, no one regards it, unlefs he be forced by the fear of a power equal or fuperior to his own.

facred,

sacred, what can be the plea of a savage inhabitant of a woody district, from which a stronger savage had driven him out?

What right have you, he would say, to drive me from my possession?

What right have you, says the other, to that possession?

Chance, replies the first, led my steps thither: it belongs to me because I inhabit it, and land belongs to the first occupier.

What is that right of the first occupier (24)? replies the other; if chance first led you to this spot, the same chance has given me the force necessary to drive you from it. Which of these two rights deserves the preference? Would you know all the superiority of mine? Look up to heaven and see the eagle that darts upon the dove: turn thine eyes to the earth, and see the lion that preys upon the stag: look toward the sea, and behold the goldfish devoured by the shark. All things in nature show that the weak is a prey to the powerful. Force is the gift of the gods; by that I have a right to possess all that I can seize. Heaven, by giving me these nervous arms, has declared its will. Be gone from hence, yield to superior force, or dare the combat (25).

What answer can be given to the discourse of this savage, or with what injustice can he be accused, if the law of first occupation be not yet established?

Justice

Juſtice then ſuppoſes the eſtabliſhment of laws. The obſervance of juſtice ſuppoſes an equilibrium in the power of the inhabitants.   The maintain-ance of that equilibrium is the maſterpiece of the ſcience of legiſlation.   It is by a mutual and ſa-lutary fear that men are made to be juſt to each other.   When this fear is no longer reciprocal, then juſtice becomes a meritorious virtue, and then the legiſlation of a people is vicious.   Its perfec-tion ſuppoſes that man is compelled to juſtice.

Juſtice is unknown to the ſolitary ſavage.   If the poliſhed man have ſome idea of it, it is becauſe he knows the laws.   But does he love juſtice for itſelf?   It is experience that muſt inſtruct us in this matter.

C   H   A   P.   IX.

Of juſtice conſidered in poliſhed man and nations.

WHAT is the love man has for juſtice? To determine this queſtion, we muſt place him above all hope and fear: make him an oriental monarch.

When ſeated on his throne, he can levy on his people taxes without limits.   Ought he to do it? No.   The meaſure of all taxes is the wants of the ſtate.   Every tax, when puſhed beyond thoſe wants, is a robbery, an injuſtice.   No truth more evident than this. Yet, notwithſtanding man's pre-

I   tended

tended love for equity, there is no Afiatic monarch who does not commit this injuftice, and commit it without remorfe. What can we infer from this fact? That man's love for juftice is founded either on a fear of the evil attendants on iniquity, or from the hope of the good confequences of efteem, confideration, and, in fhort, from the power attached to the practice of juftice.

The neceffity we are under to form virtuous men, to reward and punifh, to inftitute wife laws, and to eftablifh a regular form of government, are fo many evident proofs of this truth.

Let what I have faid of man be applied to nations. Two nations are neighbours; they are, in certain refpects, in a reciprocal dependence: they are confequently forced to make conventions between them, and to form the law of nations. Do they regard it? Yes, fo long as they reciprocally fear each other, fo long as a certain balance of power fubfifts between them. When this balance is deftroyed, the ftrongeft nation violates their conventions without concern (26). It becomes unjuft, becaufe it can be fo with impunity.

The fo much boafted refpect in man for juftice, is never * any thing more than a refpect for power.

---

* *Perhaps there are many men, there are certainly fome, who on a clofe examination of their own hearts, cannot affent to this ftrong affertion of our author. Whether the real love of juftice in thefe men proceeds from principles ftrongly inculcated and long practifed, that is from education; or from an innate principle, is here immaterial.*

Yet

Yet there are no people who do not in war say justice is on our side. But when, and in what situation ? When surrounded by powerful nations, who may take part in their quarrels. What is then the object of their pretence ? To show their enemy to be unjust, ambitious, and dreadful : to excite the jealousy of other nations against them, and by making allies to become strong by the force of others. The object of a nation in such appeals to justice, is to increase its power, and to secure a superiority over a rival nation. The pretended love of nations for justice, is therefore nothing but a real love of power.

To confirm this truth, suppose the neighbours of two rival nations to be fully employed with their own affairs, and not able to take any part in the quarrel, what then happens ? The most powerful of the two nations, without any appeal to justice, or regard to equity, carries fire and sword into the country of its enemy. Force then becomes right: and miserable is the condition of the weak and conquered.

When Brennus at the head of the Gauls attacked the Clusians, " What offence, said the Ro-
" man ambassadors, have the Clusians given you ?"
Brennus laughed at the question. " Their of-
" fence, he replied, is the refusal they make to
" divide their country with me. It is the same
" offence that the people of Albi, the Fidenats
" and

" and Ardeats formerly gave you, and lately the
" Vienians, the Falifci, and the Volfci. To
" avenge yourfelves, you took up arms, and
" wafhed away the injury with their blood ; you
" fubdued the people, pillaged their houfes, and
" laid wafte their cities and their countries : and
" in this you did no wrong or injuftice : you
" obeyed the moft ancient laws, which give
" to the ftrong the poffeffions of the weak; the
" fovereign law of nature, that begins with God,
" and ends with animals. Supprefs, therefore, O
" Romans, your pity for the Clufians. Compaf-
" fion is yet unknown to the Gauls : do not in-
" fpire them with that fentiment, left they fhould
" have compaffion on thofe you opprefs."

Few chiefs have the boldnefs and candour of
Brennus. Their language is different, but their
actions are the fame ; and, in fact, they have all
the fame contempt for juftice (27).

The hiftory of the world is a vaft collection of
reiterated proofs of this truth (28). The invafions
of the Huns, the Goths, the Vandals, the Suevi,
and the Romans ; the conquefts of the Spaniards
and Portuguefe in both Indies, and laftly our croifades; all prove that nations in their enterprizes
confult force, not juftice. Such is the picture hiftory prefents us. Now the fame principle that
actuates nations, muft neceffarily, and in like manner actuate the individuals who compofe them.

Let

Let the conduct of nations, therefore, elucidate that of individuals.

C H A P. X.

Individuals, like nations, esteem justice solely for the consideration and power it procures them.

IS not a man, with regard to his fellow-citizens, nearly in the same state of independence, that one people are to another? Man then loves justice (29) merely for the power and happiness it procures him. To what other cause, in fact, except to the extreme love of power, can we attribute our admiration of conquerors (30)? " The " conqueror, said the pirate Demetrius to Alex- " ander, is a man, who at the head of a hundred " thousand soldiers, takes at once a hundred thou- " sand purses, and cut the throats of a hundred " thousand citizens, does in great what the rob- " ber does in little ; and who, by being more un- " just than the latter, is more destructive to so- " ciety." The robber is a terror to an indivi- dual. The conqueror, like the tyrant, is the scourge of a nation. What makes us respect Alexander and Cortez, and despise Cartouch and Rassiat. The power of the one, and the impo- tence of the other. In the robber, it is not pro- perly the crime, but the weakness we despise (31). The conqueror appears as invested with great

power,

power; we would be invefted with the fame power, and we cannot defpife what we wifh to attain.

The love man has for power is fuch, that in all cafes the exercife of it is agreeable to him, becaufe it makes him recollect his poffeffion of it. Every man would have great power, and every man knows that it is almoft impoffible to be at once conftantly juft and powerful. Man makes, without doubt, a better or worfe ufe of his power, according to the education he has received. But be it as good as it may, there is no great man who does not commit fome acts of injuftice. The abufe of power is connected with its exiftence, as the effect with the caufe. Corneille fays,

Qui peut tout ce qu'il veut, veut plus que ce qu'il doit (32).

He who can do whatever he will, wills more than he ought.

This verfe is a moral axiom confirmed by experience; and yet no one refufes a great place for fear of expofing himfelf to the temptation of injuftice *.

Our love of equity, therefore, is always fubordinate to our love of power. Man, folely anxious for himfelf, feeks nothing but his own happinefs. If he refpects equity, it is want that compels him to it (33).

---

* This muft be underftood with limitation: many men have refufed power, from a fear of temptation, and a confcioufnefs of their own weaknefs.

If

If a difference arife between two men nearly equal in power, each of them, reftrained by a reciprocal fear, has recourfe to juftice; each of them fubmits to its decifion; that he may intereft the public in his favour, and by that mean acquire a certain fuperiority over his adverfary.

But let one of thefe two men be greatly fuperior in power to the other, fo that he can rob him with impunity; and then, deaf to the voice of juftice, he does not litigate, but command. It is not equity, nor even the appearance of equity, that determines between the weak and the powerful; but force, crime, and tyranny. It is thus the divan gives the name of feditious to the remonftrances of the impotent, whom it oppreffes.

To fhow ftill more ftrongly the great love that men have for power, I fhall add but one proof to the foregoing, and which is the ftrongeft.

C H A P. XI.

The love of power, under every form of government, is the fole motive of man's actions.

" UNDER every form of government, fays
" M. Montefquieu, there is a different prin-
" ciple of action." " Fear in defpotic ftates,
" honour under monarchies, and virtue in repub-
" lics, are the feveral motive principles."
                                          But

But on what proof does M. Montefquieu found this affertion *. Is it quite evident that fear, honour, and the love of virtue, are the different motives in different governments ? May we not affert on the contrary, that one caufe alone, but varied in its applications, is equally the principle of

* Fear, fays M. Montefquieu, is the motive principle in defpotic empires. He is miftaken. Fear does not increafe, but weaken the fpring of the mind. I can admit nothing for the active principle of a nation, but the conftant objects of the defire of almoft all the inhabitants. Now, in defpotic ftates there are but two; one is the defire of money, and the other the favour of the monarch.

In the two other forms of government there are, according to the fame writer, two other motive principles, of a nature, fays he, very different: the one is bonour, under monarchal ftates ; the other virtue, which is applicable to republics only.

The words Honour and Virtue are not indeed perfectly fynonimous. Yet if the word Honour conftantly brings to the mind the idea of fome virtue, thefe terms differ only in the extent of their fignification. Honour and virtue are therefore principles of the fame nature.

If M. Montefquieu had not propofed to give each form of government a different principle of action, he would have perceived the fame principle in all. This principle is the love of power, and confequently perfonal intereft modified according to the different conftitutions of the ftates, and their feveral legiflations. If virtue be, as he fays, the active principle in republics, it is at moft only in poor and warlike republics. The love of gold is that of commercial republics.

It appears, therefore, that in all governments man obeys his own intereft ; but that his intereft is not the fame in all. The more we examine in this refpect the manners of a people, the more convinced we are, that it is to their legiflation they owe their vices and their virtues. The principles of M. Montefquien on this matter appear to me to be more fhowey than folid.

activity

activity in all empires; and that if M. Montefquieu, less affected by the show of his division, had
more scrupulously discussed this question, he would
have attained more profound, clear, and general
ideas : he would have perceived in the love of
power, the motive principle of every individual :
he would have found in the various means of acquiring power, the principle to which we ought,
in all ages and all countries, refer the different conduct of men. In effect, power is in every nation
either concentered in one man, as in Morocco and
Turky; or, as in Venice and Poland, distributed
among several; or, as in Sparta, Rome, and
England, divided among the whole body of the
nation. According to these several partitions of
authority, we are sensible the inhabitants will contract different habits and manners, and yet all pro-
pose the same object, which is that of pleasing the
supreme power, of rendering it propitious to them,
and by that mean obtaining some portion or
emanation of its authority.

Of the GOVERNMENT of a SINGLE PERSON.

If this government be strictly arbitrary, the supreme power resides in the hands of a sultan: who
is in general badly educated. Does he grant
his protection to certain vices; is he without humanity, without love of glory; and does he sacrifice to his humour the happiness of his subjects ?
The courtiers, jealous of his favour only, model
their

their conduct by his, and in proportion as the defpot fhews more indifference for the patriotic virtues, they affect to hold them in the greater contempt.

In this country we find no fuch men as Timoleon, Leonidas, Regulus, &c. Such citizens cannot flourifh without that degree of confideration and refpect which was fhown to the virtuous man; who in Rome and Greece, being fecure of the national efteem, faw nothing above him.

In a defpotic ftate, what refpect will be paid to the honeft man? The fultan, fole difpofer of rewards and punifhments, centers all confideration within himfelf. No one can there fhine but by his reflected light, and the vileft favourite holds an equal rank with the greateft hero. In every government of this fort, emulation muft be extinguifhed. The intereft of the defpot being frequently oppofite to the intereft of the public, muft obfcure every idea of virtue; and the love of power, the motive principle of each individual, cannot there form juft and virtuous men.

Of the Government of Several.

In governments of this fort the fupreme power is in the hands of a certain number of great men. The body of the nobles is the defpot (34). Their object is to keep the people in a fhameful and inhuman poverty and flavery. Now what is to be done to gain their protection and favour? Enter

into

into their views; favour their tyranny, and perpetually sacrifice the happiness of a great number, to
the pride of a few.   In such a nation, it is also
impossible that the love of power should produce
good citizens.

Of the Government of All.

In this state, the supreme power is equally divided
among all the orders of the inhabitants.   The nation is then the despot.   What does it require?
The happiness of the greatest number.   By what
means is its favour to be attained?   By services
rendered it.   Therefore, every action conformable
to the interest of the greatest member is just and
tuous: consequently, the love of power, the motive
principle of the inhabitants, must compel them to
the love of justice and of talents.

What does this love produce?   The public
happiness.

The supreme power divided among all the orders of inhabitants, is the soul that is equally dif-
fused through all the members of the state; ani-
mates it, and renders it healthful and vigorous.

It cannot therefore be wonderful, that this form
of government is always cited as the best.   Free
and happy citizens will obey no legislation but
what themselves have formed: they own nothing
above them but equity and the laws.   They live
in peace; for in morality, as in physics, it is the
equilibrium of force that produces tranquility.   If
an

an ambitious man deftroy this equilibrium, and
there no longer exifts a mutual dependence
among the feveral orders of citizens ; or if there be,
as in Perfia, one man, or, as in Poland, a body of
men, who have an intereft feparate from that of
their nation : nothing is then to be feen but op-
preffors and oppreffed ; the inhabitants are divided
into two claffes only, tyrants and flaves.

If M. Montefquieu had thought deeply on thefe
matters, he would have perceived, that in every
country men are united by the love of power, but
that power is obtained by different means, according as the fupreme authority is centered, as in the
Eaft, in the hands of a fingle perfon ; or divided,
as in Poland, among the body of the nobles ; or,
as in Rome and Sparta, among the feveral orders
of the ftate : and that it is to the different manners
by which power is acquired, that men owe their
vices and their virtues : and that they do not love
juftice merely for itfelf.

One of the ftrongeft proofs of this truth, is the
bafenefs with which kings themfelves honoured injuftice in the perfon of Cromwell. This Cromwell, the blind and criminal inftrument of the future liberty of his country, was nothing more
than a lawlefs and formidable robber. Yet fcarce
was he ftyled Protector, when all the Chriftian
princes courted his friendfhip, and all of them offered, by their deputations and their embaffies, to
legitimate, as far as was in their power, the ufur-

per's

per's crimes. No one then was offended at the bafenefs with which his alliance was courted. Injuftice, therefore, is never defpifed but in the weak. Now if the motive principle of monarchs and whole nations be that of the individuals who compofe them, we may reft affured that man, folely folicitous to increafe his importance, loves not in juftice any thing but the power and happinefs it procures him.

It is to the fame motive he owes his love of virtue.

C H A P.   XII.

Of virtue.

THE word Virtue, equally applicable to prudence, courage, and charity *, has, therefore, only a vague fignification. However it conftantly recalls to the mind the confufed idea of fome quality ufeful to fociety.

When qualities of this fort are common to the greateft part of the citizens a nation is happy within itfelf, formidable without, and worthy of imitation by pofterity †. Virtue, always ufeful to

---

* *Virtue*, fays Cicero, is derived from the word *vis*: its natural fignification is *fortitude*. It has the fame root in Greek. Force and courage are the firft ideas that men could form of virtue.

† *Virtuous and vicious ev'ry man muſt be,*
   Few in th' extreme, but all in the degree,

ſhe

man, and confequently always refpectable, ought, at leaft in certain countries, to reflect power and confideration on its poffeffors. Now it is the love of confideration that man takes to be in him the love of virtue. Each one pretends to love it for itfelf. This phrafe is in every one's mouth, but in no one's heart. What motive makes the monk faft, wear a hair cloth, and flog himfelf? The hope of eternal happinefs: the fear of hell, and the defire of heaven.

Pleafure and pain, thofe productive principles of monachal virtue, are the principles of the patriotic virtues alfo. The hope of rewards makes them flourifh. Whatever difinterefted love we may effect to have, *without intereft to love virtue there is no virtue.* To know man, is this refpect, we muft ftudy him ; not by his converfation, but his actions. When I fpeak I put on a mafk ; when I act I am forced to take it off. It is not, therefore, by what I fay, but what I do, that men are to judge me ; and they will judge me rightly.

Who more than the clergy preach the love of humility and poverty ? And what better than the hiftory of the clergy itfelf, proves the falfity of that love.

The rogue and fool by fits is fair and wife ;
And e'en the beft, by fits what they defpife.
'Tis but by parts we follow good or ill ;
For, vice or virtue, felf directs it ftill.

POPE.

X 4   The

The elector of Bavaria, they say, has not, for maintaining his troops, his police, and his court, so large a revenue as the church has for maintaining its priests. Yet in Bavaria, as every where else, the clergy preach up the virtue of poverty. It is therefore the poverty of others they extol.

To know the real esteem in which virtue is held, let us suppose it banished to the dominion of a monarch where it can expect no grace or favour. What respect will be paid at his court to virtue? None. Nothing can be there respected but baseness, intrigue, and cruelty, disguised under the names of decency, wisdom, and firmness. Does the vizir there give audience. The nobles, prostrate at his feet, can scarce vouchsafe to cast a look upon merit. But, they will say, the homage of these courtiers is forced; it is the effect of their fear. Be it so. More respect then is paid to fear, than to virtue. These courtiers, they will add, despise the idol they worship. It is no such matter. Men hate the powerful; they do not despise them. It is not the wrath of the giant, but of the pigmy, we despise. His impotence renders him ridiculous. Whatever may be said, we do not really despise him, whom we dare not despise to his face. Secret contempt proves weakness and what men pretend to in this case, is nothing more than the boastings of an impotent hatred (35). The man in power is the moral giant; he is always

ways honoured. The homage rendered to virtue is tranfient, that to force eternal. In the foreft, it is the lion, and not the ftag, that is refpected. Force is all upon the earth. Virtue without importance becomes infignificant. If in the ages of oppreffion it has fometimes fhone with the greateft luftre, if when Thebes and Rome groaned under tyranny, the intrepid Pelopidas, and the virtuous Brutus, arofe and armed, it was becaufe the fceptre then fhook in the hands of tyranny: becaufe virtue could ftill open a paffage to grandeur and power. When it can no longer make its way, when tyranny, by the aid of luxury and bafenefs, is feated firm on its throne, and has bowed the people down to flavery, then no longer are feen thofe fublime virtues, that, by the influence of example, might ftill be fo ufeful to mankind. The feeds of heroifm are fuffocated.

In the Eaft, a mafculine virtue would be a folly, even in the fight of thofe who ftill pique themfelves on honefty. Whoever fhould there plead the caufe of the people, would pafs for feditious.

Thamas Kauli-Kan entered India with his army; rapine and defolation followed him. A bold Indian ftopped him: " O Thamas, he faid, " if thou art a god, act like a god. If thou art " a prophet, conduct us to the way of falvation. If " thou art a king, ceafe to be a barbarian; pro-" tect the people, and do not deftroy them." " I " am not, replied Thamas, a god, to act like a god;

2 " nor

"nor a prophet, to lead you to falvation; nor a
"king; to make you happy: but I am a man,
"fent by the wrath of heaven to chaftife thefe na-
"tions (36)." The difcourfe of the Indian was regarded as feditious (37), and the anfwer of Thamas
applauded by the army.

If there be on the theatre a character univerfally
admired, it is that of Leontine.   Yet in what
efteem would fuch a character have been in the
court of a Phocas?   His magnanimity would have
alarmed the favourites, and the people, ever at
length the echo of the great, would have condemned his noble boldnefs.

Four and twenty hours refidence in an Oriental
court would prove what I here advance.   Fortune and authority are there alone refpected.   How
fhould virtue be there efteemed, or even known?
To form clear ideas of it, we muft live in a country where (38) public utility is the only meafure
of human actions.   That country is yet unknown
to geographers.   But the Europeans, they will
fay, are at leaft in this refpect very different from
the Afiatics.   If they be not free, they are at leaft
not entirely degraded to flavery.   They, therefore, may know what virtue is, and efteem it.

CHAP.

C H A P. XIII.

Of the manner in which the greatest part of Europeans
consider virtue.

THE greatest part of the people of Europe
honour virtue in speculation : this is an effect of their education.   They despise it in practice : that is an effect of the form of their governments.

If the European admire in history, and applaud
on the theatre, generous actions, to which the
Asiatic is frequently infensible, that is, as I have
just said, the effect of his instruction.

The study of the Greek and Roman history,
makes a part of his instruction.   In the course
of this study, what mind, without interest and
without prejudice, is not affected with the same
patriotic sentiments that   animated the ancient
heroes ?   Youth cannot refuse its esteem to those
virtues, that, consecrated by universal respect, have
been celebrated by the most illustrious writers of
every age.

For want of the same instruction, the Asiatic
feels not the fame sentiments, nor conceives the
fame veneration for the masculine virtues of great
men. If Europeans admire them without imitation, it is because there is scarce any government

where thefe virtues lead to great employments, and nothing is really efteemed but power.

When I fee reprefented in hiftory, or on the theatre, a great character of Greece, Rome, Britain, or Scandinavia, I admire it. The principles of virtue imbibed in my infancy force me to it; and I the more readily encourage this fentiment, as I do not in any manner compare myfelf with this hero. If his virtue be ftrong and mine weak, I difguife its weaknefs : I refer to place, time, and circumftances, the difference I obferve between him and myfelf. But if this great man be my fellow-citizen, why do I not imitate his conduct ? His prefence humbles my pride. If I can avenge my-felf of him, I do it : I blame in him what I ap-plaud in the ancients. I rail at his generous actions : I depreciate his merit, and at leaft in ap-pearance, defpife his impotence.

My reafon, that judges the virtue of the dead, obliges me to efteem in fpeculation the heroes that have rendered themfelves ufeful to their coun-try. The picture of ancient heroifm produces an involuntary refpect in every mind that is not entirely debafed. But in my cotemporary, that heroifm is odious to me. I feel in his prefence two contradictory fentiments, one efteem, the other envy. Subject to thefe two different impul-fions, I hate the living hero, but erect a trophy on his tomb, and thus fatisfy at once my pride and my reafon. When virtue is without authority,

rity, its impotence gives me a right to defpife it, and I avail myfelf of that right. Weaknefs attracts fcorn and infult (39).

To be honoured while we live, we muft be powerful (40). Thus power is the only objeĉt of man's defire. He who had the choice of the ftrength of Encladus, and the virtues of Ariftides, would give the preference to the former. In the opinion of all the critics, the charaĉter of Eneas is more juft and virtuous than that of Achilles. Why then does the latter excite greater admiration ? Becaufe Achilles was ftrong, and we have more defire to be powerful than juft, and we always admire what we would be.

It is always power and importance that we feek, under the name of virtue. Why do they require on the theatre, that virtue fhould always triumph over vice ? From whence arofe that rule ? From an interior and confufed preception, that we only love in virtue the confideration it procures. Men are ferioufly anxious about nothing but authority, and it is the love of power that furnifhes the legiflator with the means of rendering them more virtuous and more happy.

CHAP.

C H A P. XIV.

*The love of power is in man the most favourable dis-
position to virtue.*

IF virtue were in us the effect of a particular
organisation, or a gift of the Divinity, there
would be no honest men but such as were so organised by nature, or predestined by Heaven. Laws,
good or bad, forms of government, more or less
perfect, would have little influence on the manners
of a people.   Sovereigns would not have it in
their power to form good citizens, and the sublime employment of a legislature would be, so to
say, without functions.   But if we regard, on the
contrary, virtue as the effect of a desire common
to all (as is the desire of command) the legislature
being always able to annex esteem and riches, in
a word, power, under some denomination, to the
practice of virtue, it can always compel men to it.
Under a good legislation, the only vicious must
then be the fools.   It is therefore always to the
greater or less absurdity in the laws, that we must
attribute the greater or less stupidity or iniquity
of the citizens.

Heaven, by inspiring all men with the love of
power, has given them a most precious gift. What
imports it whether all men be born virtuous, if all
be

be born with a paffion, that will render them fuch.

This truth being fully proved, it is for the magiftrate to difcover, in the univerfal love that men have for power, the means of fecuring the virtue of the citizens, and the happinefs of the nation.

As to what regards myfelf, I have accomplifhed my tafk if I have proved, that man directs, and ever will direct, his defires, his ideas, and his actions, to his felicity : that the love of virtue is always founded in him on the defire of happinefs : that he only loves in virtue the riches and happinefs it procures; and laftly, that even to the defire of glory, all is in man nothing more than a difguifed love of power. It is in this laft love that there is ftill concealed the principle of intolerance; which is of two kinds, the one civil, the other religious.

C H A P. XV.

Of civil intolerance.

MAN is born furrounded with pains and pleafures. If he defire the fword of power, it is to drive away the one, and to poffefs the other. His thirft for power is in this refpect infatiable. Not content with commanding a people, he would command their opinions alfo : he is not lefs anxious of fubduing the reafon of his fel-

low-

low-citizens, than a conqueror is of ufurping the treafures, and the provinces of his neighbours.

He does not think himfelf truly their mafter if he do not bring their minds into fubjection. To effect this he employs force : he at length fubdues reafon. Men are completely degraded by believing opinions they are forced to profefs. What reafoning begins is finifhed by violence.

The intolerance of monarchs is always the effect of their love of power. Not to think as they do, is to fet a bound to their authority ; it is to affume a power equal to theirs. By this they are enraged.

What is in certain countries the crime moft feverely punifhed ? Contradiction. For what crime was the Oriental punifhment of an iron cage invented in France ? On whom was it inflicted ? Was it fome cowardly or ignorant general who conducted a fiege, or defended a place badly ; or who by incapacity, jealoufy, or treafon, fuffered provinces to be ravaged ? Or was it fome minifter who loaded the people with intolerable taxes (41) and whofe edicts were deftructive of the public felicity ? No : the wretch condemned to this punifhment, was the writer of a Dutch gazette, who criticized, perhaps too feverely, the projects of fome French minifters (42), and made all Europe laugh at their expence (43).

Whom in Spain and Italy do they fuffer to rot in a dungeon ? Is it a judge that fells juftice, or a

governor

governor that abuſes his power? No: it is the
hawker who ſells for bread books, in which doubt
is made of the humility and poverty of the clergy.
To whom in ſome countries do they give the name
of a bad citizen? Is it to the thief, who purloins
and diſſipates the national treaſure? No: ſuch
crimes go almoſt every where unpuniſhed; for
they every where find protectors. He alone is
called a bad citizen, who in a ſong or an epigram
laughs at the knavery or futility (44) of a man in
power.

I have ſeen the country where the infamous is
not he who does the evil, but he that diſcovers
the author of it. Is a houſe ſet on fire?
The incendiary is careſſed, and he that diſcovers him is puniſhed. Under ſuch governments,
the greateſt of crimes is frequently the love of our
country, and a reſiſtance to the unjuſt commands
of thoſe in power.

Why is merit always ſuſpected by a weak miniſter? From whence his hatred to men of letters (45)? Becauſe he regards them as ſo many
torches that may diſcover the groſſneſs of his
blunders (46).

There was formerly about the perſon of a
prince, a ſubtile fellow, who, under the denomination of a fool, was ſometimes permitted to
ſpeak the truth (47). Theſe fools diſguſted: their
employment has been every where ſuppreſſed,
and it is perhaps the only general alteration that

fovereigns have made in their dependents. Thefe fools were the laft wife men that were fuffered to attend the great. If we would be admitted to their prefence, and be found agreeable, we muft talk as they do, and confirm them in their errors. But this is not the part of a man, fagacious, candid, and loyal. He will think for himfelf, and fpeak what he thinks; the great know it, and hate him. They find in him a boundary to their authority. It is men of this fort who are above all others prohibited from thinking and writing on matters of government. From whence it comes that kings, deprived of the advice of intelligent men, facrifice their real and durable power to a momentaneous fear of contradiction. In fact, if a prince be only ftrong by the ftrength of his people; his people only ftrong by the wifdom of adminiftration, and if that adminiftration be neceffarily taken from the body of the people, it is impoffible under a government that perfecutes the man who thinks, and where the people are all kept in darknefs, that fuch a nation fhould produce great minifters. The danger of acquiring inftruction there, deftroys inftruction. The people groan under the fcepter of a haughty ignorance, that foon precipitates the tyrant and his nation in one common ruin (48). This fort of intolerance is a rock, againft which, fooner or later, the greateft empires are dafhed in ruins.

CHAP.

C H A P. XVI.

Intolerance frequently fatal to princes.

PRESENT power and pleafure are frequently deftructive of future pleafure and power. A prince, to command with more fovereign
authority, would have his fubjects without ideas,
without fpirit, without character (49); in a word,
automata; always obedient to the impreffion he
gives them. If they become fuch, he will be
powerful at home, and impotent abroad: he will
be the tyrant of his fubjects, and the contempt of
his neighbours.

Such is the fituation of a defpotic monarch,
produced by a momentary pride. He fays to himfelf, it is over my people I habitually exercife my
power: it is therefore their oppofition, that frequently recalling to my mind the idea of a want
of fufficient power, makes it the more infupportable. If in confequence of this, he prohibit
the liberty of thought to his fubjects, he by that
act declares, that, indifferent to the greatnefs and
happinefs of his people, it is of little importance
to him, whether he govern badly or not, but of
great importance that he govern without control.
Now, from the moment the ftrong fpeaks, the
weak becomes filent, he bows the head, and no

longer thinks; for why fhould he think, when he cannot communicate his thoughts?

But, it will be faid, if the ftupor in which fear holds the minds of men be hurtful to a ftate, are we to conclude that the liberty of thinking and writing is without inconvenience.

In Perfia, fays Chardin, they may, even in cof-fee-houfes cenfure aloud, and with impunity, the conduct of the vizir; for the minifter, defirous of knowing the evil he does, is fenfible that he cannot know it but from the voice of the public. Perhaps there are countries in Europe more bar-barous than Perfia.

But ftill, if every one might think and write, what books would they make on fubjects they do not underftand! What abfurdities would be pub-lifhed! So much the better: they would leave fewer abfurdities to be committed by the vizirs. The critic would expofe the errors of the author; the public would laugh at him; and that is all the punifhment he would deferve. If legiflation be a fcience, its perfection muft be the work of time and experience. On any fubject, one excel-lent book fuppofes an infinity of bad. The tra-gedies of the paffion muft have preceded Hera-clius, Phedra, Mahomet, &c. If the prefs ceafe to be free (50), the man in place, ignorant of his failings, will inceffantly commit new blunders, and commit almoft as many abfurdities as the author wrote (51). Now, it is of little import-

ance

ance to a nation, that an author publishes absurdities; so much the worse for him: but it is of great importance that the minister do not make them; for if he do, so much the worse for them.

The liberty of the press is in no sort contrary to the general interest (52); that liberty is to a people the support of emulation. Who are they that should maintain this emulation? The people in power. Let them watch carefully over its preservation, for when once extinguished, it is almost impossible to kindle it again. If a people once polished fall into a state of barbarity, what can relieve them? Nothing but a conquest. That alone can give new manners to a people, and render them again powerful and renowned. If a people be degraded, let them be conquered. It is the desire of an honest citizen, a man that interests himself in the glory of his nation, who thinks himself great in its grandeur, and happy in its prosperity. The view of the despot is not the same, because he does not confound himself with his slaves: so that, indifferent to their glory and their happiness, nothing affects him (53) but their servile obedience.

The tyrant when blindly obeyed is content. If his subjects be without virtue, if his empire be enfeebled, if it perish by a consumption, it is of little moment to him: it is enough if the duration of the disease conceal the true cause, and that the physician cannot be accused of ignorance. The

only

only fear of fultans and vizirs is, that a fudden convulfion fhould feize the empire. There are vizirs like furgeons, whofe fole care is, that the ftate or the patient do not expire under their hands. If one or other of them die under a regimen prefcribed, the reputation of the minifter or the furgeon is fafe, and they give themfelves no concern about it.

In arbitrary governments all concern is confined to the prefent moment. They afk not of the people induftry and virtue, but money and fubmiffion. The defpot, the more filently to devour his people, like the fpider that inceffantly twines round the infect it has made his prey new threads, loads them daily with new chains (54): When he has at laft by fear fufpended in them all activity, where is his refource againft the attack of a neighbouring power? He does not forefce that he and his fubjects muft confequently foon fubmit to the yoke of the conqueror. But defpotifm forefees nothing.

Every remonftrance difgufts and irritates a defpot. He refembles the ill-taught child that eats the poifonous fruit, and beats his mother who would take it from him. What account is made of a faithful and courageous citizen under fuch a reign? He is regarded and punifhed as a fool (55). What regard under fuch a reign is had to a mean and bad citizen (56)? He is regarded and recompenfed as a wife man. Sultans will be flattered

ed (57), and they are. Who can conftantly refufe their demands? Who, under fuch a government, can earneftly intereft himfelf in the public welfare? If there be a wife man here and
there in the empire, every one is deaf to his
counfel. They are like lamps that burn in a fe-
pulchre, their lights fhine on no man. The tyrant confides in men grown old in attendance,
and that have the fpirit and manners of the court.
They were flatterers of this fort, that hurried on
the Stuarts to their ruin. " Certain prelates, fays
" an illuftrious Englifh writer, perceiving the bi-
" gotted weaknefs of James I. made ufe of it to
" perfuade him that the public tranquility de-
" pended on the uniformity of public worfhip, that
" is on certain religious ceremonies. James em-
" braced this opinion, and tranfmited it to his de-
" fcendants. What was the confequence? The
" exile and ruin of his houfe."

" When heaven, fays Velleius Paterculus,
" would chaftife a fovereign, it infpires him with
" a love of flattery (58), and a hatred of contra-
" diction. At that inftant the underftanding of
" the fovereign is obfcured. He fhuns the com-
" pany of wife men, walks in darknefs, falls into
" a fathomlefs pit, and, as the Latin proverb fays,
" paffes from the fmoke to the fire." If fuch be
the figns of the wrath of heaven, againft what fultan is it not irritated? Which among them choofes
his favourites from the moft faithful and intelligent

of

of his fubjects ? The philofopher Anacharfis, they fay, bafely flattered a king of Scythia, and was by his order pounded in a mortar ; but that mortar is loft.

" What do they report of me and my govern-
" ment ? faid an emperor of China to Confucius.
" Every one, replied the philofopher, keeps a
" mournful filence.   That is what what I would
" have them do, faid the emperor ; and it is what
" you ought to fear, replied the philofopher.
" The fick man when flattered is abandoned ; his
" end is near.   A monarch ought to be informed
" of the diforder of his mind, as a fick man of
" that of his body : without this liberty the ftate
" and the prince are loft."

This anfwer difpleafed the emperor ; he wanted to be praifed.   The prefent intereft almoft always weighs more with pride than the intereft that is to come, and in this refpect the people are princes.

C H A P. XVII.

Flattery is not lefs pleafing to the people than to fovereigns.

THE people, like kings, would be courted and flattered.   The greateft part of the Athenian orators were nothing better than vile adulators of the populace. Prince, people, indi-vidual,

vidual (59), all are greedy of praife. To what can we refer this univerfal paffion ? To the love of power.

Whoever praifes a man awakens in him the idea of power, with which the idea of happinefs is always connected.

Whoever contradicts him, on the contrary, awakens in him the idea of weaknefs, to which is always joined the idea of misfortune. The love of praife is common to all; but the people, too fen- fible of praife, have fometimes given the name of good patriots to their meaneft flatterers. Let every man extol with tranfport the virtues of his country, but let him not be blind to its vices. The pupil moft fincerely beloved is not the moft praifed. A true friend is never a flatterer.

Private perfons are too much difpofed to extol the virtues of their fellow-citizens ; they regard it as a common caufe. Adulation of our country- men is not the meafure of our love for our coun- try ; in general, every man loves thofe of his own country : the love of Frenchmen is natural to the French. To render me a bad citizen, the law muft make me fuch by detaching my intereft from that of the public.

The virtuous man is known by the defire he has to render his compatriots, if it be poffible, more illuftrious and more happy. In England the true patriots are thofe that exert their utmoft force againft the abufe of government ; but to
whom

whom do they give that title in Portugal ? To him who moft fervilely adulates the man in power ; yet what a citizen! what a patriot!

It is to a thorough knowledge of the motives of our love for flattery, and our hatred for contra-diction, that we owe the folution of an infinity of moral problems, otherwife inexplicable.   Why is every new truth at firft fo badly received ? Becaufe every truth of that fort always contradicts fome opinion generally received, fhews the weaknefs or falfity of an infinity of judgments, and confe-quently an infinity of people have an intereft in hating and perfecuting the author.

M. Come improved the inftrument ufed in li-thotomy ; it operates in a manner lefs dangerous and painful than the other.   What of that ? The pride of the celebrated furgeons was fhocked ; they perfecuted and would have banifhed him from France : they folicited a lettre de cachet, but by chance they were refufed.   If the man of genius be almoft every where more rigoroufly punifhed than the affaffin, it is becaufe the one has for enemies only the relations of the murdered, the other all his fellow-citizens.

I have known a devout woman afk of a minifter, at the fame time, the pardon of a robber, and the imprifonment of a Janfenift and a deift ; What was her motive ? Pride.   What is it to me, fhe would have freely faid, that they rob and mur-der, provided it be not me, nor my confeffor ;

what

what I want is, that men be religious, and that the deift do not by his arguments fhock my vanity.

By endeavouring to inftruct we humiliate. Let in the light upon a neft of young owls, and they cry out againft the injury you have done them.   Men of mediocrity are young owls? when you prefent them with ftrong and brilliant ideas, they exclaim againft them as falfe, dangerous, and deferving of punifhment (60).

Under what prince, and in what country, can a man be great with impunity ? In England, and under the reign of a Trajan or a Frederic ; under every other form of government, and every other fovereign, the reward of talents is perfecution. Strong and great ideas are almoft every where profcribed. The authors moft generally read are thofe that render common ideas in a new and ftriking manner ; they are praifed becaufe they are not worthy of praife ; becaufe they do not contradict any one. Contradiction is is intolerable to all, but efpecially to the great. To what degree did it not raife up the wrath of Charles V. againft the Lutherans ? That prince, they fay, repented of having perfecuted them ; it may be fo : but at what time was it ? When after having abdicated the empire he lived in retreat. He then faid to himfelf, I have thirty watches on my table, and no two of them mark precifely the fame time :

time* : how could I imagine then, that in matters
of religion I could make all men think alike?
What was my folly and my pride! Would to
heaven that Charles had made this reflection
fooner; he would have been more juft, more tolerant, and more virtuous. What feeds of war he
would have deftroyed! how much human blood
would he have fpared!

No prince, not even any private man, affigns
bounds to his power. It is not enough to reign
over our fellow-citizens, and command their ideas,
we would even command their taftes. M. Rouffeau loves not French mufic; in this he agrees
with all the other nations in Europe. When he
publifhed his opinion, a thoufand voices were raifed
againft him: he deferved to rot in a dungeon.
They folicited a lettre de cachet, but the minifter
was luckily too prudent to grant it, and expofe the
French nation to ridicule.

There are no crimes to which human intolerance does not lead. To pretend in this matter
to correct man, is to defire that he fhould prefer
others to himfelf; that is, to defire him to change
his nature. A wife man never defires impoffi-
bilities; his aim is to difarm and not deftroy in-

* A domeftic carelefly entered his cell and threw down the
table with the thirty watches; Charles laughed, and faid to
the fervant, you are more lucky than I, for you have found
the way to make them all go together.

tolerance,

tollerance. But what shall reftrain it? A reciprocal fear. When two men of equal force differ in opinion, neither of them infult the other; for men rarely attack thofe they think they cannot injure with impunity.

Why do military men difpute with fo much politenefs? For fear of a duel. From whence arifes the fame politenefs among men of letters? From the fear of ridicule: no man likes to be confounded with the pedants of a college. Now from thofe two inftances we may judge what the ftill more efficacious fear of the law would produce among citizens.

Severe laws would fupprefs intolerance as well as robbery. If while I have the free ufe of my taftes and opinions, the law forbids me to infult thofe of others; my intolerance then checked by the edicts of the magiftrate, will not extend to acts of violence; but if through imprudence the government free me from the fear of a duel, ridicule, and the law, my intolerance unreftrained will again render me favage and inhuman. The atrocious ferocity with which different religious fects profecute each other, is a proof of what is here afferted.

CHAP.

CHAP. XVIII.

Of religious intolerance.

THIS is the moſt dangerous of all intoléª
rance; its motive is the love of power, religion its pretence. What is it they would puniſh
in a heretic or unbeliever? The audacity of the
man who would think for himſelf; who would believe his own reaſon before that of the prieſts, and
thereby declare himſelf their equal. The pretence
of avenging Heaven is never any thing more than
that of his offended pride. Prieſts of almoſt all
religions are the ſame.

In the ſight of a mufti, as in that of a bonze,
an infidel is an impious wretch that ought to be
deſtroyed by fire from heaven; a man ſo deſtructive to ſociety as to deſerve to be burned alive.

In the eyes of a wiſe man however, this ſame
infidel is a man who does not believe the tale of
mother Gooſe: for what is there wanting to make
that tale a religion? A number of people to maintain its veracity.

Whence comes it that men covered with the
rags of penitence and the maſk of charity have
been in all times the moſt atrocious? How can it
be poſſible that the light of toleration has not yet
broke forth? What! muſt honeſt men hate and
perſecute each other without remorſe for diſputes
about

about words, frequently about the choice of errors, and becaufe they are diftinguifhed by the different names of Lutherans, Calvinifts, Catholics,
Mahometans, &c.

When in a convocation the monk anathema-
tifes the dervife, can he be ignorant that in the
fight of the dervife the truly impious, the real infidel, is the Chriftian, pope or monk who does
not believe in Mahomet? Can each fect, eternally
condemned to ftupidity, approve in itfelf what it
detefts in others?

Let them fometimes recollect the ingenious pa-
rable of a celebrated painter. Tranfported in a
dream to the gates of heaven, fays he, the firft object that ftruck me was a venerable old man; by
his keys, his bald head, and his long beard, I
knew him to be St. Peter. The apoftle fat on
the threfhold of the celeftial gates; a crowd of
people advanced towards him; the firft who prefented himfelf was a papift; I have, faid he, all
my life been a religious man, and yet honeft
enough. Go in, replies the faint, and place yourfelf upon the bench for catholics. The next was
a proteftant, who gave a like account of himfelf;
the faint faid in like manner, place yourfelf among
the reformed. Then came merchants of Bagdat,
Balfora, &c. thefe were all mufulmans who had
been conftantly virtuous; St. Peter made them fet
down among the mufulmans. At laft came an
infidel; What is thy fect? faid the apoftle, I am
of

of no fect, he replied, but I have always been
honeft; Then you may go in.   But where fhall I
feat myfelf? Next thofe who appear to you moft
rational.

Would to heaven that, elucidated by this fable,
men would no longer pretend to command the
opinions of others! God will have that truth be
recompence of inquiry.   The moft efficacious
prayers for obtaining it are, they fay, ftudy and application.   O ftupid monks! have you ever made
thofe prayers?

What is truth? You do not know: yet you perfecute him who, you fay, knows it not, and have
canonifed the dragoons of Cevennes, and elevated
to the dignity of a faint one Dominick, a barbarian, who founded the tribunal of the inquifition,
and maffacred the Albigois (61).   Under Charles
IX. you made it the duty of the catholics to murder the proteftants; and even in this age, fo enlightened and philofophic, when the toleration recommended in the gofpel ought to be the virtue of
all men, there are Caveiracs who treat toleration as
a crime and an indifference for religion, and who
would again behold that day of blood and maffacre, that horrid day of St. Bartholomew, when facerdotal pride ftalked through the ftreets commanding the death of Frenchmen; like the fultan
who paffed through the ftreets of Conftantinople,
followed by an executioner, demanding the blood
of the Chriftian who wore the red breeches.

More

More barbarous than the fultan, you put fwords in the hands of Chriftians to cut the throat of each other.

O religions, (I fpeak here of the falfe), you have ever been palpably ridiculous! and even if you were merely ridiculous, the man of under-ftanding would not expofe your abfurdities. If he thinks himfelf obliged to do it, it is becaufe thofe abfurdities in men armed with the fword of intolerance (63) are one of the moft cruel fcourges of humanity.

Among the diverfity of religions, which are thofe that bear the greateft hatred to others? The Catholic and the Jewifh. Is this hatred the effect of ambition in their minifters, or that of a ftupid and ill-advifed zeal? The difference betwen true and falfe zeal is remarkable; they cannot be mif-taken (64). The firft is all gentlenefs, humanity, and charity; it pardons all, and offends none. Such at leaft is the idea we muft form of it from the words and actions of the Son of God (65).

C H A P.   XIX.

Intolerance and perfecution are not of divine com-mandment.

TO whom gave Jefus the appellation of race of vipers? Was it to the Pagans, the Effenes, or Saducees (66), who denied the immortality of

the foul, and even the exiſtence of the Divinity?
No: it was was to the Phariſees and Jewiſh
prieſts.

Will the Catholic prieſts by the fury of their
intolerance continue to merit the ſame appellation? By what right do they perſecute a heretic?
He does not think as we do, they will ſay: but
to deſire to unite all men preciſely in the ſame
belief, is to require them all to have the ſame
eyes and the ſame complexion; a deſire contrary
to nature. Hereſy is a name thoſe in power give
to opinions commonly various, but contradictory
to their own. Hereſy, like orthodoxy, is local.
The heretic belongs to a ſect not predominant in
the country where he lives: this man having leſs
protection, and being conſequently weaker than
others, may be inſulted with impunity. But why
is he inſulted? Becauſe the ſtrong perſecute the
weak even in their opinions.

If the miniſters of Neufchatel, the accuſers of
M. Rouſſeau (67), had been born Athenians or
Jews, they would, by virtue of being the ſtrongeſt, in like manner have perſecuted Socrates or
Jeſus. Oh, eloquent Rouſſeau! regard the favour
of the great prince who protects you againſt ſuch
fanatics as a full recompence for their inſults! you
muſt have bluſhed at the approbation of thoſe
wretches; it would have inferred ſome analogy
between your ideas and theirs, and have ſtained
your talents. You were perſecuted in the name
of the Divinity, but not by him.

Who more forcibly oppofed intolerance than the Son of God? His apoftles would have had him call down fire from heaven on the Samaritans; he reproved them fharply. The apoftles, ftill animated with the fpirit of the world, had not then received that of God; fcarce were they enlightened when they became profcribed, not profcribers.

Heaven has given to no one the power to maffacre a heretic. John does not command the Chriftians to arm themfelves againft the Pagans: (68) *Love one another*, he repeats inceffantly, *for fuch is the will of God; by obferving this precept you fulfil the law.*

Nero, I know, perfecuted among the firft Chriftians men of a different opinion from his own; but Nero was a tyrant, horrible to humanity. They who commit the fame barbarities, who violate without remorfe the natural and divine laws, which commands us *to do unto others as we would they fhould do unto us,* ought equally to be accurfed of God and man.

They who tolerate intolerants render themfelves guilty of their crimes. If a church complain of being perfecuted, when its right to perfecute is oppofed, the prince fhould be deaf to its complaints. The church ought to regulate its conduct by that of the Son of God. But Jefus and his apoftles left to men the free exercife of reafon. Why then does the church forbid them the ufe of it?

No:

No man has authority over the noble function of my mind, that of judging for myfelf, any more than over the air I breathe. Shall I abandon to others the eare of thinking for me? I have my own confcience, reafon, and religion, and do not defire to have the confcience, reafon, or religion of the pope. I will not model my belief after that of another, faid an archbifhop of Canterbury. Each one is to anfwer for his own foul; it therefore belongs to each one to examine,

What he believes;

On what motive he believes;

What is the belief that appears to him the moft rational.

What! faid John Gerfon, chancellor of the univerfity of Paris, has heaven given me a foul, a faculty of judging, and fhall I fubmit it to that of others; and fhall they guide me in my manner of living and dying?

But ought a man to prefer his own reafon to that of a nation? Is fuch a prefumption lawful? Why not? If Jupiter fhould again take in hand the balance with which he formerly weighed the deftiny of heroes; if in one fcale he fhould put the opinion of Locke, Fontenelle, Bayle, &c. and in the other that of the Italian, French, and Spanifh nations, the laft fcale would rife up, as if loaded with no weight. The diverfity and abfurdity of

1   different

different forms of worſhip ſhew in how little eſteem we ought to hold the opinion of the people. The divine wiſdom itſelf appeared, ſays the ſcripture, a ſcandal to the Jews, and to the nations fooliſhneſs; *Judæis ſcandalum, gentibus ſtultitiam.* In matters of religion I owe no reſpect to the opinion of a people; it is to myſelf alone that I owe an account of my belief; all that immediately relates to God, ſhould have no judge but him. The magiſtrate himſelf, ſolely charged with the temporal happineſs of men, has no right to puniſh any crimes not committed againſt ſociety: no prince or prieſt has a right to perſecute in me the pretended crime of not thinking as he does.

From what principle does the law forbid my neighbour to diſpoſe of my property, and permit him to diſpoſe of my reaſon and my ſoul? My ſoul is my property. It is from nature that I hold the right of thinking, and of ſpeaking what I think. When the firſt Chriſtians laid before the nations of the earth their belief, and the motives for that belief; when they permitted the Gentiles to judge between the Chriſtian religion and their own, and to make uſe of the reaſon given to man to diſtinguiſh between vice and virtue, truth and falſhood; the expoſition of their ſentiments had certainly nothing criminal in it. At what period did the Chriſtians deſerve the hatred and contempt of the world? When by burning the temples of the idols, they would have forced the pagans to re

Z 3

linquiſh

linquifh the religion they thought the beft (69) ;
What was the defign of that violence? Force im-
pofes filence on reafon ; it can profcribe any worfhip rendered the Divinity.   But what power has
it over belief? To believe fuppofes a motive to believe.   Force is no motive.   Now without motive
we cannot really believe; the moft we can do is to
think we believe (70).

There can be no pretence for admitting an intolerance condemned by reafon and the law of nature: that law is holy; it is from God ; it cannot
be difannulled ; on the contrary, God has confirmed it by his gofpel.

Every prieft, who under the name of an angel
of peace excites men to perfecution, is not, as is
imagined, the dupe of a ftupid and ill-informed
zeal (71); it is not by his zeal but by his ambition
he is directed.

C H A P.   XX.

*Intolerance is the foundation of the grandeur of the
clergy.*

THE doctrine and practice of the prieft both
prove his love of power.   What does he
protect? Ignorance.   Why? Becaufe the ignorant
are credulous, make little ufe of their reafon, think
after others, are eafy to be deceived, and are the
dupes of the groffeft fophiftry (72).

W hat

What does the prieſt perſecute ? Learning.
Why ? Becauſe a man of learning will not believe
without examination ; he will ſee with his own
eyes, and is hard to be deceived. · The enemies
of learning are the bonze, the dervis, the bramin,
in ſhort, every prieſt of every religion. In Europe
the prieſts roſe up againſt Galileo; excommunicated
Polydore Virgil and Scheiner for the diſcovery the
one made of the antipodes, and the other of the
ſpots in the ſun ; they have proſcribed ſound logic
in Bayle, and in Deſcartes the only method of acquiring knowledge ; they forced that philoſopher
to leave his country (73) ; they formerly accuſed
all great men of magic (74); and now magic is no
longer in faſhion, they accuſe thoſe of atheiſm and
materialiſm, whom they formerly burned as forcerers.

The care of the prieſt has ever been to keep
men at a diſtance from the truth : all inſtructive
ſtudy is forbid. The prieſt ſhuts himſelf up with
them in a dark chamber, and carefully ſtops up
every crevice by which the light might enter. He
hates, and ever will hate, the philoſopher : he is
in continual fear leſt men of ſcience ſhould overthrow an empire founded on error and intellectual
darkneſs.

Without love for talents, the prieſt is a ſecret
enemy to the virtues of humanity ; he frequently
denies their very exiſtence. There are, in his
opinion, no virtuous actions but what are con-

Z 4   formable

formable to his doctrine, that is, to his interest.
The first of virtues with him are faith, and a submission to sacerdotal power : it is to slaves only
that he gives the name of saints and virtuous
men.

What, however, are more distinct than the ideas
of virtue and sanctity ? He is virtuous who promotes the prosperity of his fellow-citizens: the
word Virtue always includes the idea of some public utility. It is not the same with sanctity. A
hermit or monk imposes on himself the law of silence, flogs himself every night, lives on pulse and
water, sleeps on straw, offers to God his nastiness
and his ignorance, and thinks by virtue of maceration to make a fortune in Heaven. He may be
decorated with a glory ; but if he do no good on
earth, he is not honest. A villain is converted at
the hour of death ; he is saved, and is happy : but
he is not virtuous. That title is not to be obtaind
but by a conduct habitually just and noble.

It is from the cloisters they commonly take the
saints ; but what in general are monks ? Idle and
litigious men, dangerous to society, and whose vi-
cinity is to be dreaded. Their conduct proves that
there is nothing in common between religion and
virtue. To obtain a just idea of it, we must substitute a new morality in the place of that theological morality, which, always indulgent to the
perfidious arts practised by the different sects (76),
sanctifies to this day the atrocious crimes with
which

which the Janfenifts and Molinifts reciprocally charge each other (77), and which, in fhort, commands them to plunder their fellow-citizens of their property and their liberty.

An Afiatic tyrant would have his fubjects promote his pleafures with all their power, and pay down at his feet their homage and their riches : the popifh priefts exact in like manner the homage and the riches of the catholics.

Are there any means of increafing their power and wealth that they have not employed ? When it was neceffary for that purpofe to have recourfe to barbarity and cruelty, they became cruel and barbarous.

From the moment the priefts, inftructed by experience, found that men paid more regard to fear than to love, that more offerings were prefented to Ariman than Oromaza, to the cruel Molva than the gentle Jefus, it was on terror they founded their empire. They fought to have it in their power to burn the Jew, imprifon the Janfenift and Deift ; and notwithftanding the horror with which the tribunal of the inquifition fills every fenfible and humane foul, they then conceived the project of its eftablifhment. It was by dint of intrigues they accomplifhed this defign in Spain, Italy, Portugal, &c.

The more arbitrary the proceedings of this tribunal became, the more it was dreaded. The priefts, perceiving that the facerdotal power increafed

creafed by the terrors with which it ftruck the imagination of mankind, foon became obdurate. The monk, deaf with impunity to the cry of compaffion, to the tears of mifery, and the groans of tortures, fpared neither virtue nor talents; it was by confifcation of property, by the aid of tortures and butcheries they at laft ufurped over the people an authority fuperior to that of the magiftrates, and frequently even to that of kings. The bold hand of facerdotal ambition dared in a Chriftian country to lay the foundation of fuch a tribunal; and the ftupidity of the people, and of princes, fuffered it to be completed.

Are there no longer in the Catholic church a Fenelon or a Fitzjames, who, touched with the misfortunes of their brethren, behold this tribunal with horror? There are ftill Janfenifts virtuous enough to deteft the inquifition, even though it fhould burn a Jefuit; but in general men are not at once religious and tolerant: humanity fuppofes intelligence.

A man of an enlightened mind knows that force makes hypocrites, and perfuafion Chriftians; that a heretic is a brother who does not think as he does on certain metaphyfical dogmas; that this brother, deprived of the gift of faith, is to be pitied, not perfecuted (78); and that if no one can believe that to be true, which appears to him to be falfe, no human power can command belief.

The

The confequence of religious intolerance is the mifery of nations. What fanctifies intolerance? Sacerdotal ambition. The exceffive love of the monk for power produces his exceffive barbarity. The monk, cruel by fyftem, is ftill more fo by education. Weak, hypocrital, cowardly by fitu-ation, every Catholic prieft ought in general to be atrocious (79); fo that in countries fubject to his power he exercifes perpetually all that the moft refined cruelty and injuftice can imagine. If, while profeffing a religion inftituted to infpire gen-tlenefs and charity, he become the inftrument of perfecutions and maffacres; if, all dropping with the blood fpilt at an auto de fe, he dare at the al-tar to lift his murdering hands to Heaven, let no one wonder: the monk is as he ought to be. Co-vered with the blood of a heretic, he regards himfelf as the avenger of the divine wrath. But can he at fuch a time implore the clemency of Heaven? Can his hands be pure becaufe the church has declared them fo? What community has not legitimated the moft abominable crimes, when they ferved to increafe its power?

The approbation of the chnrch is fufficient to fanctify any crime. I have regarded the different religions, and have feen their feveral followers fnatch the torch from each other's hands to burn their brethren; I have feen the feveral fuperftitions ferve as footftools to ecclefiaftical pride. Who

is

is then, I have said to myself, the truly impious? Is it the infidel? No: the ambitious fanatic (80). It is he that persecutes and murders his brethren; it is he who, wishing to execute the vengeance of Heaven on the infernal regions, anticipates that horrid function on earth; who, regarding an infidel as a damned soul, is desirous by a violent death to hasten his perdition, and by an unheard-of progression of cruelty, to cause his brother to be at the same instant arrested, imprisoned, judged, condemned, burned, and damned.

C H A P.   XXI.

The impossibility of suppressing in man the sentiment of
intolerance.   Means of counteracting its effects.

THE leaven of intolerance is indestructible. It is only practicable to suppress its increase and action. Severe laws ought therefore to be employed in restraining it, as they do robbery.

Does it regard personal interest? The magistrate, by preventing its action, will bind the hands of intolerance; and why should they be unbound, when under the mask of religion intolerance will exercise the greatest cruelties?

Man is by nature intolerant. If the sun of reason enlighten him for a moment, he should seize the opportunity to bind himself down by sagacious laws, and put himself in a happy state of impotency,

tency, that he may not injure others if he fhould be again feized with the rage of intolerance.

Good laws can equally reftrain the furious devout, and the perfidious prieft. England, Holland, and a part of Germany are proofs of this truth. Multiplied crimes and miferies have opened the eyes of the people on this matter ; they have perceived that liberty of thought is a natural right ; that thinking produces a defire of communicating our thoughts, and that in a people, as an individual, indifference in this matter is a fign of ftupidity.

He who does not feel the want of thought never thinks. It is with the body as with the mind ; if the faculties of the one or the other are not exerted they become impotent. When intolerance has weighed down the minds of men, and has broken their fpring, they then become ftupid, and darknefs is fpread over a nation.

The touch of Midas, the poets fay, turned all into gold ; the head of Medufa transformed all into ftone : intolerance, in like manner, transforms into hypocrites, fools, and ideots (81), all that it finds within the fphere of its attraction. It was intolerance that in the Eaft fcattered the firft feeds of ftupidity, which fince the inftitution of defpotifm have there fprung up. It is intolerance that has condemned to the contempt of the prefent and future ages all thofe fuperftitious countries whofe

whofe inhabitants in fact appear to belong rather
to the clafs of brutes than men.

There is only one cafe in which toleration cari
be detrimental to a people, and that is when it to-
lerates a religion that is intolerant, fuch as the Catholic (82). This religion, becoming the moft
powerful in a ftate, will always fhed the blood of
its ftupid protectors ; it is the ferpent that ftings
the bofom which has warmed it. Let Germany
beware ! its princes have an intereft in embracing
popery ; it affords them refpectable eftablifhments
for their brothers, children, &c. Thefe princes
becoming Catholics would force the belief of their
fubjects, and if they found it neceffary, would
again make human blood to ftream ; the torch of
fuperftition and intolerance would again blaze.
A light breath would kindle it, and fet all Europe in flames. Where would the conflagration
ftop ? I know not. Would Holland efcape ?
Would the Briton himfelf, from the height of his
rocks, for any long time brave the Catholic fury ?
The ftraits of the fea would prove an impotent
barrier againft the rage of fanaticifm. What
could hinder the preaching up a new croifade, and
of arming all Europe againft England, of making
a defcent in that country, and of one day treating
the Britons as they formerly treated the Albigois.

Let not the infinuating manner of the Catholics
impofe on the Proteftants. The fame prieft who
in Pruffia regards intolerance as an abomination,

and

and an infraction of the natural and divine law, looks on toleration in France as a crime and a herefy (83). What renders the fame man fo different in different countries? His weaknefs in Pruffia, and his power in France.

When we confider the conduct of Catholic Chriftians, they at firft, when feeble, appear to be lambs; but when ftrong, they are tygers.

Will the nations, inftructed by paft misfortunes, never fee the neceffity of reftraining fanaticifm, and of banifhing from every religion the monftrous doctrine of intolerance? What is it at this hour that fhakes the throne of Turky, and ravages Poland? Fanaticifm. It is that prevents the Catholic Poles from admiting the Diffidents to a partition of their privileges, and makes them prefer war to toleration. In vain do they impute the prefent miferies of thofe countries merely to the pride of the nobility; without religion the great men could never have armed the nation, and the impotence of their pride would have preferved peace in their country. Popery has been the fecret caufe of the miferies of Poland.

At Conftantinople it is the fanaticifm of the Muffulmans, that by loading the Greek Chriftians with ignominy, has armed it in fecret againft the empire it ought to have defended.

Would to Heaven that thefe two examples now before us, and glaring with the evils produced by religious intolerance, may be the laft of the kind; and

and that hereafter, indifferent to all modes of worship, governments may judge men by their actions, and not by their opinions. That they may regard virtue and genius as the only recommendations to public favour; and be convinced that it is not of a Romiſh, Turkiſh, or Reformed mechanic, but of the moſt accompliſhed workman we ſhould purchaſe a watch: in ſhort, that it is not to the extent of faith, but that of talents, offices ought to be intruſted.

As long as the doctrine of intolerance ſubſiſts, the moral world will contain within its boſom the ſeeds of new calamities. It is a volcano half extinguiſhed, that may one day blaze forth with greater violence, and produce freſh conflagrations and deſtruction.

Such are the fears of a citizen, who, the ſincere friend of mankind, earneſtly wiſhes their happineſs.

I think I have ſufficiently proved in this ſection, that in general all the factitious paſſions, and in particular civil and religious intolerance, are nothing more in man than a diſguiſed love of power. The long detail into which the proofs of this truth has led me, has doubtleſs made the reader forget the motives that forced me into this diſcuſſion.

My object was to ſhew, that if in man all the paſſions above cited be factitious, all men are in conſequence ſuſceptible of them. To make this
truth

truth ftill more evident, I fhall here prefent him with the genealogy of the paffions.

C H A P. XXII.

The genealogy of the paffions.

MAN is animated by a principle of life, which is corporeal fenfibility : this fenfibility is produced in us by a love of pleafure and a hatred for pain : it is from thofe two fentiments united in man, and always prefent to his mind, that is formed what we call the paffion of felf-love (84). The love of felf produces the defire of happinefs, the defire of happinefs that of power, and the love of power gives birth to envy, avarice, ambition, and in general all thofe factitious paffions * (85), that under various denominations are nothing more in us than a love of power difguifed, and applied to the feveral means of attaining it.

---

* *Paffions, like elements, tho' bern to fight,*
Yet, mixed and foftened, in his work unite
Love, hope, and joy, fair Pleafure's fmiling train,
Hate, fear, and grief, the family of Pain ;
Thefe mixed with art, and to due bounds confined,
Make and maintain the ballance of the mind :
The lights and fhades, whofe well accorded ftrife
Gives all the ftrength and colour of our life.

POPE.

VOL. I.   A a   Thefe

These means being different, we see man, according to his situation or the form of government under which he is placed, advance to power by the path of riches, intrigue, ambition, glory, talents, &c. but constantly direct his steps toward it.

If we here recollect what is said in the second, third, and fourth sections of this work, which is,

1. That all men have an equal aptitude to understanding.

2. That this equal aptitude is a dead power in them, when not vivified by the passions.

3. That the passion of glory is that which most commonly sets them in action.

4. That all men are susceptible of it in countries where glory conducts to power.

The general conclusion I draw from hence is, that all men organised in the common manner may be animated by the sort of passion proper to elevate them to the highest truths.

The only objection that remains for me to answer is the following. All men, they will say, may love glory (86), but can this passion be carried by each of them to a degree of force sufficient to put in action the equal aptitude they have to understanding?

To resolve this question, I will suppose that I have concentered all my happiness in the possession of glory; this passion being then as lively in me as the love of myself, will necessarily be confounded

founded in me with that fentiment. It is required therefore to prove, that the paffion of felf-love, common to all men, is the fame in all ; and that it may at leaft endow them all with that energy and force of attention that is requifite to the acquiring the greateft ideas.

C H A P. XXIII.

Of the force of the fentiment of felf-love.

THE fentiment of felf-love, differently modified in different men, is effentially the fame in all. This fentiment is independent of the greater or lefs perfection of the organs. A man may be deaf, blind, lame, and infirm, and yet have the fame folicitude for his prefervation, the fame averfion to pain, and the fame love for pleafure.

Neither the force nor weaknefs of temperament, nor the perfection of the organs, augment or diminifh in us the force of the fentiment of felf-love. Women have no lefs love for themfelves than men, and yet have not the fame organifation. If there were a way to meafure the force of this fentiment, it fhould be by its *conftancy*, its *unity*, and if I may fo fay, its *habitual prefence* ; now in all thefe refpects the fentiment of felf-love is the fame in all men.

It

It is this fentiment that fometimes arms men
with an obftinate courage, as with a fword, to triumph over the greateft obftacles, and that fometimes gives them a prudent fear, as a fhield, to
avoid danger ; in a word, it is this fentiment
that, always bufied in promoting the happinefs of each individual, watches inceffantly over
his prefervation.   Now if the love of felf be in
this refpect the fame in all, all are therefore fufceptible of the fame degree of paffion, and confequently of the degree proper to put in action the
equal aptitude they have to underftanding.   But
admitting, for a moment, that the fentiment of
felf-love acts not fo ftrongly in one as in another :
it is certain that this difference, not yet perceived
by experience, muft be confequently very fmall,
and that it can have no influence on the mind.

A mechanician turns afide no more of a river
than is neceffary to move the wheels and the ma-
chinery placed on its banks ; he lets the reft of the
water run into the fea.   In like manner it is not
neceffary to turn afide any more of the whole fentiment of felf-love than the part neceffary to put
in action the equal aptitude all men have to underftanding.   Now this portion is confiderably
lefs than is imagined.   If we confult experience
in this matter, it will teach us that the fear of
the rod, or a punifhment ftill more flight, is fufficient to endow a child with the attention neceffary
for attaining of languages (87).   Now this fort of

attention is either the moſt, or at leaſt one of the moſt laborious and fatiguing of all others *.

Experience teaches us alſo that all our diſco-veries are the gifts of chance ; that we owe to chance the firſt hint of every new truth ; that all truths of this ſort are, ſo to ſay, catched without attention ; that their diſcovery, for this reaſon, has always been regarded as an inſpiration, and conſequently that there is no poet or philoſopher whom the harmony, brilliancy, perſpicuity, and preciſion of expreſſion, have not coſt more time and pains than his moſt happy ideas.

From whence it reſults, that all men organiſed in the common manner are ſuſceptible of the de-gree of attention requiſite for raiſing themſelves to the higheſt truths, and that on the hypotheſis that the ſentiment of ſelf-love is not the ſame in all men, (an hypotheſis doubtleſs impoſſible,) the ſmall difference that is found in this reſpect among them, cannot have any influence on their under-ſtandings.

In fact, if we ſuppoſe ſelf-love to be ſtronger in ſome than in others, yet this paſſion, as expe-rience proves, will not be leſs equally habitual in

---

* If the ſtudy of their native tongue appear in general leſs laborious to children than the ſtudy of geometry, it is becauſe children find more habitually the neceſſity of talking, than of comparing geometric figures ; and the perception of the ne-ceſſity of attention renders it continually leſs diſagreeable and laborious.

them.

them. Now if all fuperiority of underftanding *
depends lefs on a lively than an habitual attention, it is evident on this fuppofition, all men
muft be ftill endowed with the degree of paffion
proper to put in action the equal aptitude they have
to underftanding.

* When I mention the underftanding or judgment, the
reader, clearly to conceive my ideas, fhould recollect that the
underftanding is the produce of the attention, and the attention that of any paffion whatever, but efpecially of glory. In
vain does chance or education offer us, in reading, converfation, &c. objects of comparifon from which new ideas might refult; thofe objects will be to us barren feeds, if attention do
not render them fertile, that is, if we have not an intereft, a
lively defire, to compare them, and obferve the refemblances
and differences, the agreements and difagreements thofe objects
have with each other and with us.

If they frequently fay of a great man that he is the child of
misfortune, it is becaufe in general being continually forced to
ftrive with adverfity, a man becomes more thoughtful and
acute; he is therefore always what his fituation makes him.
But is adverfity fo falutary as fuppofed? Yes: in the prime
of life, when a habit of thinking and reflecting may be yet acquired. That age paffed, misfortune afflicts a man but affords
him little information. *Adverfity*, fays the Scotch proverb, *is
wholefome at breakfaft, indifferent at dinner, and mortal at fupper.*
Befide, adverfity frequently excites in us only a lively and momentaneous effervefcence, that is often tranfient. A paffion
for glory is more durable, and for that reafon more proper to
produce great men and form great talents.

CHAP.

C H A P. XXIV.

The discovery of great ideas is the effect of constant attention.

A Vehement desire frequently occasions an effort of the mind more lively than lasting. Now the acquisition of great talents supposes an obstinate application, and a desire of instruction more habitual than vehement.

However engaged people of the world may be with their fortune and their pleasure, they feel by intervals the desire of glory. But why does this desire prove fruitless to them? Because it is not sufficiently durable. It is to the constancy of desires that great success is annexed. If an Agnes always deceives an Arnolph, it is because the desire of a woman to meet a lover is always more habitual than the desire of preventing it is in those that watch over her.

The inhabitants of Kamschatka are in some things of an unequalled stupidity; in others they have a marvellous industry. In the making of cloths, says their historian, they surpass the Europeans *. Why? Because, inhabiting one of

---

* If the inhabitants of Kamschatka surpass us in certain acts, they may equal us in all. Talents are nothing more than different applications of the same understanding to different subjects.

He

the moft inclement climates of the earth, they are moft habitually fenfible of the want of covering. Now an habitual want always produces induftry. A man who is fenfible of the value of confidera-tion, that it procures power, (the common object of the defire of men), will do his utmoft to attain it. It is in the poffeffion of that efteem he cen-tres all his happinefs, and it is then the defire of glory is identified with the love of ourfelves. Now this laft fentiment, as is proved by expe-rience, being habitually prefent to all men, ought to endow them with that fort of attention to which the fuperiority of the underftanding is annexed.

All men organifed in the common manner are therefore fufceptible not only of paffions, but of the habitual degree of paffions, fufficient to elevate them to the higheft ideas.

From whence then proceeds the extreme in-equality of underftandings? Becaufe nobody fees precifely (88) the fame objects; nor is precifely in the fame fituation (89); nor has received the fame education; and becaufe, finally, chance, that prefides over our inftruction, does not conduct all men to mines equally rich and fruitful.

He that can lift a pound of feathers or wool, can lift a pound of iron or lead. The difference therefore perceived be-tween the induftry of the inhabitants of Kamfchatka and ours, arifes from the different wants that a favage or polifhed nation muft fee in different climates,

It

It is therefore to education, taken in its fulleſt extent we can underſtand the term, and in which the idea of chance is alſo included *, that we are to refer the inequality of underſtandings.

To complete the proofs of this truth, it only remains for me to ſhew, in the following ſection, the errors and contradictions into which they fall, who on the ſame ſubject adopt principles different from mine.

I ſhall take M. Rouſſeau for an example. He is of all others the writer who in his works has treated this queſtion with the moſt acuteneſs and eloquence. I ſhall therefore diſcuſs his principal opinions ; and if I demonſtrate their falſity and contradiction, I imagine that the public then leſs

---

* Becauſe chance has always a part in our inſtruction, are we from thence to infer the inutility of education ? No : education will never make all the inhabitants of a nation men of ſuperior underſtanding ; but by improving it, by inventing new means of exciting in us the deſire of glory, and putting men frequently in ſituations where chance places them rarely, there is no doubt but its empire may be greatly contracted.

There are in Rome conſervatories or ſchools of muſic, from whence conſtantly iſſue good muſicians, and in which are every year formed ſome men of genius. At Paris there is alſo a ſchool for bridges and public roads that produces intelligent artiſts, among whom are found ſome men of ſuperior talents.

An excellent education may therefore increaſe the talents of a nation, and may make of the meaneſt of the people men of ſenſe and intelligence. Now thoſe advantages of an improved education are ſufficient to encourage men to the ſtudy of a ſcience, the perfection of which is in part connected with the happineſs of humanity.

attached

attached to its ancient prejudices, will judge of my principles without partiality, and will find it-self in that calm and happy difpofition that makes men adopt every juft idea, however paradoxical it may at firft appear.

NOTES.

N O T E S.

1. (page 272.) SOME have regarded the impetuofity of attack in a battle, as one of the charac-teriftics of the French : but this impetuofity they have in com-mon with the Turks, and in general with all nations not ac-cuftomed to a fevere difcipline. The French, however, are fufceptible of it. The king of Pruffia has fome of them in his army, and all are there exercifed in the Pruffian manner.

2. (p. 273.) The words loyal and polifhed are not the fame. A people of flaves may be polifhed. The habit of fear will make them reverential. Such a people are often more civil, and always lefs loyal, than one that is free. The merchants of all nations atteft the loyalty of the Englifh traders. The man that is free, is in general a man of probity.

3. (ibid.) In a degraded nation, we do not find, even among the firft of the citizens, charaéters of a certain eleva-tion. Free and bold fpirits would be there too difcordant from the others.

4. (p. 274.) Who, in the Eaft, is the man the moft extolled ? The greateft tyrant: he is the man moft feared and moft deteft-ed. This tyrant, fo much praifed while living, may, therefore, always think himfelf the idol and delight of his people. If hi-ftory draw his portrait truly, it muft be a long time after his death. What method then has an Eaftern monarch to know, if he really carries with him to the tomb the efteem and regret of his fubjeéts ? He has but one : which is to refleét within him-felf, and examine, if he be always employed in promoting the happinefs of his people, and if in all his aétions he have never confulted any thing but the national intereft. Has he been al-ways indifferent about it ? He may reft affured, whatever eu-logy they give him, that his name will be defpifed by pofterity. Death is the lance of Ithuriel ; it deftroys the charm of falf-hood and flattery.

Difgrace operates in the fame manner on a vizir, as death does on a fultan. While the former is in place, there are no eulogies with which he is not loaded, no talents that were not
ascribed

afcribed to him : but when difcharged, he is, as he was before his elevation, frequently one of the meaneft of the people.

5. (p. 274.) Can an arbitrary monarch, always regardlefs of his foreign enemies, flatter himfelf that a people habituated to tremble at the fcourge of his power, and bafe enough tamely to fuffer themfelves to be plundered of their property, their lives, and their liberty, will defend him againft the attack of a powerful enemy ? A monarch ought to know, that in dividing the chain which unites the intereft of each individual, with the general intereft, he deftroys all virtue, and that the virtue of an empire once deftroyed, it precipitates into ruin. That the props of a defpotic throne muft fink under its weight. That merely ftrong in the ftrength of his army, that army defeated, his fubjects, freed from their fears, will no longer fight for him. That two or three battles have in the Eaft decided the fate of the greateft empires. Witnefs Darius, Tigranes, and Antiochus. The Romans fought four hundred years to fubjugate Italy, when free, but to conquer fervile Afia they only prefented themfelves before it.

6. (p. 275.) The defpot, for his glory and his fecurity, ought to regard thofe very philofophers he hates, as his friends, and thofe courtiers whom he cherifhes, and whofe vile flatteries of his vices excite him to crimes that lead on to his perdition, as his enemies.

7. (p. 276.) By what fign do we diftinguifh an arbitrary power from a legitimate ? Both make laws ; both inflict capital or leffer punifhments on the violators of thofe laws. Both employ the power of the community, that is, the power of the nation, to maintain their edicts, or repel the attack of an enemy. True: but they differ, fays Locke, in this; the firft employs the public authority to gratify his caprice or enflave the inhabitants, and the other employs it to render himfelf refpectable to his neighbours, to fecure to the inhabitants their property, their laws, and their liberty. In fhort, the employing the national force to any other purpofe than the general welfare is a crime. It is therefore the different manner of employing the national force that diftinguifhes the arbitrary power from the legitimate.

8 (ibid.) Defpotifm appeared in fuch a light to the virtuous Tullius, the feventh king of Rome, that he had the courage to fix himfelf the bounds to royal authority.

9. (p. 277.)

9. (p. 277.) Among the various caufes of the little fuccefs of France, in the laft war, when we reckon the jealoufy and inexperience of the generals, and their indifference for the public welfare, perhaps we fhould not forget the gangrene of religious flavery, which began at that time to fpread itfelf over all minds. The Frenchman now no longer dares to think for himfelf. From day to day, he thinks lefs, and will, from day to day, becomes lefs refpectable.

10. (p. 282.) The love of power is fuch, that in England itfelf there is fcarce a minifter who would not inveft his prince with arbitrary power. The intoxication of a great place, makes the minifter forget, that weighed down by the power he erects, he and his pofterity will perhaps be its firft victims.

Why do men feek great employments? Is it from a defire of doing good? He that is not animated by this motive, muft regard them as burdens. When men defire them, it is lefs for public utility than their own. Men are not, therefore, born fo good as fome pretend. Goodnefs fuppofes a love for others, and it is in ourfelves only we center all our love.

11. (ibid.) The defire of power is general, and if to obtain it all men do not expofe themfelves to the fame dangers, it is becaufe the love of felf-prefervation is in the greateft part of them an equipoife to their love of power.

12. (p. 283.) In almoft every country, force is preferred to juftice. In France, they make the advocate pay taxes, but not the lieutenant. Why? Becaufe one is to a certain degree the reprefentative of juftice, and the other of power.

13. (p. 285.) Who are the enemies of an illuftrious man? His rivals, and almoft all his cotemporaries. His prefence humbles them. By whom is he praifed? By the ftranger; he is without envy: he makes a part of living pofterity: the diftance of place equals that of time. The approbation of ftrangers is to a man of letters almoft the only recompence that he can now expect.

14. (p. 290.) When we are inwardly conftrained to acknowledge another to have a fuperior underftanding, we hate him; his prefence is difguftful: we would be revenged and get rid of him: for that purpofe we force him to leave his country, like Defcartes, Bayle, Maupertuis, &c. or we perfecute him like Montefquieu, Diderot, &c.

There

There is no great man, they say, in the fight of his wife, or his valet de chambre. I well believe it. How can we continually live with a man we are too often forced to admire? In this cafe, we muft either leave him, or ceafe to efteem him. Riches and dignities may for a time impofe filence on envy; but then it is fecretly irritated. We are unwilling that a man already our fuperior by birth and dignity, fhould alfo excel us in talents. Does a man write like Frederic? We ridicule in him the talent for writing which we admire in Cæfar, Cicero, &c. we fee him with regret eftablifh his merit by a good work. But is not his converfation alone fufficient to prove his genius? No: in converfation the ideas fucceed fo rapidly, that we have not time to confider them in every light, nor to fee their propriety; befide, the tone and gefture of the fpeaker, and the difpofition of the hearer, may all help to impofe on us. We may therefore always difpute a merit of this fort: we do, and confole ourfelves by it.

Perhaps to be loved we fhould merit but little efteem; all fuperiority attracts awe and averfion. Why does affability render merit fupportable? Becaufe it makes a man in fome degree defpicable.

A referved merit gives at once a difpofition to refpect and hatred, and an affable merit a difpofition to love and contempt. He who would be careffed by thofe that furround him fhould be content with little efteem. We pardon merit by forgetting it. Great talents have fome admirers and few friends. The fecret and general defire of the majority is not that genius exalt itfelf, but that folly be extended.

15. (p. 290.) From what motive do men purchafe fatiric pamphlets? From the fcandal they caft on great men, and the praifes they give to thofe of little ability. Human nature is not changed in this refpect. If the Athenians, fays Plutarch, fo haftily advanced young Cymon to the higheft offices, it was to mortify Themiftocles; they were tired of efteeming the fame man fo long together: Why do we extol to excefs rifing talents? Frequently to deprefs thofe already in efteem. When we penetrate, fays Plutarch, profoundly into the human heart, and fee its principal motives, we find that the defire of obliging one man arifes lefs from the pleafure of ferving him, than the gratification of envy in depreciating another.

16. (p. 291.) Fathers in general, though honeft, yet ignorant, fee with impatience their fons frequent the company of men of

letters,

letters, and give their company the preference to all others : their paternal pride is thereby mortified.

17. (p. 291.) If, as they say, letters and philosophy be in France without protectors, we may, without the spirit of prophecy, affirm that the succeeding generation will be without learning or genius ; and that of all the arts, those of luxury will alone be cultivated.

18. (p. 292.) Violence and persecution are in general proportioned to the merit of the persecuted. In every country illustrious men have undergone disgrace. It is scarce one hundred and fifty years since a man in England could not have been with impunity a great man.

19. (ibid.) Few authors think for themselves. The greatest part of books are made after other books ; yet he that has not a manner of his own, ought not to expect esteem from posterity.

20. (ibid.) Formerly all men bowed down before the ancients, and whoever in secret preferred Tasso to Virgil or Homer never owned it. What reason however have we for concealing our opinion, when we do not give it as a law ? What better than the diversity of opinions, can improve the taste of the public ?

21. (ibid.) When princes or magistrates regard the opinion of posterity, they commonly merit its esteem ; they will be just in their edicts and their sentences. It is the same with authors. When a writer has posterity present to his mind, his manner of comparing objects becomes great ; he discovers important truths, and he secures to himself the general esteem, because he writes for men of all ages and all countries.

22. (p. 293.) The theological libel intitled the Censure of Belisarius, excites horror by the barbarity and cruelty of its assertions : it always recalls to my mind that fine verse of Racine.

Eh quoi, Mathan ! d'un prétre est-ce la le langage ?

What, Mathan ! is this the language of a priest ?

23. (ibid.) The citizens to whom we owe the greatest respect are, first, those generals and ministers whose valour or sagacity have secured the grandeur or felicity of empires. The next most useful citizens are such as improve the arts and sciences, that supply the wants of men, or preserve them from discontent.

content. Why then do we ſhew more reſpect to a man of wealth or power than to a great mathematician, poet, or phi-loſopher? Becauſe our firſt reſpect is for a power or poſſeſſion to which we conſtantly join the idea of happineſs and pleaſure.

Power is the idol of youth, and even of thoſe of maturer age; ſo long as they can twine the myrtles with their laurels.

If power be ſometimes diſdained by age, it is becauſe it no longer affords its former advantage.

24. (p. 297.) It is at the period that men, by increaſing, are forced to manure the earth, that they perceive the neceſſity of ſecuring to the labourer his harveſt, and the property of the land he cultivates. Before cultivation it is no wonder that the ſtrongeſt ſhould think he has as much right over a piece of barren ground as the firſt occupier.

25. (ibid.) A reſiſtance to him who is poſſeſſed of power is reputed ſedition and a crime even in poliſhed nations. No proof of this can be more clear than the complaint an Engliſh merchant made to the houſe of commons: " Gentlemen, ſaid " he, you can never imagine how perfidiouſly the negroes treat " us; their wickedneſs is ſo great, that on ſome of the coaſts of " Africa they prefer death to ſlavery. When we have bought " them, they ſtab themſelves, or plunge into the ſea; which " is ſo much loſs to the purchaſers. Judge by this action of " the perverſity of that abominable race."

26. (p. 299.) At what time do a people violate the law of na-tion? When they can do it with impunity. Rome while weak was equitable and virtuous: when it had conquered Ma-cedonia no nation could reſiſt it: then become more ſtrong it ceaſed to be juſt. Its inhabitants were from that time without honour, and without faith. The powerful are always unjuſt. Juſtice between nations is conſtantly founded on a reciprocal fear, and from hence that political axiom: *If you deſire peace, prepare for war. Si vis pacem, para bellum.*

27. (p. 301.) Ariſtotle places robbery among the different kinds of hunting; and Solon, among the ſeveral profeſſions, reckons that of theft: he obſerves only that we ſhould not rob either our fellow-citizens, or the allies of our republic. Rome, under the firſt of her kings, was a den of robbers. The Ger-mans, ſays Cæſar, regard devaſtation and pillage as the only

exerciſe

exercife proper for youth ; and the only one that can keep them from idlenefs, and make them finifhed men.

28 (p. 301) There is, they fay, a law of nations between the Englifh, French, Germans, Italians, &c. I believe it. The fear of reprifals will eftablifh it among nations of a force nearly equal; but when they are freed from that fear, and have to do with a favage people, from that moment the law of nations appears to them nothing more than a chimera.

Is it for the Chriftians to talk of the law of nations, the law of nature and of virtue? They, who without any injury received from the Indians of the Eaft, invade their coafts, lay wafte their cities, and drive out the inhabitants. They, who with their European merchandize carry to the African towns a fpirit of difcord, and availing themfelves of the wars they have kindled, purchafe the vanquifhed for flaves. They, who without offence, or even the appearance of offence on the part of the weftern Indians, landed in America, deftroyed the palaces of Montezuma and the Incas, maffacred their fubjects, and feized on their dominions, without regard to the law, *primo occupanti*.

The church boafts of caufing treafures that have been ftole to be reftored ; but has it caufed to be reftored to their legal proprietors the empires of Mexico and Peru? Has it not on the contrary, in concert with princes, pillaged the new world? Has it not enriched itfelf with the fpoils, and by its conduct brought into contempt thofe precepts of the natural law, which it fays are engraved on every heart by the hand of God?

What can be more abfurd and pitiful than the morality of the church? If a prince take a miftrefs, it is in their opinion a matter of indifference, if fhe do not oppofe the projects of the church, for then the priefts cry aloud againft the impiety. But if the fame prince carry war and devaftation among a people that have not offended him, if he caufe 400,000 men to perifh in an expediton, and bow down his people with taxes, the priefts are filent. Curious morality this of the catholic church !

29. (p. 302.) Men love juftice, they fay ; but the magiftrates are the inftruments of juftice, and charged by the ftate to adminifter it ; they therefore ought, above all, to protect innocence. But do they in reality protect it? A criminal caufe is conducted in two different manners in Spain and in England:

Vol. I.   B b   that

that in which an advocate is given to the accused, and where his trial is conducted in a public manner, is without doubt that where innocence is moft protected againft the corruption and partiality of the judges, and confequently the beft. Why then is it not adopted? Why do not the magiftrates folicit its admiffion? Becaufe they imagine that the more arbitrary their fentences are, the more fear they will infpire, and the more authority they will have over the people. The fo much boafted love of equity is not therefore either natural or common to men. Now how can we call them the friends of humanity, when they are not even friends to juftice?

30. (p. 302.) The idea of happinefs is fo clofely connected in the mind with that of power, that they are not without difficulty feparated. We refpect even the appearance of power: it is to this fentiment that we owe perhaps a certain admiration of fuicide. We imagine him to be poffeffed of great power who can fo defpife life as to put himfelf to death. To what caufe but the love of power can we attribute the exceffive hatred of fagacious women for men of a certain inclination? Alexander, Socrates, Solon, and Catinat* were heroes, faithful friends, and worthy citizens: a man may therefore have this inclination, and be ufeful to his family and his country. From whence then proceeds the horror of women for men fufpected of it? Becaufe they have lefs power over them. Now this defect of power is to them infupportable; they are fo many flaves to it, at leaft in their empire, men of this fort are therefore guilty of a crime that death alone can expiate.

31. (ibid.) It is power that makes one monarch refpectable to another. While Philip II. was bufied in his clofet, he called for a fervant, and nobody came; his fool laughed: What do you laugh at? faid the king: To think of the awe and fear in which you hold all Europe, and of the contempt in which they would hold you if you were not powerful, and the reft of your fubjects did not ferve you better than your domeftics.

* *That thofe men were really addicted to this perverfe inclination feems to be mere conjecture; it was doubtlefs very common in Greece, and therefore every ancient Greek is fuppofed to have been infected with it: juft as we fuppofe every Dutchman to be a lover of money, and every Frenchman fond of gallantry.*

32. (p. 303.)

32. (p. 303.) Princes rarely feel the enthufiafm of equity: few among them are animated with a noble love of humanity. In all antiquity Gelon alone affords an example of it. He held human facrifices in horror; he carried the war into Africa, and obliged the vanquifhed Carthagenians to abolifh that deteftable cuftom. Catherine, in like manner, armed to force the Poles to toleration. Of all wars thofe two perhaps have been alone undertaken for the happinefs of nations. Gelon and Catherine II. will therefore, in this refpect, divide the efteem of pofterity. If we would judge of the merit of fovereigns, we fhould do it, not by the little broils that may arife in their families, but by the great benefits they have done, or would have done to mankind. The defire of doing good is rare among them. The only time at which the public good commonly operates is that when the intereft of the prince coincides with that of the people. At what periods have the kings of France promoted the liberty of their fubjects, and weakened the feudal power? When the haughty vaffals of the crown equalled themfelves with their fovereigns; then the ambition of the monarchs gave freedom to the people

Let not the princes of the Eaft boaft of their love of equity. He that would make brutes of his fubjects cannot love them. It is a folly to imagine the people would be then more docile and eafy to govern. The more enlightened a nation is, the more readily it fubmits to the juft demands of an equitable adminiftration. He that would blind his fubjects, would be unjuft with impunity. Such in general are men, and yet they dare to call themfelves the friends of juftice. O felf-ignorance and hypocrify!

33. (ibid.) Are there, as they fay, men who facrifice their deareft intereft to juftice? No: but there are, who hold nothing dearer than juftice. This generous fentiment is in them the effect of an excellent education. By what method can this principle be engraved on every heart? By prefenting on one hand, the unjuft man as bafe, defpifed, and confequently impotent; and on the other hand, the juft man as efteemed, honoured, and confequently powerful.

When the idea of juftice is by thefe means connected in the mind with thofe of power and happinefs, they will be confounded, and form but one; and when we have a habit of recalling them together, it will foon become impoffible to divide them.

This

This habit once contracted, we shall be proud of appearing just
and virtuous ; and then there is nothing we shall not sacrifice to
that noble pride.

It is thus the love of power and importance begets the love of
justice.   This last love, it is true, is a stranger to man ; that of
power, on the contrary, is natural to him ; it is common to all,
to the honest man and the knave, the savage and the polished
citizen.

The love of power is the immediate effect of corporeal sensibility, and the desire of justice is the effect of instruction ; consequently, it is on the sagacity of the laws that depends the virtue of a people.   How many virtuous men are there among a
people where justice is respected, that would be unjust among a
ferocious nation, where equity is regarded as weakness and
cowardice ? Men therefore do not love equity for itself.   This
question has been at all times decided by the conduct and manners of all nations, and all despots.

34. (p. 307.) Under a feudal government who are the tyrants ? The lords.   Tyrants therefore, they will say, are more
numerous here than under a despotic government: I doubt it.
The sultan has under him vizirs, pachas, beys, receivers and di-
rectors of taxes, with an infinity of underlings and sub-tyrants,
who are still more indifferent to the happiness of the vassals
than the proprietors.

35. (p. 312.) In England, if iniquity in a great man be
despised by low people, it is because those people, being protected by the law, have nothing to fear from the great.   If in
every other country the vices of the great be on the contrary
respected, it is because vice is there armed with power, and
power we can abhor and not despise.

36 (p. 314.) Attila, as well as Thomas, gloried in being the
scourge of the Almighty.

37. (ibid.) Seditious and rebellious are the injurious titles
the powerful oppressor gives to the impotent oppressed.

38. (ibid.) In every empire where the momentary desire of a prince is a law, all the laws are contradictory, and
there are no appearances of moral principles, either in the go-
vernors or those that are governed.

39. (p. 317.) Contempt is the portion of weakness.   This is
perhaps the only truth of which princes are not ignorant.   If a
monarch lose a province or a town, he appears despicable even

in

in his own eyes : but if he unjuftly take a town or province from his neighbour, he thinks himfelf refpe&able. He has always feen injuftice honoured in the potent, and the world remain filent before power.

40. (p. 317.) The ftrong and wicked, fays an Englifh poet, fear thofe only that are ftronger and worfe than themfelves ; but the juft and virtuous ought to fear all men ; he has all his fellow-citizens, even his very friends, for perfecutors ; all attack him. His virtue frees them from the fear of revenge. Humanity in him is equal to weaknefs in others ; and under a vicious government, the good and weak are born vi&ims to the wicked and ftrong.

41. (p. 320.) An Englifh nobleman landed in Italy, ran over the country about Rome, and embarked haftily for England. Why, they faid, do you quit this fine country ? " I can no " longer bear to fee, he faid, the wretched looks of the Roman " peafants ; their mifery torments me ; they have not even a " human afpe&." This nobleman perhaps exaggerated ; but he did not falfify.

42. (ibid.) The murder of Clytus was the difgrace of Alexander, and the punifhment of the Dutch gazetteer that of the French minifter. The crime of thofe two unfortunate men was the fame ; they were both imprudent enough to fpeak the truth. In the laft century mankind were enraged at the treatment given the gazetteer. There are ages ftill more bafe, when the punifhment of a man of veracity is applauded.

43. (ibid.) When we are concerned for this gazetteer, and compare his crime with his punifhment, we feem to be tranfported to the dominion of the fultan of the Indies, who hanged his vifir for having put three grains of pepper into a cream tart. The illuftrious, but unfortunate, M. Chalotois was very near fuffering the fame fate, for having, in like manner, put three grains of falt into a letter, wrote, they fay, to a comptroller-general.

44. (p. 321.) In France, why do they not dare to exhibit the futility of the great on the ftage ? Becaufe, they fay, comedies of that fort would produce little reformation : it is true. The poet who flatters himfelf with corre&ing the frivolity of the French by a ridiculous portrait is deceived. There is no filling the veffels of the Dana'des. Men of found fenfe are not to be formed under a government where priefts and wo-

men

men have a powerful influence. A light and trifling spirit can alone be there cultivated ; for it is that only which leads to fortune.

45. (p. 321.) It is not to his genius, but conftantly to fome particular event, that a man of talents owes the protection of the ignorant. If the ugly feek the company of the blind, ignorance flies that of the fharp-fighted.

46. (ibid.) An ignorant vifir always views with an evil eye the man who travels into the countries of learned people and wife princes. The vifir fears that the traveller on his return fhould defpife him : an enemy to men of ability, he boafts of his contempt for them, and it is by this contempt the ftranger judges him. Great minifters and great princes have always been protectors of letters ; witnefs the prince of Brunfwick, Catherine II. Prince Henry of Pruffia, &c.

47. (ibid.) It was formerly the privilege of fools to fometimes fpeak the truth to princes ; but ftill with what caution and at what moments ! Let us imitate, fays one of them, the prudence of the cats ; they do not think themfelves fecure in an apartment till they have fmelled to every corner of it.

48. (p. 322.) It is to the liberty the Englifh and Dutch ftill enjoy that Europe owes the little of it that ftill remains. Except them there is fcarce any nation that does not groan under the yoke of ignorance and defpotifm. Every virtuous man, every good citizen, fhould therefore intereft himfelf in the liberty of thofe two people.

49. (p. 323.) It is only over automata that defpotifm commands. There are no characters but in a free nation. The Englifh have one ; the Eaftern nation have not : fear and fervility ftifles it among them.

50. (p. 324.) When a government prohibits writing on matters of adminiftration, it makes a vow of blindnefs, and that vow is common enough : " As long as my finances are well regulated, and my army well difciplined, faid a great prince, " let who will write againft my difcipline and my adminiftra- " tion ; but if I neglect either of thefe, who knows whether I " fhould not have the weaknefs to compel fuch writers to " filence."

51. (ibid.) When a man becomes a minifter, it is no longer his time to form principles, but to apply them ; carried away by the current of bufinefs, what he then learns is nothing more

more than details, always unknown to thofe that are not in place.

52. (p. 325.) To limit the prefs is to infult the nation : to prohibit the reading of certain books is to declare the inhabitants to be either fools or flaves : fuch a prohibition ought to fill them with difdain. But it will be faid, it is almoft always after the opinion of the powerful that a book is approved or condemned ; yes, at the beginning : but this firft judgment is nothing ; it is the voice of prejudice for or againft. The judgment truly interefting to an author is the judgment of the people, after reflection, which is almoft always juft.

53. (ibid.) The age at which men attain great places is frequently that when attention becomes the moft irkfome. At that age he who compels me to ftudy is my enemy ; I feek his punifhment and wifh his death. I can very well pardon a poet for his fine verfes ; I can read them without attention : but I cannot pardon a moralift for his acute reafonings ; for the importance of the fubject obliges me to reflect, and if he combats my prejudices, he wounds my pride, he robs me of my indolence, and forces me to think ; now every conftraint produces hatred.

54. (p. 326.) The land of defpotifm is fruitful in miferies as well as monfters. Defpotifm is the luxury of power, of no fignificance to the happinefs of a fovereign. The very idea of this power would have made a Roman tremble. It is the terror of an Englifhman. Judge Pratt fays on this fubject, "Let "us be cautious that the ftudy of the Italian and the French "does not debafe a free people."

What are in the eyes of the Englifh the nobility of Europe ? Men who join to the quality of flaves that of oppreffers of the people ; of citizens whom the law itfelf cannot protect againft the man in place. A nobleman in Portugal is neither proprietor of his life, his eftate, or his liberty : he is a domeftic negro, who, flogged by the immediate order of his mafter, defpifes the negro flogged by order of the overfeer of a plantation. This, in almoft all the courts of Europe, is the only difference between the humble citizen and the haughty nobleman.

55. (ibid.) We muft either creep, or keep at a diftance from the court. He who cannot live but by its favours, muft degrade his nature, or die of hunger. Few men prefer the latter.

56. (ibid.) The late king of Pruffia being at fupper with the Englifh ambaffador, afked him what he thought of mo-

B b 4

narchs.

narchs. " In general, he replied, I think them a worthlefs
" race ; they are ignorant, and debauched by flattery. The
" only thing in which they fucceed, is riding a horfe ; and at
" the fame time, of all thofe that approach them, the horfe is
" the only one that does not flatter them ; for he breaks their
" neck if they do not govern him well "

57. (p. 327.) The more defpotic a government is, and the
more degraded the minds of the people are, the more they
boaft of a love for their tyrant. The flaves at Morocco blefs
their fate and their prince, at the very time he condefcends to
cut their throats with his own hands.

58 (ibid.) Sovereigns corrupted by flattery are fpoiled
children. Habituated to command over flaves, they frequently
attempt to behave in the fame manner to their equals, and are
fometimes punifhed by the lofs of a part of their dominions.
It was the challifement the Romans inflicted on Tigranes, Antiochus, &c. when thofe tyrants dared to equal themfelves to a
free people.

59. (p. 329.) When a man is rich he would be admired for
his wealth ; when he is of quality, he would be admired for his
rank ; when he is well made, for his figure. It is not difficult
to praife : all have fomething they think commendable.

60. (p. 331.) The man of genius thinks for himfelf; his
opinions are fometimes contrary to thofe commonly received ;
he therefore fhocks the vanity of the greater number. To
offend nobody we fhould have no ideas but thofe of the world :
a man is then without genius and without enemies.

61. (p. 336) The Albigois were treated in the fame manner as the Vaudois. The excefs to which the rage of intolerance was carried againft them is not to be conceived. The
frightful picture of the barbarities exercifed on the Vaudois is
left us by Samuel Morland the Englifh ambaffador at Savoy,
then refident on the fpot. " Never, fays he, did Chriftians
" commit fuch cruelties on Chriftians : they cut off the heads of
" the barbes, (the teachers of the people), boiled and eat them :
" they cut open the bellies of the women, to the navel, with
" flints ; from others they cut off their breafts, broiled and eat
" them. They applied fire to the private parts of fome ; they
" broke the limbs of others, and expofed them to fcorching
" fires ; from others they plucked off their nails with pincers :
" they tied men, half dead, to the tails of horfes, and drew
" them in that manner over rocks. The leaft of their punifh-
" ments

" ments was to be thrown from a fleep rock, from whence they
" frequently fell among trees, to which they hung till they
" perifhed by hunger, cold, and their wounds. They cut
" fome of them into a thoufand pieces, and ftrewed their limbs
" and flefh about the country. They impaled the virgins by
" their private parts, and carried them about like ftandards.
" Among others they drew a young man, named Pelanchion,
" about the ftreets of Lucerne, which are every where ftrewed
" with pointed flint ftones; and if the pain made him lift up
" his head or his hands, they were prefently beat down : they
" at laft cut off his fecret parts, and by ftuffing them into his
" mouth, ftrangled him ; then cut off his head, and threw the
" trunk into the river. The Catholics tore to pieces with
" their hands the infants they fnatched from the cradle. They
" roafted young girls alive, cut off their, breafts, and eat them.
" From others they cut off the nofe, the ears, and other parts
" of their bodies. They filled the mouth of fome with gun-
" powder, to which they fet fire. They flead others alive, and
" hung the fkin before the windows of Lucerne. They beat
" out the brains of others, which they roafted or boiled, and
" then eat. The leaft punifhments were to cut out their
" hearts, to burn them alive, to disfigure their faces, cut them
" into a thoufand pieces, and then drown them. But they
" fhewed themfelves true Catholics, and worthy Romans,
" when at Gareiglian they heated an oven, and forced eleven
" Vaudois to throw each other into it, till the laft, whom the
" murderers threw in themfelves. Nothing was to be feen in
" all the vallies but bodies dead or dying. The fnow of the
" Alps was ftained with their blood. Here was feen a head,
" there a trunk, legs, arms, bowels torn out, and a heart yet
" beating."

For what pretended crime did they punifh the Vaudois with
fo much barbarity ? For that of rebellion, they faid. They
were reproached with not having abandoned their dwellings and
the place of their birth to the firft order of Gaftall and the
pope; of not having exiled themfelves from a country they
had poffeffed for 1500 years, and where they had always enjoyed the free exercife of their religious worfhip. It is thus
the gentle Catholic religion, its gentle minifters and faints
have at all times treated mankind. What could the apoftles
of the devil do worfe ?

62. (p. 336.)

62. (p. 356) No man can cast a penetrative look on the various false religions, without conceiving the greatest contempt for the human race in general, and for himself in particular. What! he will say, were thousands of years necessary to convince men equally intelligent with myself of the folly of paganism? Do the Jews and the Guebres still persist in their errors! Do the Mussulmans still believe in Mahomet; and may it be thousands of years before they are convinced of the falsity of the Koran! Man must certainly be a very weak and credulous animal, and in short, this planet of ours must be, as a wise man said, the mad-house of the universe.

63. (p. 357.) Why is the clergyman generally esteemed in England? Because he is tolerant: the laws tying his hands, and giving him no share in administration. Because he does not, and cannot injure any one; because the maintenance of the English clergy is not so burthensome to the state as the Catholic clergy; and lastly, because in that country religion is properly nothing more than a philosophical opinion.

64. (ibid.) What I say of zeal I say also of humility. Whatever sect we may suppose a cardinal to be, he can never really think himself humble when he sets himself up at Rome for the protector of such a kingdom as France. True humility would refuse so fastuous a title. I do not mean however to deny the stupidity of some prelates; but their ambitious pretensions prove less the ability of the clergy than the folly of the people. During my stay at Japan, said a traveller to me, whenever I heard the words Donoo-Sury-Sama, that is to say, My Lord Crane, they forced me to think on the name of some bishop.

65. (ibid.) Jesus exercised no authority upon earth. If he had desired that the sacerdotal power should command, he would have at first left that command with his apostles. Now their successors have not yet shewn us their commission, or title to such a legacy.

66. (ibid.) The Saducees were regarded as the most virtuous among the Jews. The word Saduc in Hebrew is synonimous to *just*. The Saducees therefore were, and ought to have been less hateful to God than the Pharisees: the latter demanded the death and the blood of Jesus Christ. Now incredulity is, and ever will be, less contrary to the spirit of the Gospel than inhumanity and deicide.

67. (p. 358.)

67. (p. 338.) To the difgrace of France, M. Roufleau has not been lefs perfecuted at Paris than at Neufchatel. The Sorbonnifts could not forgive him his dialogue of the Reafoner and the Infpired. That dialogue, they fay, is too bold. What anfwer is tnere to this? but the reafonings of M. Roufleau are either true or falfe. To refute juft reafons by violence is injuftice; to refute bad reafons by the fame method is folly: it is to confefs ftupidity; to injure our own caufe. Sophifms refute themfelves: the truth is eafily defended.

Befide, what are the objections of M. Roufleau? Thofe that every bonze, dervis, and mandarin makes to the monk he would convert. Are thofe objections infoluble? What then do the monks in China? Why do they afk affiftance, alms, and gratifications of princes, to defray the expence of a miffion where they can make no converts? But the monks who travel over the Eaft have no other object than to enrich themfelves by commerce; they employ the treafures that have been lavifhed on them by the people to no other purpofe than to deprive thofe very people of the profit of legitimate commerce. In this cafe what juft reproaches have not the nations to make them? And what accufations can they bring againft M. *Roufleau? He has preached, they fay, the religion of nature: but it is not contrary to the revealed. M. Roufleau has been honeft in his criticifms; he was not the author of thofe infamous libels intitled, *Gazette Ecclefiaftique*, yet he is banifhed, and the novelift is tolerated. Who then were thy judges, O illuftrious Roufleau? Fanatics, who would, if it were in their power, blaft the memory of Marcus Aurelius, Antoninus, and Trajan, and would accufe the greateft prince of Europe of his fuperior talents as a crime. What regard is to be had to fuch judgments? None. Let us appeal to pofterity, and defpife all thofe judgments that are not pronounced by reafon and equity. Pofterity will judge the judges, and if the moft intolerant have not been the greateft knaves, they have at leaft been the greateft fools.

A butt for the cabals of priefts, M. Roufleau is treated in this age as Abelard was in the twelfth by the monks of St. Denis. He denied that their founder was Denis the Areopagite mentioned in the New Teftament. From that moment they declared him an enemy to the glory and crown of France: he was confequently defamed, perfecuted, and profcribed by the faints of his century.

Who.ver

Whoever oppofes the pretenfions of a monk is an impious
wretch.   From hence the accufations of blafphemy and atheifm
are now become fo puerile and ridiculous.   I hope, for the honour of the human underftanding, that the great men of the
earth, the princes, minifters, and magiftrates will one day blufh
at having been the vile inftruments of monachal rage and vengeance; they will fear to make exile and punifhment honour-
able by the merit of thofe on whom thofe punifhments are inflicted.

The Athenians, to fecure their liberty, fometimes banifhed a
too popular citizen : the fear of a mafter made them profcribe
a great man.   The nations of Europe, fecure from that danger,
have not the fame pretence for committing the fame injuftice.

68. (p. 339.) Caffidor thought like St. John.   Religion, he
faid, cannot be commanded.   Force makes hypocrites, and not
believers.   *Religio imperari non poteft, quia nemo cogitur ut cre-
dat.*   Faith, fays St. Bernard, ought to be perfuaded, not commanded : *fides fuadenda, non imperanda.*   Nothing is more voluntary, fays Lactantius, than religion ; it is nothing in him to
whom it is repugnant.   *Nihil eft tam voluntariam quam religionem in qua, fe animus averfus eft, jam fublata, jam nulla eft.*
Nothing more contrary to religion, fays Tertullian, than to endeavour to force belief; it is not by violence, but freely we
muft believe.   *Non eft religionis religionem cogere velle, cum
fponte fufcipi debeat, non vi.*

69 (p. 342.) The Pagans, they will fay, believed in priefts
that were impoftors.   Be it fo : but did that belief give them a
right to perfecute ?   There are thoufands who believe in a
mountebank, or an old woman, rather than a phyfician.   Has
the latter a right to demand the death of the infidels in medicine ?   In corporeal as well as fpiritual maladies, every one
ought to choofe his own phyfician.

70. (ibid.) Frequently, fays M. Lambert of Pruffia in his *Novum
Organum*, we think, believe we think, and believe more than we
really think and believe.   This is the fource of a thoufand errors.   If a man forbear, for example, to read prohibited books,
he thinks he believes, and fufpects in fecret the falfity of his belief: he is like a falfe pleader, who fears to read the defence of
the adverfe party.

71. (ibid.) The pilots of the veffels of fuperftition are fkilful; as for the failors, the greateft part of them are ignorant.
The governing clergy require but little underftanding in the
                                                                    clergy

clergy governed; and on this account we have nothing to reproach the latter. How does your brother the priest employ
himself? somebody asked Fontenelle: In the morning, replied
the philosopher, he says mass, and in the evening he does not
know what he says.

72. (p. 342.) Nothing can be more abfurdly fubtle, fay the
Englifh, than the arguments of the theologians, to prove to the
ignorant Catholics the veracity of papifm. Thefe arguments
would do equally well to prove the truth of the Koran, that of
the Thoufand and One Nights, or the tale of Mother Goofe.
To be convinced of this, let them apply to thofe ftories the
fophifms and diftinctions of the fchools, and they will find nothing in them theologically incredible.

73. (p. 343.) Defcartes, when perfecuted, quitted France,
taking, like Æneas, his penates with him, that is, the efteem
and regret of men of fagacity. The parliament, then Ariftote-
lian, publifhed an arret againft the Cartefians: their doctrine was
therein condemned; as has fince been that of the Encyclopedia,
l'Efprit, and Emilius. There is nothing different in thefe
arrets but their dates. Now the prefent parliaments laugh at
the former; future parliaments will laugh at the prefent.

74. (ibid.) See the apology by Naudé, for great men ac-
cufed of magic. The author there thinks himfelf obliged to
prove that Homer, Virgil, Zoroafter, Orpheus, Democritus,
Solomon, pope Sylvefter, Empedocles, Apollonius, Agrippa,
Albert le Grand, Paracelfus, &c. never were forcerers.

75. (ibid.) The theologians have fo much abufed the word
materialift, of which they have never been able to give a clear
idea, that the term at laft became fynonimous to a clear underftanding. They now mean by that word thofe celebrated
writers whofe works are read with avidity.

76. (p. 344.) With what odious imputations have not the Catholics loaded the Proteftants? What tricks have not the monks
employed to irritate princes againft their faithful fubjects!
What art to make them appear no other than rebels, who with
rage in their hearts, and arms in their hands, are ever ready to
fcale the throne! Such, O monks, is your juftice and your charity! On what do you found your calumnies? Which of the
churches, the Roman or the Proteftant, has the moft frequently
arrogated the right of dethroning kings, and depriving them
at once of fcepter and life? and which has moft frequently put
it in practice? If we examine hiftory, and calculate the number

and

and kind of attempts made by one and the other, the question will soon be decided.

The reformed, they will say, have made war on princes. No : but princes have made war on them. When I am unjustly attacked, defence is a law of nature, and numerous persecutors always avail themselves of this law. It is by irritating the sovereign against his faithful subjects, that the monks put arms into the hands of the reformed. All the different sects of Christians are at this day tolerated in Holland, England, and Germany ; and what troubles do they there excite ? Peace is established in that empire on the plan of toleration, and doubtless will remain there as long as the government shall restrain the ambition of the ecclesiastics.

To conclude ; if, as I have already said, governments take no part in theologic quarrels, the people will regard them as matters of no more importance than the disputes about the ancient and modern writers.

77. (p. 345.) Who has not laughed to see the Jesuits so often accuse the parliaments of revolt, and cite them before the king, as a scholar before his preceptor ? France, they then said, is a nation of slaves, where each one accuses the other of sedition.

78. (p. 346.) The monks are employed incessantly in searching the scriptures for passages whose interpretation may be favourable to intolerance ; but who does not know that though the scriptures are of God, the interpretations are of men.

79. (p. 347.) The warrior, frank and brave, is commonly humane ; his freedom and courage set him above all fear. The priest, on the contrary, is cruel. Why ? Because he is weak, false, and cowardly. Now of all creatures, says Montaigne, if women be the most cruel, it is because in general they are weak and destitute of courage. *Cruelty is always the effect of fear, weakness, and cowardice.*

80. (p. 348.) Nothing is more indeterminate than the signification of the word *impious*, to which is annexed a vague, confused idea of villainy. Do they by this word mean an atheist, and apply it to one who has only obscure ideas of the Deity ? In this sense all men are atheists ; for no one can comprehend incomprehensibility. Do they apply it to those who call themselves materialists ? But if we have not yet any clear, adequate ideas of matter, we can have no clear idea of the impiety of materialism. Are we to regard as atheists those who have not

the

the fame idea of God as the Catholics? We muſt then call by
this name the pagans, heretics, and infidels. Now in the laſt
fenſe atheiſt is not a fynonimous term with villain; it figniñes
a man who on certain metaphyſical or theological points does
not think with the monk and the Sorbonne. That the word
atheiſm or impiety may recal to the mind fome idea of villainy,
to whom ſhould it be applied? To perſecutors.

81. (p. 349.) It is not to be imagined to what a degree intolerance has of late years carried idotiſm in France. A man of
fenſe informed me that during the laſt war a hundred idiots,
when with their confeſſors, accuſed the Encyclopediſts of the de-
rangement in the finances; and God knows if any one of them
ever had the leaſt hand in their adminiſtration. Others reproached the philoſophers with the little love for glory in our
generals; and at that time theſe fame philoſophers were ex-
poſed to a perſecution, that nothing but the love of glory and
the public welfare could ſupport. Others again attributed to
the publication of the Encyclopedia, and the progreſs of the
philoſophic ſpirit, the defeats of the French armies; yet it was
then that the very philoſophic king of Pruſſia, and the very
philoſophic people of England, every where defeated thoſe armies. Philoſophy was the ſpright in the ſtory that did all the
miſchief.

Yet, faid a great prince on this ſubject, every people who
baniſh philoſophy and good fenſe from among them, cannot
promiſe themſelves either great fucceſs in war, or a ſpeedy re-
eſtabliſhment in peace.

In Portugal there are few philoſophers to be found; and perhaps the weakneſs of the ſtate is there in proportion to the fot-
tiſm and ſuperſtition of the people.

82. (p. 350.) Without the aid of the Catholic princes the
Papiſts, as ſtupid, and perhaps more intolerant than the Jews,
would fall into the fame contempt.

83. (p. 351.) Intolerance was never greater in France:
perhaps they would not now print, without caſtrations, M.
Fleury's Eccleſiaſtical Hiſtory, nor permit the impreſſion of Fontaine's Fables. What impiety might they not find in theſe
lines of the ſculptor and the ſtatue of Jupiter * ?

* The poet formerly owed but little to the weakneſs of the ſculptor,
who dreaded the wrath and hatred of the gods of his own making:
for in this he was a child, and children are jealy concerned that
their dolls be not offended.

84. (p. 353.) All things in us, even to felf-love, is acquifi-tion ; we learn to love ourfelves, to be humane or inhuman, vir-tuous or vicious. The moral man is all education and imitation.

85. (ibid.) Our various characters are the produce of our factitious paffions; that they are not the effect of organifation or particular temperament is evident by their being attached to certain profeffions : fuch, according to M. Hume, is that of a foldier, and that of a minifter of the altar, which are nearly the fame in all ages, countries, and religions.

86. (p. 354.) The love of glory elevates a man above him-felf ; it extends the faculties of the mind and foul : but he who regards that paffion as the effect of a particular organifation de-ceives himfelf. The defire of glory is a paffion fo truly facti-tious and dependent on the form of government, that the legif-lature can always at its pleafure kindle or extinguifh it in a nation.

87. (p. 356.) There is no art or fcience that has not its par-ticular language : and it is the ftudy of this language that at an advanced age renders us incapable of the ftudy of a new fcience.

88. (p. 360.) There are in every country a certain number of objects, that education offers equally to all ; and it is the uniform impreffion of thofe objects that produces in the inhabit-ants that refemblance of ideas and fentiments to which we give the name of the fpirit and character of the nation.

There is befide, a certain number of different objects that chance and education prefent to each individual, and it is the different impreffions of thefe objects which produces in the fame individuals that diverfity of ideas and fentiments to which we give the name of particular fpirit and character.

89. (ibid.) I fuppofe a man cannot make himfelf illuftri-ous in letters without dividing his time between the world and retirement ; that it is in the defert he muft pick up diamonds, and in the world cut, polifh, and fet them : it is evident that chance and fortune, which have permitted me to live by turns in the city and in the country, have done more for me than fome others.

END of the FIRST VOLUME.

www.ingramcontent.com/pod-product-compliance
Lightning Source LLC
Chambersburg PA
CBHW021328110726
47900CB00005B/1400